Chris

Best wishes

JOINING FORCES

BY

STEVE LITTLE

ISBN 978-0-9576894-1-1

First published in the UK in 2014 by
Medehollow Productions
3 Crabtree Drive, Leatherhead, Surrey, KT22 8LW
Telephone: 0044 1372 375574
Email: info@medehollow.co.uk

'Joining Forces' is dedicated to my family

With thanks to my editor, Lucy McCarraher, Patrick Roberts for help with the production and the Cobham Writing Group for all their suggestions and advice

Steve Little's first novel, *'More Than Just A Life'*, was published in 2010 to critical acclaim.

"... touching ...sensitive ... emotional... thoughtful ... immensely moving ...personal ... enthralling ...gripping ...sad ... critical of the awfulness of the establishment ...a tremendous insight into a mind disturbed ... quite, quite excellent." – Howard Swan

"... well written and very engrossing" – Western Front Association

A hard-hitting drama set in World War One it tells the story of Eddie Wilson, a young soldier who escapes from the horrors of the trenches at Passchendaele only to be captured and Court Martialled. It is a harrowing tale of how the Army dealt with deserters, many of whom were suffering from shell shock or combat stress as we would call it today. It also tells of Eddie's remarkable friendship with his captor, an equally young military policeman, Frank Shipley.

'Joining Forces' is the sequel and it takes us on an exciting journey through Frank's post war life. From the relatively sedate life as a village policeman Frank, overcoming personal tragedy, becomes an ace marksman to be used by MI5 in covert operations involving him in episodes that might have changed the course of history. The story culminates in his desperate attempt to evacuate the beaches at Dunkirk in 1940.

Steve has also written and published *'Days We'll Remember All Our Lives'*, a collection of humorous, true, short stories about life for a group of baby boomers during the 1960s. He also published *'Living The Claret Dream'* in 2013, telling the story of the Chelmsford City FC's glory years in the late 1950s and 1960s.

You can find out more about Steve's current and future writing at www.stevelittlebooks.com

FOREWORD

'Joining Forces', like *'More Than Just A Life'* before it, is a drama built around actual historical events. Quite naturally I have had to include historical figures and texts of radio broadcasts made before and during World War Two. However, most of the characters are completely fictitious, but in a few instances I have changed the names of real people so as not to cause any difficulties with living relatives.

In *'More Than Just A Life'* I based most of the action from the trenches (and beyond) on the experiences of my maternal grandfather, Bill Harris, as told to my teenage mother in the 1940s.

In *'Joining Forces'* much of the action relating to the evacuation from Dunkirk is directly based on what happened to my paternal grandfather, Ted Little. He lived long enough to tell me what he went through despite not being able to talk about it at all for many years. In fact, his experiences of making his way to the coast and trying to get onto a boat and away from the Dunkirk beach were so dramatic and traumatic as to be almost unbelievable!

I asked him what it felt like to be under constant threat of death and with the Germans actually visible behind him as he and his disparate group of fellow soldiers made for Dunkirk. He said, 'It was a bit of an adventure really!'

Truly remarkable men: matched by those ordinary folk who left England in an armada of small boats to save those on the beaches across the Channel. Nearly three hundred thousand were rescued and, whilst Dunkirk signalled a defeat for the British Expeditionary Force in 1940, getting those men home would enable the Allies to re-group and return four years later to ultimate victory.

Steve Little 2014

1

Marie opened the bedroom curtains and pulled the sash window down a few inches. She felt the cold blast of December air. Light snow was already settling on the grey rooftops towards the centre of Calais, where gas lights twinkled in the late afternoon gloom. Her father stirred. She turned to see his pale face on the pillow and leant over to touch his forehead; it was still burning and damp. She kissed the side of his head before picking up his dinner plate from the bedside table. He had eaten very little.

In the kitchen downstairs, she left the plate on the draining board to wash up later and took a bowl, warming on the stove, to the table. Her spoon hovered over the warm broth before she put it down and pulled a handkerchief from her apron; she bit on it as she held it in front of her face and then used it to wipe her eyes.

A tap on the window was followed by a knock on the back door. Marie quickly blew her nose, returned the handkerchief to her pocket and the bowl to the stove. Smoothing her hair she opened the door.

'Frank! Frank Shipley. A surprise, my goodness,' she exclaimed in a heavy accent. 'Entrez! Please, you must be very cold!'

Frank ducked his six feet three inches through the doorway, wiped his feet on the doormat and leant forward to kiss Marie on each cheek.

'Thanks. It's a bit brass monkeys out there.'

Marie looked a little bemused.

'What is a brass monkey, Frank? I am sorry but it is some time since I spoke English. I am very rusty and is that even the right word?'

'Sorry, Marie, I forgot. It means it's extremely cold and 'Yes' rusty is correct. You'll soon pick up the English again and anyway you're not too bad, a little more of an accent perhaps than before.'

He removed his red trimmed Military Police cap and ruffled his wavy black hair into place. Marie helped him off with his greatcoat wiping the wisps of snow from its shoulders. Underneath Frank was wearing his dress uniform with its red and black MP armband.

'My, Frank, you do look smart.'

'Thank you; there was a fancy lunch in the Officers' Mess today.'

'You are an officer now?'

'Oh no, still only a sergeant, but I wangled an invite.'

'Wangled?'

'Sorry, Marie; managed to obtain I should say.'

'I see, well do sit down, please. I was only thinking about you earlier today as I have been sent a letter from Mrs Wilson – you know, Eddie's mother. Can I get you anything – a hot drink or perhaps a brandy?'

'No, I'm fine thanks. What letter's this?'

'Oh, it was just a short note thanking me for looking after him, nothing more. So, what brings you here on this cold afternoon?'

'Nothing really; I was on my way back from the Mess and was passing. I'd heard the school had given you time off and thought I'd see how you were. Are you all right, has anything happened?'

Marie's expression changed and her eyes welled up. She looked at the floor then the ceiling and her bottom lip quivered. Frank came to her side of the table and put his arm round her shoulders.

'What's up? Is it your father?'

She shook her head and wiped her nose.

'I am not coping well. Papa has a severe chill and that has not helped – maybe it is this sickness that has been sweeping your army camps. I just cannot get Eddie from my mind and you know how close we were. I am also having trouble sleeping.'

'Have you both seen a doctor?'

'The school called one in when I broke down during a class. It frightened the children and I felt awful about it. He told the school I should have plenty of rest, so they said I must stay away until after Christmas and then see how I feel. I have not had him call on Papa yet.'

Frank returned to his chair. Marie blew her nose and dabbed her eyes.

'Sorry, Frank, but it has all become too much.'

'Look try not to worry it's not surprising after what you've been through. Would you like an Army doctor to examine you? One of them is a chap I knew from before the war. He might be able to give you something to help you sleep and look at your father too.'

'Oh ... I am not sure ... I do not want to put you to any trouble.'

'It's not a problem; I'll contact him tomorrow and ask him to drop round.'

'You do not have to do this, Frank, just to please me. I have already told you I do not, how do you say, bear a grudge; you were only doing your duty with Eddie and could not have done more to help him afterwards. You did not shoot him, your Army did.'

She broke away. Frank decided to change the subject.

'I've been busy lately. It's chaos in and around Calais. Since the Armistice the men have been stuck in their camps waiting to be sent home.'

'Yes, I have seen them in the town causing trouble.'

'You local French people must be sick of the sight of them. Discipline's gone out of the window and you're right, many are now quite ill and some have died already. Everyone's blaming the Americans for bringing it over.'

Marie smiled.

'So, Frank, what are you and your men up to?'

'Still looking for deserters, I'm afraid. Three in total and it's just as hard to track them down especially as they can now mix with the troops hanging around towns like Calais. I'm hoping everyone will be shipped home in the New Year, me included.'

'Did these men run away from the action, like Eddie, or are they wanted for something else?'

'One's for attempted murder, but the other two disappeared in the last few days of the war and they've been on the run ever since. I've only recently joined the search as I was tied up with Eddie's Court Martial as you know. The trouble is we're stretched a bit thinly now, plus we're called out at all hours to sort out the fights in the bars and whatever. I can't believe it's taking so long for the men to be shipped out; you can understand their frustration.'

A sudden shout from upstairs caused Marie to run to help her father. When she returned she found Frank reading a handwritten letter.

'What's that?' she asked, standing over him.

'This is my other reason for coming.' He coughed nervously, 'Remember that Major Burnside from the Court Martial, that helpful officer we spoke to? Well he's written me a private note.'

Marie put her elbows on the table and rested her chin in her upturned palms as Frank read aloud.

'"Dear Sergeant Shipley, you will recall we met at Private Wilson's Court Martial. I have to tell you, entirely off the record, that the letter so eagerly awaited, which might have at least saved Wilson from the firing squad, did arrive a day or so later; there had been some foul up with the shipping. You know I agreed with you that Wilson should have been spared execution and this news adds to my disappointment. This is all I can say, but there is more to the story. I would appreciate it if you would destroy this note as soon as you have read it. Yours, Burnside."'

Frank returned the piece of paper to his pocket and looked at Marie for a reaction. She started to say something, but stopped.

'Interesting, isn't it?' said Frank.

'I do not know what I can say,' she managed, holding her hands to her face.

Frank looked concerned.

'I'm really sorry but I thought you'd want to hear what it said.'

'Yes of course I do. I am fine, but what does he mean by "more to the story"?'

'I'm not sure. I would like to know, but probably we'll never find out.'

He looked at Marie. She was composed and thoughtful.

'I thought you might be more upset by the news about that delayed letter,' Frank continued.

Marie held his hand,

'I do miss Eddie terribly but hearing that isn't changing anything now.'

Frank squeezed her hand.

'That's the right attitude. You must try to move on.' He looked at his watch. 'Look, I'm sorry, but I have to go; I'm late back as it is. I'll have a word with this doctor friend, his name's Ingleby – a Major, and see if he can visit. Are you happy with that?'

'I'll leave it up to you. I'm feeling better each day, just tired all the time. I'm really more concerned about Papa; if your friend could take a look at him as well that would be even better.'

'Fine, I'll sort it out in the next day or so and, by the way, your English is coming back already, well done!' He stood up and moved towards the door. 'What plans do you have for Christmas?'

'With all that's gone on I haven't given it much consideration. I suppose it depends how we both feel, but we'll certainly be staying here. What about you? Have you any leave?'

'I do, for a change. Just the two days though.'

'Well, you must join us and stay over. Come over Christmas Day morning, I might even buy you a present!'

'No, don't do that – then I'll have to get you one.'

She playfully punched his chest and passed him his coat. As he put his arms into the sleeves she put hers round his waist and, standing on tiptoe, kissed him lightly on his cheek. Stepping back she spoke softly.

'It's been so good seeing you again. If there's a problem with Christmas I'll get word to you. Thank you so much for coming over; I do appreciate it.'

***

The following morning Frank dropped into the makeshift medical centre in the Town Hall. He gave his name to the soldier at the front desk and asked for Major Ingleby. As he sat waiting on a bench in the narrow corridor leading to the wards, a group of nurses and orderlies swept past heading towards the front doors; they returned carrying two stretchers with a soldier on each. A single nurse behind them stopped and asked Frank if he was waiting to be treated or just visiting. He told her was waiting for Major Ingleby and explained his visit was urgent but would be brief. She looked sympathetic, said she would see what she could do and returned to the ward. A constant stream of soldiers came past Frank, some walking but many were supported by their friends, others were on stretchers; they all looked pale and dishevelled. An orderly stood in the doorway to the wards and checked off the names as the men passed.

'Where are all these men coming from?' Frank asked him.

The orderly looked up wearily then came to attention when he saw Frank's uniform.

'Oh we're clearing one of the camps, bringing the bad ones here but the rest are being shipped home.'

At that moment, Jack Ingleby appeared from a room to Frank's left.

'It is you, old chap, and now a sergeant!' Frank stood up and they shook hands. Ingleby was shorter, but still nearly six feet. He had lost weight since Frank had last seen him in Somerset before the war; now there were flecks of grey in his brown hair and he looked tired. The two of them had been at school together in Wells where Ingleby's father was the Dean at the Cathedral.

"Thanks for seeing me, Jack. I heard you had recently arrived here from down on the Somme, you must be really busy.'

'You can say that again, old chap! This bloody virus thing is rampant. I have patients dying by the hour in there.' He pointed to the door behind him. 'I hoped I'd be home by now and dare say you feel the same.'

'I most certainly do and I feel sorry for the men –' Frank started.

'They survived the war,' interrupted Ingleby, 'but now they're dropping like flies. Anyway, what can I do to help? Are you ill?'

'No, I'm fine and I won't take more than a few minutes of your time but could you do me a favour? A young Frenchwoman and her father living a few streets away are really quite ill. He has this Spanish flu and she's had a minor breakdown, not able to sleep very well.'

'Frank, I'm very busy here; I can't help the locals too, you know.'

'I appreciate that, Jack, but a favour for old times' sake?'

Ingleby hesitated.

'Go on, give me the details,' he said, with an air of resignation.

'Well, the lady's name is Marie Coutteau and I met her when I captured a deserter she'd been sheltering for almost a year. Rightly or wrongly I became friendly with them both and tried to help the soldier as I felt he had lost his marbles. I failed miserably and he was shot last month. I have to say it's affected me too; I've this sense of guilt and can't get him out of my mind. But enough of me, do you think you could find time to pay them a visit, it needn't take long?'

'Bloody hell, Frank, you're involved a bit above and beyond!'

Frank shrugged. 'Maybe, but can you drop in later today? I'd be really grateful.'

'You know my French is bloody awful, don't you, old man?'

'Don't worry; she speaks pretty good English. She used to teach in Kent before the war. Her father also worked over there – Diplomatic Service, I think, so he speaks decent English too. She's twenty-two, same as me, but widowed already; her husband was killed at Verdun. She's been through so much, what with this soldier, Wilson, being close to her as well.'

'How close?'

'Very.'

'As it's you, Frank, I'll do what I can. Give me their address, old boy.'

Frank handed over a piece of paper, 'It's on there; they're expecting you. Leave a message at the Military Police Office if there's anything serious I should know about and thanks. I'll buy you a beer and we can catch up about home when we have more time.'

'Fine. Good, leave it with me. Sorry but I really must go.' They shook hands before Ingleby returned to his room.

***

'Madame Coutteau?' Ingleby asked, doffing his army hat.

'Yes, you must be Major Ingleby, do come in.' Marie stepped back, took Ingleby's hat and placed it on the hall table. 'Can I get you a coffee?'

'Oh yes please; thank you very much.' He followed Marie into the kitchen, 'I shall be pleased to help you and your father but am rather pressed for time, I'm afraid, so whilst you get the coffee can I examine your father?'

'Of course, I'll take you upstairs, follow me.'

Marie finished making the drinks and brought them through to the parlour table as Ingleby arrived at the bottom of the stairs. He smiled at Marie and sat down.

'Well, Madame, I'm pleased to say your father is over the worst. It is what many of our men have, a virus. It will take time but will work its way out of his system. He'll be weak for a while and he has this cough, which is quite common, there is little I can do for him other than suggest he stays in the warm and gets plenty of rest; now what about you?'

Ingleby sipped his coffee whilst Marie explained what had happened to her since the autumn. He listened sympathetically, nodding an understanding from time to time as he let Marie unburden herself as she explained what had led to her breakdown at the school. She became tearful. He passed her a clean handkerchief and she dabbed her eyes.

'Sorry,' she said, 'I know I am being, how you say it, silly?'

'Not at all, not at all. You have been through so much it's not surprising you now feel the way you do and Sergeant Shipley did mention you were having trouble sleeping. I can give you some tablets to help with that and you can see how you go with them; I'll have then dropped round later. Like your father you need a little more time but perhaps after Christmas you'll feel better and be able to return to work. If you still need my advice you can always catch me at the temporary medical centre near the Town Hall.'

Ingleby finished his coffee and stood up to leave. Marie collected his hat from the hall.

'Thank you so much, Major, it has been very helpful and comforting. Just one more thing, you know Sergeant Shipley from your schooldays and I have been drawn close to him over Eddie Wilson, but what is he really like?'

Ingleby took his hat, shuffled his feet and felt his cheeks go red.

'I, I ...,' he blustered, 'I'm not prepared for that question!' He laughed. Marie said nothing but clearly wanted an answer. Ingleby knew this was no idle question and that there was more to it than met his eye. He composed himself before continuing.

'Although Frank is younger than me, we were at the same school and hit it off through sport mainly. He is a first class chap. I've never seen him lose his temper; he's clever, kind and would never hurt a soul. How he came to be a Military Policeman always surprised me but he is extremely well thought of, although his help for your friend Eddie was somewhat frowned upon within the army but it truly showed what he is like as a human being.'

Ingleby moved towards the front door, 'Madame, please take care of yourself and your father but do come to me if I can help.'

Marie opened the door and Ingleby put on his hat. She offered her hand and he took it, kissing her fingers.

'Thank you again,' she said, 'and for what you said about Frank.' Closing the door she leant her back against it and sighed.

***

Frank heard nothing from Marie or Ingleby, but when he arrived on Christmas Day he found Marie considerably improved; the short course of pills prescribed by Ingleby had given her the much needed sleep, but her father's virus was taking time to clear.

Over the two days' holiday Frank did what he could to lift Marie's spirits but she was often tearful. They attended church on Christmas Day followed by a walk to the quayside then dinner with her father. They finished off two bottles of wine whilst playing Canasta and by the end of the afternoon her father had returned to his bed. Marie was giggly, relaxed and soon asleep in an armchair.

Frank smiled as he looked at her. Her cheeks were flushed from the alcohol. Her silky brown hair had settled on her shoulders but was still windswept from earlier. She looked no more than a schoolgirl with her petite figure: young, innocent and not with the look of someone who had already endured a lifetime of emotions. He recalled when they had first met, the day his men had crashed into her house to arrest Wilson, and how frightened and timid she had been. At Eddie's Court Martial Frank had seen a different side to her as she showed such strength and bravery giving her evidence. But days later she was to collapse into his arms as the shots of the firing squad had rung out on that foggy November morning.

***

They did not meet again until the end of January, but exchanged regular letters. Marie had now returned to the school and her father was up and about, much improved but with a persistent cough. Frank was away in England for a week whilst he delivered two captured deserters to their Court Martial in Aldershot. On his return he immediately rushed to see Marie and found her in good spirits - much more like her old self.

She had clearly gone to some trouble with her hair and make-up, the first time Frank had seen her wearing rouge since the Court Martial. In a high-necked sweater and tight skirt her normally slim figure was a little more rounded and her face fuller, but to Frank this was no bad thing. Her eyes were alive and not dull and sunken inside the rings around them as they had been at Christmas.

They decided to walk into town and looked for somewhere quiet to enjoy a drink. There were places to avoid where soldiers were milling around with nothing better to do than drink. They found a little place by the docks run by a woman whose two boys were at Marie's school. She gave them a warm welcome and insisted they stay as long as they liked. They chose a small table in one corner overlooking the cross channel ferry berth but said nothing to each other as they watched the comings and goings outside until Frank took hold of Marie's hand,

'How are you, really?' he asked.

'Fine after what the Major –'

'No I mean after Eddie.'

Marie looked annoyed and pulled her hand away but Frank held it again.

'Marie, love, it's all right there's no need to be like that. Not only was there Eddie but your husband too. Gracious you're only, what, twenty-two? That's such a tender age to have gone through all of what you have had thrown at you. I know you're not alone with your grief and there are thousands of women like you, but that doesn't make it any easier.'

'I know, Frank, but I feel guilty about Eddie. I mean he was a deserter and I should have handed him over to your army as soon as he arrived on my doorstep, but I couldn't, I just couldn't. I now feel I was responsible for him being found guilty when he might have been treated leniently if he had returned straightaway.'

'No, you did what any caring person would have done; that's your loving nature and I saw how close you two were at the time of his Court Martial. It was my army that killed him and I wish I could have done more for him.'

Marie grasped his hand tightly,

'You were wonderful in what you did, Frank - not just for him but me too, rebelling against your own army like that. I shall always be so grateful.'

She turned to see if anyone was watching before she leaned across the table, looked straight into his eyes and kissed him softly on the lips. As she pulled away she looked down before sheepishly lifting her head slightly. Frank stroked her temple with the back of his fingers and returned her kiss, but more strongly than before.

Having said their goodbyes and settled the bill they left arm in arm. Marie shivered in the cold easterly wind blowing off the sea and cuddled in close as they walked along the quayside towards the town centre. It was now dark. Behind them three soldiers suddenly appeared from an alleyway. They were all drunk with two supporting the other between them. They were noisy, shouting at the top of their voices. They followed Frank and Marie for a hundred yards or so before one of the soldiers called out at Marie with a crude suggestion. With Frank having borrowed an overcoat belonging to Marie's father and hatless, he looked from the rear like any other Frenchman out for a stroll. The soldier repeated the remark. Frank spun round; the men were only yards away and immediately spotted Frank's Military Police uniform. The two dropped their friend onto the pavement and ran off. Frank picked up the remaining soldier who, once he too saw the uniform, staggered off towards his friends waiting at the entrance to the alley.

Meanwhile Marie had sheltered in the doorway of a ladies' fashion shop and was looking through the window. Frank came up behind and put his arms on her shoulders.

'I am so sorry you had to witness that, the sooner these men are shipped home the better.'

Marie said nothing but turned and looked up at Frank. He eased her further into the doorway so her back was up against the locked door. She smiled as he gently held her shoulders before holding his hands to each cheek and kissed her on the lips with an open mouth. He was surprised with the passion she showed as she returned his kiss, touching his tongue with hers. It was as if she was unburdening herself of all her pent up frustrations and emotions. Finally they broke apart but said nothing and walked on to the house, where they kissed again at the front door before entering.

***

Throughout February, Frank spent as much time with Marie as he could and they grew closer. He was often away for days at a time or busy dealing with the disturbances in Calais, but, finally, the bulk of the remaining soldiers had been shipped home and his life became quieter. The unit in Calais was reduced to Frank and two others. He was happy to stay, for a short while at least, so he could remain near Marie. But he knew his return home would not be long in coming and he would need to find work, as he had no intention of staying in the

Army any longer than he must. He hoped Marie would want to be with him, but knew she could not leave her father behind. The old man was only slowly improving and still frail, with the cough remaining troublesome. There could be a new life for Frank in France, but he concluded it would be better to leave. He had no intention of returning to the painting and decorating business with his father in Somerset but, instead, to make a fresh start.

As spring arrived, news reached him that police forces at home were keen to recruit ex-military policemen once they were demobbed. This was an opportunity he would certainly wish to grasp and he pondered on how to raise the matter with Marie and her father. However, before he could decide what to do he had a surprise visit at his office one morning from a breathless Jack Ingleby.

'Christ, Jack! What's up?'

Ingleby bent forward, resting his hands on his knees as he gasped for breath.

'It's Marie's father. He's collapsed.' Ingleby took another deep breath. 'She wasn't sure you were in Calais and, as I was nearer, came for me. It looks bad. He's on his way to hospital.'

Frank grabbed his greatcoat and followed Ingleby out of the door. Outside a staff car driven by one of Frank's men was pulling up to the side of the road. As the man stepped out of the car, Frank shouted over,

'I need the car, turn it over with the starting handle,' Frank ordered. The driver ran to the front, gave it two turns and the engine burst into life. With Ingleby in the passenger seat Frank drove off at speed across town.

In the hospital ward, Marie was sitting at her father's bedside. He was asleep. She looked up as they joined her.

'He's very ill. It is a brain bleed like you suggested, Major.'

Ingleby nodded.

'I'll leave you to it. I'll be outside,' he said, backing out into the corridor.

Frank pulled up a chair. Marie was composed; he'd expected her to be more upset.

'They say he's in a bad way and seriously paralysed. Sorry I didn't let you know but I was under the impression you were away. The Major was near...'

Frank gently held her hand and stroked a lock of hair from her forehead, 'You did the right thing. When did it happen?'

'I heard a thump on the bedroom floor at about seven o'clock this morning and left my neighbour to attend to him whilst I found the Major.'

'Well, let's pray he comes through it but he does look so weak.'

For two days and nights they shared a vigil at the bedside. In the early hours of the third day Marie was dozing in an armchair when a nurse shook her awake. Her father was dead. She sat there for almost an hour holding his cold hand. No tears came.

Frank only received the news when he arrived at the hospital after breakfast but Marie had already left for home. He rushed round to the house expecting to find her distraught; instead she was composed, stripping her father's bed and tidying up the bedroom. Frank held her close.

'I am so sorry, this on top of everything else. I can't begin to understand –'

'I'm fine,' she interrupted. 'Papa wasn't likely to recover and would have hated being unable to do much, a cripple maybe.'

She bundled up the sheets and blankets.

'We ought to tell the Major; he was so kind. Would you mind letting him know?'

Later Frank found the billet Ingleby shared with two other doctors; he was leaving the house when Frank arrived. They walked to a bar around the corner and sat at a pavement table.

'I knew he was in a bad way,' said Ingleby, 'and was certainly paralysed down one side plus his brain might have been further damaged. How's Marie?'

'Remarkably calm and yet I imagined she'd be more upset.'

'She might be later; shock sometimes takes a while to come out so keep an eye on her. Where does that leave you now? You said the other week you might stay here after demob.'

'It does change everything, that's for sure. She has no ties here. She's only lived in Calais for a year since being moved from near the Belgium border during the fighting around Ypres. That's where she met Eddie when he turned up on her doorstep. I've been told the London Police are looking to recruit ex-military police as they're short of men. If Marie agrees I'll probably take that option. There are worse jobs. What about you?'

'Oh, I'm returning to Somerset, but not sure for how long. The doctor in Wells is near to retirement and the last time I was home on leave he asked if I would join him with a view to eventually taking over. That seemed a good idea with my parents still living there, but now an old university pal has approached me. He is setting up a special intelligence unit within the Civil Service. I don't quite know why, but he's asked me to join it. Bloody good money and it all appears rather exciting!'

'Well whatever you do I know you'll do it well. I'll be visiting Somerset as soon as I can to see my father, so perhaps I can come over.' Frank looked at his watch, 'Look, I'd better return to Marie. Give my regards to your parents.'

'Of course and do let me know when the funeral is, won't you?'

***

The funeral and burial took place the following week. When they arrived home, Marie removed her coat and scarf, dropped them onto the back of the sofa and slumped into the cushions. Frank poured her a brandy.

She stretched out her legs and kicked off her shoes.

'That went off well – there were more there than I expected. It was kind of the Major to come.'

Frank sat in the chair opposite, 'I think he feels a bit guilty that he didn't do more for your father.'

'He shouldn't feel like that; he had enough to cope with at the hospital.'

'True, but he told me at the cemetery that an examination of your father showed there was a tumour on his lung. That explains the cough. Jack feels he should have thought of it, although apparently the cancer was advanced.'

Marie said nothing. Frank leant over and kissed the top of her head. She half smiled. He raised his glass.

'Well, here's to the future.'

They sat quietly. Marie shut her eyes. She wore no make up; her hair, recently cut shorter, enhanced her elfin features. Suddenly she opened her eyes and swilled the brandy around the bottom of the glass.

'Where do we go from here, Frank?'

'Er, well –'he stammered.

She laughed at Frank's confusion. 'You must have thought about it,' she continued. 'You could be sent home any day now and where does that leave me? Perhaps we should marry.'

'We're not even engaged yet!' he said, laughing. 'Are you ready for it after all that's happened?'

Looking serious, Marie grasped his hand.

'I've kept this from you, but I've been writing to an old friend in England, Josie Walmsley. I knew her from when I was teaching in Dover. She's now Head of French at a girl's secondary school in Chelmsford and says there's a post there if I want it. There's no reason for us to stay here once you've received orders to return to England.'

'You sly old thing.'

'And I could start as early as next month,' Marie continued. 'It's an easier decision for me now Papa's no longer with us.'

'You should have told me about the school,' Frank lightly chided her. 'It sounds like a great opportunity and it's almost certain I'll be in England by the late summer. I might be kicking my heels for a while waiting for demob, but, anyway, first things first.' He eased himself onto one knee and held her hands in his. 'Marie Coutteau, will you do me the greatest honour of becoming my wife?'

'Silly fool!' said Marie as she lent forward and kissed him. He fell backwards and she lay on top of him. Taking her lips away from his she asked softly, 'Is that the answer you were looking for?'

***

With the remaining deserter captured boarding a ship in Le Havre, Frank's workload reduced to almost nothing. Shortly after receiving a letter from the Metropolitan Police offering him a post in London, orders were issued returning him to his old barracks at Aldershot to await his release. He was surprised by Marie's lukewarm reaction to his news.

'How long before they actually release you?' she asked. 'Weeks, maybe months?'

'I don't know, but as the London Police urgently want me I'm sure they'll speed things up.'

'That's another thing, this job in London. I don't want to be travelling such a long way to school every day. Could there possibly be a posting available nearer Chelmsford? The war must have left everywhere short of officers.'

'I can see your point, but London's the place to be and we can still live near Chelmsford. I'll catch the train up to London; it's only an hour away.'

'But that's still a long day and then you'll be on shifts. With my teaching pay we will not need you to earn so much. You could find a post as a village policeman, perhaps. If it doesn't suit you, you can always look for something else, no?'

He understood. Since being posted to France nearly three years ago he had barely had a break from the long hours on duty. Perhaps she was right, opt for a quiet life for a while and see where it took him.

***

A few days later Frank wrote to decline the London offer, but asked for his details to be forwarded to the Essex Police Force. He was surprised to receive an early reply. It gave no details but he was told to inform Chelmsford Police Station as soon as he was available.

Marie was delighted. She had already written to Josie accepting the teaching position and set a date to leave Calais.

***

The quayside was crowded as the ferry slowly docked. Frank carried Marie's one suitcase. It was a clear, calm, early morning with a gentle warm breeze.

Across the sea a low sun highlighted the cliffs at Dover. Here, though, it was noisy: a unit of soldiers stood to one side, most smoking and laughing. A loud shout brought order and the men formed up, hastily casting their cigarettes to the ground.

'I wish I was coming with you,' said Frank.

'Me too, but it will not be long.'

A fleet of ambulances drew up behind them and they had to step out of the way. Orderlies dropped from the cabs and opened the rear doors.

An army truck pulled up and Jack Ingleby stepped onto the quayside. Holding a large clipboard, he called the orderlies to him and read out a list of instructions; the men climbed into the ambulances and unloaded the patients on stretchers or helped those who could walk. He spotted Frank and Marie and waved.

The soldiers were called over to carry the stretchers straight up the gangway and onto the ship. The orderlies assisted the less ill who walked along wrapped in blankets.

'That's about the end of it all, then,' said Frank. 'There's only a few of us left now. This must be the last of the soldiers; that platoon is made up of men from the prisoners' compound – I recognise some of them!'

Having delivered the stretchers, the soldiers began to line the deck on the side of the ship. The noise of their banter filled the air again.

As other passengers began to board, Marie cuddled into Frank and looked up at his face. He smiled and kissed her cheek.

'Let me know as soon as you arrive in Aldershot,' she said softly, 'and when you will be released. You have Josie's address, yes?'

'Yes, it's in my diary. I might be given a spot of leave straightaway at Aldershot. If that's the case I'll come over but I'll write first. I hope it goes well at the school; I'm sure it will. Look, they're calling for all remaining passengers.'

He kissed her lightly on the lips aware that those standing on the rails were watching. A few wolf whistles followed and Frank turned glaring at the men, who simply laughed. He recognised one face as one of the drunks from the quayside a few months before. Marie hugged him more tightly and looked up again at his face. He kissed a tear from her cheek but neither spoke. She stepped away and walked up the gangway to more whistles. At the top she turned, waved and blew him a kiss. She was crying.

Ingleby came over.

'A fond adieu?'

'Yes,' Frank said quietly. 'She's off to Essex to take up her teaching post.'

'When are you leaving?' asked Ingleby.

'Saturday.'

'Me, too. That's the last of the patients apart from those who won't make it: only three, thankfully. We've lost over two hundred at this hospital alone since the Armistice last November. It's a bloody tragedy. Anyway, what have you in mind after you are demobbed?'

'I hope to be in Chelmsford or nearby. Ideally I'd like a village or similar. Marie and I decided that London wasn't for me, or us really, and a village should have a police house. After all that's happened, a quieter life will be most welcome. Oh yes, and we're to marry!'

'Well good for you, old chap! Congratulations, you make a lovely couple. Have you set a date yet?'

'No, it depends when I'm released. Are you still off to Wells?'

'Yes, that's still the plan but only to use as a base as I'll take that other post I told you about. Look, old chap, I'm glad I've seen you before you leave. I've decided to write about how the shelling and whatnot affected the men and the way the Army dealt with it, but of course from a doctor's point of view. You might be able to help by giving me a soldier's because you knew that Wilson chap and saw what he was like. Would you mind if I tapped your brain for more information?'

'I'd be pleased to. Perhaps we could talk more when I visit my father?'

'Jolly good. Look, you have my parents' address so you can let me know when you're arriving. Perhaps you could jot down your experiences with Wilson for me before you come, old chap.'

'You're in luck there, Jack, I kept a full diary; I'll dig it out.'

'Excellent! Right, I'm off. Now you take care and all the best with the nuptials!' Frank offered his hand, but Ingleby clasped him in a bear hug.

***

When he arrived at Aldershot, Frank found a letter waiting for him from Marie.

"Mon plus cher Frank,

I am safely arrived at the Walmsley house and I am settled in comfortably with them. I have already been to the school to meet the headmistress – who is un peu feroce! Josie wants me to teach conversation as well as grammaire. The headmistress, though, has reservations, but is prepared to see if I can accomplish this. I cannot wait to see you again and miss you terribly. Write as soon as possible with news of your return to me!

Je t'embrasse

Marie"

The notepaper smelled of her perfume and Frank felt a pang of longing as he slipped it inside his diary. Stretched out on his bed, he sifted through the entries from last year written during his time with Wilson. The detail surprised him as he re-read how Wilson explained what he had been through on the front line; the devastating effect of death all around him and how his mind had slowly disintegrated. From these notes Frank would certainly be able to prepare some interesting material to pass on to Ingleby.

***

Two days later Frank was called in to see his commanding officer.

'Ah, Shipley, sit down,' said the Colonel pointing at the chair in front of his desk. He held a brown file and shuffled some sheets of paper inside it. He looked over the top of his half moon glasses then removed them and shut them in a case.

'You have been very lucky, Sergeant, the Army took a very dim view of what you did for that Wilson fellow. If it hadn't been for this Major Burnside speaking up for you, you might have been facing a disciplinary charge yourself. I can tell you another thing, too, more than simple campaign medals would have come your way but for what you did. Anyway, I now have a letter from Essex Police asking for your immediate release. It seems they have an urgent posting for you. I've a mind to tell them to wait but, as it's the Police, I feel obliged to sign you off. You can leave tomorrow and here are the details.'

He handed over an official looking letter and curtly waved Frank away. Outside on the parade ground, Frank did a little jig of delight.

Returning to his quarters he hastily wrote to Marie.

"My Dearest

Thank you for your letter. I am on my way. I shall be with you Wednesday evening. I have to go to the Chelmsford Police Station first to meet the officer in charge. I have a posting to a village called Broomfield. Apparently it is not far outside Chelmsford so it will be just right for us and, most importantly, we should get a police house. It could not have worked out better. I am immediately being sent on a training course so will be put up in the Police Hostel near you for a while, before being moved to Broomfield.

I so miss you too. I can't wait to be there with you and to hold you again.

With all my love

Frank"

***

The following morning Frank caught the early London train. He had been allowed to keep his army uniform on the proviso he gave it up for his police uniform. With nothing more than his kitbag, he headed straight to the Police Station from Chelmsford Railway Station. There he met Superintendent Allen.

'Take a seat, Shipley; this is a surprise to have you here already but a pleasant one nevertheless. Now let's get straight down to business. Before we sort out anything there's one fact I need to know about you. Are you married?'

'No, sir, but I'm sort of engaged, although I've not bought the ring yet. She's a French girl – woman, I should say. She's over here already, about to start teaching at the Girls' High School.'

'Excellent,' Allen clapped his hands, 'because what we have in mind for you is Sub Station Officer out at Broomfield, a few miles north of here and the position comes with a house. Perhaps I should say that the Station Office is based in a normal house. Our rules only allow married couples to live there, so have you set a date yet?'

'No, sir, the engagement's all happened rather quickly. Marie is living with a fellow teacher here in Chelmsford for the time being. We haven't talked about when just yet, but there's no reason why we should delay it!'

'Good. As you know, I've arranged for you to lodge in one of our hostels for now until you've sorted something out. You'll need some training but as you've been running a police unit out in France that shouldn't take long. Have you any clothes or belongings with you?'

'Only my kitbag with a few essentials, that's all. I'll need to change out of this uniform.'

'Well, we can give you the police uniform almost straight away. I'll sort that out in the next few days and you'll have to give up what you're wearing now but you'll need some civilian clothes. There should be some at the hostel and you might like to sift through what's there to find if anything fits but the rest you'll have to buy.'

'Thank you, sir. Could I take my wife-to-be to view the police house in the next few days?'

'Of course, of course. Have a word with the sergeant outside; he'll be able to help with a key and directions. He'll also tell you about the hostel. All it needs is for me to thank you for coming and to wish you good luck!'

'Thank you very much, sir. I won't let you down.'

***

Once he had seen the sergeant and dropped off his kitbag at the hostel, Frank hurried to Marie. Excited by his arrival she led him into the parlour and introduced him to Josie and Norman.

'Pleased to meet you,' he said shaking hands with them both, 'Thank you very much for offering Marie a room. I have received confirmation that we definitely have the police house in Broomfield. We can look at it now and move in as soon as we're married!'

'Oh, that's excellent news,' beamed Josie. 'It's not far from the school either – nice village, too.'

'Quiet, two nice pubs and a little school for your children,' added Norman.

'Norman!' said Josie, 'please!'

Marie blushed and smiled at Frank.

'Well that is the plan, isn't it?' grinned Frank, with a knowing look at Marie and they all laughed.

'Come on, Marie, help me with the tea from the kitchen,' said Josie changing the subject.

As they left, Norman sat down and offered Frank the other armchair.

'A Sergeant in the MPs; I've heard all about you. Surprised you're still in uniform. I did my bit, but got shrapnel in my side. A blasted painful wound as it turned septic and I nearly died. Still gives me gyp!'

'You're lucky it wasn't worse, I suppose. I receive my police uniform later in the week, but I didn't bring much from France and the rest of my stuff is at the family home in Somerset.'

Josie put her head round the door.

'We heard that out here. Norman, you've clothes upstairs you never wear. You're a bit shorter than Frank, but some'll fit. Sort out some items and Frank can take them away to try on.'

Five minutes later Norman returned with two shirts, a pair of trousers and a jacket.

'Here, they might be a bit small for you, but you're welcome to them.'

'That's very kind of you, Norman, thanks a lot!' Frank stood up and tried on the jacket. It fitted.

Norman pulled Frank by the arm towards the window and spoke so the women would not hear.

'Josie's so pleased Marie found you. We were so worried about her; any letter she sent to Josie during the last year or so was pitiful – and even worse following the execution. You make sure you look after her now, won't you?' Norman moved his face closer and looked Frank straight in the eye. Frank leant back and Norman smiled.

'You have my word,' said Frank. 'I watched her suffer too you know but you should have seen her at Eddie's Court Martial. She is made of strong stuff underneath it all, but that's not to say she hasn't been through the mill.'

'Good man, she's a gem!' said Norman returning to his chair. The two women came through from the kitchen with trays of tea and sandwiches.

They chatted for over an hour and Frank developed a strong liking for Josie and Norman; a happy couple in their late forties with two grown up children. Josie was tall and elegant with long blond hair and the confident air of a good teacher. Norman, tall but slightly stooped with thick grey hair and moustache, worked as a draughtsman for the local council. With both their salaries they had a comfortable living in a three bed roomed house on the edge of the town.

Frank asked more about Broomfield.

'I know it well,' said Josie. 'If you carry on past the school it's about two miles along the same road. Nice place. The usual: a couple of pubs and a school, as Norman said; a church, a few shops, not much, but also an airfield between there and Springfield, a little way past the river that runs through the village. There's a ford across the road and the planes are in the field on the other side. We've been up there for a walk and watched them; it's fascinating. You'll like it in the village and it's easy for Marie to travel into school, too. I have seen the Police Station and it's set into the front of the house.'

'It sounds charming,' said Marie. 'And much better than London!' She shot a glance at Frank who ignored her.

Norman decided to change the subject again.

'So, just how soon can you get married?'

'No idea!' said Frank. 'Do either of you know?'

'It depends,' said Josie. 'Church weddings take a while to sort out, but you could opt for the Register Office.'

Frank and Marie looked at each other and nodded.

'You could always have a church blessing after,' Josie added.

'I can help with the Registrar,' Norman offered. 'His office is next to mine at the Council and I have lunch with him in our canteen. There are restrictions on timings and all that for weddings what with residency and so on, but given your position with the police I'm sure he'll move things along if I ask.'

'Oh that is so kind of you, Norman. We will be happy to be married as soon as it is possible,' said Marie. Frank stood up and shook Norman's hand.

***

When Frank and Marie arrived to view the police house, they found a young constable in the office. He showed them through to the living quarters at the rear, which, he explained, had remained empty since the middle years of the war.

'Someone has cleaned in here recently,' said Marie, examining her finger after running it along the mantelpiece, 'and the window frames have been painted. It smells a little; I'll open a window.' She had to force the lattice window open as the paint had hardened, sealing the window to the frame. She looked at the long back garden. 'Come and look at this, Frank, and how big it is but somewhat overgrown, that will keep you busy!'

'So you'll do the decorating inside, will you, love?'

'Not me. Remember what Norman said: I'm here to have babies!'

'First things first, my dear, don't rush me.' They both laughed.

The house was partly furnished with sheets draped over the chairs. Beyond the parlour, a kitchen stretched narrowly along the side of the house with a door onto a side passage. Upstairs were two good-sized bedrooms with a wardrobe and bed in each. A small empty room and a toilet completed the living quarters. The wallpaper throughout was old and would need replacing.

Having locked up behind them and returned the key to the constable, they caught the bus into Chelmsford and separated, Frank to the Police Station and Marie to the School to complete her preparations for the start of term the following day. That afternoon Frank started his training after which he was due to start his Broomfield duties the following week.

***

Their wedding took place on the last Saturday in September at Chelmsford Register Office. It was a low-key affair attended by a few of Frank's colleagues, the Walmsleys who acted as witnesses and Frank's aunt from Taunton. His father felt unable to travel due to an attack of gout. A small reception followed at The Saracen's Head nearby, but there was no time for a honeymoon and the wedding night was to be spent at the police house.

Later that evening and having checked all the doors downstairs were locked Frank joined Marie in the bedroom. She was already under the bedclothes. He quickly undressed and started to put on his pyjamas.

'Don't worry about them; get into bed as you are, mon cher,' she said with more than an accent than usual.

Frank pulled back the covers. Marie was completely naked, the first time he had seen her like that. He felt that sudden unease with this being the first time he had been with a woman, an experienced one at that.

2

Josie's idea of encouraging Marie to teach more conversational French proved popular with the senior girls and, with Marie not being much older, she was able to connect with them far more easily than the older teachers. For the first time since her first husband died Marie felt settled in her life, happy in her marriage and with no regrets about her decision to move to England.

After the frantic finale to his war, Frank was pleased to have this time to settle into the sort of life he had enjoyed in Somerset before the hostilities had begun. He spent much of his spare time writing up the notes from his diary and finally passed them to Jack Ingleby when visiting his father during the summer. Ingleby wrote to Frank soon afterwards thanking him for his thoroughness and promised to forward a copy of his book when completed. In his letter Ingleby confirmed he had taken the job offered with the Intelligence Service but gave no further information as to what this entailed.

Broomfield gradually picked up the pieces following the effects of the war and was expanding with people moving into the village as new houses were built. However, Frank's duties remained rarely more than routine - the occasional theft, the odd drunk at closing time and a few stern words for youngsters up to no good. Restless and in need of a new challenge he put in for his sergeant's exam in early 1921 as the routine promotion to a larger station, promised when he agreed to take the posting, had not materialised.

Marie had felt unwell for most of January and had taken time off from the school. Although she had said nothing to Frank she suspected she was pregnant and visited her doctor.

On that same afternoon Frank was cycling back to his office after his last sweep through the village before his overnight relief arrived when he saw Marie walking purposefully along the main road towards the house. He braked beside her, 'What's the hurry, have you a train to catch?' She swung round beaming but said nothing as she went through the garden gate.

'What is it?' Frank called after her. She ran ahead and unlocked the front doors while Frank left his bicycle in the passage.

'What is it?' he repeated as he caught up with her.

'Well, Constable Shipley, that second bedroom upstairs will have to be decorated!' she exclaimed excitedly.

'You're joking! You mean...?"

'I'm not likely to joke about such a thing, am I?' she kissed him. 'Our baby is due in July, that's why I've been feeling unwell since Christmas and it's just been confirmed by the doctor!'

'I don't believe it. Oh how lovely – and there was me thinking life was becoming a bit stale.'

Marie pulled away, looking surprised and hurt.

'Oh not with you, the job,' explained Frank hastily. 'I've put in for my sergeant's exam. We'll need more money when the baby arrives. Look, sit down. Come on sit down!'

'Frank, don't be so silly. I am perfectly fine; now, put the kettle on.'

Once his relief arrived, Frank headed to the pub having already arranged to meet with a few friends on this his night off. As he walked along the garden path he did a little dance, swinging around an imaginary partner. Marie watched through the upstairs' window and smiled.

She was in bed when he returned a few hours later. Two friends had helped him home, but ran off once they had opened the front door. He was tipsy rather than drunk, but when he crept into the bedroom Marie feigned annoyance. In fact she found his attempt to undress quite hilarious yet hid this from him but couldn't help laughing at his failed attempt to tell her the punch line of a story about an elephant and a kangaroo. He was most apologetic the following morning as he nursed his hangover and Marie pretended to be upset before she dissolved into giggles when she told him how he had been the previous evening.

***

As the months passed, plans were agreed with the school. Marie knew she might be able to stay on long enough to see out the summer term provided she and the baby remained healthy. Josie, delighted with Marie's news, promised to ensure her workload would be as light as possible. Almost immediately, the school decided to bring in a new French teacher at the beginning of the summer term so Marie could dovetail with her and then hand over the reins when she felt she had to leave. The senior girls gave her great support and were interested to know how she was coping. They often chatted with her about the pregnancy, what it involved and what childbirth might be like, they were equally keen to know when she would be returning to the school.

***

Frank completed his sergeant's exam in the last week of May and was confident of success. He felt a degree of fulfilment but all that mattered now was the safe arrival of their baby.

In early June he was invited by the local Parish Clerk onto a committee to consider the erection of a monument in memory of the fallen during the war. Towns and villages were being encouraged to remember the dead in this way. Broomfield was not without its casualties, albeit with fewer than in many other places, but such losses were felt as deeply in this close-knit little village as anywhere else.

The committee decided to recommend to the Parish Council a series of fund raising initiatives for a war memorial. The usual winter and summer fairs were planned together with concerts, flower shows, raffles and jumble sales.

The Council agreed and suggested an official launch including a timely reminder of what the men from the village had faced in the war, not only those who died, but also those who returned. With this in mind they approached Frank and asked whether he would give a talk on his experiences

'I'm no public speaker,' he said to Marie later that evening, 'and I'm not sure what I could say. I feel a bit of a fraud not having been in a fighting unit.'

'Well, you're no Lloyd George, that's for sure,' she said laughing before adding more seriously, 'but people here look up to you. Why don't you talk about

Eddie and what he went through? You might wish to leave out the desertion part as that might not be so well received; you had better say he was killed in action. His would be an interesting story and I can help you with it. When do you have to let them know?'

'Oh, in a week or so, but you might have a point; Eddie's life in the trenches is quite a story and powerful stuff. I wrote plenty in my diary which I know was useful to Jack Ingleby and Eddie must have told you much more.'

***

The village hall was packed. Frank and Marie were on the stage with the Chairman of the Council and a local man who had lost a leg in the fighting. The Chairman outlined the plans for the memorial and the funds required; the audience were enthusiastic and warmly applauded when Frank was introduced. He started hesitantly, glancing at Marie who nodded encouragingly.

By the time he reached the end of Eddie's story, so rapt was the audience you could hear a pin drop. The whole room remained quiet as he said 'Thank you,' and sat down. Marie nodded and smiled; he nervously smiled back. The audience shuffled in their seats and talked to each other in hushed tones with much shaking of heads and tutting. Eventually one man rose to his feet and applauded shouting, 'Bravo!' Gradually everyone did the same. Frank looked embarrassed but stood and waved to acknowledge the clapping. The Chairman slapped him on the back and Marie, with tears in her eyes, hugged him tightly.

Those on the stage remained in the hall as the audience filed out, dropping contributions into buckets by the door as they left for home. One woman remained and, as Frank and Marie came down the steps to leave, she came over.

'Constable Shipley, I would like to thank you for tonight. My son also died in the war; he was only eighteen like your friend and I've had trouble accepting what he had to put up with. The story of your friend's experience has made me understand I'm not the only one - not the only mother to have lost a son. You mentioned all those men that this Eddie knew who didn't make it, they had mothers too and sisters, brothers and fathers. Thank you again.'

Before Frank could say anything, she turned and hurried out. He turned to Marie, 'Who was that?'

'I think it's Mrs Parmenter – Phyllis. She lives with her husband in Mill Lane. They have a daughter called Joan, about our age. You certainly made an impression on her, and everyone else, with your talk. You were splendid.'

'You don't think it had too much detail?

'No, it was just right. This should really help the fund-raising off to a good start. Did you see how much money was being dropped into those buckets?'

3

As the summer unfolded, Marie became more and more uncomfortable. The extra weight she was carrying made it difficult to sleep, especially in the hot weather and this made her tired and irritable. She constantly apologised to Frank for her short temper but he simply shrugged it off as being one of those things you have to expect.

By chance, on one of his routine visits to the main Chelmsford Police Station, Frank met Josie Walmsley in the High Street.

'I'm sorry I haven't been over to see Marie for a while, how is she?' she asked.

'She's not bad, thanks, but struggling with this heat; fortunately there's not long left now.'

Frank looked at Josie's bulging carrier bag, 'Catching up on some shopping, are we?'

Josie laughed.

'School finished early as it was Speech Day and I thought I would stock up on clothes for the next year at the school. Would it be convenient if I came to visit Marie in the next couple of days? I've scarcely seen her since she left the school.'

'Oh, would you? She'd appreciate the company. I think she finds it boring being at home, not able to do much. You must know what that feels like?'

'Of course, but it was a long time ago. Perhaps I could come over the day after tomorrow?'

'Yes, do. Come for the day. I'm working but I'll be in the office some of the time.'

'I'll aim for late morning. Tell Marie not to go to any trouble; I'll have my dinner when I get home.'

'I can't wait to tell Marie, she'll be thrilled. Thanks, Josie, and I hope to see you on Thursday,' said Frank, kissing her on the cheek.

***

Josie found Marie sitting in the garden.

'My God you are big, Frank said you were,' she said. 'How long do you think you have left?'

'It's about a week and the sooner the better. It's so uncomfortable.'

'Yes, I can imagine and with this heat! Still,' Josie added, looking at the cloudless, blue sky, 'at least you can sit outside. Where's Frank?'

'Oh, he's had a call out to The King's Arms; some money has gone missing. Can I get you a cup of tea?'

'It's all right, I'll make a pot for us both, you just sit there.' Josie went into the kitchen.

'The milk's in the pantry,' Marie called after her.

As they sat sipping their tea Josie updated Marie on the news and gossip from the school; who was coming in and who was leaving over the summer.

After a while Marie stood up, stretched her arms as high as she could reach and suggested the two of them take a short walk. She left a note for Frank and locked up the house. The two women walked slowly along the path next to the main road, arm in arm. A number of carts and the occasional car or lorry passed by but once they turned left into a narrow lane leading to the ford, there was no traffic at all.

'This leads to the airfield, doesn't it?' asked Josie.

'Yes, then to Springfield. The airfield's the other side of the ford. Aren't these gardens lovely?' Marie stopped and pointed at the neat gardens of two semi-detached bungalows. 'Just look at those pansies, they are beautiful.'

A man appeared from inside the garden shed of the first bungalow.

'Hello, Mr Parmenter,' said Marie, 'We were saying how lovely your pansies are.'

'It's been the best year for them since before the war, Mrs Shipley. Would you like a bunch and one for your friend too?'

'Oh that would be nice, thank you. May I introduce Mrs Walmsley, a fellow teacher from the High School?

'Pleased to meet you,' said Mr Parmenter touching the peak of his cap, 'how are you keeping, Mrs Shipley? The baby must be due soon.'

'Not long now. How is Mrs Parmenter?'

'She has Joan here with her little one – though she still misses Maurice.' He handed her the flowers. 'Good luck with your baby. Pop along and see Joan and her daughter when yours arrives.'

'I'll do that. Thank you for the flowers and please give my best to Mrs P.'

'Thanks very much,' added Josie.

'It's a pleasure; all the best!' replied Mr Parmenter as he waved and returned to his shed.

They continued along the lane, which opened out briefly then narrowed again at the ford.

'We'd be best off stopping here,' said Josie. 'These hedges make it very narrow and I'm not sure I want wet feet!'

Marie laughed, 'It is only shallow, Josie, and I would like to cool my feet a little in this heat.'

'But if something comes along the road it could be dangerous.'

'It will be fine; nothing much comes along here,' said Marie, 'I should like to sit on the riverbank in the field on the other side and rest in the shade there before we leave for home.'

Marie set off along the middle of the road. A few yards short of the ford she spotted early blackberries growing in the hedgerow. She led Josie over to pick some.

'Not quite ripe,' Marie grimaced as she bit into the fruit, 'a bit early for them, but they'll do for a pie with plenty of sugar. We can make it this afternoon. Come on, Josie, help me pick them.'

Josie half smiled and laid the flowers on the ground at the side of the road.

Marie pulled a small shopping bag from her handbag and handed it to Josie. 'You unfold it and I'll reach for the berries.'

She leaned up to pick some and giggled: her dress was caught on the bush where it bulged over her midriff.

Josie tried to release her.

'You should be more careful doing all this; you'll have to let me do the picking.'

Suddenly a lorry appeared on the other side of the ford. There was a loud screeching of its brakes.

Water sprayed up either side of its wheels as it ploughed into the water. As Josie looked up she saw the driver struggling with the steering wheel, trying to gain control. He was only yards from them and braked again. The lorry slewed and its engine spluttered. It was now moving broadside towards them. Marie tried to move away, but the blackberry thorns held her back. Josie pulled at her as the front of the lorry hit Marie on her left side, spinning her round and throwing her deeper into the hedgerow. Still holding her hand, Josie fell on top of her.

The lorry's tyres threw up smoke as the brakes finally gripped. It spun round and was now pointing in the direction it had come from. The driver leaped from the cab and ran towards them. He grabbed Josie's arm, pulled her out of the hedge and onto her feet.

'Are you all right?' he asked.

'Yes, I'm fine, but help my friend.'

They both knelt down.

'Marie ... Marie, can you hear me?' shouted Josie.

Marie remained motionless and quiet. Josie could see her breathing was shallow. She looked at the driver. He looked shocked and pale but said nothing.

'You must help me pull her out, I can't manage her on my own she's too heavy,' Josie told him. The driver leaned past Josie and grabbed Marie's shoulder to ease her onto her back. She screamed out and he pulled away.

Mr Parmenter arrived panting heavily. 'I heard the lorry ... oh my God,' he exclaimed.

Josie stopped him getting too close.

'Please fetch Constable Shipley. Is there a local ambulance?'

'Yes,' said Mr Parmenter, 'up at the airfield, up there.' He said pointing up the road. 'I'll get the constable.'

'If he's not at the police house try The King's Arms!' shouted Josie after him. He waved in acknowledgement.

'I know where the ambulance is,' said the driver, 'I've come from there.'

'Please fetch it and hurry!' said Josie.

Marie was still quiet but now conscious. She lifted her head slightly.

'My arm, I think it's smashed and my hip hurts too,' she moaned.

Josie looked at Marie's blood stained dress.

'Mr Parmenter's looking for Frank and the lorry driver's collecting the ambulance stationed at the airfield; it won't be long before they're here. Just rest easy.'

Marie lost consciousness again.

Josie looked round frantically. Mr Parmenter was pedalling round the corner onto the main road, but coming towards her was a middle-aged woman carrying a blanket and two pillows.

'Perhaps you could do with these,' she said as she knelt beside Josie. They covered Marie with the blanket but could only put the pillows under her feet.

'She's lost consciousness; she was hit by the lorry and I think she's broken her arm. Her hip's damaged too and, oh God, look at the blood.' Josie touched the soaked dress.

'Let's hope the baby's all right?' The woman moved in closer. 'Marie ... Marie? It's Phyllis Parmenter, can you hear me?' She turned to Josie. 'She's out cold. We need a piece of wood for her arm to make a splint, see what you can find over there,' she said, pointing into the undergrowth below an ash tree. Josie moved away.

Phyllis pulled away the brambles and touched Marie's head. It felt very hot. She was able to move one of the pillows beneath it. Marie groaned but her eyes remained shut. A car drew up carrying two policemen.

'Can we help?' shouted one. 'We were up at the airfield and heard there was an accident.'

'One of you go to my house, it's number four. In the kitchen you'll find a box with a red cross. It's on the shelf near the back door. Bring it here; there are bandages in it for a splint. The front door's open. I used to be a nurse,' she said by way of explanation.

As one left, the other crouched beside Phyllis, who whispered, 'This looks bad and she's almost nine months gone with a baby. She's Constable Shipley's wife.'

Josie returned with an armful of small branches.

'Well done, put them there; we'll wait for the bandages,' said Phyllis. 'She's still unconscious.' She turned to the policeman. 'Can you return to the airfield and check on what's happening with the ambulance?'

'Right,' said the constable as he ran to the car, then shouted, 'Here comes Frank.'

Frank braked hard as he arrived by the group and threw down his bicycle. He stood above his stricken wife and the two women kneeling next to her. All he could do was stand there for a moment with his hand clasped over his mouth.

'She must be nearly at nine months.' Phyllis whispered to Josie.

'Only a week short as far as I know.'

Marie had come to again and was whimpering quietly as Phyllis felt round her bulge.

The first policeman arrived with the first aid box and handed it to Josie. He said nothing and stood next to Frank with his arm around him. All four looked round when they heard the bell of the ambulance in the distance.

Josie tied two bandages round the stoutest suitable branch and handed it to Phyllis to put into place on Marie's arm.

The ambulance, driven by Arthur Lightfoot the caretaker at the airfield, splashed through the ford and stopped behind the lorry. The lorry driver was in the cab but when he saw the policemen he jumped down and ran off towards the village. No one followed.

Phyllis attempted to set the splint in place. Marie opened her eyes and tried to sit up but screamed out, grabbing her stomach with her good arm. She fell back, crying.

Frank tried to push past Josie but she put an arm across his chest.

'Frank, move out of the way. It could be the baby.'

'But I want to speak to her!'

'Wait a minute,' Josie said sternly.

Marie was moaning; she lay there with her knees pulled right up to her waist, but held out her damaged arm so Phyllis could finish securing the splint.

Josie leant forward and spoke into Marie's ear.

'The pain, is it the baby?'

Marie moaned. 'I'm very wet between my legs; I think my waters might have broken.'

Josie looked at Phyllis. She told the men behind her to stand back. Josie lifted Marie's skirt and grimaced. The cloth was damp between her legs; the wetness was streaked with blood.

'Maybe that blood's from her dress,' said Phyllis quietly.

'I hope so. We'd better move her and get her to hospital as soon as we can,' Josie whispered.

Lightfoot waited with the unfurled stretcher. The ambulance doors were now wide open and ready with the folding steps pulled out.

Mr Parmenter restrained a small crowd of neighbours who had gathered in the road.

'Bring the stretcher over,' Phyllis called out.

Lightfoot laid it out in front of Marie's feet whilst the men stood waiting.

'Two of you push into the bush behind her to lift her by the shoulders; we'll hold her feet. Arthur, you place the stretcher under her when I say.' Frank and the policeman eased into the brambles and held each shoulder.

Frank bent forward, 'This might hurt, love, but we'll be as gentle as we can.' He stroked her hand. Marie looked up and smiled.

'Right ... now!' shouted Phyllis. They gently lifted Marie and Lightfoot ensured she dropped easily onto the stretcher. Marie groaned and passed out again. Carefully, they carried her into the ambulance. Phyllis and Josie followed and sat next to her. Frank hovered by the door as the men went outside.

'Frank,' said Phyllis, 'I think it would be better if you joined Arthur round the front.'

'But I –'Frank complained.

'No, Frank,' Josie intervened. 'You'll be in our way. She'll be fine and we'll take good care of her; let's get her into hospital as soon as we can. Off you go!'

Frank stepped onto the road and helped Lightfoot close the rear doors before climbing into the cab. As they did so, the police car driven by the second policeman returned. He called out of the window.

'Is there anything we can do to help?'

Frank leaned out of the ambulance's window.

'Best you move the lorry. The driver's run off, try and find him. The people here will tell you what he looks like. I'll catch up with you later – see me tomorrow at the police house.'

Frank closed the window and they drove off.

Marie lapsed in and out of consciousness on the journey. Josie eased off the wet knickers and looked at them closely.

'Thank God, it looks like it's not blood from inside her.'

Phyllis felt around the lower abdomen.

'I think the baby's coming.'

She stood up and banged on the closed partition of the cab. 'Drive as quick as you can!' she shouted.

'What is it?' Frank called out.

'It's just the baby, but don't worry we both know what to do.'

Minutes later they pulled into the hospital forecourt. Frank was already on the running board as the ambulance slowed. A group of nurses stood chatting outside the main entrance. Seeing Frank in his uniform hanging onto the open door, two of them ran inside for help and the other two hurried to the rear doors, which sprang open from the inside as they arrived. Josie was at the top of the steps.

'She's about to have her baby; she's already on a stretcher so we can carry her in!'

Phyllis was bent over Marie.

'Marie, dear, we're at the hospital, hold on while we carry you inside!'

As they were about to lift each corner of the stretcher, Marie's body began to twitch and she nearly fell off.

'Put her down,' said one of the nurses. 'Get the doctor, quick!' she told the other.

Frank came up the steps.

'What's happening?'

Josie moved forward.

'We don't know; she's having a fit or something. We need a doctor, we daren't move her.'

Frank looked at Marie over Josie's shoulder.

'God, she's grey and look at that sweat!'

'It's fine, Frank, don't worry!'

'Out of the way, please, clear a path.' It was the doctor. 'Can I have you all outside please, except the nurse? They filed down the steps. Two nurses stood there waiting with a trolley. Josie put her arm round Frank, but he pulled away.

Phyllis came up next to Josie and whispered in her ear,

'I'm worried, she could be having a heart attack; I've seen it before.'

***

A nurse ushered them to a waiting room. Arthur Lightfoot arrived, but said nothing. Frank sat forward staring blankly at the floor, with his elbows on his knees and his chin cupped in his hands. Josie wiped her eyes and blew her nose. Phyllis stood up and went to the window, looking at nothing in particular; Arthur picked up a newspaper from the table and read the front page.

The door opened and they all turned. It was only two more visitors; they came in, nodded and sat down. After a few minutes the door opened again. It was the Matron with a nurse.

'Would you and your friends like to come with us?' the nurse asked Frank.

They followed her out into the corridor. She opened the next door along and beckoned them inside. It was a small consulting room with a desk and only two chairs. They all remained standing and the Matron stood in front of them with her back to the window.

She spoke impassively.

'We have taken the patient to a treatment room. The baby seems well on its way but we have a problem with the lady. Is she your wife?' she asked Frank, who nodded. 'We suspect she has had a heart attack. She remains unconscious which is helping the baby who is our priority right now. They are both in very good hands and everything will be done to help your wife as soon as we can. The nurse here will find you more comfortable seats outside in the corridor where you can wait. I shall let you know more as soon as I can. Try not to worry.'

As she left, the nurse showed them to the chairs in the corridor.

'Would you like a cup of tea?' she asked, but they all refused. She left them momentarily and soon returned with a printed form and a pencil. She sat next to Josie, quietly asking questions and filling out the form.

Arthur excused himself and left for the front doors.

'Probably having a smoke,' announced Phyllis.

There was some activity along the corridor. Josie and Phyllis looked up, but Frank continued to stare at the floor. Two doctors hurriedly came along the corridor; a door opened and the Matron looked out, beckoning the doctors inside.

'That must be where Marie is being treated,' whispered Josie to Phyllis. 'I don't like the look of this!'

Frank sat with his chin still resting on his hands. Phyllis sat next to him and placed a comforting arm across his shoulders.

'Don't worry too much; they'll be fine, you'll see. Do you remember me? Phyllis Parmenter; we met when you gave that moving talk?'

Frank nodded but said nothing.

Nearly an hour passed, during which Frank barely moved whereas the two women were unable to sit still and paced up and down the corridor. The door to the treatment room eventually opened and one by one the staff filed out. Frank stood up. Josie and Phyllis held his hands. Only the Matron came towards them and Frank slumped into his seat.

'Oh no, oh my God, no!' he moaned as Josie crouched next to him still holding his hand.

'Perhaps you could return to my room,' said the Matron solemnly.

As they filed through the door Arthur appeared.

'What –?' he started, but Phyllis put her finger to her lips and pointed to a seat in the corridor.

A nurse brought extra chairs into the Matron's room and they all sat down with the Matron seated behind her desk. Before she could say anything, the door opened and a doctor came in; he stood behind the Matron. They both looked solemn and serious. Phyllis dabbed her eyes with her handkerchief. The Matron spoke slowly.

'Mr Shipley, your baby boy is fine. We are cleaning him up and checking him over, but he appears to be perfectly normal and healthy. I am so sorry to have to tell you this, but your wife has passed away. There was nothing we could do for her. She had one heart attack in the ambulance and another one as the baby was born. We did everything we could. I am so sorry for you, as are all my staff.' She bowed her head.

For a moment there was quiet. The nurse left with the doctor. Phyllis cried gently into her handkerchief as Josie squatted in front of Frank and clasped both his hands.

The Matron came round from behind the desk.

'I'll leave you here, but the nurse will be outside if you need someone.'

Frank started to cry uncontrollably and loudly, his whole body convulsing. He turned his head into Josie, resting it between her breast and shoulder. She hugged him tighter. Phyllis leant forward and kissed his head, but said nothing and left the room.

He tried to speak.

'Why? Why Marie?' He sobbed again.

'Yes. I know, it's hard,' comforted Josie; now in tears.

'It's only been a couple of ...' he broke away, slipping to the floor. He was now crying out so loudly that the nurse came in.

'Can I help?' she asked.

'Yes, dear,' said Josie, 'a cup of tea would be nice for us all. Strong and sweet, please.'

'She doesn't deserve to die ... I don't deserve this!' wailed Frank.

Arthur opened the door and put his head round.

'Anything I can do?'

'Not now, just look after Phyllis.' Arthur quietly shut the door.

Frank sat leaning against the wall with his knees pulled up to his chin. Josie was beside him. She jumped as he let out a piercing scream. He continued to shout out loudly; it sounded more like a roaring laugh. The nurse returned with the two cups and saucers on a tray.

'I heard that, it's shock. Quite common and better for him to let it out; if it continues I'll have the doctor look at him.'

'Thanks,' said Josie. The nurse put the tray on the floor next to them both.

'Mind, it's hot and I've put three sugars in. Is there anything else I can do for you?'

Josie shook her head. Frank waved away the tea.

'Come on Frank, drink it, please love.'

He ignored her, but was quieter now. Josie sipped from her cup. The nurse left as Phyllis came in. She looked enquiringly at Josie who shrugged, saying nothing. Still on the floor Frank sat with his head between his knees. There he remained for several minutes before suddenly standing up. He drank the cup of tea in one and pulled himself up to his full height.

'I'd better go to my son.'

The nurse was waiting outside in the corridor.

'I'd like to see them, please,' he asked.

'Follow me, your little boy's in here.' She opened the door and let him through. In the middle of the room stood a cot with a single bed to one side that had been stripped to its mattress, but Marie's body was not there.

The baby was quiet. Wrapped in a blue blanket and with his eyes closed, his face looked a little flushed and wrinkled. Frank leant forward, kissed the baby's head and stroked his arm. Frank looked round to ask the nurse if he could pick him up, but she had left. He stood there staring at his tiny son.

There was a knock at the door. The Matron came in followed by Josie.

'Can I pick him up?' asked Frank.

'Of course you can, but gently now,' said the Matron. 'Here, let me help.'

She wrapped the blanket round the baby as Frank cuddled him, kissing his head and bouncing him very lightly.

'Are you sure he's fine?' he asked the Matron.

'Oh, yes, he had a difficult time, but was delivered normally in the end. He's a good weight considering he was a little early; six pounds, two ounces.'

Frank looked up.

'Excellent. Would you like to hold him?' he asked Josie.

She smiled, took the baby and slowly walked round the room, gently swinging him across her chest.

Frank sat on the bed.

'What's happened to my wife?'

'We took her out through here to the Chapel of Rest,' said the Matron, pointing at the double doors behind her. 'You can visit her any time you wish. Would you like to now?'

'I would, actually.' He turned and looked at Josie.

'You go and I'll look after the little one. He's so lovely,' said Josie, 'I'll show him to Phyllis.'

The Matron led Frank across the quadrangle to the chapel.

'As you would expect,' she explained, 'we shall have to keep your little boy in the hospital for a while, but you can come in every day.'

'Thanks, of course I will. Is that any time? I'll have shifts to work.'

'We'll make special arrangements given the circumstances, don't worry.' She opened the door and let Frank through. 'Just wait here a moment, I'll check everything's in order.'

Frank looked round the small waiting area as the Matron entered the chapel itself. There was a painting on one wall of Christ with a crown of thorns, a single cross on another, but the others were plain. He sat on one of the two chairs.

Matron returned closing the door behind her.

'Won't be a few minutes,' she said, sitting beside him. 'Whilst we're waiting perhaps we can talk about a name for the baby? Had you decided on one?'

'Er, not really. We'd talked about a few.'

'There's no rush but we like to have one. The nurses will be mothering him, of course, so it would be nice for them.'

Frank's mind raced. He immediately considered Frank; it was a tradition in his family to continue with that, although the second name was the one used. He would not want to do this without Marie knowing. He had to link the name to her. Then it came to him.

'George, after Marie's first husband, and Edward after a good friend of ours,' he blurted out.

'Right,' said Matron, 'that was quick!'

'It's what Marie would have wanted.'

'Right, George Edward it is!'

A man appeared from the chapel.

'We're ready for you now.'

'You go through, I'll wait for you here,' said Matron.

The man stayed in the waiting area as Frank stepped into the dark chapel. A soft paraffin lamp flickered in the corner providing an eerie light across the table where Marie lay. A sheet covered all but her face and a single rose had been placed on her chest above her clasped hands. He touched her cheek with the back of his hand: she was cold. He felt a tear on his cheek and wiped it away. He stroked her hair for several minutes while looking at her lifeless face. Finally, he leant over, kissed her forehead and left.

Outside Matron was now alone.

'I'm so sorry, Mr Shipley. Are you all right?' she enquired kindly.

'Yes. I think so. Thanks.'

'One more thing, Mr Shipley, you will have to decide what to do when George is due to leave here. Please do give it some consideration. We'll keep him here for a fortnight or so, but perhaps next week we can talk it through.'

'Yes. I will. Thank you.'

'Also we need to make arrangements for your wife. Would you like us to contact a funeral parlour for you?'

'Could you? I'd be grateful and I'll come in on Monday to sort everything out.'

'That's fine, now I'll leave you with George and your friends.'

They walked to where Josie and Phyllis waited with George and carried him to his cot. Frank stood looking at his son who was now asleep. Josie linked her arm in his.

'He's beautiful, isn't he? He has Marie's eyes.'

Frank bit his lip and said nothing. Josie left him alone with his thoughts.

Ten minutes later, she and Phyllis returned.

'The nurses need to check him over. Are you ready to leave now?' said Josie.

'Yes, I think so.' Frank turned to Josie with tears in his eyes. 'Marie looked so peaceful, so beautiful.'

'We know,' replied Phyllis. 'We saw her and paid our respects. Arthur is still here with the ambulance; he can take us home, happy with that?'

Frank nodded and put his arm around Josie. They walked out into the corridor and towards the front door. Phyllis followed a few yards behind. Parked where he had dropped them off, Arthur was sitting on the rear steps to the ambulance smoking a cigarette, which he immediately dropped to the ground and stamped on it. Standing up he said, 'Frank, I'm so sorry about your wife.'

'You heard about my boy George did you?' Frank managed.

'I did. Lovely,' said Arthur, as he walked round to the cab.

Josie gave Frank a hug.

'I can walk home from here. I need to be there for when Norman gets home,' she said, 'I wish I could come with you, but I'll visit tomorrow. We can talk more then.'

'Thanks and thank you for all you did today...' Frank meant to say more, but caught his breath as he felt the tears well up and his voice falter.

She hugged him again and shut the ambulance door behind him as he sat down. As it pulled away, Phyllis used both her hands to hold his one, but neither said a word until they arrived at the house. Arthur left them standing in the road as he drove to the airfield.

'I'll come in with you, Frank.'

'No, it's fine, Phyllis, I would rather be on my own, if you don't mind.'

'I'll drop back later; would you like something to eat?'

'Not now, but perhaps later in the evening.'

Inside, the house felt cool and quiet. He stepped into the kitchen and poured himself a glass of water. Through the window he could see the teacups still on the table in the garden where Marie and Josie had left them; he picked them up, brought them back to the kitchen and put them on the draining board. The late afternoon sun appeared from behind a cloud and he squinted at its brightness. He carried his water to the bedroom. He placed the glass on the bedside table and fell onto the bed. Looking around he was overwhelmed by memories of Marie: her nightdress neatly folded on the pillow, a necklace on the dressing table, a cardigan on the chair and her hairbrush lying between the pillows. He picked it up, pulled out the long brown hairs and rolled them into a ball. As he held them tightly, the tears flowed once more. After a while he drifted off to sleep, hugging the pillow with the nightdress close to his face. He could smell her scent, sweet and strong.

4

Frank heard a woman's voice calling followed by loud knocking on a door. It was dark now and for a moment he was unsure where he was. He quickly tidied the bed, ran down the stairs, turned on the office light and opened the front door. There stood Phyllis holding a large saucepan.

'Hello Frank, I've some soup for you.'

'That's kind, thank you,' he said, yawning. 'Sorry. I must have been asleep.'

Phyllis smiled and walked past him towards the kitchen.

'I'll put it on the cooker; you can warm it up when I've left or wait until tomorrow.'

'Thanks – ... and thanks for all you did today.'

'How are you feeling?'

'Pretty ropey!'

'What's that stuck to your elbow?'

Frank turned his arm to see the ball of Marie's hair hanging there. He picked it off and put it in his pocket.

'It's Marie's,' he explained sheepishly.

Phyllis touched his arm in sympathy, 'Is there anything else I can do for you before I leave?'

'No, I don't think so, and thanks, thanks a lot.'

'That's no trouble, we'll all pull together for you and don't worry about feeding yourself; come round to our house for your meals, won't you? We'll help with the funeral and little George and you must ask us for anything.' She kissed him lightly on his cheek and turned back into the office. 'I must go; we all need an early night. You take care now; I'll pop round first thing tomorrow.'

Frank closed the front door, turned off the lights and returned to the kitchen. He looked at the saucepan of soup but decided he could not face any. Returning to his bed, he pulled the lock of hair from his pocket, smelt it and started to cry, loudly and uncontrollably.

***

After fitful sleep Frank woke with the sun shining brightly into the bedroom and, looking at his watch, realised he was late for duty. Still wearing his police shirt and trousers he was bathed in sweat, so, stripping down to his underwear, washed and put on a fresh uniform. The only thing he could face eating was an apple, so he poured Phyllis's soup into the sink and went through to the office. There he was surprised to find Stan Hebden from the Springfield station.

'Stan.'

'Hello, Frank,' said Hebden sombrely. 'I don't know what to say about your wife. I heard about it from our chaps who turned up at the accident. I received a message to come over here and cover for you, today.'

'Fine,' said Frank indifferently.

'The Super's due any time.'

'Right, I won't be a minute.' Frank returned to the kitchen and was sick into the sink bringing the apple back up. He wiped his mouth with a flannel and looked into the shaving mirror. His unshaven face was pale, in contrast to his red eyes; his hair was dishevelled. He turned away, took a tumbler from a cupboard and filled it with water from the tap. He drank slowly. Twice he retched but nothing more came up.

Hebden put his head round the door.

'Super's arrived, are you all right?'

'Not really, but tell him to come through.'

Allen looked solemn as he shook Frank's hand.

'I know there's nothing much I can say to help you over your loss, but please accept the condolences of all the men. It's a tragedy and nothing less but I'm pleased your little boy is fine.'

Frank was surprised how word of what had happened had spread so quickly.

'Thank you, sir. Yes, he's bonny.'

'I wanted to tell you right away that I'm putting you on three month's compassionate leave. Of course, you can stay living here and, as you've seen already, I've asked Constable Hebden to take over the village in the interim. The benevolent fund will help make up your wages. After the three months you might be able to decide what to do, what with your son and all.'

Frank had not even considered George and the future.

After all three had briefly discussed any outstanding items, Frank left Hebden and the Superintendent to return to his bed. He felt his despair deepening.

In the early afternoon, he shuffled into the kitchen and found Phyllis at the sink filling the kettle.

'The constable let me in,' she said, as she turned round. 'Good grief, Frank, you look terrible, have you eaten? What happened to the soup?'

'Sorry, I had to pour it away; I can't stomach anything.'

'But you must eat; I'll make you something light after I've made a cup of tea.'

Frank felt better for the sweet tea and cheese sandwich. Phyllis sat with him in the kitchen.

'I know it's early days Frank, but what about Marie's funeral?'

'Oh, the hospital are sorting it out, they have contacted a firm to deal with things,' he said without much interest.

'What about George?'

'They'll keep him for two weeks or more.'

'And then what?'

'I don't know.'

'I see, well come to us for your tea at about six – or will you be visiting George? – We have our Joan living with us now; you won't have met her. She's recently had a baby. But what about George?'

He hesitated; he had not given visiting George any thought.

'No, I'll leave it today, but I'll come round, thank you. Your daughter and her husband, do they live with you?'

'There is no husband.'

'Oh, I see.'

'She did summer work last year near Norwich, on a farm,' said Phyllis feeling she needed to explain further. 'She met this young man from Lincolnshire. Turns out he's married with a family. It was awful for Joan; they met a couple of times but he took advantage of her. She'd had a few glasses too many of rhubarb wine believing it to be cordial.'

'You mean ...?' Frank broke away.

'Well, I called it rape but she blamed herself. It wasn't until she came home that she found she was expecting. The folk round here don't take kindly to that sort of thing and we nearly sent her away, but she stuck it out. In the end it was not too bad, especially when people heard of the circumstances.'

'She should have told me when she came home; we could have tracked down this man. He shouldn't be allowed to escape punishment for that sort of thing.'

'Maybe, but it's tricky, her word against his.'

'But still –'

'Anyway, Lizzie's lovely. Not the way we'd like to have our first grandchild, but after losing Maurice in the war it's nice.'

'How is Joan coping with what happened – any lasting scars?'

'Not that I've seen, the only good thing was that she was so drunk she can't remember the ordeal at all. Anyway, come and meet her later, about six. If you like, one of us can come with you to visit George and perhaps help with the funeral arrangements in the next few days.'

She left and Hebden came through from the office.

'I'm off now, I'll do a sweep of the village then return to The Kings Arms and pick up from where you left off with the missing money. I'll see you tomorrow.'

Frank followed him out of the front doors and turned along the side passage to the end of the back garden. As he looked across the open fields to the west and towards the orange glow of the setting sun, he suddenly felt faint and giddy. He grabbed hold of the linen post for support. He felt cold but was sweating profusely. He shut his eyes and a wave of nausea came and went but there was a sudden vision of Joan's rape, but she had Marie's face. As quickly as the condition arrived it went away again.

Above his head there were still clothes on the washing line from the day before, including two of Marie's blouses, in an extra large size to cover her bump. He felt them; they were warm and dry. They smelt of Lux, her favourite. He removed them from the line and held one in each hand. She had last worn them at the weekend. He carried them to the dustbin and threw them in. From there he marched upstairs and pulled all Marie's clothes out of the drawers and wardrobe. He bundled them up and, returning to the dustbin, rammed them in. What was left over, he tossed into the garden shed.

'What on earth are you doing, Frank?'

It was Josie.

Frank looked shame-faced and neither said anything for a few moments.

'Sorry you had to witness that, but I feel annoyed; frustrated, maybe.'

'Would you like me to take Marie's clothes away?'

'Could you? I know it's a bit soon, but that's how I feel.'

'Of course, it's only natural. If you let me have a suitcase, I'll take them today.'

Josie stayed for nearly an hour. She had brought a collection of cards and letters from girls at the school. Frank insisted she read them out. They were heartfelt and sad.

***

The funeral was held at Broomfield church but Frank had no family there, yet the church was full. Most of the staff from the school came and they were joined by a large number of the older pupils. The villagers turned out in large numbers and the police too were well represented. Josie read the eulogy.

The *Essex Chronicle* had carried Marie's accident as their main story confirming the lorry driver had been arrested and charged with causing Marie's death by driving dangerously. He now faced a possible prison term and had been sacked by his employer. He wrote to Frank, full of remorse and begging forgiveness, but Frank screwed up his letter and threw it away.

Despite the care and affection all around him, these were dark days for Frank. It was as if his world had fallen apart. He rarely saw Hebden, who kept his distance apart from the occasional question or request for information. Frank spent hours curled up on his bed only leaving the house for his meals at the Parmenter's which he only picked at. Every other afternoon he had to force himself to visit George. Josie visited regularly but Frank rarely said much yet seemed to welcome her company.

Joan often joined him for his hospital visits and Phyllis mothered him; her Maurice would have been about the same age. Husband Harry was a quiet man, always in the garden tending his vegetables and flowers and he often offered to take Frank to the pub to lift his black mood, but Frank always turned him down.

Joan, a few years younger than Frank, was the one bright light for him. She coped well with her little daughter only a few weeks older than George. She had found work at the local primary school where Harry was the caretaker. She only worked mornings so was free to join Frank at the hospital and they often chatted in the late evenings after the others were in bed, but all Frank would talk about was Marie. Joan listened patiently and sympathetically, but Frank remained morose and depressed.

On one hospital visit, Frank, alone this time, was about to leave when the Matron called him into her office.

'Mr Shipley, do come in and take a seat.'

She pulled up a chair and sat right next to him. She held his hand.

'George will be strong enough to leave here in the next few days. I am worried about how you are. You look tired and pale. Of course, we would normally be happy for a baby to be with a sole parent, but I'm not sure you can cope. We could have him looked after by foster parents once he leaves here and the Almoner can help with that. Once you feel able to return to work you will have a problem if you have George yourself. Have you any family that can help such as parents, sisters or brothers?'

Frank shook his head.

'What about Mrs Shipley's? Has she anyone?

Frank drew his breath in sharply and bit his lip. He shook his head and looked at the floor.

'I'm sorry, Mr Shipley, I know this is upsetting for you and I can stretch to another week for George to stay here but that's all, I'm afraid. I suggest we make an appointment for you with the Almoner in the next few days, but in the meantime, perhaps you could consider what would be best for George. If not foster parents then possibly a housekeeper. You could advertise, perhaps or could the Force help at all?'

Frank continued to stare at the floor.

'Mr Shipley?' she prompted.

He looked up.

'Sorry. Sorry, Matron, no I can't think of anyone to help right now. Maybe a housekeeper would be the answer. I know I must do something but it's been hard.' His voice faltered again.

'Yes I know it's always hard in these circumstances. Look, I'll drop you a note when I've spoken to the Almoner about this appointment. She will be a great help and provide better advice than I can. May I also suggest you consult your doctor, as he will give you advice about your health and perhaps a tonic or similar to help? You do look tired out.'

Frank's mood darkened even more on the bus journey home. He sat with his head pressed against the window, staring out without really looking at anything. Fortunately for him, the conductor reminded him they were at his stop in Broomfield.

When he arrived indoors, he searched through the sideboard and the kitchen cupboards. He knew there was a full bottle of brandy somewhere and eventually he found it in the cupboard under the stairs, still in its box.

Early the next morning Hebden found Frank slumped in the armchair with the bottle by his feet with very little brandy left. He helped Frank stumble to his bed to sleep it off.

Frank failed to arrive for his lunch, so Phyllis took him round a plate of stew. Frank was still in bed, but awake. His hair was unkempt, his face unshaven and drawn, his clothes all crumpled. With the room smelling like rotten fruit, Phyllis opened a window to let in some air.

'Come on, Frank, you must do better than this. I've brought a stew; now, come downstairs and I'll serve it up for you.'

Frank said nothing but followed Phyllis to the kitchen. He poured himself a glass of water and gulped it down whilst Phyllis put the stew onto a plate and cut him a thick slice of bread off the loaf from the bread bin. He poured himself another glassful and sat at the table.

He picked at the food as Phyllis sat opposite. He felt queasy and had no appetite.

'What would Marie say about all this? It's not a place you can bring your boy home to, is it? I know I'm being rude, but you're in no fit state to look after anyone, let alone a baby a few weeks old!'

'I know, I know,' was all Frank could manage.

'Have the hospital said when they will allow him home?'

'Yes. Last night the Matron told me it would be in about a week, but first I have a meeting with the Almoner about George's care. I feel afraid because I know I can't possibly look after him, but I don't want him in a foster home or worse. Maybe a housekeeper would be the answer and perhaps I should advertise or ask around?'

'That would seem to be the answer, Frank. I'll ask around the village and you could put an advert in the paper or one in the post office window; there's bound to be someone. Now, look, eat the stew and smarten yourself up; you must get a grip, then perhaps we can sort all this out.'

She swept out taking the empty pot of stew. Frank pushed the plate away and folded his arms. He sat staring into space.

The following day he was sitting in the garden reading the paper when Hebden came out from the office with Phyllis. She was wearing a brightly coloured dress and looked completely different out of her everyday working clothes and with her long grey hair tied in a neat ponytail with a red ribbon.

'Going to a wedding?' said Frank rather brusquely.

'No. Just off to a W.I. meeting. I'm glad you've smartened up too, after yesterday.'

'Yes, I'm sorry about that and thanks, you were only being kind and I was rude.' She smiled but said nothing.

Hebden pulled up the other garden chair for Phyllis and returned to the office. Frank was fond of Phyllis. She reminded him of his mother who, had she lived, would have been about the same age. He poured her a glass of lemonade from the jug on the small table in front of him and they chatted for a while before Phyllis began to shuffle nervously in her chair. Frank looked at her quizzically.

'Was there something else you came here for?'

'Well, yes. With Joan likely to stay with us and me looking after Lizzie so Joan can remain at work, Harry and me thought we could look after George as well. I'd love to and it would at least solve one of your problems. What do you think?'

For a moment Frank was stunned. This would suit the welfare people at the hospital as well as the Police, allowing him to return to work and, hopefully, they would agree to let him stay here in the house, at least for now. He looked at Phyllis; she was nodding waiting expectantly for his answer.

'What do I think? I think it would be bloody marvellous, if you'll excuse my language!'

***

Within a few days Frank had spoken with Superintendent Allen, who was happy to let him remain at the house in the circumstances. The Almoner, following a meeting with Frank and Phyllis, gave the go-ahead for George to be in their joint care.

Four weeks to the day after Marie's accident Frank was due to collect George from the hospital and to bring him home to the Parmenter's. Dressed and ready to leave, he suddenly had another attack of the dizziness and nausea. He managed to stumble through to Hebden in the office and asked him to take a message to Phyllis and Joan telling them not to wait and to continue on without him and collect George.

After a sleep Frank felt better and headed to the Parmenter's.

'How are you now?' welcomed Phyllis, 'I hope it wasn't my cooking!'

'No. No not at all. I had mushrooms for my breakfast, it must've been them,' he lied.

He looked at George asleep in his pram. He had put on weight, had a mop of black hair and had lost the wrinkles on his face. He opened his eyes: they were brown like his mother's and Frank carried him into the sitting room where Joan sat with Lizzie who, despite being a month older, looked smaller than George and so different with her blond curls and fair complexion.

For a while Joan and Frank were alone with the babies.

'How are you, Frank, will you soon be ready to return to work?' asked Joan sympathetically.

'I should, but I don't feel like it. I can't raise any enthusiasm to do much. All I want to do is sleep or laze around and I don't even want to leave the house; it's as much as I can do to come round here. I even ran here, not wanting to meet anyone and I keep having these funny turns, feeling faint and dizzy.'

'You should see the doctor.'

'I know, but I become nervous and jittery about a small thing like attending his surgery.'

'Sounds like your nerves, Frank; you must have something for them. Would you like me to ask the doctor to call round?' I'm due at his surgery with Lizzie later this week.'

'Would you? I'm not sure what he can do, but anything will help.'

'Leave it with me but had you considered having a break away? What about your parents? They'd love to meet George.'

'Actually it would only be my father as my mother died years ago. Yes I could visit him, but I can't look after George, can I?'

Joan was deep in thought. Suddenly a look of excitement came across her face.

'I tell you what Frank,' she said grabbing his hand, 'why don't I come with you and bring Lizzie? I could look after George as well; the school breaks up this week so I'll have the time.'

'I can't expect you to do that.'

'Oh go on, it'll give Mum and Dad a rest too!'

'I'll think about it; it's very kind of you to offer and Dad has plenty of room for all of us.'

Phyllis came through from the kitchen.

'Mum, Frank and me are thinking of a holiday in Somerset with the children and to stay with his father.'

Phyllis looked concerned.

Joan saw her mother's expression.

'Mum, it's only a holiday. It'll give you a break.'

'Of course,' smiled Phyllis. 'You go; it'll be good for you both.'

***

Two weeks later they were at Frank's father's house in Wedmore, a few miles from Wells. The doctor had indeed paid a visit and prescribed pills to help Frank relax. He now slept better and felt more positive about life in general. He and Joan found his father in good spirits, delighted to have his son home and to meet his little grandson. He was working during the day leaving Joan and Frank plenty of time together to enjoy walks around the village, pushing the two babies in the one pram.

Frank liked Joan; she was easy going with a ready smile, attractive without being pretty, with wavy, blond hair held back by clips. Tall for a woman and with a rounded bosom and wide hips, she walked with a poise and elegance unusual for a country girl. Despite his reservations about the trip, he had managed it without the panic he had felt previously.

Sitting in the garden in the afternoon sun whilst the babies slept in their pram, Frank stretched his arms towards the sky.

'Joan, this idea of yours to come here has really helped me.'

'I knew it would because you need families at such a time. You were in a rut at home with nothing to think about except Marie and to feel sorry for yourself.'

'But Joan, you have coped really well with what you went through; Phyllis told me what happened.'

'She shouldn't have said anything,' said Joan, slightly embarrassed.

'It's not something a woman can recover from that easily. I could have arranged to have the man tracked down.'

'I know, but the damage was done and I wanted nothing to do with him. When I found I was expecting that sort of helped and I knew that something good would come out of it all.'

'Well, I think you're very brave and there's me feeling sorry for myself all the time.'

'We're all different, Frank!'

They sat for a while not speaking before Joan broke the silence.

'You must know a number of people round here. Have you always lived in these parts?'

'No. I was born in London; can't you tell by my accent? I came here when I was young, then my mum died and, after that, the war started. I attended school in Wells and have friends there and I was close friends with one. He is older than me, but we became friends and, in fact, met up in France: he helped Marie and her father right at the end of the war and after. He's a doctor or, at least was, but the last I heard he was thinking of joining the Intelligence people.'

'Does he still live round here?'

'I don't know. His folks do; his father is the Dean at Wells Cathedral.'

'You should visit the family; I'll look after George, so why not tomorrow?'

Frank thought for a few moments. 'Do you know what, that is a good idea, as long as you don't mind?'

'No, not at all. You go.'

***

Frank pulled the bell hanging above the front door of the Dean's house and Mrs Ingleby answered. She failed to recognise him at first but once he introduced himself she excitedly invited him inside where they chatted for over an hour. Mrs Ingleby was moved to tears when Frank told him what had happened to Marie.

'Goodness me, Frank, you've been through so much. Jack mentioned he'd seen you in France after the war ended.'

'Where is Jack these days?'

'He's in London now. He didn't carry on with his medical work; he's in the Civil Service. He doesn't say much about what he's doing, but he has a nice car which means it must pay well. By coincidence, he's coming home on Friday for the weekend, so if you're still around, why not come over?'

'I hope to still be here and could come over on Saturday morning.'

'That'll be fine. It's a shame, but Mr Ingleby and I will be at a service in Bath because I would love to meet the young lady and the children. Perhaps another time, but do come over; Jack will be pleased, I'm sure. Did you know Jack has been writing a book?'

'Yes, he mentioned it when we were in France and I gave him details about my experiences of shell-shock. I knew a soldier who had it badly.'

'Well, he has almost finished it and has a publisher; a fellow he knew from university. He hopes it will be out some time next year.'

'Good for him, I'll certainly buy a copy.'

Mrs Ingleby laughed.

'Oh, I'm sure he'll give you one for free, Frank, especially if you've helped him with it!'

Shortly afterwards, Mr Ingleby arrived home and, following a pleasant lunch, Frank caught the bus back to Wedmore.

***

Frank decided to see Ingleby on the Saturday without Joan and the children. When he arrived at the Inglebys' house there was a smart blue Bentley parked outside. Jack came out of the house to greet Frank.

'Is this yours?' said Frank in mock surprise, looking back at the car.

'Most definitely, old boy; I don't really own it but don't tell my parents! My friend in London lets me borrow it in return for me letting out the spare room in my flat.'

They stood on the veranda overlooking the garden.

'I was deeply sorry to hear from mother about your wife. How awful! Marie was such a sweet girl. How have you been since it happened?'

'Pretty depressed, Jack: scared and panicky to even leave the house at times, hot and cold sweats, feeling queasy and I'm still on sick leave but have some tablets from my doctor to help. You must have come across this sort of thing when you were a doctor is there anything I can do?'

'Not really, old man, you've been through so much. It's probably an anxiety thing, not dissimilar to shell-shock. Can you see the similarities with your friend, Eddie?'

Frank thought for a moment, 'Do you know, Jack, I can. I hadn't thought of it before.'

'Well, all you can do is ride it out and be as positive as you can. Keep active, push yourself to do things and remember your little boy needs you.'

'I have been trying, but it's hard.'

'I know, Frank, I know. You'll be fine, you'll see.

'Thanks. I do hope so.'

Ingleby decided to change the subject.

'Frank, you know those notes you gave me about that Wilson fellow? Well, I've used most of them and added in some other research. If you wait a moment, I'll show you my draft manuscript.' He returned from the room next door with a large wad of typed sheets.

'Something of a magnum opus I'm afraid, Frank, but I have a publisher.'

'Yes, your mother told me.'

'If you turn to chapter fifteen, you'll find that's the one all about your friend Eddie. Read it, it'll not take long; I'll make us some tea.'

Frank found the right pages. He could recognise many of his own words and the facts were faithfully repeated without too much embellishment. It brought back memories: Marie's words were there, too, detailing what it was like nursing Eddie during his breakdown; followed by Eddie's last days in Poperinghe as he waited for his execution.

Ingleby sat drinking his tea and waited for Frank to finish reading.

'Powerful stuff, Jack, bloody good actually.'

'Have I told your part right? Have I reflected Wilson's moods after his breakdown and what your wife saw during it?

'Oh, I think you have, most definitely,' said Frank, handing Ingleby the sheets of paper.

'It'll probably come out under a pseudonym. It's more than a little anti-establishment and conflicts a little with my work. My superior knows about it and I've shown him the more controversial parts. He seems happy with it, but it will have to be read by more senior people, apparently.'

'You can't be too careful, Jack, and it is early in your career.'

'Well, I'll take that chance, old boy! Anyway, it's not quite finished yet. Funnily enough, I was about to contact you but, now you're here, you've saved me the bother. What I would like is to obtain the views of Wilson's family for that part of the book because at present it has a little too much scientific stuff and needs a wider, more human story. Wilson must have found a way to write home when he was on the run, don't you think? He might have told them how he was feeling. Are you in contact with his family?'

'No, but I do have their address and Marie and me did say we would visit. It would kill two birds with one stone if I came with you. I know they had at least one letter from him because I posted it!'

'So let's go together and it might help with your recuperation too. Where do they live?'

'Just outside Burnley.'

Ingleby was thoughtful for a moment, 'That's Lancashire isn't it? By chance, I've a meeting to attend in Blackpool during October. I could stop off and interview them when you're there. What do you think?'

'It sounds good to me and if you let me have the dates when you'll be there, I'll contact them to ask if they're willing to help you.'

Soon after, they left for a pint at the local pub where Frank asked Jack about his work in Intelligence.

'I can't tell you too much,' said Ingleby in hushed tones and looking round the bar to make sure no one could overhear. 'What I can say is that we're watching subversives; you know those from abroad looking to prey on the weak here. Following the Russian revolution there'll be Bolsheviks here feeding off the unrest and economic problems. Who knows the Germans might also rise again for round two; they won't be happy with the terms of that treaty signed a couple of years ago.'

'Phew,' said Frank, 'I hadn't considered that at all, perhaps I've been too wrapped up in my own problems. I understand your point and how important a lid is kept on it.'

They parted, promising to finalise the arrangements once Frank heard from the Wilsons and by Monday he, Joan and the children were back in Broomfield. It had been a good break for Frank with plenty to take his mind off his problems and to spend more time with George. He had felt a cloud lifting from above his head, but within days he returned to his gloom as George became ill. Phyllis had to call out the doctor during the night, as she was worried by a rash on George's back and his temperature was high. Joan ran round to tell Frank who immediately feared the worst. Back at the Parmenter's the doctor decided to take George into hospital for a thorough check but for Frank it was too much and he took to his bed.

Later that day, Hebden came to the bottom of the stairs.

'Frank, there's a Josie Walmsley asking for you. Shall I show her in?'

Frank swore to himself.

'No,' he shouted, 'I don't want to see anyone!'

Hebden returned to Josie.

'I'm sorry. You probably heard that, but he's depressed again. He was recovering, but his little one's now sick and he's worried.'

'Don't worry, it's fine,' said Josie. 'I'll drop round to Mrs Parmenter's to see how George is.'

Arriving at the Parmenters' she found everyone lifted by the news that George has a mild attack of measles and had just arrived home.

'Frank should be told. He wouldn't see me when I called round; he was a bit rude, actually.'

'That's not like him,' said Phyllis, 'but he was worried about George. Frank's been sitting around not doing much until last week when he visited his father. My Joan joined him to look after the children and George must have picked up the measles on the trip.' She called out to Joan,

'Can you tell Frank about George?'

'I'm on my way,' shouted Joan from the hall.

'I'll come with you,' said Josie.

Frank was buoyed when they told him.

'Josie, I'm sorry I said what I did earlier; you caught me at a bad moment.'

Josie looked at him sternly.

'Joan has told me what you've been like. Think how you are letting yourself down and your little boy. He needs you; we all need you. Yes, you lost Marie and we all felt that loss, but think of all those families round the world that lost their nearest and dearest in the war. You're not special. Look how you encouraged Marie to move. For goodness sake stop feeling sorry for yourself and get on with your life!'

For a moment Frank was lost for words. He put his arms round Josie.

'You're right, of course you are. I'm being stupid, but it's hard to break out of it. I will try, I promise I will try.'

'And don't forget, we'll all help you,' said Joan. 'Now what about sorting out that trip to your friend's family up north? Jack Ingleby will be waiting to hear.'

***

After the women left, Frank looked for his diary. He found it in the drawer of the bedside table. Turning to the inside back page, he found the scrawled address in pencil, written whilst he was with Eddie out in Belgium.

In his letter to the Wilsons, he explained how he knew Eddie and told them about Marie. He also mentioned the book and what Ingleby would like from them, suggesting a date for the visit to coincide with Ingleby's trip to Blackpool. Within a few days he had received a reply from Mrs Wilson inviting them to stay for a weekend.

He travelled up by train on the following Friday, having arranged to meet Ingleby at Preston. The long journey gave Frank the chance to decide exactly what he would say to Eddie's family. He was aware they knew of the Court Martial, but beyond that he was not sure what else they had been told. He simply mentioned in his letter about being with Eddie in Belgium shortly before the outcome of the Court Martial was known.

He had an hour's wait at Preston for the Blackpool train before he and Ingleby travelled on to Burnley where they parted. Not wishing to inconvenience the Wilsons with an extra guest, Ingleby had booked into the Sparrow Hawk hotel in the centre of Burnley. He intended to come over to the Wilson's on the Saturday morning.

The family lived a few miles out of Burnley in the small village of Padiham. Not sure how to get there, Frank saw the sign for the Police Station as he left the Burnley station concourse. Inside, he presented his warrant card to the desk sergeant and asked for directions. The sergeant told him he was due to drive out to the Padiham area later and offered Frank a lift in one of the police wagons. Frank waited in the canteen and after the sergeant joined him for a cup of tea, they set off.

When they pulled up outside the Wilson house, a woman came rushing out to speak with them.

'Is it me husband?'

Frank leapt out.

'Mrs Wilson, it's me, Frank Shipley.'

'Oh, thank God. I thought summat must have 'appened to Tommy when I saw you. Come inside, lad; don't worry about thy feet. We do appreciate you coming all this way. Weren't you bringing a Mr Ingleby?'

'I have, but he's staying in Burnley. He didn't want to inconvenience you; he'll come over tomorrow.'

'Perhaps just as well 'cause the two of you would've snuggled up in our Eddie's old room. We are all reet sorry to hear about thy wife. Dreadful, what about t'little lad - How's he doing?'

'He's fine, thanks. I have a lovely lady looking after him. I'll be returning to work shortly, but Marie's death hit me hard and I've been on extended leave.'

She ushered him through the dark hall, past the front room and into the parlour. A young woman was standing by the open fire.

'Frank, this is Eddie's sister, Hilda.'

'Hello Hilda pleased to meet you.'

The slim young girl smiled and shook Frank's offered hand. She was tall with rosy cheeks and Frank could see a likeness to Eddie around the eyes, with similar laughter lines at their corners.

Mrs Wilson guided Frank into one of the four armchairs in the small room.

'Tommy'll be home soon, once he's finished shift at t'mill. Let's wait to hear all about our Eddie when he arrives. I've kept some hotpot. Hilda, fetch it for t'lad.'

Hilda returned carrying a tray with a plate of steaming meat and vegetables, together with a thick slice of bread and a glass of stout. They chatted, first about George and then Marie. Frank told them how close Eddie and Marie had been, but they already seemed to know that. They explained that Eddie had managed to send letters through to them, but these were sketchy and a little strange at times.

As Frank finished his meal, Tommy Wilson arrived home. He was much taller than Eddie and very thick set. He had a heavy accent, more Yorkshire than Lancashire, and much stronger than the rest of the family. At first Frank had trouble in following what he was saying, which they all found extremely amusing.

Tommy poured himself a glass of stout and another one for Frank; they all sat round, making a circle with the armchairs. Mrs Wilson spoke first.

'We do appreciate what thee did for our Eddie; he often mentioned you in his later letters. Whilst we miss him so, we're over the worst. Don't spare us any of the details, will thee?'

Having given the matter much consideration on the journey, Frank was well prepared and started with a question.

'First of all, it would be interesting to hear what you do know and what you were told at the time.'

Hilda looked at her parents as if waiting for them to say something, but they both looked at her, so she explained.

'We had a letter from a Major Burnside telling us Eddie was presumed dead after he was reported as missing after an artillery attack at or near the Front. He doesn't have a grave.'

Hilda looked at Frank. He remained impassive, although he knew this story to be untrue. It was interesting that Burnside had written to them, too.

Hilda continued.

'Apparently, his name is to be placed on a memorial out in Belgium, but it hasn't been built yet.'

'There's one to be built round here too,' chipped in Mrs Wilson.

'They will be everywhere. Our village is raising funds for one,' said Frank. 'What else did they tell you?'

'Only that Eddie had been cleared of all charges against him and had returned to the fighting,' confirmed Hilda. 'Did you know this Major Burnside?'

'No,' he lied, a little unconvincingly. He could only think Burnside sent this letter under orders.

Tommy had remained quiet, but then asked,

'Is there owt more we should know?'

Frank flushed a little.

'No – not at all. As you know, I was close to Eddie, but I was not really fully aware of the circumstances of his death. I heard he'd been killed, but we lost touch after his Court Martial, that's all.'

Tommy was satisfied and Hilda asked,

'Tell us about how you captured Eddie and what happened up to and including the Court Martial.'

He told them all he felt he could. It was upsetting for both women. Tommy, too, was visibly moved by the story. He left the room and returned with two more bottles of stout, but said nothing.

Hilda opened a drawer in the sideboard and pulled out a letter.

'This was from Eddie, written from his cell.' She gave it to Frank to read.

'Dear Ma Pa and Hilda

Are you well I am fair. All bad news out here with this blasted war but keep some hope. I did ask Marie to write about what has happened to me. She is so kind. I am waiting my trial I don't know how it will go. Marie and this MP have offered to help. A good lad called Frank. We have much in common. He captured me and we came back here – just the two of us and a lot happened on the way. I might not get a letter to you again and if the worst happens try and be strong. Give my regards to any of the lads you see although most are over here. We are told it all could be over soon. I could see you at Christmas you never know so please don't worry about me I have got this far.

God bless you all

Your loving son Eddie'

When Frank looked up he saw the women wiping their eyes.

'What you don't know is that I put this letter in the post for Eddie, but I'd not seen what was in it until now. It's very sad, did you hear from him again?'

They all shook their heads.

'I'm off to me bed,' said Tommy, rising from his chair.

'Oh, Tommy, that writer's coming over in't morning so we can help with his book. He's at t'Sparrow Hawk right now,' said Mrs Wilson.

'Right. I'll take t'lad here to football after.'

Hilda shut the door behind her father.

'That's the football at Turf Moor in Burnley. Do you follow it?'

'Of course and I often chatted about it with Eddie. He used to play for Burnley, didn't he?'

'He should be playing there now; he was that good before the war and only fifteen.'

***

Ingleby arrived shortly after nine the next morning. Frank met him at the Wilson's front door and took him into the garden. Checking they could not be overheard Frank spoke quietly.

'I must warn you that they know little about what really happened to their son, but instead they've been given a cock and bull story about him being found innocent and subsequently killed at the Front, so tread carefully with your questions.'

'Right,' said Ingleby. 'I will. Thanks. I'm only really interested in the effect Wilson's breakdown had on them being this far away. They must have had letters.'

'They did. His sister read one to me and it referred to another sent to an aunt, which suggests there may be more.'

Frank took Ingleby inside to meet the Wilsons. True to his word Ingleby only kept to questions about Eddie's state of mind, but after some soup and a sandwich for lunch it was time for Tommy and Frank to leave for the match. Ingleby decided to stay at the house to write up his notes, promising to join the other two after the game.

Outside the ground in the middle of Burnley, the throng of people was enormous, with queues forming along the road outside the ground. The pair met up with Tommy's friends and they stood on the terraces at the packed cricket field end. Burnley were riding high in the league and the large crowd saw their team secure another win. When Frank and the others arrived at the Sparrow Hawk after the match, Ingleby was already there. He bought everyone in the group a drink, endearing him to them immediately.

After discussing every aspect of the game, the group pooled their money. Ingleby offered to hold onto this kitty and order the drinks when needed.

Whilst Ingleby was up at the bar buying the next round, one of the men asked Frank,

'How did thee know young Eddie then, lad?'

A little uncertain of what these friends might or might not know, Frank hesitated.

'I was with him in the war.'

'You don't sound like you're from round here so how come you fought together.'

'Oh no, we met away from the frontline; I wasn't in the East Lancs.' Frank felt embarrassed, but Tommy came to his rescue.

'Don't worry, lad, they all know about t'Court Martial.'

Looking relieved Frank added,

'It was me that captured Eddie. It's a long story but we became best mates and I helped him at his trial.'

'Well, thy must have done a bloody good job, that's all I can say!' The man looked round at the rest of the group who all nodded in agreement. He continued.

'So yon mate here's writing a book on shell-shock, Tommy tells us.'

'That's right; it will have a chapter on Eddie. I've given my two pennyworths and the Wilsons have too.'

'Good,' the man added. 'None of us here was called up, too old, but we saw them what's come home: broken men some of 'em, especially them that has legs and arms and whatnot missing. Those what look fit still ain't able t'work: it's their minds.'

A drink-fuelled argument followed about shell-shock and how dismissive the Army had been about it. Ingleby sat and made notes, pleased with this additional material.

Just after ten, Tommy stood up a little unsteadily.

'Come on, lad, time to catch us bus.'

After handshakes all round, everyone but Ingleby left. He saw them off at the door and, as he walked across the bar on his way back to his room, there was a loud blast from across the road. Frank and the other men fell back through the door with its force. They crouched. Ingleby had thrown himself to the floor and now crawled towards them. The glass from the door was slowly dropping onto the floor.

'Jesus,' someone shouted, 'what the bloody hell was that? It sounded like a bomb.'

Frank said nothing but carefully stood up, easing the door open. Shouts came from the men and women in the bar behind him and they moved forward for a better look.

'Stand back!' Frank shouted at them. 'There might be another one.' He opened the door further and peered out. People were scurrying away from a small black hole in the road. In the building opposite a man was shouting out of a window above the butcher's shop. Frank was unable to hear exactly what he was saying but it was high pitched and manic.

He called out to Ingleby.

'Jack, make sure they stay here and move back.' He slipped out of the door and pressed himself against the outside wall of the hotel. He looked up at the man in the window, who continued to shout and wave his arms. Frank could make out a few words; it was about the war and how he had been badly treated. A policeman arrived and ushered the remaining onlookers further along the road. As he did so, the man threw something out of the window and Frank saw the unmistakeable shape of a grenade. It bounced on the road and rolled towards the kerb about ten yards away. He dived to the ground and the grenade exploded, shattering the rest of the hotel's front windows.

'Get out of here!' shouted one of the policemen to Frank, 'it's not safe.' But Frank, crouching, moved to the policeman's side.

'I told you to bugger off!' said the policeman.

'I'm a copper like you. I was at the Station yesterday and saw your sergeant, Mattocks is it? The name's Shipley; I'm visiting. Where's this bloke obtained grenades from?'

'I don't know. It must be from the war. What's he been saying, can you make it out?'

'Something about being badly treated since he came home. Do you know who he is?'

'That's Sid Mulhearn, nearly bought it in France. Lost a leg and been locked up for a while. His mind's gone.'

'Come on, let's cross to the other side of the road and shelter in the butcher's doorway,' said Frank. Half way across a shot rang out. Frank saw the bullet make a spark as it hit the road. The policeman screamed out and fell. Frank pulled him into the shop's doorway.

'Shit, he shot me in the leg,' shouted the policeman. 'God that hurts, shit!'

Frank looked at the hole in the trousers and prised it open. Blood was seeping from the wound above the knee. The shot had missed the bone and imbedded itself deep into the thigh.

'It's not that bad, you'll be fine,' Frank said calmly. He undid the man's belt from his trousers and tied it round the thigh as a light tourniquet.

Frank looked out along the street. It was clear; apart from three more policemen crouched at the crossroads further down. Frank recognised one of them as Sergeant Mattocks.

Across the road the hotel door slowly opened. Ingleby shouted,

'Frank, what's happening? I saw a man fall.'

'Careful, Jack, the bloke has a gun and a man's down with a leg injury. Can you check to see if the hotel has a rear exit?' Ingleby turned and spoke to someone inside.

'Apparently it has,' Ingleby shouted. 'To a garden.'

'Well, take everyone out through there and, if you can, to the end of the street to my right. A police sergeant is waiting there with more officers. Tell them to move close to the buildings along this side of the street and bring a stretcher or at least something to carry this injured bloke on. Tell them to be careful, the man upstairs might have more grenades.'

Minutes later Ingleby was talking to Mattocks. One of the other policemen ran off towards the police station. The policeman at Frank's side was quiet now. Frank looked up towards the window, but a ledge was in his way.

'Hey, you, you up there, can you hear me?' There was no answer.

'Perhaps he's given up,' said the policeman.

'Give me your helmet,' said Frank. Frank put it on his hand and dangled it out towards the road. A shot rang out and missed the helmet by a few feet.

'Well, that answers that question. It's like the trenches all over again; we used to do that to tempt the old Hun snipers. Always worked,' said the policeman mournfully.

Frank could see the policemen led by Mattocks edging their way along the building with a stretcher.

'Who are you?' asked Mattocks when he arrived next to Frank.

'We met yesterday; you gave me a lift. I'm from Essex Police, remember?'

'Yes of course. Sorry, I didn't recognise you. Thanks, thanks for this,' said Mattocks genuinely. The two policemen with him loaded up their colleague and carried him away.

'Our man is a Sid Mulhearn, do you know him?' asked Frank.

'Yes I do. He has a tin leg and damage to his brain. God knows how he has a gun. Was the explosion down to him, too?'

'Grenades,' Frank chipped in.

'Bloody hell, that sounds more serious. We can't reach him through the shop very easily because it's too secure. We would have to break the door down and that might aggravate him. Perhaps we can talk him down. If that fails we'll have to take him out; we can't put people's lives in danger any more than we have to!'

'When you say take him out, do you mean shoot him?' asked Frank.

'We've not much choice, have we? I'll need permission and a gunman. The trouble is the nearest one is likely to be Manchester way. He'd never arrive here in time.'

'Have you any decent rifles at the station?' asked Frank.

'Actually we have, but my blokes couldn't hit a barn door from ten paces.'

'I could take him out'"

'How come?'

'I was brought up in the country – shooting rabbits, that sort of thing. I was trained by the Army to be a sniper at one point, but instead I was sent to the Military Police.'

'We'll use you as last resort, but I'll need permission. I think we should try and talk him down first, he might be more amenable now.'

Frank stuck out the helmet again. Another shot rang out and sparked up off the road. Frank looked at Mattocks.

'I don't think so, do you, Sergeant?'

'Right, Shipley, I'll obtain the gun and the authorisation I need for this. I'll return as soon as I can, but why don't you move away and double back round to the Hawk. The best view of this bloke'll be from the upstairs there.'

Mulhearn started up again. It was mainly incoherent but appeared to be about a land fit for heroes being nothing more than a broken promise.

'No jobs, no money and no life!' he shouted. 'The bastards nearly had me killed; now they want me to die! They don't care. All those lives given up – all for nothing!'

Frank was surprised to find Tommy and Ingleby waiting in the garden.

'Tommy, it'll be safer for you to go home,' said Frank.

'Nay, lad, I'll wait for thee and make sure you're alreet.'

'I should be helping you,' said Ingleby, 'you know, rank and all that! Not that I mind you doing it all, you've had the experience and I haven't.'

Frank looked at him and smiled. He told them what the police had decided to do. Leaving Tommy in the garden, Frank and Ingleby took a position upstairs in the front room above the bar. It had a good view of the house opposite and Frank slowly opened the window. Mulhearn stopped his shouting for a moment. Frank saw the rifle raised and ducked down into the room.

'What do you want?' shouted Mulhearn. 'Are you the bloody police?'

'No,' Frank lied, 'an old soldier like you. Look, this is serving no purpose. Come out, but lay down the gun and the grenades first. We can sort this out over a pint; why don't you simply calm down and come out into the street. I promise you won't be harmed; we can all sit and have a chat. There's no telling what might happen if the police have to rush you.'

'Sod off. I've had enough, I'm making a stand.' He pulled away from the window.

'Do you think he'll shoot himself before too long?' whispered Ingleby.

'Possibly,' said Frank, 'but I've had these stand offs in France in the war with deserters. If he wanted to kill himself he'd have done it already. Perhaps he wants us to do it.'

For almost an hour nothing was said apart from Mulhearn asking a few times, 'Are you still, there, coppers?' No one replied.

Mattocks joined them carrying a rifle wrapped in a cloth.

'That's great: an Enfield and with a sight fixed,' enthused Frank as he removed the cloth. 'These were used in the war and were damned effective. I wasn't aware they were now issued to the police.'

'They're not. Let's just say the station commander likes collecting souvenirs!' said Mattocks. 'But we've a problem: I have to wait for authorisation and there's no one around. One of my men has taken a motorcycle to Manchester to collect it, but he could be an hour or more!'

Ingleby stepped forward.

'Perhaps I can help here.' He produced a warrant card from his jacket pocket. 'With this rank and position, I have the necessary authorisation for this.'

Mattocks read the card, looked up at Ingleby and Frank before handing it back.

'Christ! That's a bit unexpected. We don't have many like you around here! Fine, right, Shipley do what you have to!'

Frank moved closer to the window keeping out of any line of fire from across the street.

'He's quiet at the moment, Sergeant. I can take him out, wing him like, and your men can storm in through the front door. Have you a key?'

Mattocks held up a key ring containing a number of different keys.

'Good, we need to have him fully exposed so I have a clear shot. I can wing his shoulder. What do you think?' Frank looked at them both.

'You might have been a good shot in the past but may I ask if you've done this sort of thing before. Are you convinced you can just wing him?' said Mattocks.

Frank laughed, 'I've not shot a man before, but all through the years when I was growing up I could shoot rabbits dead from fifty yards away. They were smaller and on the run too!'

'I can vouch for that,' said Ingleby, 'we knew each other before the war.'

'Well, if you're sure there's no other way, it'll have to be like that. I'll have the men in position ready to charge in. We'll have to give you a signal when we're ready and you can give the order.'

'Fine,' said Frank, 'I need you to distract him so he comes to the window and is a bigger target, I can then make sure. Cut out the back here and underneath him. Give him some abuse and annoy him but, for goodness sake, don't get yourself shot. Mr Ingleby here will hold up a handkerchief to tell you when to start shouting. As soon as I shoot him, Mr Ingleby'll wave the handkerchief from side to side for you to burst in. Do you understand?'

'Absolutely, and Good Luck.' He left via the garden and made for the far end of the street. After briefing his men, two headed to the rear of the butcher's and two came with him along the walls of the shop buildings until they were in position.

Frank set about checking the Enfield and adjusting the sight. He looked around the room and, with Ingleby's help, pulled a narrow chest of drawers across in front of the window.

'I can rest my elbows on here ready for the shot when he appears.' Frank positioned himself. 'Right, can you see the sergeant yet?'

'Yes, he's there with two men.'

'Now give him the first signal.'

Mattocks started shouting up at Mulhearn. Frank looked through the sight. A net curtain across the window flapped a little in the evening breeze. The two policemen joined in with Mattocks. Still Mulhearn failed to appear.

Frank became tense and was finding it difficult to focus on the window opposite. He looked at Ingleby and then outside; everything began to spin round. He was now sweating and closed his eyes, feeling he was about to be sick. He gulped and took a deep breath. He knew it was not the drink.

'Are you all right, old boy? Ingleby asked. 'You look awful?'

'I'll be fine in a moment,' he gulped again. Gradually the nausea subsided. He looked across for Mulhearn but there was still no sign. A shout came from the street. It was Mattocks.

'Mulhearn, you don't deserve any help from anyone; you're nothing but a waste of time.'

Mulhearn appeared in full view. A shot rang out and echoed amongst the buildings. Mulhearn was thrown backwards.

'Give the second signal!' Frank shouted to Ingleby. Seeing it, Mattocks unlocked the shop door and seconds later appeared at the upstairs window and shouted,

'We have him. He's alive, but his shoulder's shattered.'

Ingleby shook Frank's hand.

'Bloody brilliant shot! Are you feeling better now? You had me worried for a moment there!'

'Fine thanks, Jack, and thanks for your help; it was probably nerves.'

They left to re-join Tommy in the garden. With him were Mattocks and a man in civilian clothes. He came over and spoke to Frank.

'Well done, young man. Shipley, isn't it?' We can't thank you enough, what a shot! Have you had special training for this sort of thing?'

'No, sir, but I had plenty from my father when I was young and, of course, further training in the Army during the war.'

'I'm the local Commander here and I'll write to yours telling him what you've done for us. Are you only an ordinary constable?'

'Yes sir, just a village bobby.'

'Well, you're wasted, that's all I can say. Are you staying here for long?'

'No, I'm off home tomorrow, first thing.'

'You'd better give the Sergeant here what he needs before you leave.'

The Commander and Mattocks left.

After another half an hour helping fill out a report and giving his details, Frank met Tommy in the bar. Ingleby was about to leave for his room.

'Frank, I've a couple of matters to attend to in the morning,' he said, 'I'll meet you at Preston station at about ten thirty.'

A policeman drove Frank and Tommy home to Padiham where a concerned Mrs Wilson was waiting up for them. Annoyed at first she soon softened when Tommy told of the events of the evening calling Frank 'the hero of the hour'. Frank felt a little embarrassed and was not sure she believed it all, but she gave him a kiss goodnight and said 'Well done'.

***

When Frank left at nine the next morning, they all promised to keep in touch and Mrs Wilson said she would knit some baby clothes in the coming weeks and send them on.

His bus passed the hotel and the butcher's on its way to the station. Although it was still early, a few locals were on the streets: a small crowd was gathered outside the shop talking earnestly and pointing at both windows facing each other across the street. Frank smiled. It seemed last night had been nothing but a dream.

The early train was almost empty and very few people waited on Preston station when he arrived to pick up the connecting train. He looked out for Ingleby, but there was no sign of him. With a fifteen-minute wait before his train left for London he bought a newspaper and entered the station buffet. A log fire raged in the corner and the room was extremely warm, contrasting with the cold morning outside. The windows were steamed up and the room smelt of cigarette smoke and fried eggs. Three customers sat round one table and a middle-aged woman prepared the eggs in a frying pan behind a tall counter. She had a scarf knotted on her head and a cigarette hanging out of her mouth with a long piece of ash about to drop off.

Frank approached her. She said nothing but cocked her head as if to ask 'What?' He ordered a cup of tea and the woman told him to sit down as she'd bring it over. She left the steaming mug of tea in front of him and, as she moved away, the ash fell from her cigarette and dropped onto his trousers. Without saying a word she smiled, shrugged and used the back of her hand to sweep the ash onto the floor.

Ingleby appeared in the doorway wearing a pinstriped suit and carrying a briefcase. Frank stood up as he came over.

'Jack, you look like you've been to a funeral!'

Ingleby smiled and joined him at the table.

'No, government business here in Preston, even on a Sunday; we never stop!'

'Cup of tea?'

'Thanks.'

Frank called over to the woman for another cup, but she was in the back room and chose not to hear. He collected one himself and handed it to Ingleby.

'Cheers,' said Ingleby, 'did you sleep last night after all that excitement?'

'It was a while before I dropped off.'

'Me too and I was thinking about what you'd done and how you did it. In my line of work certain situations arise which, how can I put it, need dramatic solutions. We have trained marksmen already, but if push came to shove would you be prepared to work with me? I can always use another good man.'

Frank sat for a moment staring into space not sure what to say. The platform guard shouted from outside, announcing the arrival of the train from Glasgow and calling all passengers for Crewe and London. Frank paid for the tea and stepped out onto the platform. He could hear the engine in the distance.

'I need the 'Gents'; won't be a minute.' When he came out everyone except Ingleby had boarded the train. The guard was ready to wave it off.

They ran to the nearest door. The guard blew his whistle and waved his flag towards the driver leaning out of his cab; with a jerk the train pulled away.

They passed along the corridor looking through the glass panels of the compartments. The first two had families with young children, but the next was free. Frank placed his rucksack on the luggage rack above his head then sat opposite Ingleby.

'Where's your case, Jack?'

'Ah well, my driver's taken it. I met up with him earlier and he's taken it to Shrewsbury. I'm only with you until Crewe. I could have travelled with him, but I wanted a chat. You didn't answer my question.'

'Would this involve actually killing someone?'

'It might, but not necessarily.'

'I'm not sure I could do that, Jack.'

'It would only be taking out an enemy of the state or similar. We don't make a habit of it. It may be that I won't call upon you at all, but I'd like you up my sleeve. Occasionally, I need help from outside the Service for various reasons and you'd be an ideal man.'

'Well, if you put it like that you know where I am.'

'Good man, Frank, and there is something else. You were right about the Wilsons. They had been told a pack of lies about their son and it smells of a cover up by the Army. I wonder why they went to all this trouble. Clearly this Burnside chap knows all about it. I might track him down; it won't be difficult. I'll let you know if I find anything.'

'Thanks. Did you obtain much from the Wilsons about what they went through?'

'They did have quite a few letters. Fascinating stuff of a mind disturbed; a unique insight and I can't wait to write it up.'

'Make sure I receive a copy, won't you?'

'I'll post it, old boy, probably be ready next year.'

They were soon approaching Crewe and Ingleby stood up.

'One thing, Frank, about this weekend, you've come alive and look much better than when I saw you in Wells. I hope George fully recovers from his measles and do try to return to work soon, it'll give you a purpose and help you forget all that's happened.'

He pulled the sliding door and stepped into the corridor.

'One other thing; that Joan? Sounds like a lovely girl!' He shut the door quickly and waved through the window, laughing. Frank smiled sheepishly.

5

A week after his trip north, Frank returned to work. Waiting for him on his desk was an invitation from the Chief Constable to attend the Chelmsford Station the following Friday in dress uniform. He couldn't think why, but when he arrived the station was alive with excitement. He joined a group of officers gathered in the courtyard behind the station. The Chief Constable arrived and stood on the steps to read out a letter. It was from his counterpart in Lancashire detailing Frank's part in the standoff with Mulhearn. He also read an official citation and presented Frank with the Police Medal, bringing a cheer from his colleagues.

As they dispersed, Frank was invited to the Superintendent's office. The Chief Constable was there and spoke first.

'Shipley, we've also had a letter from a man called Ingleby; he's from the Home Office. I understand you met him when you were in Burnley. I won't read it, but he's recommending you be marked down as a specialist gunman and, as necessary, be used in the type of situation you encountered when he was there with you. Now, we have no problem with that, but, of course, these situations are, fortunately, few and far between. This will, however, be placed on your file and you may well be called upon in the future to carry out a similar exercise either in Essex or further afield.'

All present looked expectantly at Frank, but he was unmoved and the Chief Constable continued.

'It seems you've made a real name for yourself. However, you will have to be patient and see what unfolds. Hopefully, you'll move up to Sergeant soon. All I can say for now is 'well done' and 'good luck'.'

Returning to his normal duties, Frank read through the files and reports made by Hebden bringing him up to date with events in the village. He made sure he was seen out and about and everyone had a word for him or simply a wave. A parcel arrived from Mrs Wilson with two cardigans for George and a short letter enclosing a full-page article from the *Lancashire Telegraph* all about the siege and Frank's part in it. It also highlighted the reason why he was visiting the town, mentioning Frank's friendship with Eddie and the Wilson family.

Not a day would pass without him calling on George who was thriving and fully recovered from his measles. Invariably, Frank would join Harry and Phyllis for a meal either during his dinner breaks or for his late afternoon tea.

Phyllis was perfect for both George and Lizzie treating them as if they were her own children. Harry spent much of his spare time building toys for the two little ones. Although they were a little young to use them yet, they could look forward to a double-seated rocking horse, a swing with a double basket seat and even a little two-seater pedal cart with a wooden steering wheel.

Frank could not believe his luck in finding such wonderful people to look after his son, but he often sat alone in the evenings feeling morose and sad. He missed Marie deeply: her infectious smile, her cheeky giggle and her tender love – now sadly gone. Had it not been for George, he would have completely fallen to pieces. His police work remained less than challenging and he wanted to move on, but now he had to think of his little son and the care the Parmenters were providing.

For the next few months, life continued much the same. He had received no call from Ingleby's in respect of the special duties for which he had been earmarked. George enjoyed his first Christmas with the Parmenter family; Frank was on call, but nothing happened. He was able to spend plenty of time with his son, but felt the pain of missing Marie even more at such a family time with many dark, unhappy moments. He had continued to have many bad days especially when things remained quiet in the village and his policing duties were minimal. If he was busy he was fine, but too often he had nothing better to do than feel sorry for himself.

One thing that lifted his spirits was being with Joan. Neither her Lizzie nor his George was crawling yet, but rolled around on the floor playing together. At Christmas they enjoyed opening their presents and playing with the wrapping paper like most small children. Frank bought the Parmenters a new china teapot.

Harry had dropped their old one and they were making do with Frank's metal one from the police house.

Frank treated Joan to a pair of gloves and she gave him a thick pair of socks. Taking a break from his duties, Frank invited her to The Angel for a drink before their Christmas dinner. Joan was excellent company, telling him funny stories about some of the villagers gathered in the bar. Many came over for a chat.

Joan was still at the school, but now working the full school hours. To supplement her income, she served in the local grocery store on a Saturday. She was able to pay her parents for her keep, but rarely socialised; content instead to stay at home to look after Lizzie and George in the evenings. She told everyone she was steering clear of men after what had happened in Norfolk. Despite this, she enjoyed Frank's company; she felt drawn to him, but kept her distance, mindful of his loss and how he felt about Marie.

After their Christmas dinner, they walked with the two babies in their pram past the cricket field and towards the ford in Mill Lane. It was already becoming dark. They stood silently next to where Marie's accident had happened. The two posies were still there, now wilted and brown. Joan picked them up as Frank bent down and placed a small wreath on the grass verge. He stood hunched in his thick policeman's coat. He pulled a handkerchief from his trouser pocket and blew his nose. He looked at Joan. She smiled and held his hand, squeezing it tight. She pulled him to her and gave him a hug.

***

Frank was in his office one early afternoon in the spring when Joan burst in. He jumped out of his chair and helped her into it. She was trying to speak but was too breathless. Eventually, she managed to say,

'Alf Harber's causing trouble at the school; threatening the Headmaster.'

Frank grabbed his helmet, collected his bicycle from the shed and headed off to the school. There he found only calm, with Alf Harber and the Headmaster drinking tea in the school office.

Alf was head of the Harber family, gipsies who lived in their caravans a short distance from the school. His eight-year-old son, Willy, had told his mother at dinnertime he was being suspended from school. When Alf had arrived home after a few drinks at The Angel and heard the story, he had stormed off to confront the Head.

'Come in, Constable Shipley, have a seat,' said the Headmaster. 'Mr Harber has calmed down now; it's all been a misunderstanding.'

'I'm glad to hear it,' said Frank, looking reproachfully at Mr Harber, who looked sheepishly away. 'But, Alf,' Frank continued, 'you can't upset Miss Parmenter in the office and threaten the Headmaster like this.'

Alf looked up, said nothing, but shook his head.

'You must watch your drinking, Alf; I've told you before about it and, if something like this happens again, I'll have you charged. What sort of example are you setting for Willy?'

'I'm sorry.'

'And one other thing: don't take it out on Willy just because he didn't understand. Do I make myself clear?'

Alf nodded.

'Sorry,' he said meekly and left. Frank followed him out and as he neared the school gates, Joan came hurrying towards him, looking concerned.

'It's fine, Joan, all sorted out. A misunderstanding and no harm done, we've sent Alf Harber off with a flea in his ear!'

'Thank goodness! Sorry to have dragged you out unnecessarily, but it looked like it might become out of hand.'

'No, you did the right thing.'

'Before you go, can I offer you a drink? Tea, perhaps?'

'Yes, I do have a little spare time,' Frank said, looking at his watch. 'I'm due in Chelmsford later, but not until four.'

They sat in the empty staff room, chatting about what had happened. Joan looked pretty in her flowery dress, cream with large red flowers matching the colour of her cardigan. Her eyes were icy blue and complemented her blond hair. She was slimmer than when they had first met, having lost the extra weight she carried after Lizzie was born. Frank was fascinated by her smile and now, as she spoke, he was barely listening. He interrupted her.

'I have Friday night off. Would you like to come to the pictures with me?' he blurted out.

Joan was taken by surprise and hesitated. Gathering herself, she held his hand.

'That would be lovely. What's on?'

'It's that Charlie Chaplin film we were talking about at Christmas. It's doing the rounds for the second time.'

'Oh, even better!'

***

By the time Friday arrived, Frank was as nervous as a kitten. He took the old suit his father had given him when they were in Somerset out of the wardrobe in readiness, but had to put it outside on the clothesline to remove the smell of mothballs. When he put it on it was a little tight around the middle and still smelled slightly; he could not find the tie that matched it and all he had was his police one. Not wanting to be seen out with a girl wearing a police tie, he borrowed one from his neighbour.

He wanted to slick down his hair with a centre parting, but found the hair oil left over from his war service now smelled rank and he had to pour it into the sink. Instead, he opted for a side parting using water.

He looked in the mirror and was satisfied. He had arranged to meet Joan at the bus stop. The clock on his mantelpiece said two minutes to seven and they had agreed to catch the five past. The picture started at eight fifteen leaving them plenty of time and to queue if necessary.

Joan was already at the bus stop. She was wearing a calf length skirt in beige with a blue blouse that matched her eyes. Her hair was soft and wavy; a touch of rouge on her cheeks served to accentuate her high cheekbones.

'You look lovely,' said Frank.

'Thank you,' she replied, looking at the ground, slightly embarrassed.

Once seated on the top deck of the bus, they chatted about their day until Joan laughed.

'What's so funny?' asked Frank.

'The whiff of mothballs.' She laughed again.

'It's a long time since I was all dressed up. I did my best to air it.'

'No, it's fine,' said Joan more seriously. 'Perhaps you'll have a chance to wear it more often now.'

Frank looked at her knowingly and smiled.

A queue was forming outside the cinema with the immaculately dressed commissionaire keeping order. After buying their tickets, they headed through the double doors to the stalls and an usherette moved towards them and showed them to the back row. Frank was about to ask to be seated nearer the front when Joan pulled him towards the row, giggling as she did so.

Taking off their coats and settling in their seats, they looked at each other and laughed. Most of the other couples in that row were already kissing and cuddling, not paying any attention to anything else.

The Pathe newsreels carried the latest news from around the world. Finally, the pianist started playing and the film began. Joan reached out to hold Frank's hand. During the film, which had them roaring with laughter at Charlie Chaplin's antics, Frank slipped his arm around Joan's shoulders and pulled her towards him. She nestled her head into his neck.

When the film ended they headed for the bus station, arm in arm. Their bus was not due for at least ten minutes. It was chilly now and Joan cuddled into Frank as they chatted and laughed about the film. She looked up and kissed him fully on the lips. The kiss was long and passionate. As she broke away she looked up and smiled.

'Have you enjoyed yourself tonight?' she asked.

'It's been the best I've had since –'he broke away.

'Well, it's been great for me too. I've not been out with anyone since Lizzie arrived. Thank you for inviting me.'

'To be honest, Joan, I've been trying to pluck up courage since Christmas when we were in the pub and had that walk.'

'You shouldn't have waited all this time, you chump!' She kissed him again but more softly this time.

***

As spring gave way to summer their relationship became stronger. When Frank's duties allowed, he played a few games of cricket for the village club. With their ground being close to where Marie was killed, he always left a small bunch of flowers by the side of the road each time he played a home match. Joan often brought the two children along to watch. George and Lizzie were now toddling around and into everything; they still lived with Harry and Phyllis.

In the early autumn, Frank was called to a meeting at the main station with Superintendent Allen who looked on edge when Frank came into his office. Sitting at his desk, he twiddled his pen nervously.

'Sit down, Constable. I'm pleased to say you are being made up to Sergeant. I know it has been a long time coming, but we have had no local vacancies and I knew you would not wish to be moved too far because of your son. I will be putting you in charge of the station being built on that new development between here and Broomfield. It will eventually be very large with shops, schools and hundreds of houses – even its own pub.'

Allen waited for a reaction from Frank, but he said nothing. Allen opened a file, put on his glasses, read something before carefully placing the glasses on the desk. His hands were shaking slightly.

'I have to raise another matter. It's the question of your marital position, sadly we discussed this before in different circumstances and you are aware the police rules state that, to live in the family police house, you must be married. I've been able to allow leeway on this given the tragic events of last year, but regrettably we have to deal with your possible move out of where you are now and, of course, the same rules will apply to the house you'll be offered on the new development. However, should you have any plans to remarry that would put a different light on the matter. Is this likely in the foreseeable future?'

'Actually, sir, I do have a girlfriend and I've already made up my mind to ask her to marry me. Could you allow me to stay on at least until mid April next year, by which time I'm sure I'll be married? If my girlfriend says 'No' to the engagement and marriage, I'll move out as soon as possible, but I'm confident this will not be the case.'

Allen looked relieved.

"Oh, that is good news. You've been through hell and you've coped really well. I was proud of what you did up in Lancashire. In view of Broomfield's expansion, we're moving in Constable Hebden to work with you there for now, with a view to him taking over when you move on. This will not be long in coming, as the station will open as soon as the new residents start to move in. Once there you'll have a team of at least two constables working under you.'

Allen stood up and offered his hand.

'Well done, Frank, do let me know what the little lady says won't you?' They shook hands and Frank left. Allen sat in his chair and blew out his cheeks.

Frank could hardly wait to tell Joan and her parents of his promotion. After he completed his rounds of the village and before returning to his office, he dropped in, as usual, to see George, helping to put him to bed. Phyllis poured a cup of tea and gave him a plate of sandwiches. There were kisses and handshakes all round when he told them. Later, he and Joan left for The Angel and, once in the corner of the bar with their drinks, he asked his question. Joan stood up and came round the table to him, held him round his neck and kissed him several times.

'I'll take that as a 'yes' then' was all he could say.

After finishing their drinks they hurriedly returned to the house. Excited, Joan ran straight inside and was jumping up and down as she told her mother and father. More kissing and hugging followed.

Frank led Harry away from the women.

'Sorry, Harry, that I didn't formally ask your permission before all this happened.'

'That's fine, son. Me and Phyllis thought you'd never get round to asking!' He slapped Frank on his back and they returned to the others. Phyllis opened a bottle of sherry and Harry proposed a toast.

Returning to his office, Frank completed the paperwork left from earlier in the day. He locked the front door and went into his rooms. As he relaxed into an armchair and stretched out his legs, he reflected on what a day it had been. He stood up in front of the mantelpiece and picked up the only picture he had of Marie before kissing it.

6

The excitement and sense of fulfilment with his promotion and engagement soon left Frank when he was called out to an accident in School Lane a few days later.

Willy Harber and his younger sister, Susie, had been on their way home after finishing school. Willy had been dribbling an old tennis ball and playing it back and forward to the grass verge ignoring his five-year-old sister. She had been jumping from the verge and into the road and back again. Suddenly she had missed the jump to the flat part of the verge and twisted her ankle on its edge. This had thrown her off balance and she had staggered across the road, knocking Willy over. A passing delivery van had braked and swerved, but caught Susie a glancing blow that had knocked her up into the air and straight out of her shoes; she had landed awkwardly on her shoulder and rolled onto her side, unconscious. The shocked van driver had pulled up and ran over to help the little girl while Willy had knelt next to her, crying.

Two women, walking further along the road, had come to help. They sent the driver to the Police House to use the telephone for an ambulance. Frank had been there and, having made the call, returned to the accident.

When he arrived the Harber family were there, too. He froze as he stood over Susie. This reminded him too clearly of Marie's accident and he felt that same chill inside. Susie soon regained consciousness but her shoulder was damaged and she wept softly, comforted by her mother. Frank, realising his duty, took statements from the driver and the passers-by before seeing off the Harbers in the ambulance. Still feeling a little shaken he slowly made his way back to his office with that memory of Marie constant in his thoughts. Despite his love for Joan, he knew how much Marie was a part of him and would probably remain so for some time to come, particularly through little George.

That evening he sat staring at Marie's photograph on a table in front of him. When in bed the image of her dead body in the mortuary was all he could see. It made him feel sick inside and he found sleep impossible. He recalled that Eddie Wilson had spoken of such flashbacks and how he was tipped back into his anxiety, though in his case it had been to the horror of the trenches.

The next morning Frank remained anxious and depressed. Stan Hebden, now in place at Broomfield, arrived to start his shift at eight o'clock. Frank told him he felt unwell and was returning to bed.

He stayed away from his work for three more days. His depression remained and he hardly ate anything nor slept well. Joan came in every day after she finished at the school, staying until the early evening before leaving to put the children to bed. She tried to bring him out of his mood but nothing worked and she encouraged him to visit the doctor.

Frank began to have doubts about what lay ahead and how he would cope: there would be the wedding, the new posting and the move to the new house to deal with in a short space of time. Right now he did not feel he could handle any of it. Despite his love for Joan and the children, it was all becoming too much. He felt too embarrassed by his weakness to see the doctor. He did not want more pills; they were not the answer.

Despite her comforting words, Frank knew he was worrying Joan and he needed help, but was not sure where to turn. He could see much of Eddie Wilson's state of mind in himself: a defeatist attitude in the mire of misery.

In desperation, he decided to visit the Walmsleys, his one connection with the past – and with Marie.

Josie was surprised to find him on her doorstep at nine one evening. He had cycled all the way across town in the rain. Having dried off, he sat in front of the fire with a mug of cocoa.

'Norman's at Rotary and won't be home until eleven,' Josie told him.

'I'm sorry to call on you like this, Josie, but I didn't know what to do for the best.'

He explained what he had been through over the past few days and his recurring problem since he had returned from France.

'Look, Frank, I'm no expert on this and you should, at least, consult your doctor, but you might remember we had a similar conversation when you were feeling depressed after Marie died. It seems to be the same problem, but you now have Joan and her child and George, of course. You've just been given a well-deserved promotion and face a new work challenge; you should be feeling on top of the world not in this pit of depression.'

She looked at him enquiringly.

'I know you're right, Josie, but it's hard for me. The whole thing is like Eddie and Marie's story being played out again, with tragedy upon tragedy. Being about to be married to Joan is like repeating how it was with Marie. Even small things, like the Police wanting me married in order to have one of their houses: it's become like the same dream, or perhaps a nightmare, over and over. Seeing that little girl lying by the roadside like Marie has triggered all this off again.'

'Of course, dear, but look at the positives because these changes are all good things and you have so much to look forward to. It's a settling down after all that you have been through. Try to see it as a new chapter; perhaps even a new book.'

'I will. Of course, I will. But just when I think I'm over it, the bloody thing starts up again.'

'Frank, I know you'll come through. I've been trying to put this into perspective for you and all I have come up with is for you to look at what you have now and compare it with something really awful.'

'Like what?'

'The men in the trenches, maybe? You might not have been there, but your friend, Eddie, must have told you what it was like and you would have heard other stories. They had real problems with death possible at any moment and awful living conditions. Now that is something to make you depressed and your friend Eddie's experiences would have sent the sanest man off his head.'

She looked Frank straight in his eyes. He nodded and she continued,

'Well, there you are, Frank. All I can suggest is that, each time you feel sorry for yourself, you just think of what it must have been like for him and those other men and how they would have happily changed places with your circumstances right now.'

Frank was thoughtful. He knew she was right. For a while, they chatted on about Joan and the children until it was time for him to leave.

'Josie, you've been such a help. I knew coming here was the right thing to do and I'll try my best. You've already lifted my spirits.'

'Well, simply remember what I said and, if you still struggle, ask for expert help.'

'I will. Now come here.'

He held his arms outstretched. They hugged and she kissed him on each cheek.

'Marry that lovely girl. Enjoy the children. That's the best advice I can give you.'

'Thanks, Josie, and give my regards to Norman; I'm sorry I missed him.'

He set off for home. The rain had stopped and the moon was bright in the clear sky. He felt this was a sign.

***

Frank soon settled into his police work and felt much better. With Hebden now full time, there was added responsibility. Frank joined the Territorial Army at the suggestion of Hebden, who was already a member. There Frank specifically requested to be allowed to hone and maintain his shooting skills, as the Police and Jack Ingleby had suggested.

Frank also spent as much time as possible with Joan and the children. When he was working at the police house, the children would often play in the garden with Joan or Phyllis. Harry had built a swing and a wooden climbing frame with a little house at the top for George and Lizzie to enjoy and also tidied the garden, planting vegetables and an array of winter flowers and shrubs.

Soon, daffodils flooded the garden with their spring flowers and the wedding arrangements were in place. Frank felt uncomfortable about holding the ceremony at Chelmsford Cathedral, where he and Marie had their blessing or at Broomfield Church, where her funeral had taken place. Joan and her family were very understanding; they decided on a civil ceremony with a reception afterwards at The Angel.

It was a glorious time: the children were excited to be pageboy and bridesmaid; Frank's father came up from Somerset and stayed with Harry and Phyllis for a few days; whilst Jack Ingleby travelled from London for the wedding day in the blue Bentley. It seemed the whole village crowded into The Angel to celebrate with them and wave the couple off to their honeymoon in Torquay.

Shortly before they left, Josie had a quiet word with Frank.

'You look wonderfully happy today, Frank, much better than when I last saw you. You must think you've turned a corner?'

'I have, Josie, I have, and much of it is thanks to you.'

***

In the summer of following year, Frank received an unexpected visit from Superintendent Allen. Frank was working in his office and Hebden was out on his rounds when Allen appeared in the doorway.

'Good morning, Sergeant, I have brought someone along with me.'

He turned and ushered his companion through the door.

'Hello, old chap, long time no see.' It was Ingleby.

'Jack! Hello, this is a pleasant surprise. How are you?'

'Fine. How's married life?'

'Good, thanks.'

'I'll leave you to it,' said Allen and he returned to his car.

Ingleby pulled up a chair next to Frank's.

"That was a lovely wedding, Frank, and is it really two years since we were up in Burnley? Despite what was said then, you probably weren't expecting to be asked to carry out a job like that one again were you?'

'Well I –' Frank started, but Ingleby continued.

'I've moved on to a different department since I last saw you, but there's a special task I want done and you came to mind. It is of utmost importance, national importance in fact, with orders coming from the Prime Minister himself. It could be dangerous, but with your expertise it might not be so. I can outline the task and you can let me know if you'll do it, but I need an answer today.'

Frank blew out his cheeks and raised his eyebrows. Ingleby continued.

'It will be very similar to what you did to that fellow in Burnley, taking someone out but not killing them.' He reached inside his jacket and pulled out an envelope, removed a photograph from it and passed it over.

'Take a close look; this is the target. He's a German called Neusen and a nasty piece of work. He's over here at the German Embassy and difficult for us to touch. I can only tell you a certain amount, but he's been stirring up anti-Semitic hatred in and around the East End of London where many Jews live. We suspect this is work supported by certain German factions and possibly the thin end of a larger wedge. As I say, he's protected by the immunity that being at the embassy brings. Consequently, we want him out of the way. To have him killed would be too much and cause awkward questions from the Germans. What we want is for him to be taken out whilst giving one of his anti-Jewish speeches, being caught in the act as it were. The Germans won't want to make too much of it, but we'll make sure it's in all the papers. They'll have to send him home. Problem solved, old boy!'

Frank was still looking at the photograph and said nothing at first. Neusen looked sullen and menacing: he had fierce, unsmiling eyes below bushy eyebrows matching his dark hair and trimmed moustache.

'National importance, you say?' Frank eventually said.

'Definitely!' said Ingleby eagerly.

'If you don't mind me asking but why me? Surely you must have men in whatever organisation you are in to do this sort of work?'

'That's a fair point, but, at most, only half a dozen people are aware of this and you know who three of them are! Double agents, for want of a better word, flourish in all areas of intelligence, but you are outside of all of this. That's why I thought of you and the fact you're a bloody good shot. What do you say?'

'How long will it be for?'

'It will mean a couple of days away. We'll probably require you next week as soon as we know when and where he'll next be speaking: I can let you know via your Super. Neusen usually speaks at open-air meetings, which will make things easier and we already have most of the arrangements set up. So?'

'I'll do it, assuming you have an adequate rifle, and I'll need some practice. What exactly did you have in mind in terms of the injury to this Neusen?'

'I would say enough for them to ship him home, but not enough to kill him. I'm told the rifle we have for you will be accurate enough to shatter a man's shoulder or knee from a distance. What about the knee?'

'Perfect, I'd say.'

'Good. You're right about getting used to the rifle. I can arrange that for the day before and we'll put you up overnight. You must not tell anyone of this, not even your wife and family. I'll square this with your boss before I leave and let him know as soon as I can next week. One of my men will help set you up at the location. All the planning is in place, we've been working on it for a while.'

'Fine, Jack, I'll wait to hear. By the way, you know we spoke when we were visiting the Wilsons about that Major Burnside, the chap who wrote to me and to the Wilson family? Did you find out anything about him?'

'Sorry, old chap, I meant to mention it. I tried. Bloody classified to such a level even I had no access. This means it must be serious and something important people do not want us to know about. This Burnside fellow seems to have gone to ground; no trace of him that I can find. I'll keep trying, old chap, but I shouldn't hold your breath.'

***

True to his word a letter arrived from Ingleby the following week. As Frank packed an overnight bag, he decided he had to tell Joan something. He found her hanging out the washing.

'Sorry to spring this on you, love, but Jack Ingleby's sent a missive and wants me in London for a couple of nights. I can't tell you much but it's linked to what happened up in Burnley.'

Joan looked disappointed.

'Do you have to?' she asked, knowing there would be no answer.

'Sorry, love, you know how it is but, look, I have to go. I'll be fine, don't worry and give the kids a hug from me.' Before Joan could say anything he kissed her and left.

'Be careful!' she shouted after him.

He travelled by train to Liverpool Street and was met at the platform gate by the agent, introducing himself as Langley. His car was parked in Bishopsgate and they drove to an old military camp in East Ham. Frank was billeted in a large, empty hut that in years previously would have been filled with recruits, but with the post war cutbacks, had clearly not been used for some time. The intelligence was that Neusen would be speaking the next evening from the bandstand in Victoria Park, Bethnal Green.

The next morning Frank was taken to the firing range. He was pleased to be given a Canadian Ross rifle, whose sight was much better than the Enfield he had used before, and he soon came to grips with its adjustment. He was rarely more than half an inch out at any target up to a two hundred and fifty yards - the work with the TA had paid off. Alone that night at the camp, Frank sat cleaning the rifle and checking the sight once again.

Langley returned in mid-afternoon the next day. He brought with him a hand drawn map of Victoria Park and the surrounding roads which he laid out on the table. Together they discussed the plan.

'Neusen will almost certainly come from the road behind the bandstand,' said Langley, pointing at the right hand corner of the map. 'He's spoken here before. Last time a taxi dropped him off and he walked through the one gate there. Fortunately, workshops are set into the arches of the railway as it passes by above the level of the park. One of these is empty and has been commandeered. A window in the loft provides a clear line of sight to the bandstand, but one important point is that you must not shoot until he starts speaking.'

'How far, roughly, from where he'll be standing will I be?' asked Frank.

'I measured it yesterday and, give or take, it's two hundred and eight paces.'

'No problem, but I'll have to adjust the sight a little. We're lucky there's this place close enough for a clear shot.'

'Well, we've been following this chap for ages and know his routine. He rarely speaks at more than three different places. We've looked at each one and planned accordingly.'

'After I shoot him, what's the plan?' said Frank, looking again at the drawing.

'Hopefully, there'll be a large crowd; several hundred gathered last time he spoke here. You're bound to cause confusion and some panic, but don't hang around even if you fail to hit him because you'll probably only have the one shot.'

'I'd better not miss then!' said Frank.

'I've a large overcoat for you to wear,' continued Langley, ignoring the comment. 'With the rifle hidden inside, walk out into the service road where you cannot be seen from the park. From there, pass under the bridge beneath the railway line and, when on the other side, you'll see my car. I'll bring you back here and you'll be able to return home tomorrow as if nothing has happened. Do you have any questions?'

'What if something goes wrong?'

'You're on your own and we'll deny all knowledge of you; you'll be simply a random chancer. Sorry, but that's the way it is!'

'I somehow knew you would say that.'

'It might be an idea to tell the police you're a Communist because that's the sort of thing we expect them to do.'

'Yes, well ...' said Frank, not totally convinced. 'Come on, let's go.'

The short drive through East London took less than ten minutes. It was quiet in the road running alongside the workshops beneath the railway line apart from the occasional train passing overhead. When they arrived at the workshop doors, Langley stood and looked round to check no one was watching before removing the padlock. As Frank started to follow Langley into the building a face appeared at the door to the unit next door.

'Can I help guv'nor?'

'No. It's fine thanks,' said Frank, pausing. 'We've only come to have a look. We might rent it, you see.'

'About bloody time as it's been empty for ages. What trade?'

'Oh, we just need it for storage. Import, export that sort of thing.'

'Righto, mate but anythin' you need to know, I'll be 'ere 'til five, so might see you again.'

'Thanks,' said Frank, relieved he could now go inside.

'Well done,' said Langley as he looked down from the open loft space. 'Shut the door behind you and come up the ladder. We'll set you up.'

The window opened just enough to allow the rifle butt to be poked through and for Frank to see the whole of the bandstand. By kneeling on the floor, he was able to rest the rifle on the windowsill and have a perfect view.

'I'll be in the road as planned,' explained Langley. 'Remember – escape as quickly as you can once you've fired. Here's the coat. Good luck!'

Frank settled down to wait and heard Langley drive off, but, shortly after, the door opened downstairs.

'Anyone here?' It was the man from earlier.

Frank cursed before calling out and moving to the top of the ladder,

'Yes, I'm up here.'

The man climbed onto the first step of the ladder, 'Oh, there you are,' he said.

'I was just up here taking in the view whilst my friend's gone to collect our business partner – looks like we'll take it,' explained Frank, coming down the ladder.

'Oh righto, mate, that's good,' said the man, backing away to the door. 'I'm off home for me tea. We might meet again.' He closed the door behind him and ambled off along the street, singing tunelessly to himself.

Frank leant against the ladder and whistled softly in relief. He was sweating and wiped his face with the coat.

Soon the crowd began to gather in the park milling around in front of the bandstand and talking in groups. Frank saw three policemen patrolling the edges of the park away from the main throng.

He checked his sight for the umpteenth time using the microphone on the main stage as his target. He was reminded of Burnley and hoped that, this time, he could keep his anxiety in check.

A young woman climbed onto the bandstand. She was applauded as if she was well known to the audience. She railed against the Government and its policies receiving tumultuous applause when she finished.

Frank readied himself. He could feel his heart pounding in his chest. His mouth was dry, but with no nausea this time, no dizziness. A stagehand came on to adjust the height of the microphone. Frank looked through the sight and followed the man across the stage to make one final adjustment.

The normal hubbub of a large crowd erupted into a loud cheer as a small figure leapt up to the stand with two heavily built men in suits by his side. Frank recognised him immediately – it was Neusen.

Momentarily, Frank felt his hands shake, but it passed. A bead of sweat formed on his temple as he lined up the sight onto his target, but he only had a clear view of Neusen's head.

The German began whipping up the crowd with his anti-Semitic, right wing rhetoric. Frank was surprised the policemen didn't intervene, but perhaps they had orders. Neusen's protection stood with arms folded at the front of the stage facing the crowd. Neusen, having dispensed with the microphone, was walking along the stage from one side to the other waving his arms and shouting.

This was unexpected, but Frank remained impassive; the point of his rifle followed the moving target. Neusen edged to the rear of the stage, Frank's finger squeezed the trigger slightly, but not enough to fire. The sight was now fixed on the back of Neusen's leg.

'Turn round,' Frank whispered, 'come on ... a bit more.'

Neusen obliged and was now standing still. Frank fired. Neusen reeled and fell to his left, screaming as his heavies ran to him. The crowd stood in stunned silence.

Frank pulled the rifle inside the window and slipped it into the deep pocket of the coat as he put it on. He wedged the butt under his armpit and climbed down the ladder. He slowly opened the door and looked out, but nobody was there. He shut it, fixed the padlock and ran into the archway. He came to a sudden halt and swore under his breath. The neighbour from earlier was walking towards him on the other side of the road and waved.

'Did he turn up?' The man shouted.

'Who? What?'

'Yer know, yer partner. Did he like it?' The man came across the road.

'Ah yes, thanks, fine, we'll be taking it.'

'Blimey, mate, you don't 'arf look hot, you're sweating buckets.'

'I'm in a bit of a hurry, actually,' Frank tried to edge away. The shouting from the park distracted the man.

'I came to see what the bloody gunshot was about. Is it a riot or somefin'?'

'I don't know. Look, must dash, 'bye.' Frank turned and hurried off leaving the man shaking his head.

'Bleeding posh git!' he said, as he reached for his packet of cigarettes and headed towards the park.

Langley was waiting with the engine running. Frank leapt into the passenger seat and Langley drove off.

'Did you get him? Langley asked.

'Right on his knee-cap, shattered it,' said Frank, proudly.

'Excellent! The Major will be pleased. I'll take a longer route back just to be on the safe side.'

Within half an hour they were back at the hut and Langley left immediately taking the rifle with him. Frank sat on his bed and, still feeling that tingle of excitement, knew he had coped better with his nerves this time. This was work he could handle and he hoped Ingleby would be pleased enough to use him again.

Two days later the papers were full of the news about a political shooting in the East End, blaming it on the Communists. Joan held the paper under Frank's nose at breakfast.

'I won't ask,' was all she said.

The following day a letter arrived in a plain brown envelope. Inside was a small sheet of white paper containing one typed sentence 'N on way to Berlin. Thanks.'

***

After the Bethnal Green assignment and the note, Frank heard nothing further directly from Ingleby until Superintendent Allen called Frank to his office a fortnight later with some news.

'Ah, Shipley,' said Allen, as Frank knocked and entered, 'I won't detain you long but I have a very favourable report from Major Ingleby – very favourable indeed. Those comments will be placed on your record but there is something else in that he particularly asks that you maintain your shooting prowess with the TA because almost certainly you will be called upon again.' Allen paused, 'Sorry, Sergeant, please do take a seat.'

Frank picked up a chair from behind the door and brought it to Allen's desk.

'Now, Sergeant,' Allen continued, 'I do not know, of course, what it was you did for the Major but from experience I can surmise it was important to him and, with the nature of his work, something of national significance. Are you content to continue with this type of work?'

Frank thought carefully for a moment recalling what he felt like after the Neusen shooting.

'Do you know sir,' he ventured, 'it could be dangerous, this work as you call it. I'm a family man and have to think of them but to be quite honest I found the assignment exciting and exhilarating. I would jump at the chance of working for Major Ingleby again.'

'So be it, Sergeant, but it worries me a little that the mundane life of a country bobby does not hold the same attraction, so I hope you'll stick with us until the call comes again.'

'Oh I will, sir, absolutely.'

'Good man. That's all for now, you'd better get back to your less than exciting duties.'

As Frank cycled back to his office he thought of the family. With the children still young, he did not wish to worry Joan unduly and he knew she had realised from the newspaper report of the Neusen shooting exactly what he was involved with. Part of him regretted giving her an inkling of what he was being asked to do but on the other hand he would not wish to hide things from her and he knew he would have tread carefully to ensure Joan did not worry unduly about what he might be involved with in the future.

***

George and Lizzie would be starting school the following year, but, now that 1925 was here, they spent three days a week at the local nursery school and their names had been put down at the primary school where Joan worked. It was likely, however, that their new house, provided with Frank's posting, would become available before that.

The planned development on the north side of Chelmsford was well under way. Some residents had already moved in, but street upon street remained under construction. The houses had large gardens and there were plans in place to add communal greenswards across the estate with a large park for sport and recreation at its edge. It would be an ideal place for the children to grow up in and Frank and Joan had already visited their new house which was waiting for its roof to be added. Their move there would not be long in coming and, this time, the Police House would be separate from the Station.

The new Police Station was almost complete and, as expected, Frank was confirmed as its Sergeant. Stan Hebden and a young constable would remain two miles away at Broomfield, but still under Frank's control with the two further constables working under him at the new Station. During the summer, Frank and the family moved into their new house.

It was a larger semi-detached property and included a small front garden with a long narrow one at the rear. Downstairs were a living room, dining room and sizeable kitchen supplemented by a toilet and pantry. There were two large bedrooms upstairs with a small box room, bathroom and toilet. Joan was delighted, especially to be separate from Frank's office. Although Harry and Phyllis were no longer close at hand to help with the children, the house was near to a new school with plenty of local amenities and shops. As Station Sergeant, Frank's pay would be considerably higher and this would help towards the family costs especially as the children grew older. For the Neusen shooting he received a separate single payment of two day's wages at quadruple rate which came as a surprise. Frank knew he had another reason to welcome another call from Jack Ingleby.

7

The family settled into their new life and Frank's workload was far greater than he had experienced at any time since he first arrived in Essex. Three years passed by without any word from Ingleby. The Superintendent was as mystified as Frank who threw himself into his job and soon dismissed from his mind any thoughts of the exciting work he expected with the Intelligence Services. He had tried to make contact with Ingleby but had met a wall of bureaucratic unhelpfulness and gave up.

The local population on Frank's manor, as he called it, grew considerably as the new housing was completed; yet its growth coincided with the economic slump being experienced not only in the Britain, but also around the world.

Chelmsford did not escape the downturn. Many of the large, local employers laid off workers as they struggled to come to terms with the recession. In desperation, many men turned to petty crime. Pilfering and more serious theft became a problem on the estate, giving Frank and his men a difficult time. Fights in the local pub, The Old Barn, became regular occurrences, as despair gave way to frustration.

Husbands and fathers were separated from their families, who were often put into the most basic care facilities. Some men became down and outs, drunks fuelling their problem by thieving. The Essex Home School for youngsters in care came within the area under Frank's control. This School was a strictly disciplined unit with military-like standards. The older children there, despairing of any sort of future, seemed set on a life of crime and would often target shops, houses, the community centre and even the chapels to steal anything they could. Frank's men seemingly spent half their time at this School tracking culprits and a wide range of stolen goods.

It certainly was a particularly difficult time for the country as it dipped even further into a financial and social quagmire with the forces of law and order stretched to their limits.

***

Out of the blue a manila, typed envelope arrived at Frank's home address and was marked with a red stamp of 'Confidential' with a London postmark. Before he even opened it Frank knew it would contain a letter from Ingleby. He was right and it invited him to a meeting at an address in London the following day. He knew what this meant and a twinge of excitement swept through his body. He immediately telephoned the Superintendent who already knew of Ingleby's request having also received a letter that morning.

With Joan at the park with the children Frank was unable to give her the news; news she might not welcome – a problem Frank would have to deal with later. Instead he cycled to the Station where he found one of his constables sifting through a file at the main desk.

'Morning, Sergeant,' the young man said without looking up.

'Good morning, Constable,' replied Frank, a little mockingly. 'Before we get down to the nitty-gritty of the overnight report I have to tell you I'm not here tomorrow as I have to attend a meeting in London. You'll have to sort out your shifts to cover for me. Can you manage that?'

Suddenly the young man looked up, more interested than before.

'I'm sure we can, Sarge. A meeting ... that sounds intriguing. They offering you a job up there, do you think?'

Frank laughed.

'I doubt it! Look, I need to sort out a few things at home, so can I leave you to cover until six when your relief arrives? But first though let's go through the happenings of the night.'

***

Arriving home well before lunch time Frank found Joan in a deck chair in the garden reading.

'You back already?'

Frank sat on the grass at her feet.

'Where are the children?' he asked.

'Oh Mum came round and took them on the bus into town.'

'Good, well look, love, I've heard from Jack Ingleby after all this time.'

'I see,' she said with a lack of enthusiasm.

'He wants me at a meeting in London tomorrow morning. You can guess what that could mean.'

'Something dangerous, I suspect?'

'Not necessarily.'

'Did he say anything in his letter?'

'No just that he was sorry he had not been in contact and would explain more at this meeting.'

'You know what, Frank? I worry about these things. I hoped that one job for him might be the end of it. What's it been, three years or more?'

'Something like that, love, anyway you're not supposed to know anything about that job!'

'Don't worry, I wouldn't mention it to anyone, but two and two makes four. I knew when I read the newspaper report about the shooting of that German chap it was down to you. A sort of sixth sense! You just be careful, sweetheart, that's all.'

'Thanks, love, I know it's hard for you if I have to go away but let's wait and see what Jack has to say as we might be jumping the gun.'

He knelt and kissed her fully on the lips before starting to move away, but she pulled him to her and they kissed again. She lost her balance, toppled off the deck chair onto the grass and rolled on her back. Frank was still on his knees and he fell on top of her. He kissed her open-mouthed and she responded.

'How long before Phyllis gets back?' asked Frank with a grin.

'Long enough, sweetie,' replied Phyllis getting to her feet and heading to the back door.

***

Frank showed his warrant card at the main desk of the Home Office. The commissionaire picked up the telephone, announced Frank's arrival and invited him to sit in the waiting area.

'My dear chap, how good to see you after all this time!' Ingleby called over as he came out of the lift. Frank was surprised by how much Ingleby had aged since they last met. Walking with a stoop, hair now very grey and with gaunt features he looked much older than someone should in their mid-thirties.

'You haven't seen the last of me after all,' Ingleby added. 'Well you nearly had. Turns out I have a heart problem. Do you remember I had rheumatic fever when I was five? It's left me with this problem.'

'Good God, Jack, I am sorry, but I don't remember you being ill and, don't forget, I'm four years younger than you. But I did wonder why I hadn't heard from you in ages.'

'Of course, but, anyway, I'm feeling much better. Come along, we've a load to get through.'

Ingleby led the way to the lift cage. Two floors up they entered a large office with a table surrounded by chairs. A man in a black suit, winged collar and black tie sat at the far end. He stood up when they entered and came over. Frank had seen his face before, but could not think where.

'Sir, this is the man I told you about, Frank Shipley.' Frank blushed a little. Ingleby did not give the man's name.

They sat at one corner of the table where Ingleby opened a thick folder in front of him and pulled out a large envelope.

'It goes without saying,' Ingleby added, 'that what we discuss here must be treated with absolute secrecy. What I am about to tell you is of such importance that, if it leaks out, goodness knows what might happen.'

The other man shuffled in his seat, coughed and nodded.

'Frank, of course you've heard of this Hitler fellow in Germany? He's a coming power over there. You might have read about his rally last year at Nuremberg? It was full of anti-Jewish rhetoric and pledging to get even over the Versailles Treaty.'

'I did read an article in the papers but hadn't realised –.'

'His National Socialists,' Ingleby interrupted, 'are a dangerous lot and certain factions here and, I think it's safe to say, some of our allies want to, let's say, nullify his threat.'

Ingleby looked at the other man.

'Oh, absolutely,' he confirmed.

Frank was surprised and looked at both in turn.

'When you say, 'nullify', what exactly do you mean?'

The two senior men exchanged glances, but said nothing. They looked at Frank knowingly.

'You mean kill him?' exclaimed Frank.

'Quite so, old man,' agreed Ingleby.

Frank stood up and walked round the table then turned to face them.

'Sorry, but why me?'

'As with Neusen, and for other reasons, we don't want to use a known agent for such a job,' said Ingleby.

'But, Jack, I've never killed anyone before. This is quite different. Is this Hitler that much of a danger to us? From what I recall reading in the papers, he's not being taken very seriously in Germany.'

'Well, Frank, he should be. Certain agencies and governments,' Ingleby flashed a look at the other man, 'have been following him, listening, watching and are running scared. I appreciate this is asking much of you to kill a man, but we see him as a real danger, not simply to our country, but the rest of the world.'

Frank was thoughtful for a moment and returned to his seat. He felt confused, worried and excited all at the same time. He tried to remember what he had read about Hitler. A great speaker and he headed a party with a few seats in their equivalent of our parliament and soon expected to add more. He was playing on the economic problems in Germany, which were far worse than elsewhere in Europe.

'I know you don't want to, Jack, but can you tell me exactly who is driving this? Surely, it's unheard of – at least at this level and, as you say, being approved by Governments?'

Ingleby hesitated and looked at the other man, who nodded.

'Let me just say, old man, that you must know the Jewish community holds a considerable amount of sway in business, the newspapers and in these Governments. It is they who are behind this, Frank.'

'But, Jack, from what I know of this man, he's not considered a serious threat.

'Are you aware that he has set out in a book what sort of world he wants in his lifetime?'

'No, I didn't know that.'

'Well, it was not taken very seriously at first when it came out five years ago, but with the current problems in Germany many believe him and his party to be a coming power. To be honest, we are all worried and, from a very high level, I have been approached to remove him.'

Ingleby looked again at the other man, who explained,

'Shipley, as the Commander here says, we have all the intelligence you need and a cover for you. You will only be able to have one try at this and if you fail so be it. We both know it's difficult and not without risk. You can refuse, but we need you; this man is highly dangerous and a greater threat than many imagine ...' His voice tailed off.

'Where would this take place?' Frank asked.

'Don't worry, Frank, it's all in here,' said Ingleby, holding up an envelope. 'All sorts of planning has been put into this and through a wide range of different sources, yet no one person in the field suspects what we might actually be doing. You can have a few days to think about it and let me know by dropping me a note, but to a different address than here – it's in the envelope.'

Frank looked inside the envelope.

'Frank, you'll find all you need in there, but you must burn most of it when you have taken on board all the information; I've marked the pieces to keep. All I can say, old chap, is that we really do need you for this.'

'I'll read it tonight and send the note tomorrow, without fail.'

'Good man. This time only a very small number will know everything of what is planned. Your cover over here is perfect and we can easily set you up to travel around Europe without anyone suspecting you.'

They all shook hands and Ingleby led Frank to the door stepping outside with him.

'Frank, I do appreciate you have your concerns. It is not easy to ask one man to kill another and I will understand if you turn us down, but I would not ask if it was not one of the most important things this Government, any Government come to that, has ever contemplated. Now, I'll have to leave you to see yourself out, as I need a chat with the Secretary. I'll await your reply. Goodbye, old man, and thanks for coming. Do give my regards to the family.''

Frank walked slowly down the stairs instead of taking the lift. Ingleby mentioned the Secretary and Frank now remembered where he had seen the man's face before: in the newspapers. The commissionaire opened the front doors and saluted as Frank walked past. On the pavement outside, he stood rock still for a moment.

'Bloody hell!' he said out loud. He looked round hoping no one had heard, but he was alone. He turned to his left and headed towards Westminster Underground Station.

He was home by lunchtime.

'Were we right about it?' Joan asked.

'You know I can't tell you anything but it's big, very big and might mean me spending time away, but I've been given the choice whether to take it on or not.'

'You'll do it,' said Joan coolly. 'Do you want something to eat before you return to work?'

'Yes, please. I shall be here until after three as I've some material to read first. Can you put it on a tray and I'll take it to the front room?'

He sat at the table and opened the envelope, removed the sheaves of paper and started reading. The instructions were detailed and thorough. He was to become Charles Adamson, a civil servant, and an aide to a minister shortly due to attend a Trade Fair in Salzburg.

Joan brought in the tray, but said nothing.

Frank read that Intelligence had discovered Hitler was planning a visit to his hometown of Braunau in Austria, on the border with Germany and north of Salzburg. This was, by chance, likely to happen in the same week as the Fair. The Minister would be making his way to Salzburg with his Private Secretary and Frank would travel on his own, staying in a separate hotel.

Two pages gave details of Hitler's proposed visit, with dates and times when he would address meetings. One was outdoors and was scheduled to take place on September 24th. Numbered photographs of the area were included with the site inserted on a map where each one was taken. Three likely positions for a sniper were also marked.

Frank was to use the Fair as his cover and alibi, staying in Salzburg for the rest of the week before heading to the British Embassy in Vienna. Once there, arrangements would be made to bring him home. Telephone numbers were provided together with coded phrases he had to use at certain times.

He carefully read through everything twice. He stood up and looked out of the window, but stared at nothing in particular. Having been excited when Ingleby had first outlined the plan, Frank was now not so sure. He picked up the photographs and sifted through them again. The more he considered it, the more he realised the risks involved.

Joan put her head round the door.

'I'm just off to the shops, sweetheart. Shall I expect you at about six?'

'Yes, love, about then.'

He read through the instructions again before returning them to the envelope, which he placed on top of the wardrobe in the bedroom before leaving for the Station.

Frank was unable to settle to his work but kept thinking of Joan and the children; did he need to put himself at such risk? The Neusen job was one thing, but that was with some support and not far from home. This was a much different proposition. What would happen if it all went wrong and he was caught? He assumed the security around Hitler would be considerable.

Still undecided he left for home early and found Joan in the kitchen. She asked pointedly,

'And?'

It forced his decision.

'I'm accepting it. I'll be travelling quite a bit and might be away for a week or more, but no need to worry though, it'll be fine.'

'Really,' said Joan sarcastically. 'You know, I wish you'd never become involved in this. It's all due to that bloody visit to see Wilson's family all those years ago; that bloke runs your life even from beyond the grave.'

Frank felt a sudden fury rise in him and was about to argue when he saw from her face how worried she was for him. He decided to let it pass and sat at the kitchen table watching her cleaning the stove. He loved her with all his heart and just as much as he had loved Marie. He knew Joan would prefer him to remain an ordinary policeman and the last thing he wanted was to upset the happy family life she had given him after all his problems, but he felt he had to do what Ingleby asked. He also suspected Joan knew that too.

He turned her round, looking into her eyes.

'My lovely girl, I know how you must be feeling and I love you more than anything else and would normally not do anything to hurt your feelings, but this is work I am cut out for and Jack Ingleby needs me for it. He says it is of national importance and, when I met him recently, he had a government minister with him. You must try to understand that the last thing I want is for you and the kids to worry because I'll be fine. It's not like wartime where I might have my head blown off.'

She held him close.

'I know, sweetie, but I wish you didn't have to. I'm sorry I spoke about your friend like that as I know how much you felt for him, but just be careful and return to me as soon as you can.' She kissed him strongly on the lips.

Frank collected the envelope from the bedroom, kept what he needed and tore up the rest before putting the pieces of paper into the boiler in the kitchen.

The next morning he wrote to Ingleby accepting the assignment. Two days later he was in Ingleby's office to collect the final instructions and documents.

'Frank,' Ingleby explained, 'you need to catch a train to Liverpool tomorrow and a taxi to the Lee Enfield factory there. They have put together a special rifle with a telescopic sight and silencer. They want to make a few minor adjustments to suit you before you try it out.'

Frank raised his eyebrows but said nothing.

'After that we need you in Hull for the boat. The final details are in here.' Ingleby handed over an envelope.

Frank removed the one sheet of paper and read through the list of instructions. Left inside the envelope were the pre-booked tickets for the boat and trains with an overnight crossing.

'You should arrive in Salzburg on the 20th,' continued Ingleby, 'where the hotel is booked for a week. I am told the rifle splits into three parts, making it easy to transport and hide but all the rest of the information you need is in the notes. Make sure you telephone the number we've given you when you arrive at the hotel, but we will have another agent keeping an eye on you. Although the Minister has no knowledge of you at all, his Parliamentary Private Secretary does. I suggest you do visit the Trade Fair and introduce yourself to the PPS. At least make it known to the hotel that you are about to attend, even if you don't. Is all that clear?'

'Yes, Jack, and it is very thorough. I take it I can pull out if the circumstances dictate? And it'll be my decision and mine alone.'

'Yes, of course it is. With Hitler making a very rare trip outside of Germany we saw this as our one chance. It is an excellent one, but it will not be the only one.'

'That's it, Jack?' asked Frank.

Ingleby added, gravely,

'One more thing: we'll disown you if you're caught, old man. Of course, was that to happen the normal channels will try and help you, but ostensibly you're on your own. Do you understand?'

'Yes, that's fine. I'd expect that, just as with the Neusen job.'

'Fine, old boy, and it only leaves me to wish you good luck and, hopefully, I'll see you in early October.'

***

Frank passed Superintendent Allen a letter from Ingleby explaining his forthcoming absence on some spurious pretence. Allen knew it, but said nothing and wished him well. That night Joan was edgy and short tempered with the children when they arrived home after another day with Phyllis and Harry. Joan barely spoke to Frank all evening. He packed his holdall, checked he had everything he needed and had one final read of the instructions. Confident he knew them word for word, he put all but the tickets into the boiler.

In bed, Joan finally spoke about his trip.

'Could you be killed?'

'We can get killed walking along the pavement.'

'Don't be stupid, you know what I mean,' she snapped back.

'It'll be fine and I'll be home before you know it. But don't say anything to the children or anyone else come to that; tell anyone who wishes to know that I'm away on a training course or something like that.'

She lay quiet and still, but was close to him. He could feel her breath on his neck. Her hand moved across him and she pulled him towards her kissing him with an open mouth. He clutched her breast and squeezed lightly until he felt her fully relax. He leant over and turned out the bedside lamp.

Joan vaguely remembered a kiss as it was getting light, but when she awoke she was alone.

8

Frank spent the day at the Liverpool factory testing the new rifle before leaving in the early evening. With the rifle split into its three parts, it easily fitted into his holdall. It was the first time he had used a rifle with a silencer and, after shooting normal rifles from an early age, it took a little getting used to.

He arrived in Hull shortly before ten in the evening and, once on the boat, was shown to his cabin. He lay on his bunk staring at the metal ceiling inches above his head, contemplating the task ahead and running through the plan again. He knew the intelligence was not enough. Photographs were one thing, but actually scouting the site would prove much more valuable. He was very happy with the rifle knowing its high degree of accuracy would most adequately serve the purpose. But there were variables - weather for one, especially with the wind. Only having that one day and one opportunity to complete his task the strength of the wind and its direction could play a crucial part in the accuracy of his shot and the ultimate success of his assignment.

Frank arrived in Ostend in the early morning after a smooth crossing and a good night's sleep. From there he caught the train to Brussels and onto Salzburg with a change at Frankfurt.

Salzburg's Myriad Hotel was situated in a quiet back street a short walk from the railway station. Shops stood either side of the hotel's entrance with the two storeys of the hotel's rooms set above. The reception area was small with a low table and two chairs in front of a counter behind which a middle-aged woman, wearing a neat white blouse, red waistcoat and black skirt, stood checking through a large ledger. She looked up as Frank approached.

'Herzlich willkommen auf der Myriad.'

'Thank you,' replied Frank.

Before the woman could say any more, a man appeared from the inner office.

'Ah, you must be Mr Adamson. Welcome to Austria. Did you have a pleasant journey?' he asked in English with the hint of a West Country accent.

'Yes, thank you. You speak very good English.'

'Well I am English, you see. Althorp, Simon Althorp. Are you here for the Trade Fair?'

'That's right, and perhaps a little sightseeing later in the week. I'll hope to visit Vienna from here and perhaps over the border; I have friends in Germany.'

'Well, Mr Adamson, it is very beautiful around here, particularly in the city itself. Everyone is excited and we have many visitors at present, what with the Fair and Herr Hitler speaking not far from here this week. Great man, don't you think?'

'I don't know that much about him or what he's doing, I'm afraid.' Frank needed to change the subject. 'Do you have a safe deposit facility?' he asked.

'Of course, Mr Adamson, we have a cellar we use, and inside are the secure boxes. The cellar is behind the locked door to your left there.' He pointed at a pine door near the front, glass door. 'Here's your room key for now; it's number twenty-four at the top of the stairs. Dinner from seven, breakfast from six thirty. Will you be dining in tonight?'

'Oh yes, it's been a long day. And thanks. By the way, do you have a telephone I can use?'

'Certainly, there's one in the hallway through the door behind you leading to the stairs.

Frank waited in the hall until he was alone and, using the phrase he had learnt, asked the operator for the number Ingleby had given him. An English voice answered with a sullen, 'Hello?' It was obviously not the Embassy's main number.

'The frankincense has been delivered,' whispered Frank.

'Fine,' said the voice from the other end and hung up. Frank looked at the mouthpiece and shrugged before putting it onto its catch.

As Frank climbed the stairs carrying his holdall, Althorp opened the door from reception and called to him,

'Sorry, Mr Adamson, can I ask you to fill in a form for me? I forgot earlier; it's here in reception.'

They walked back to the counter.

'It's required for the local police,' added Althorp. 'We don't normally have to ask guests to do this, but we understand it's because of Herr Hitler's visit. This is his home area, of course.'

Frank looked closely at Althorp as he answered the routine questions.

Althorp had a nasty scar from the left eye socket to his neck and walked with a pronounced limp. He was about the same age as Frank.

'How come you're working here in Salzburg?' Frank asked.

Althorp placed the form in a drawer of a filing cabinet and walked to the counter.

'I was badly wounded in the war, as you can see,' he pointed to his scar, 'and my leg, too. The Germans picked me up and I was eventually brought to a camp near here to recuperate. This is where I met my wife. She's Austrian and was a nurse in the war. After the Armistice I stayed on and we were eventually married. I originally lived near Bristol and was in the Somersets. What about you?'

'Oh, Military Police.' Frank regretted saying this as soon as he did so, wishing he had lied instead.

'Really?' Althorp became more interested. 'Where were you?'

'France – I used to live in the West Country like you but was born in London. My folks bought a place in Wedmore near Cheddar Gorge, do you know it?'

'Would I have to pass through it on my way to Wells?'

'Almost certainly.'

'Lovely part of the world, like round here really. Look, I must get on, but do let me know if there's anything you need; I'll see you at dinner.'

Frank's room was pleasant enough, with a view over the square outside and included a single bed, chest of drawers with a mirror, a small washbasin and a wardrobe. He unpacked all but the rifle from his holdall and lay on the bed with his hands behind his head. He felt cold and shivered, although it was warm in the room. He was disappointed to have unwittingly drawn attention to himself as he stumbled over Althorp's questions. With Althorp there, it would be less easy to come and go – unnoticed. The reality of what he had to do was making him more nervous than he had been ahead of the Neusen job and he felt alone; this felt all very new to him. What might it be like killing a man? Rabbits, foxes and pheasants were one thing, but another human being? He had not fired a shot at anyone during the war, although he had been trained to do so. But this was not the war.

Before dinner, he collected the keys for the box in the cellar from the woman on reception. She also gave him a candle and a box of matches. Carrying his holdall, he opened the pine door and stepped down into the dark cellar. At the bottom of the stairs he lit the candle and looked around the room. Amongst a block of black wooden, upright lockers with badly painted numbers on the front, he found his. They did not seem particularly secure, but he placed the three parts to the rifle inside, but retained the sight. Having locked the door, he blew out the candle and started up the stairs.

Althorp appeared in the doorway above him.

'You've found it, Mr Adamson? I saw the door open.'

'Yes, all done.

'What are you doing at the Fair?'

'Oh,' said Frank casually, 'I work for the Trade Minister. You might wonder why I'm here and not with him, apparently it's a question of cost, but this is fine for me.'

'So, Mr Adamson, you're a civil servant?'

'I am, indeed.

'I don't suppose you know a chap called Ingleby; he would have lived near you.'

Frank felt his cheeks flush.

'No, I don't think so. Why?'

'Oh nothing, really, but he works for the Civil Service in London. Did you know him perhaps from your schooldays? He's a bit older than you I would guess. Trained as a doctor at the same university as me and was in France too.

'No – never came across him. Right, my dinner waits. Here, perhaps you can take these.' He handed Althorp the candle and matches.

Althorp waited for Frank to reach the dining room before he lit the candle. Satisfied he would not be seen, he ran down the stairs and checked Frank's locker. It was secure. From a large key ring he picked out a small silver one. He opened the locker and smiled; he could see the butt end of a rifle. He relocked the door and returned upstairs where he made a telephone call.

The following day, Frank caught a bus to Braunau. On the journey he again recalled the intelligence he knew about the town. Arriving there he was surprised to find it bustling with people, many more than he expected. Pictures of Hitler were everywhere. Frank made his way to the north side of the town and towards the park where Hitler was due to speak.

Braunau was set in a valley along which open fields extended into Germany. In the lane to the right of the park were small cottages, their neat gardens surrounded by hedges. Behind them the land climbed steeply, the slopes thick with vegetation above which tall trees formed a canopy. Frank followed a winding path; below him and to his left he could see the park where workmen were unloading parts of the stage from a lorry.

The path came to an end in a clearing where a bench overlooked the valley. He sat there watching the river Inn meander into the distance forming a natural boundary with Germany. Looking down the hillside, all he could see of the cottages below him was smoke rising from a chimney. Taking the rifle sight from the inside pocket of his jacket, he scanned the park and focussed on one of the men there. He estimated he was quarter of a mile from where the stage was being set up: a perfect distance for accuracy yet far enough away for him to make an unseen escape to the lane and into the town. A problem might be that local people would also come here and use this spot as a vantage point to watch Hitler.

He decided to look further up the hillside. As he climbed higher on the rough ground, there were more trees and less vegetation due to the lack of sunlight. Ahead he spotted a clump of rhododendrons stretching for some distance and set around the base of a copse of birch trees. The spring flowering was long gone, but the leaves were thick and, when he entered through a gap, it was so dark he could barely make out anything inside. Looking out to the park, he had a perfect view. Again, he checked the sight line; it was fine.

He made his way back towards the town, keeping well away from the path on this occasion, until he reached the lane. This would be the perfect route for him to take on the day.

On his way to the bus station he read one of the notices containing Hitler's image. He found clear confirmation of the timings and it was five thirty on the 24th, three days time. As he turned away from the notice, a young woman approached him; she spoke to him in English, but with a heavy accent.

'Guten morgen, do you have a light?' she asked, pointing an unlit cigarette at him.

Startled, Frank blurted out,

'No, sorry, I don't smoke.'

She shrugged and walked off.

His heart was pounding. How did she know he was English? He felt worried. He watched her until she was out of sight. No more than a teenager she had black hair tied into pigtails. Why ask him? He had no cigarette himself and there were plenty of other men and women around who did.

***

Back at the Myriad Frank was pleased to find Althorp not on duty, saving him from the possibility of more awkward questions. The receptionist looked up as he moved towards her.

'Herr Adamson.'

'Train?' Frank asked as he made the noise of an engine, as well as gesticulating with his hands and repeatedly pointing at his watch.

She hesitated, held up her finger and turned towards the table behind her, picked up a timetable and handed it to him. He thumbed through the pages, found what he wanted and gave it back.

After an early dinner in the empty hotel restaurant Frank went back to his room to collect his holdall. He returned downstairs to the cellar and placed the rifle parts into the holdall before leaving it under the bed in his room. He decided to take an early evening stroll but as he opened the hotel's front door Althorp was coming in.

'Good evening, Mr Adamson, how are –'

Before he could finish Frank had swept past into the street.

Althorp stood holding the door and shaking his head.

***

Following an early breakfast the next morning Frank returned by bus to Braunau, but this time with the rifle in the holdall. Finding the bushes from the day before, he checked the line of sight once again; he wanted to leave nothing to chance. He scraped a shallow hole with his hands and the heel of his boot. He wrapped the rifle in newspaper he had brought from the hotel, carefully placed the bundle in the hole and covered it with soil.

When he returned to the hotel Althorp was at the reception desk.

'Good day?' he asked.

'Lovely, thanks. A long walk, beautiful area.'

'Anywhere in particular?'

'No, just around the city and to the Exhibition Hall where the Fair is being held.'

'It starts tomorrow, doesn't it?'

'It does indeed,' said Frank, heading towards the stairs, eager to return to his room and cursing his luck to have this man here.

Althorp watched Frank's haste to get away with interest. He picked up the telephone and asked for a number in German. When connected, he spoke briefly.

Frank spent part of the following day at the Fair. He made himself known to the Minister's Secretary before leaving to look round Salzburg. On his way to The

Myriad in the late afternoon, he stopped at a cafe with tables and chairs outside and ordered a coffee with a piece of sponge cake. Standing on the other side of the road and smoking a cigarette was a short, balding man with a coat too thick for the warmth of the day. Frank had noticed him earlier at the Fair.

He followed Frank as he left, but kept to the other side of the road. Frank decided on a longer route than normal to his hotel. He was in no doubt the man was following him.

Once inside, Frank watched through the glass door as the man continued walking past and towards the railway station. Althorp was absent again. In his room, Frank pulled back the net curtain and looked at the street below. There was no sign of the man, but a young girl smoking a cigarette was sitting on the wall of the hotel opposite. It was the same girl who had asked him for a light out at the park.

He sat on the edge of the bed weighing up what best to do. The man in the overcoat must have been trailing him; it was too much of a coincidence to be otherwise. Who was that girl? Was one the agent Jack Ingleby talked of? Should he continue or make his way to Vienna and the Embassy, as Ingleby had told him to do if he was compromised? He opted out of dinner downstairs and had a meal brought up to his room. He had a restless night and it was almost light when he finally dropped off to sleep. He was late for breakfast and his mood was not improved to see Althorp behind the reception desk.

'Good morning! How are we today? Anything exciting planned?'

'Not too bad, a bit tired, but I'll be at the Fair for most of the day. When that closes I shall be travelling over to Munich to visit friends and staying overnight.'

'Lovely city, you'll enjoy it, but you'll miss Herr Hitler; he's up at Braunau later today. I've heard the Fair's shutting at three to allow those who wish to hear him speak to travel up there. '

"I'd forgotten that – oh well at least there won't be many on the train to Munich if I catch one at about four.'

Frank made his way to the restaurant; Althorp watched him leave through the double doors and picked up the phone.

After breakfast, Frank packed his holdall. He would almost certainly abort his mission if there were any hint of being followed that day. For now, though, he decided he would do his best to shoot Hitler, as planned.

As he left the hotel, Frank saw no sign of the man in the overcoat or the girl; he decided he would catch the train to Braunau on this occasion.

The station was busy. Frank bought his one-way ticket and sat waiting for the train to arrive. On time, it had the open carriages favoured in Europe. He chose a seat by the door to the next carriage and scrutinised those who boarded with him: most were women, some with children, but no one suspicious. He settled down as the train meandered through the Austrian countryside. Having dozed off to catch up on his sleep, he was woken suddenly by the door slamming shut next to him. The same young girl with her black pigtails brushed past, but carried on through the door to the next carriage without looking back. This was his cue to abort his mission but he remained uncertain. He stood up and walked to the door and could see the girl in the next carriage reading a magazine. It all seemed suspicious. He returned to his seat and for the rest of the journey weighed up what to do. He decided that if he were followed when walking towards the hillside at Braunau, he would return to the station and catch a train to Vienna.

Most of the passengers left the train at Braunau. Frank stopped to buy a newspaper and looked out for the young girl. She walked past and out of the station. He followed. She had disappeared by the time he stepped into the street outside.

He decided not to head straight to his vantage point above the park, but for the library he had to pass on the way. He was sure he was not being followed, but waited in the library foyer to make sure. No one he recognised came in. After a few minutes and now outside he could see nothing unusual. He felt confused. Who was she? Surely she was tailing him? Was she connected to the man from yesterday? Had she a connection with Althorp, who seemed suspicious?

Part of him knew he should head straight for Vienna, but equally the mission was important to Ingleby and those he was representing. Hitler was hardly known in Britain and, as Ingleby had told him, not being taken seriously throughout Europe, but the support Frank had witnessed here suggested Hitler was a coming force. The shooting had taken on a different dimension. He felt he had to carry it out if he could; despite the possible personal cost.

He walked on towards the park checking no one was following. A crowd was already gathering despite the fact Hitler was not due to speak until the late afternoon. In two days the park had been transformed. Flags fluttered on poles behind the stage in front of which were rows of temporary folding chairs with an area behind for those who wanted to stand. A military band practised on the stage and workmen adjusted the lighting. Police and Army personnel patrolled the perimeter.

As Frank moved up the hillside and away from the park, it was as quiet as it had been on previous days. He crept towards the clearing, but the bench was empty and he moved on. Inside the rhododendron thicket, he dug up the rifle. The wind was much stronger than it had been on his previous visits and he had to adjust the rifle sight to allow for its strength and direction. He knew this wind change meant a greater margin for error.

The weather deteriorated further. Frank cursed: the sniper's worst enemy was the gusting crosswind, now even stronger. A sighting shot down towards the park would test his adjustment and would have been helpful, but he felt this would be too risky.

Through the sight he could see the seats slowly filling yet it was still two hours before Hitler was due to speak. The flags were now fully extended near the stage and Frank adjusted his sight once more. An accurate shot was now almost impossible, but he knew that, having come this far, he would have at least one attempt.

If successful, the shooting would create confusion in the park and allow him to run to the station. If there were no immediate trains to Vienna he would head across country on foot.

Hitler was half an hour late. A previous speaker had whipped up the crowd and the roar that greeted Hitler's introduction was loud, resonating through the valley. The band came on stage followed by a group of schoolchildren each carrying a party flag. Behind came Hitler, small in stature and wearing a long black coat and trilby hat. Flanked by burly, uniformed men, he stood behind the rostrum acknowledging the waving crowd, most of whom were holding the flag of the National Socialists. He turned to sit towards the rear of the stage. Someone moved forward to speak at the rostrum. Hitler was in clear view as he waited to be introduced, but there was now less attention on him. This was Frank's opportunity. He lined up his target balancing the rifle on the limb of a birch tree. His hands were steady and he waited, hoping the wind might drop. Hitler would soon move from his seat. It had to be now. He fired and could see the bullet strike the curtain behind those seated on the stage, but narrowly missing Hitler's head. No one noticed. He adjusted the sight and fired again, but this time a splinter of wood flew up in front of Hitler's feet. Hitler moved to the rostrum to speak and Frank knew his chance had passed; only the top of Hitler's head was now visible and the accuracy required was too great.

Frank broke down the rifle and placed it in the holdall. He headed towards the town safe in the knowledge he was unlikely to be followed. He knew from his earlier visit that the library had a telephone and he needed to ring ahead as instructed.

Using mostly sign language he asked the assistant if he could make a call. He offered a selection of coins, but these were waved away.

'The frankincense is being returned.' Frank told the man who answered. It meant he was coming in, but did not need any help.

Outside, Frank was surprised to see the young girl sitting on a bench across the road, reading a magazine. He started off for the railway station, beginning to panic. He would have to shake her off. He increased his pace without looking behind. He turned a corner onto the station concourse and there, directly in front of him, was the bald man in the overcoat sitting on a bench. When he saw Frank he stood up and moved towards him. Suddenly a car's tyres screeched to a halt behind Frank. The passenger door flew open.

'Get in!' It was the girl. Frank hesitated. 'Major Ingleby has sent me,' she shouted.

Frank threw his holdall onto the back seat and fell into the passenger seat as she drove away, the door slamming shut as they sped off. The girl skilfully negotiated the tight roads, thankfully quiet with so many at Hitler's rally. Frank checked to make sure they were not being followed and soon they were alone heading east towards Vienna. Nothing was said until they reached the open countryside.

'Did you succeed?' the girl asked, without a trace of a German accent.

Frank was not sure how much she knew about his mission but assumed it must be enough for him to be open with her.

'No. I tried, but it was too windy. Where are you taking me?'

'Vienna.'

'How long will that take?'

'Over four hours, so I suggest you get some rest. I'll pull over and you can hop in the back and have a doze.'

Frank slept soundly for almost two hours and remained on the back seat for the rest of the journey when only a few words were exchanged with both aware that the less they knew about each other the better, particularly if their position were to become compromised. A little before midnight they entered Vienna.

'There we are,' said the girl, as she pulled up outside a tall imposing building where a Union Jack fluttered above a pillared entrance with steps up to a set of double doors.

'I don't know how I can thank you enough,' said Frank, picking up his holdall and stepping out onto the pavement. 'Perhaps we'll meet again.'

'Perhaps,' said the girl, with a little smile. 'Good luck!'

With the front doors locked for the night, Frank had to pull the doorbell three times before a man dressed in a dinner suit ushered him inside.

'Follow me please, Mr Shipley.'

Frank was surprised he knew his name. They walked across the ornate marble entrance hall towards a panelled oak door. The man knocked discreetly and went through beckoning Frank to follow.

Jack Ingleby and Simon Althorp stood there smiling.

'Good God!' Frank exclaimed.

'Hello, old boy, glad to see you've made it and we've heard it didn't work out. You've met Althorp, before, of course,' Ingleby laughed.

Frank pointed at Althorp and smiled. 'You didn't betray me to the Germans!'

Althorp walked over, now without his pronounced limp, and shook Frank by the hand.

'Sorry about that, Shipley.'

'Simon, or Commander Gosling to give him his correct name,' Ingleby continued, 'is the agent I told you about. He's been keeping an eye on you and reporting to me here at each stage. We've had him using his hotel work as cover.'

'But why are you here?' Frank asked Ingleby.

'Time for honesty, Frank: apart from needing to be here if Hitler was dead and to deal with the fall out that would have brought, I have to say this whole episode has partly been a way of testing you out. Yes, certain factions want Hitler removed, but I never expected you would come close to carrying it out. I assume you got a shot away?'

'Oh yes,' said Frank, 'but we were done by the strong winds.'

'I guessed as much because it's been blowing a gale here for most of the day too. But this exercise was in a small part also designed to see what you were like in the field and how you reacted in dangerous situations. If you were successful it would meet the needs of the others and, in a different way, mine too. I knew you had suffered with your nerves in the past, old chap, and I needed to make sure you could cope. I have plans to use you in other ways, if you are agreeable.'

'Well, I must say that was a supreme test, Jack, trying to remove someone like Hitler. But I didn't realise how popular he has become.'

'How close were you?' Gosling asked.

'Two shots, both narrowly missed, mainly due to that crosswind.

Ingleby patted Frank on the back.

'To be honest, old man, you did well and surpassed any expectations. Major Gosling put you in a quandary as Althorp by being over familiar. Miss Parker, the girl who followed you and picked you up, also put you to the test. You must be careful not to give yourself away quite as easily as you did when she asked you for a light. However, we shall de-brief you properly tomorrow. Did you enjoy the experience?'

'Do you know what, Jack, I think I did.'

'That's good – and we do appreciate what you've done and it was worth the effort. It didn't work out with Hitler, but we will have other chances. I will need you again, but, for now, it's a return to the humdrum of the beat in Chelmsford, I'm afraid!'

Ingleby ushered Frank towards the door.

'We'll put you up here tonight and you can be on your way tomorrow after we've had our little chat.

They shook hands. Frank hesitated.

'Jack. One further question: who was the small, balding man with the overcoat? Your Miss Parker saw him.'

'She recognised him. German Secret Service, we think. We do know they were tracking all suspicious visitors because of the Hitler thing. The Commander here believes the woman receptionist at the hotel tipped them off. She might have heard you say you were with the Minister at the Fair; something else we can talk about at the de-briefing.'

Before he left for home the following day, Frank spent an uncomfortable hour with Ingleby and Gosling. They discussed every aspect of his mission, criticising where necessary, but praising his determination and commitment. Ingleby summed up.

'We put you into this very raw and, as I said last night, it was to test your mettle as much as anything and to see how you worked under pressure. I have no doubts about your shooting capabilities, but it was more about your mental approach. To me, you appear to have coped admirably, old boy. Yes, I've been told you let yourself down on a couple of occasions, but we'll be able to refine these things with some more training. What the reports reaching me have said is that you have worked on your own through the difficulties and, most of all, have been prepared to put the needs of your country before those of yourself.' Frank looked at Gosling who nodded.

'Well thank you Jack,' said Frank, blushing a little. 'And I feel I've learnt a good few lessons.'

'Excellent. Now, old chap, I can guarantee you will hear from me again and I'll most probably have a use for you working undercover as you certainly seem to have the aptitude. There is just one more thing, you might like to think about becoming fluent in a foreign language and can I suggest French? I have several German speakers working with me, but I'm a little thin with French and you should be reasonably conversant already with your history, so it shouldn't take much to pick it up again. Just a suggestion and there's no rush.'

'I'll give it a go and start as soon as I can.'

'Good man, Frank, now follow me.'

Ingleby escorted Frank into the crowded entrance hall and then led him into a small side room.

'Frank, I didn't wish to mention this in front of the Commander, but I've tracked down that Burnside fellow for you. I spoke to him briefly on the telephone a few weeks ago, but he was not willing to say much about Wilson due to the secrecy block on the file. I now hear he is very ill and possibly on the way out. Anyway he's on sick leave. Sorry, but I tried.'

'Thanks, Jack; that's a shame and maybe we'll never know what he knows. By the way, what happened to your book?'

Ingleby laughed and shook his head.

'Because of my position, old chap, I had to submit the draft to a pretty high level. Like the Wilson thing, it's been blocked because they didn't like the criticism about shell-shock. It will probably never see the light of day – and to think how much time I spent on it! My parents have it locked away in their study. If you are down to see your father, why not drop in and have a read of it.'

'I will.' Frank looked at the clock on the wall. 'Look, I must go; my train leaves in fifteen minutes.'

***

The long journey home gave Frank plenty of chance to reflect on the events in Austria. He felt proud of his efforts despite the disappointment of not being able to complete his mission in its entirety, but Ingleby had seemed pleased and Frank could not wait to work for him again.

On arriving home the children were overjoyed to see him. They were too young to concern themselves with where their father had been or what he did when he was away. Joan knew better than to ask too many questions.

She gave him a long hard kiss when they were alone.

'Good trip; France was it?' She asked, raising her eyebrows.

'Austria, actually. Lovely place and we'll have to go there some time, but not for a while.'

9

Frank returned to the not inconsiderable task of running his new Station on the now completed housing estate. He still found time to maintain his shooting skills with the TA, yet no call came from Ingleby.

The 'land fit for heroes' promised after the war finally seemed to be emerging but Britain, like most other countries in the early thirties, was still enveloped in an economic crisis. Chelmsford, with its large industrial base, was not spared. Two further constables were added to Frank's command to deal with unrest in the local community and the rising crime levels.

While the police, in places like Chelmsford, maintained an element of control, civil unrest was becoming a major problem in the larger cities, particularly London. By 1931, Sir Oswald Mosley had formed his New Party, based on Hitler's National Socialism ideal. Frank took a keen interest once he read that Mosley was being compared with Adolf Hitler in Germany. Since the attempted shooting in Austria, Frank had followed Hitler's rise in popularity. The National Socialists were gaining seats at an alarming rate in Germany and Mosley's party, although not winning seats in local or general elections was beginning to secure a growing share of the vote.

Like Hitler, Mosley and his followers were extremely anti-Semitic. The Jewish community, particularly in London's East End, was being subjected to abuse from Mosley's more aggressive followers and formed their own militant groups. The lingering anti-British feeling amongst the Irish also simmered in the more run down areas and was strong in the East End. The Communists revelled in this unrest by not supporting any one group in particular but using each for their own benefit. Finally, the criminal fraternity, just like the Communists, took advantage of the problems both economic and political.

To Frank, these problems seemed far away from the more petty crimes rife in North Chelmsford. In the three years since he had worked for Ingleby abroad, he had spent time adding to his rudimentary French, as Ingleby had suggested.

George, in his last year at primary school, was keen on foreign languages and had joined Frank in learning basic French grammar. They also sought help from Josie Walmsley and had spent two days of every week during George's summer break honing their conversational skills. Josie no longer taught at the High School. Once her husband Norman had taken early retirement following a period of ill-health, they set up a business handling exchange visits between French and English schools during the Easter and Summer school holidays. This was proving extremely successful and also meant they only worked for six months of the year.

George was tall and strong for his age, and excelled at most sports. He was bright and had always ranked among the top pupils of his class. Aged eleven he had just secured a place at Chelmsford Grammar School.

Lizzie was a lively girl who liked to draw and paint and had a talent for art. She failed to obtain a place at the Girls' High School, but Frank and Joan promised her she could attend art college when she was older to help develop this talent, hoping this would encourage her to continue with it.

Joan kept on with her part time post at Broomfield school for a while. Despite the school being only a bus ride away the travelling added almost an hour to her day. When a similar post became available at the local school on the new housing estate, she successfully applied.

Lazing in the garden one afternoon in late spring, Frank and Joan sat watching George and Lizzie playing cricket using three sticks for the wicket, a tennis ball and an old bat. Lizzie was becoming annoyed, as George was making sure all the catches he hit to her were just out of her reach; eventually she gave up and stormed indoors. George stretched out on the grass enjoying the warm sun.

Joan put her arm round Frank.

'You know what? I like this life. I used to worry so much when you were on those special missions.'

'There were only two – and I could receive the call again. But the last one was that long ago perhaps they've forgotten about me.'

'I hope you're right, but I somehow doubt it. By the way, have you seen those pictures in today's paper of that Hitler fellow at one of those huge rallies? I read the article about him and was very impressed.'

'Dangerous, though.'

'Do you really think so, darling? He seems to be turning Germany round after all their troubles. I know old Churchill doesn't like him and keeps warning everyone, but that's about all.'

Frank laughed.

'What's the matter?' Joan asked.

'You know what, love? I saw Hitler when I was in Austria.'

'What do you mean saw him – you met him?'

'Nothing like that, but I saw the effect he was having on that part of the world. It was near the German border. He was speaking at a rally, but not one like in the papers; it was smaller. He's much more popular in Germany now than he was then. Many say he'll become their leader before long.'

Joan frowned.

'I'm putting two and two together about your trip but I hope I'm wrong.'

Frank simply shrugged, stood up and walked towards the back door.

'Frank?' Come back here ... Frank Shipley!'

He ignored her and carried on.

George had been dozing, but was woken by Joan's shouting.

'What is it, Mum?'

'Your father.'

'What about him?'

'Nothing.'

'Mum, it didn't sound like nothing.'

'Just forget it, George. It's something that happened years ago with your father's work, but thank God that's all in the past.'

***

Only a few days later Frank received a telephone call from his Assistant Chief Constable requesting a meeting.

'Ah, Shipley, take a seat, will you?' said the ACC when they met at the Police Headquarters the following morning. 'Thank you for coming in.' He lit himself a cigarette. 'You don't, do you?'

'No, sir.'

'I have received this letter from a Mr Ingleby. I believe you know him. He has requested that we release you from your duties here completely and let you join a new force he is setting up in London. This is all I know and this Ingleby appears to have no rank. However, I have another letter from none other than the Home Secretary verifying Ingleby's status and the request. The work is of a secretive nature; so secret that I am not being told what it is. You are to report immediately to Whitehall. Here is the address,' he said handing Frank a sheet of paper. 'This Ingleby will brief you when you see him tomorrow.'

'What do I tell my men, sir?'

'Nothing – except that you are being posted to the Met. We shall have to sort out the mess this sudden decision leaves us in. I am not very happy with it, but as it's the Home Secretary I have to accept it. Now, you need to see your Super; he's expecting you and you'll have to bring him up to date with what is happening on your watch. Any questions before you leave?'

'No sir, except about my family and our house. What happens there?'

'Stay there for now. London will have to offer something. I suggest you ask Mr Ingleby tomorrow.'

***

Frank met with the Superintendent to brief him on outstanding matters and issues on his patch. Later when he returned to the Station he found only one Constable there and whilst waiting until all the officers returned from their patrols, he telephoned Hebden at the Broomfield Station with the news.

'I'm happy for you, Frank,' said Hebden. 'It's what we dream of – a job in London. When do you start?'

'Tomorrow.'

'Blimey, Frank, they must be desperate. Sorry! I mean they must need you urgently. We must have a leaving do for you – next week perhaps?'

'Of course, Stan, I can't leave you all without a proper goodbye. I'll have to let you know what evening I'm free.'

'Fine, I'll arrange it. Good luck, mate, I wish it was me.'

Frank placed the receiver onto the stand and smiled. Perhaps if Stan Hebden knew what Ingleby might have in store he would not be quite so keen. Frank felt that tingle of excitement: the effect Ingleby's calls always had.

When his team returned to the station, he informed them all of his immediate move to London.

***

At first Joan was as excited with the news as Frank, until he told her it was Jack Ingleby who wanted him.

'I really did hope he'd forgotten about you. It's bound to be dangerous.'

'Not necessarily.'

'Oh, come on, Frank, you can't believe that. What you said the other day, or rather what you didn't say, told me all I needed to know. Anything you do for Jack Ingleby means danger of some sort.'

'Let's wait and see. I'll know more tomorrow. It might just be a routine posting and I've always wanted to work for the Met – I had a post lined up with them when I returned from France, but Marie didn't want me to take it which is why we came here. It'll be more money, I'm sure, and that will help with the kids.'

'If, like Marie, I said I didn't want you to do it, you'd take no notice, would you?'

'But, Joan, the circumstances are now different. It will be fine, you'll see.'

Not convinced, Joan returned to the kitchen to prepare their tea.

***

'Well, well, Frank here we are again,' said Ingleby shaking Frank's hand firmly. Ingleby looked frail. 'You're shocked, Frank; I don't look that well, do I?'

'You have looked better, Jack, that's for sure.'

'Heart attack again, much worse this time. That's why I've not been in contact. Been laid low for the best part of two years, old chap, but if you think I look bad now, you should have seen me after it happened.'

'I am sorry Jack. I was surprised not to have heard from you after what you said in Austria but now I know why and there was me thinking you'd forgotten about me.'

'Far from it, old boy, and you would almost certainly have been put to good use before now but for my problems. What about Herr Hitler? It's a pity we missed that chance, don't you think?'

'He certainly looks dangerous; you were right about him.'

'Well, never mind, Frank, and you're probably wondering what this is all about. What do you know about Sir Oswald Mosley?'

'Quite a lot, actually, because since the Hitler mission I've followed his political career and this has led me on to Mosley.'

'So, you know about his New Party and what they are about?'

'Yes. A little worrying, isn't it?'

'Absolutely, old boy, spot on. What I have lined up is for you to work in my department monitoring Mosley's crowd. I planned to take out Mosley and that would have been a job for you, but orders from on high have stopped that idea. I needn't bore you with the reasons, but suffice to say, certain factions have brought influence to bear.'

'Is it an office job?'

'Not quite, Frank. At first I want you to build up your own intelligence on them, that's true, but when that's done I want you to infiltrate them: working on your own; getting right inside their party. This will be a few months down the line because you'll also need specialist training. Are you with me on this?'

'You'd better tell me more.'

'It's like this, old chap: the Fascists from Germany and Italy are funding Mosley and he is a threat, there's no doubt about that. However, I personally believe he will have his time, but he is stirring up all this unrest with his party's anti-Jewish stance that the Communists and anti-Fascists, as well as the Jews, are setting up against him. We are fearful of civic unrest and, if Hitler's rise continues, Mosley's influence here could become even greater. So, I need someone on the inside feeding me information. The higher up Mosley's party the better.'

'You think I can do that, Jack?'

'Old chap, you would not be sitting here if I didn't! Now, I want you to start straightaway and to be based here. I'm waiting for a house in Epping to become available for you and the family. I expect that to be in a month's time.'

'That won't please Joan,' Frank interrupted.

'I know, but you cannot stay in the police house. We'll look after you financially with the move and, if you wish your son to stay at the Chelmsford Grammar School, we can pay for him to board. What's your daughter doing?'

'She's still at school. She can leave next year and we think she'll attend a college to study art.'

'I'm sure there'll be one near Epping that's suitable. I'll have that checked out for you. In the mean time, tell Joan all about it before returning here on Monday. I'll have all the information you need to start reading through. I'll also help with part of the training on how to infiltrate Mosley's crowd.'

***

Frank's leaving party held at The Saracen's Head in Chelmsford two weeks after he started in London and organised by Stan Hebden was a rip-roaring success. No one asked him about his new work.

A month further on and despite her reservations, Joan had quickly settled into their cottage situated away from Epping town centre. George, like many young teenagers, was pleased to have time away from his parents and found the independence in the boarding house much to his liking. Lizzie was her usual phlegmatic self, looking forward rather than back, and she could not wait to leave school.

Frank travelled to the London office each day by underground train. Ingleby's unit was based in Finsbury Circus, an area off Moorgate and within easy walking distance of Liverpool Street. It soon became clear that Frank was not working as part of the Metropolitan Police but MI5. Ingleby rarely appeared and Frank's trainer for the specialised work was Commander Gosling, who Frank had known as Simon Althorp in Austria. Gosling had been brought home when his position in Salzburg had become compromised.

Gosling was an excellent mentor, passing on tips from his time undercover in Europe. Together they discussed situations that might be encountered and how to deal with them. They shared the intelligence about Mosley and his followers known for wearing mostly black and had thus been dubbed 'Blackshirts'.

Within two months, Frank was ready to start his new role in the field. Unexpectedly, Ingleby arrived one morning at the Finsbury Circus office looking fitter and tanned. They chatted for a while about Gosling's work and Frank's reading up on all that he could about Mosley, his politics and the men close to him. Ingleby said he had been away in the South of France to recuperate. He mentioned he was with a woman, but gave no further details. Finally, Ingleby moved on to the real purpose for his visit.

'Frank, old chap, now you are ready for your task we want you to take on a new persona. It will not be permanent and you will still have your home life. You are now ready to become a member of Sir Oswald Mosley's party, feeding back what you can and from as far up their organisation as you can possibly manage. To friends and family, however, you will remain Frank Shipley, a Met officer.'

Ingleby looked for a reaction, but Frank remained calm and unmoved.

'What we need to do now,' Ingleby continued, 'is to give you a separate identity; one to convince our targets and one you are comfortable with. Our men often find it easier to base a new character on someone they know or have known. Can you think of anyone?'

Frank shook his head slowly as he sat staring ahead, running through a host of people he could use. He suddenly clicked his fingers.

'You have one? Right, give me the details,' said Ingleby.

'What about Eddie Wilson? I know all there is to know about him, or at least more than I know about anyone else.'

'Absolutely, old chap. Perfect! You'll need to think it all through to be convincing.'

'I'm sure I can pull it off, Jack.'

'My plan is to put you in a flat in the East End. Your work cover has already been sorted out – you have a clerk's job at the Sun Insurance offices in Bartholomew Lane, not far from here. You will not have to attend but, if anyone checks you out, we will have that covered. I'm not sure if you've been keeping up your TA work but you will have to give that up.'

'I won't need my shooting skills then?'

'You might, but not in the same way. You'll cope without practising.'

'What about Joan and the children? I can't simply disappear.'

'Don't worry about it, old chap; you can often be at home. Joan will understand, but make sure the true nature of what you are doing is kept from her and your friends. Eddie Wilson it is. I shall arrange for my secretary to draw up all you need to be Wilson. Come here this time next week to pick up what she'll have for you.'

Frank looked concerned and pensive.

'Is there something else, Frank?' asked Ingleby.

'Well ...' Frank hesitated, 'Joan does know I'm working for you and she expects it to be dangerous. She's bright enough to have put two and two together to work out what I have done for you in the past.'

'What if I drop over to Epping to see her and the family, to reassure them? I fancy a little country air.'

'Can you tell her much, Jack?'

'Enough, hopefully.'

'Fine, come for tea this Sunday, why don't you?'

***

When Frank told Joan she was annoyed at first. She had that day written to Josie and Norman Walmsley inviting them to come and stay at the weekend.

'That's not a problem, love,' said Frank, 'Jack'll muck in. He's not expecting to stay and he already knows the Walmsleys from the wedding.'

'But you'll have to give me a hand.'

Jack was in fine fettle when he arrived, more like his old self, but Joan was still surprised at the change in him. His hair was almost white and he was much thinner than when she had last seen him.

George was home for the weekend too, but Lizzie was staying over at a friend's house. Ingleby explain to Joan the importance of what Frank was now doing and how it would not be putting him in any more danger than being a policeman. Joan seemed satisfied, if not totally convinced.

As they sat at the table for their tea, Josie asked Frank about his French.

'I'm still practising it, Josie. George and I try to chat in French as much as we can to help. He's much better than me; speaking it like a native. His mother would be pleased! He also has his French friend he writes to only using French and this friend is only allowed to write in English. To be honest, though, I have let it slip somewhat and, of course, don't see George as much as I used to.'

'I would like you to keep it up, Frank,' interrupted Ingleby, 'you never know when it will come in useful.'

'I'll let you have a copy of a very helpful new book, just published, which is all conversational French.' Josie suggested. 'That's all you need, really. Marie once told me you were pretty good at it when you were with her and her father. Conversation is always the best way to learn.'

Joan, listening to this, picked up on what Ingleby had said.

'Jack, are you likely to send Frank abroad? Wasn't he supposed to be based solely in London?'

'Well, he is, Joan, but you never know.'

She was about to ask more before Frank interrupted, clapping his hands.

'Come on everyone, tuck in, s'il vous plait.' Everyone laughed.

10

Frank began his new task by frequenting the various London meetings of Mosley's followers, now called the British Union of Fascists, often introducing himself to the speakers and other officials afterwards. The outdoor rallies were beginning to draw large crowds, far greater than those for the likes of Neusen all those years before. Frank often impressed those he met by quoting directly from Hitler's *Mein Kampf,* having read this during his training with Gosling. He was soon accepted as a respected and valuable new recruit and, within six months, was often being asked to speak at these meetings and rallies mixing fierce rhetoric with a sense of humour. He was accepted as Eddie Wilson, hard-done-by northerner, thrown out of work after serving his country in the Great War. He had yet to meet Sir Oswald, but had been introduced to Neil Francis Hopkins, the BUF's Director General, and his assistant, George Donaldson. They clearly thought highly of him and told him so.

He wore a Nazi-style uniform, but only at the rallies. Frequent photographs of BUF's key supporters began to appear in newspapers and, to disguise his appearance, Frank grew a moustache and had his hair shaved short. This new look did not find any favours with Joan but Lizzie and George were highly amused by it.

Each week Frank wrote to Ingleby updating him on any intelligence gained and of future Blackshirt events. This gave the authorities time to plan ahead to control the ever-increasing clashes between Mosley's followers and the anti-Fascists. The information also included details of the funding for Mosley from Italy, Germany and a surprising number of powerful groups in Britain. Frank rarely heard from Ingleby except for an occasional question, but he did tell Frank, when they met on one occasion, that he was delighted with the depth and quality of the intelligence. Joan accepted Frank's routine of being away for five nights or more each week. He was normally home at weekends unless there was a rally.

Lizzie had been accepted at Ongar Art College, but lived at home. George still boarded during the week in Chelmsford and hoped to obtain a place at university. He kept up his correspondence with his French friend, Jean-Luc, who visited each summer while George spent part of his Easter holidays with the Fontaine family in Eastern France.

As Frank was leaving a meeting in Stratford Town Hall one evening, Hopkins passed him a note of an address in the West End near St James's Park with an instruction to report there in two days' time.

The imposing Georgian house with its black railings was halfway along King Street. It had three storeys above the street level with steps to a cellar below. Frank pulled the bell handle and, when the door opened, instantly recognised the man inside. His name was Hindley and he regularly attended the rallies held around London's East End. Frank considered him a shady character; he was surrounded by dubious looking henchmen and always plotting with others. Frank had heard many stories about him since he had been undercover and had also been briefed about him during his training.

'Ah, Wilson, come on in. Let me take yer 'at and coat.' He led Frank through the entrance hall. 'I'm sure you're keen to find out what this is all about.' His accent was most definitely cockney, his voice high pitched.

'Well, it has come a bit out of the blue.'

'Someone 'ere who wants to meet yer.'

As they passed through the tiled hall into an extensive lounge, a tall man stood up from the sofa and came towards them.

'Wilson, I'm George Donaldson. We met recently after you'd spoken one evening. I'm pleased to meet you again.'

'Likewise,' responded Frank.

'Oh, I love that accent don't you Hindley? Where's it from, Manchester?'

'North of there actually, I was brought up near Burnley.'

'That's right; I was told you were thrown out of work from the mills after war service and came down here looking for work. But insurance now, isn't it?'

'Yes, a bit boring, but it pays the rent and gives me plenty of time for the Party.'

Donaldson smiled. A man in his sixties, he was wearing a black business suit over a white high collar and bow tie. He used a monocle for his left eye, which was half closed. Smoking a cigarette in a silver holder, he flicked the ash into the open fire before sitting on the sofa. Hindley left them alone, closing the door behind him as he left.

Pointing Frank to an armchair, Donaldson spoke again. His accent was London with an attempt to mask this with a hint of upper class.

'Now, now, young Wilson, you have most certainly impressed us since you arrived, not least with Sir Oswald. The point is that we are looking for additions to Sir Oswald's support team and he and I believe you most certainly fit the bill. It will only be part time and you can carry on for now with your other office work, but we will pay you a retainer. This is an absolute feather in your cap.'

This was not what Frank had been expecting.

'You look surprised,' added Donaldson.

'I am a little,' said Frank, realising what an opportunity this provided.

'Come, come, you have shown yourself to be an excellent speaker with a great knowledge of Herr Hitler's vision. You can help Sir Oswald with his speeches and also provide protection for him. You must have been Army trained and can handle yourself; you certainly have the build for it, that is for sure.'

'Thanks. Yes, I suppose you're right. I shall welcome the opportunity to work closer with Sir Oswald. Thank you.'

'That's fine then. You will be reporting to Sutton, Sir Oswald's secretary. I shall inform him you have accepted and he will contact you. Will you be at Saturday's rally?'

'I intend to be.'

'Good. Sutton can meet you there and tell you what he wants. Now, let us have a cup of tea.' Donaldson moved towards the door, but before he reached it Hindley came through with a tray.'

''Ere we are, boys, a nice drop of Rosy Lee. 'As he gone for it?' Hindley asked.

'He most certainly has,' confirmed Donaldson.

***

Frank wrote to Ingleby updating him on this development. Within two days Ingleby had responded and arranged to meet Frank in Regent's Park.

'This is momentous to be that close. Well done, old boy! We'll provide you with more precise information on what we want you to look out for. We're already putting together the details and I'll drop them in the post when they're ready, but for now, run with it and make the most of this contact with Sutton on Saturday. One other thing – I suggest we correspond as before, but meet here if we have to. I do not want you compromised; people like Hindley take no prisoners and their contacts reach deep into all areas of Government, Police and, dare I say it, the Intelligence Services.'

Frank met Sutton at the rally and immediately became involved in the detailed planning of a major rally and the march through the East End scheduled for the first Sunday in October.

Frank supplied Ingleby with the precise plans and he, in turn, was able to pass these on to the Police. A few days ahead of the march, the two met and Ingleby had a list of instructions.

'Frank, old man, I see this as an opportunity for us to further advance your status within the BUF. This march and the rally to follow will not pass off without incident, as these things never do. I want to create a direct threat to Mosley. You will know it's coming and be able to react first. I plan to have one of our men break through any cordon when you are near the church in Cable Street and he'll be wearing a distinctive yellow balaclava so you can't possibly miss him. Get to him before he comes too close and don't spare the attack, he's expecting to be hurt.'

'The things we do for you, Jack!'

'Well, needs must, old chap.'

'And you believe this will impress Mosley and his men?'

'Of course, don't you? We both know their light is fading. They will see this march as a chance of re-kindling their ambitions. Mosley will be nervous on the day and all his entourage will be on tenterhooks. You saving the day should have a massive impact and improve your stock with them no end.'

***

Mosley himself was to lead the march with Frank and Hindley providing the armed protection. Large BUF support was expected, but a far greater number of anti-Fascists and Communists were expected to line the route. It was rumoured that these factions were set on preventing the BUF getting from their first rallying point on the edge of Cable Street and on into Stepney. Thousands of police would also be on hand to deal with the crowds.

Hindley provided Frank with a pistol to keep hidden in his pocket and only to be used if Mosley's life was seriously threatened. They drove with Mosley in his bulletproof car to a rally of followers in Royal Mint Street next to Cable Street. Mosley was tense. He was dressed in a uniform of black military jacket, grey jodhpurs, jackboots and peaked cap. When he addressed the crowd of several thousands, he was soon into his stride. But trouble had broken out in Cable Street where the police were clashing with the anti-Fascists.

Frank was at Mosley's side when Metropolitan Police Commissioner Sir Philip Game came to discuss whether the march should be cancelled in view of the rioting along the route. Mosley's plan was to speak at a rally in Limehouse and finish this off with another one in Victoria Park, where Frank had shot Neusen all those years before.

Mosley called his aides together to discuss the Commissioner's proposal. Frank stood by and listened. He was now worried that, if the march was abandoned, Ingleby's plan would fail. Eventually, it was agreed that the march would head westwards instead, passing through the City and along the Embankment for a rally in the West End. This did not fit into the Ingleby plan at all.

The marchers headed off away from the trouble in Cable Street. In their midst, Mosley had Frank and Hindley at his shoulder. Frank looked at the young men and women around him; many wore their BUF Cadets' grey uniform and most were in their early to mid teens.

Frank had now given up on seeing the man in the yellow balaclava. Once in Queen Victoria Street, south of St Paul's, a crowd of protesters suddenly arrived chased by the police. More joined the throng and lined the street, but the police were now there in sufficient numbers to hold them back. Mosley said nothing, but Frank could see he was sweating profusely and looking anxious. Mosley knew this disorder was not likely to help his cause.

Suddenly, the police cordon failed to restrain the crowd. Frank spotted the balaclava. The man was in the front row of the mob a few yards away. Momentarily his eyes met Frank's. He broke through the cordon and headed straight for Mosley's group, shouting abuse as he ran. A policeman grabbed his ankle, but the man slipped from his grasp. Frank removed the gun from his pocket, surged forward and slashed the man across the face with its barrel, then kicked him in the stomach as he lay on the ground.

Frank saw the man stagger into the crowd and he returned to Mosley's side, but Hindley sidled up and said quietly,

'Bloody brilliant, Eddie my son, now you'd better scarper in case the Bobbies saw that and come after yer. The boss don't want no trouble with them.'

Frank smiled to himself as he jogged away; pleased the plan seemed to have worked after all.

***

From that day Frank worked more closely with Hindley, but was kept away from the more sinister and criminal dealings of his dubious empire, built, as it was, on extortion, threats and violence. Frank was only used for BUF work. He was given the responsibility of the security arrangements for any future rallies.

However, the Blackshirts were on the wane. They never really recovered from the day of the 'Battle of Cable Street'. Mosley was running out of funds and, whilst Italy's Mussolini continued to provide a certain amount of money, this began to diminish as time went by. Hindley also seemed to lose interest and concentrated more on his protection rackets and other more seedy criminal activities. Donaldson, responsible for preparing for the major rallies, spent more time in Hindley's world of organised crime.

Frank had less and less information to give Ingleby, although details of these criminal activities were useful information to pass on. At one meeting, Ingleby talked of pulling Frank out now that Mosley's threat was little more than an inconvenience, but decided to leave matters as they were for the time being.

The Blackshirts saw Frank as a valued member: reliable, diligent, personable and a safe pair of hands. No one had ever checked on his background or asked him very much about it and he felt secure and settled, but knew this would change once Ingleby felt his work was done and it was time to move on.

At home Joan was helping out at a school in Epping three mornings a week. George was hoping for a university place to read French and Lizzie had finished college with a first class diploma and returned to Chelmsford to take up a post as a tracer in the Drawing Office at Hoffmanns. She was renting a room from the Walmsleys.

Frank was on the equivalent of an Executive Officer Civil Service grade and his earnings were twice what they would have been had he stayed a Police Sergeant. Financially the family were well off. Joan knew better than to ask Frank anything about his work but, as he was required less in London, she saw more of him. They even took holidays, with regular return visits to their honeymoon hotel in Torquay.

But in early 1938 there was a sudden development.

11

Frank met Donaldson for a drink at The Blind Beggar pub in the Mile End Road.

'Eddie, come and sit down I've exciting news,' said Donaldson, patting Frank on the back. 'Here's a pint for you.'

Donaldson handed Frank the jug of dark beer.

'Sir Oswald wants you as his one of his personal assistants helping George Sutton, as I'm moving on. You'll also be needed to provide protection where necessary. Of course, this will mean giving up your job, working full time and living partly with the Mosleys. That's not likely to be a problem, is it?'

It would be difficult for Joan and the family to accept, but he would have to say 'yes'.

'No, not at all, I return north to my family only rarely and the Sun only need a week's notice,' he lied. 'I'll have to delay the start for a couple of days whilst I sort that out, but I'm due time off and won't have to work for the whole week.'

Donaldson outlined Frank's new role at Mosley's side. Frank left after midnight and returned to his flat feeling a little light headed. He could not wait to meet Ingleby to pass on this news.

The next morning he made his usual contact with Ingleby. They met in Regent's Park the day after and Frank brought him up to date with the developments.

Ingleby was delighted.

'That's marvellous, old boy, and what an opportunity for us. As you know, we are not so worried about the Blackshirts as we were when you started out on this, but the Mosleys still mix with the hierarchy in Germany and then there's

Mussolini, of course. You may see and hear things that remain important intelligence. And they're paying you!'

***

As the weeks passed, Frank's work under Sutton became routine; he spent an occasional day with Mosley, sharing the protection duties with another man. Little meaningful intelligence became available for Ingleby until, one morning, Frank was sifting through Mosley's correspondence when he came upon a document in German attached to a letter from the office of Josef Goebbels. Understanding a little German, Frank could see the heading 'GEHEIM' and knew this meant it was of a secret nature. When he was alone he copied out the three pages of typing by hand and passed it onto Ingleby at their next meeting.

'Some of it is coded,' said Ingleby. 'That will mean it will contain sensitive information; a quick look suggests to me that it is about the Jews. If I can, I'll let you know what it contains once our boys have had a chance to translate it all. We have already worked out most of these codes. Well done, old boy, and to think I was about to pull you out.'

***

About to leave Sutton's office one late afternoon, Frank was asked to drop off a package to Donaldson at The Blind Beggar on his way home. Donaldson appeared to have a new role to the effect that he was building up contacts within the gangs operating in the East End. Donaldson already had his link with the murky world of Hindley and was looking to widen his influence.

Donaldson was waiting in the public bar and looked like he had been drinking for most of the day. He slurred his words as he greeted Frank.

'Sit down, my boy. Two pints over here, barman!' he shouted.

Frank handed over the large manila envelope and sat down.

'You're a good man, Eddie, top bloody notch – for a northerner.' He laughed loudly.

'Where are those drinks, barman? Bloody idiot!' Donaldson teetered to the bar.

Frank looked round the room. The Blind Beggar had an unenviable reputation as the meeting place for much of the low life in that part of the East End with small groups of tough looking men often sitting huddled together, whispering. Periodically, violence broke out as rival gangs clashed over some matter of criminal principle. The local police gave it a wide berth and only in exceptional circumstances would they attempt to intervene.

At that time in the late afternoon, men from the docks were coming through the door in a steady stream, stopping off for a drink before making their way home. The bar was crowded. Donaldson was still waiting impatiently for the beer. Four dockers burst into the bar; one left to buy the drinks and the other three came to sit at the small table next to Frank.

Frank casually glanced up at them as they passed him. Suddenly he froze. He recognised one of the men. He looked down and away, but the man looked straight at him.

''Scuse me, mate, can I nick this?' He picked up one of the chairs.

Frank hardly raised his head, but said, 'Yeah, sure, take it.'

The man moved away but suddenly stopped.

'I don't believe it!' he shouted out. 'Bloody hell it's Frank bloody Shipley, isn't it?'

Frank looked up. 'Sorry,' he managed to say, 'I think you've made a mistake.'

The man stooped and looked straight into Frank's eyes.

'No, you're Frank Shipley all right, I'd know you anywhere. You must remember me! Reg Andrews –; you know, the bloke what were driving that lorry in France when we crashed. We was escorting that prisoner to Belgium, you know, what's his name? You know, sod it, what was it? I know... it was that Wilson bloke, you know ... deserter. I was badly injured and sent back 'ere to recover. Bloody 'ell, Frank Shipley! I don't believe it. Surely you remember. I've changed a bit and so 'ave you but I'd recognise you any place. What're you doing here?'

Frank's face was flushed and he felt a trickle of perspiration running down his temple. He stood up and ushered Andrews towards the toilet door away to their left. Before they had moved more than a yard, Donaldson returned with the two pints of beer in his hand.

'What's all this?' he asked.

Before Frank could say anything, Andrews spoke.

'I was in France in the war with Frank 'ere and we nearly died in a crash, but he might've saved my life, you know. The bloody lorry blew up and I'd've been trapped in it, but 'e pulled me out.'

Donaldson looked at Frank and frowned.

'What's this about, Eddie, is this bloke a nutter? Who is this Frank? What the bloody hell's he on about?'

Frank said nothing, but looked at Andrews who grinned. Donaldson waited expectantly, but Frank placed the palms of both hands under the pints of beer and tipped them over the front of Donaldson's shirt.

'What the ...?'

Frank pushed past Andrews, knocking him out of the way. He skipped round the legs of the other drinkers, pushing past those around the bar and headed for the front door. Once out in the street, he sprinted along the Mile End Road heading for the underground station. He kept looking back, but no one was following.

At the pub, Donaldson grabbed Andrews by the lapels of his jacket and pushed him up against the wall.

'Now, tell me what that was all about,' he snarled.

Frightened, Andrews looked over Donaldson's shoulder towards his three mates standing directly behind them. They pulled Donaldson away and forced him down into a chair. Donaldson put up his hands as if to say 'enough'.

'I only want to know why you called that bloke Frank something or other when his name's Eddie, Eddie Wilson.'

Reg Andrews joined Donaldson at the table.

'That ain't Eddie Wilson. He's dead. That were Frank Shipley and I was in the Military Police with 'im over in France in the war. 'E was me Corporal, good bloke, and we was in this crash, my fault, taking this deserter Wilson to Belgium. I think it was for 'is Court Martial. As I said, 'e and Wilson probably saved my life.'

'Are you sure about this? Absolutely sure?'

'Yes, honest, mate. Look, I lived with the bloke for more than a year and slept next to him often enough; I think I know who 'e is!'

Donaldson looked up, 'Do you know what happened to this Shipley after the war?'

Andrews shook his head. Donaldson looked at the others who shrugged as if to say they knew nothing.

'But you've not seen him since the war?' Donaldson asked

'Nope.'

'Interesting,' said Donaldson. 'Now, if you'll excuse me, I'm off.' The three men stood bemused and stepped back to let Donaldson leave. One of them asked Andrews,

'What the flying fig was that all about?'

'Search me,' said Andrews. 'Bloody strange, but I wouldn't want to be in Shipley's shoes when that bloke catches up with 'im.'

***

Back at his flat, Frank sat on his bed to collect his thoughts and to weigh up his options. He could return to Joan in Epping, but that might put her at risk if Donaldson delved into who he really was. Instead he decided to go to ground; he would need Ingleby's help to have Joan moved. With no time to make the normal arrangement to meet Ingleby, he would have to call at his office. He packed his holdall and tore a page from the back of his diary. He wrote a note for the landlady and left it on the dining table with his key and a pound note to more than cover the outstanding rent on her hall table.

Outside in the street a few people passed by, but no one suspicious. Two cars were parked but Frank recognised them as belonging to the neighbouring houses. He decided to catch a bus from the stop at the end of the street and soon arrived at Ingleby's office.

The commissionaire on the front desk ushered him to the second floor. Ingleby was not in his office. His secretary explained that her boss was at a meeting and would not return for an hour or so. Frank settled down to wait but he was nervous, on edge. Accepting a cup of tea he only drank half of it as his eyes were drawn to the loudly ticking clock on the office wall. The time dragged and more than two hours later, Ingleby returned.

'Frank, old chap, you're not supposed to come here.'

'Sorry, but this is an emergency.'

Ingleby showed him into his office and shut the door.

Frank explained what had happened at The Blind Beggar.

'So I left as quickly as I could,' he concluded, 'and picked up my things from the flat. I know I shouldn't turn up like this but now my cover's blown it didn't seem to matter. It was all I could think of apart from returning to Epping.'

'You did the right thing. We'll put you up in a safe house for a couple of days before we decide what to do.' Ingleby picked up the telephone and spoke to his secretary.

'Could you contact Tompsett and ask him to come over here straightaway? Thanks.'

He looked at Frank and shrugged

'I can't believe our bad luck with this,' Frank said after a pause. 'What are the chances of that happening, Jack?'

'Never mind, old son, we've had a good run and it's time to pull you out. That document you copied was priceless; it tells us what Hitler's real intentions are. Bloody frightening, quite frankly, and if only we could have taken him out.'

Ingleby walked over to the window and stared out. He remained deep in thought for some minutes, his hands clasped behind his back and head bowed.

'Look,' he finally said, as he turned back to face Frank, 'it will not take long for Donaldson and his henchman to find out about you from their informers. I would not be surprised if they call in Hindley. He's a nasty piece of work with a wide network and will come looking for you. To be on the safe side we'd better move your family until it all calms down. The last thing we want is for them to be put in danger. What's your view?'

'Well, they are not in any immediate danger as George is boarding still and Lizzie is with the Walmsleys. I was thinking about it on the way over; perhaps we could move Joan in with the Walmsleys or even to her parents in Broomfield. No one will find her at either place.'

'Good idea, Frank, and she might prefer to be with your daughter. I'll arrange for my man collecting Joan to take her to Chelmsford. Before that I suggest you write a note to Joan for this chap to pass on; she'll then know he's genuine when he pitches up on her doorstep.'

Ingleby collected a sheet of paper, inkwell and pen from the outer office. Frank sat at Ingleby's desk and wrote:

My dearest Joan,

I am fine, but there has been a development at my end that might mean you getting some unwanted attention. The man delivering this letter is called Tompsett and is one of Jack Ingleby's men. I want you to join Lizzie at Josie and Norman's for now, but please do not worry. It is a precaution Jack and I feel would be for the best. I shall remain in London for a while but will come back as soon as I can.

All my love

Frank

He wrote *To My Dearest Joan* on an envelope so she would recognise his handwriting

***

Donaldson headed straight for the George and Dragon where he knew he would find Hindley. He was sitting at his usual table with a girl on his lap. She was drunk and the buttons on her blouse were undone exposing the top of her breasts; Hindley kissed each one in turn. She giggled. When he saw Donaldson he pushed the girl away; she swore at him and he slapped her across her bottom. One of his henchmen pulled her away towards the bar.

Donaldson pulled up a chair and sat down. Hindley leered at him with a drunken smile and offered a limp hand. Donaldson ignored it and moved closer.

'I've found out by chance down at The Blind Beggar that Eddie Wilson isn't who he says he is. He's called Shipley, he's an ex-military copper and I reckon he's been passing on information, probably to the police or worse. Now he's close to the boss, that is a real problem – and to think he's had access to sensitive material.'

Hindley looked shocked and slammed his fist onto the table.

'I'll kill the bleeder.'

'Well, quite, and I need you to use your contacts to find him and kill him. He did a runner from the pub and he'll be in hiding. Whoever he is working for will shield him, but you must have enough men on the inside of these places to find out where he is. I want you and your men onto it now. Keep me posted every hour or so. You can reach me at my office. I reckon you've two days, maximum, to find him before he's away for good. You might be lucky and find he has a family we don't know about. If he has, we could lean on them and flush him out.'

***

Joan was listening to the radio and darning a pair of socks when she heard a knock on the front door. She looked at the clock on the mantelpiece; it was nearly a quarter to eight. She opened the door slightly keeping her foot up against the inside to stop the caller forcing their way in. The man outside smiled pleasantly and lifted his trilby. He was wearing a long raincoat, open at the top, revealing a smart tie and white shirt.

'Hello, Mrs Shipley. My name is Eric Tompsett. I work with your husband and have a letter from him here as a way of introduction.' He passed the envelope through the small gap. Joan immediately recognised Frank's writing and let the door open further. Tompsett stepped inside taking off his hat.

'He is safely with us, Mrs Shipley, but as you'll see from his note we need to take drastic action.'

She twice looked up at Tompsett as she read the letter and he half smiled both times.

'What do we need to do?' she asked calmly.

'I've a car waiting outside. I shall take you to your friend's house to make sure you're not at risk. Please pack enough clothes for a few days; we'll assess what to do after that.'

She ran upstairs to the bedroom and returned with a small case. She quickly cleared the kitchen placing the crockery into the overhead cupboard and locking the back door. Tompsett waited patiently by the front door. Joan lifted her coat from the hook in the hall and put it over her arm, but as she picked up the case she asked,

'Do you think I should leave a note for my neighbour? She might worry where I am.'

'Yes, I would,' confirmed Tompsett. Joan found her writing pad and a pencil. She scrawled a message to say that she had to be away for a few days as a close relative was ill and needed looking after. She passed the note to Tompsett to approve before posting it through the neighbour's letterbox.

Within the hour she was knocking on the front door of the Walmsley house in Chelmsford.

***

At the George and Dragon, Hindley sat alone at a table in the back room with his hand on a telephone. He was more sober now. He was a small man with black, greasy hair slicked back and with a quiff; his suit was shiny and had seen better days, his shirt's top button was undone and his tie skewed at an angle. He had just taken a call. He now knew who Frank Shipley really was. His contacts even surprised him at times. He did not have a precise address, but knew the Shipleys lived in the Epping area. It would not take long for his men to find a Kelly's directory or similar with the address in it.

***

A thick set man wearing a cap and short dockers' coat stopped the Morris 10 outside the Shipley's house. He checked the address on the piece of paper, making sure he had the right place, and walked to the front door. He knocked twice but, with no answer, he put his hand to the pane of the bay window and peered through. He turned away and walked to the house next door. The lady there opened the door and smiled pleasantly. The man doffed his cap.

'I'm sorry to bother you, but I was hoping to catch Mrs Shipley in. She wanted me to do a repair on their toilet cistern, I'm a plumber.'

'She's not there, she left suddenly for a few days, but I don't know where to or exactly when she'll be coming home.'

'Oh, I see. I'll have to see her another time. Sorry to have troubled you. Thanks anyway.' He returned to the car and spoke to the driver through the open window.

'We'd better find a phone and ring the guv'nor – tell him we've had no luck here.'

Hindley put the phone down in his office in Shoreditch, picked up his diary and turned to the inside of the back page where he had a list of phone numbers. He found the one he wanted, picked up the phone and dialled.

'Hindley here again; I need the address of yer safe 'ouses in The Smoke; the family one's rubbish. I need ones where this Shipley might be. What? ... Yeah, I know you're putting yer bloody job on the line, but you ain't a choice, me old china. You know why. Do you want me to tell yer old lady that little secret?'

There was a slight pause before Hindley continued, 'No, I thought not. Now bloody get to it. I need an address by the end of today and there's a pony in it. Call the usual number.'

Donaldson arrived soon after and Hindley updated him on the current situation.

'I'm a hundred per cent we'll know where 'e is by this time tomorrow,' he said. 'My blokes'll stash 'im away before shifting 'im down the marshes. They know what they're doing and they'll cover their tracks, no problem.'

'Good,' said Donaldson. 'I told the Mosleys and they are most definitely not pleased.

***

Jupiter Crescent, Balham, South London, a row of terraced Victorian houses was one of the more prosperous areas in that part of London, the residents mainly City office workers and their families.

Frank had enough food for a few days and a selection of clothes to change into. A wireless and a selection of books gave him something to while away time, with one of Ingleby's men detailed to visit each day, yet time dragged. Frank felt relief when told Joan was safely with the Walmsleys, but worried about his own safety; every few minutes he checked the street for anyone lingering there.

***

Hindley replaced the receiver and finished writing the address on his notepad. He ripped off the sheet, walked over to the hat stand and put on his trilby and coat. At the George and Dragon he found his two trusted heavies playing cards at a table in one corner. He told them to join him in the room above the public bar where he gave them the sheet of paper and explained what it meant.

''E might be guarded so take yer shooters,' Hindley told them. 'Case the place first to make sure what's there, but don't delay more than a few hours as they might move 'im again and I want 'im now. Don't shoot 'im unless you really 'ave to and don't 'urt anyone protecting 'im, as we've enough problems without 'arf the coppers in London on our tails. Do I make myself clear?'

'Yes boss,' they answered in unison and left. Hindley stood at the bar and the landlord passed him a whisky.

Hindley's men parked the Morris at the far end of Jupiter Crescent and one walked along the row of houses. He looked a typical office worker on his way home for his tea in his smart suit and tie with a newspaper tucked under his arm. He briefly stopped outside number 27 and re-tied his shoelaces.

He returned to the car and spoke to the other man.

'There's no sign of life but we'll have to call at the house to make sure,' he explained, as he settled into the passenger seat.

'Knock on the front door,' the other said, 'and if anyone answers say you're the insurance man. You know, from the Prudential or something like that. Pretend you're looking for a Mrs someone or another about her payments. You know what I mean. I'll pull round the corner, nearer the house.'

Frank was reading his day old newspaper when he heard the knock. He jumped out of his chair. Looking through the thick net curtains he could see a well-dressed man with a trilby standing outside, staring at the door. He decided not to answer. After the third knock he heard footsteps heading away along the street and he relaxed.

Returning to the car, the man opened the rear door and climbed in.

'There's definitely someone there. I looked through the letterbox and I could see stuff on the kitchen table. We'll collect some gear and break in when it's dark.' He looked at his watch. 'We'll give it a couple of hours. Right, let's go!'

***

The house was beginning to feel cold as the fire in the living room had burnt down to almost nothing. Frank decided he would have an early night with a hot cup of cocoa and a book.

He placed the guard over the fire to prevent any remaining sparks dropping onto the rug in front of the hearth and opened the thick curtains to make the neighbours think he was up and about the next day. He gave a cursory glance outside. Three cars were parked along the road and they were all a type of Morris, he noted.

The two men in the car were now only four doors down from number 27 and sat drinking tea from a flask. It was now almost completely dark outside. One tossed the dregs from his cup out of the car window and the other screwed the cap onto the top of the flask. Both had a shotgun in the space in front of their seats. They looked at each other, nodded and picked up the guns which they placed out of sight inside their overcoats once out in the street. This was lit now with dim gas lamps flickering every ten yards or so. They edged along keeping close to the front garden walls and stopped abruptly when a downstairs light went off inside their target.

One pointed to the other to make for the alleyway leading to the back gardens whilst he walked up to Frank's front door. There he waited allowing time for the other to reach the back door. Eventually he lifted the brass knocker before giving three sharp raps.

Frank was upstairs and half out of his trousers but quickly pulled them up and fastened the buttons. He slowly crept to the top of the stairs. Gingerly he took each step down and once at the bottom went to his jacket hanging on the peg inside the front door. As he lifted his handgun from the side pocket, he caught a glimpse of the shadowy figure through the frosted glass in the door. He crouched at the bottom of the stairs.

Unbeknown to Frank the second man was already in the kitchen. He had prised the back door as quietly as he could with a long knife and now held the handle of the door into the hallway. He opened it slightly. The only light was a sliver through the front door from a streetlight opposite. He could see Frank crouching in the hallway at the bottom of the stairs with his back to him. Opening the door fully, he slipped through with the shotgun raised above his head and the butt pointing towards Frank. He hit down and Frank crumpled unconscious to the floor. He opened the front door and let in the other man. They knelt and checked Frank over. A slight trickle of blood ran from a lump on Frank's head but he was breathing lightly. The man who had hit Frank returned to the car and reversed it as close as he could to the front door.

They bundled the still unconscious Frank onto the back seat. Having secured the front door of the house, they sped off.

***

The MI5 man arrived the next morning after ten o'clock with the newspaper and a bag containing a pint of milk, chops, vegetables and a bottle of lemonade. He let himself in and shouted up the stairs before entering the kitchen where he saw the damaged rear door. Panicking, he ran upstairs; there was no sign of Frank, only a pile of his clothes worn the day before. He dropped his bag on the hall table and ran to the telephone box at the end of the road. He dialled the usual number and Ingleby answered immediately.

***

Mosley's secretary moved round the desk as he considered what Donaldson had said. He sat down in the chair and picked up the file with Wilson's name on the front; reaching for his pen, he dipped it in the inkwell, deleted Wilson and wrote Shipley instead.

'So, you think we should kill him, George?'

'Well, he's from MI5 that we do know. Sent no doubt to feed them information and that's how the police, Jews and communists knew all about the marches beforehand and came prepared. What's the boss think about it?'

'He doesn't want anything to do with it. Anyway, he's left for Italy to seek more funds off Mussolini. Whatever we do, we've to make sure that nothing incriminates us, that's why we need to use Hindley's men to deal with Shipley one way or another.'

Donaldson walked to the window, 'When you put it like that, we've little choice but to remove him. I've told Hindley to hold him for a few days whilst we make up our minds with the likely view of disposing of him down on the Essex Marshes. He might have stuff on all of us that could have serious consequences – treason, even.'

'That's it then, George. Tell Hindley to eliminate Shipley and leave no trace. He'll love that, but the Party needs to distance itself from all this. We don't need any more bad publicity; it's bad enough already.'

The Secretary closed the file and put it in the drawer of the desk.

'Right, George,' he continued, 'have Hindley dispose of Shipley somewhere we don't know about. You'd better obtain some cash from the Treasurer and take it with you as Hindley'll probably want a couple of thousand or so.'

***

Ingleby ushered Commander Gosling into an office at Moorgate Police Station.

'Thank you for coming in at such short notice, but we've not much time. The Blackshirts are holding Shipley somewhere in the East End. We need police help on the ground as he's in great danger, which is why I'm here liaising with them. I need your expertise to co-ordinate them in the field.'

'Things are bad then,' said Gosling, inadvertently rubbing the scar on the side of his face. 'I heard his cover was blown. He's really in trouble if they hand him over to Hindley; that would be curtains.'

Ingleby was quiet for a moment.

'We've a tail on Hindley all the time,' he added, 'but he's a slippery customer and well protected. He'll guess we might be watching him, but might not be expecting a tail on his two lieutenants. We've informers around the East End and the Jewish community are keeping their ears to the ground for us. They track the Fascists all the time. The Communists might receive information through their contacts, but I wouldn't trust them as far as I could throw them. Anyway, I need you to lead the search for Shipley. Try the Communists first to see how far you get. Hindley and his men will be involved somewhere along the line because the top Fascists will try and distance themselves from Shipley and leave Hindley's mob to do their dirty work. I'll let you know if we come up with anything as a result of the tail and, if you hear anything, let me know right away.'

Gosling moved towards the door.

'I'll work on this alone as far as I can, sir, but I might need all the support necessary if we need to set up a raid or similar.'

'Do whatever you think is necessary; ask and you'll have whatever you want. You know from as long ago as Austria that Shipley's a top man and we need him returned in one piece. Set off now, you might only have a couple of days at best.'

Gosling left the Station. It was early in the evening and the streets were quiet apart from the noisy starlings gathering in the trees as dusk approached. He was impressed with Shipley, having trained him and seen him in action; now he had to save his life and knew he had little time left to do so.

***

Hindley screwed up the note from Donaldson and threw it on the fire, watching it burn to nothing. He called his man Dolby in from the kitchen. Dolby brought two glasses of whisky and gave one to Hindley.

Dolby was an ex-heavyweight prospect. He had let his fists do too much talking outside the ring and from a young age had been in and out of prison until Hindley recruited him to act as his protection. Dolby had persuaded a former cellmate, Harris, to join him after they met in Pentonville. Harris, a thug with no respect for anyone or anything, was the man responsible for carrying out all the dirty jobs Hindley wanted.

With these two willing lieutenants, Hindley was able to distance himself from anything that might land him in trouble and allow him to concentrate on his other activities in the East End, where he controlled just about anything on the wrong side of the law from prostitution, extortion and, now, the benefits from the mayhem caused by the Fascists and the Communists. He played one off against the other and was rewarded handsomely from time to time by both.

He had already put the two thousand pounds in his safe before Dolby arrived at the Shoreditch flat Hindley used as his London office. His wife and children were at home in their mansion on the St George's Hill Estate in Weybridge.

He sipped the whisky and told Dolby to sit down.

'I've a job for you an' 'Arris. The bloke we 'ave in Cedars Road must be moved and disposed of – you know what I mean?'

Dolby nodded.

'First, you need to move 'im to that 'ouse down Hornchurch for a while because we must keep 'im on the move. Then take 'im out on Rainham marshes and lose 'im, you know what I mean?'

'Right, but why don't we take him straight there?'

'Because I wanna wait 'til the 'eat's off. There'll be police and maybe army looking in all the obvious places, but it'll tail off in a few days, they'll fink 'e's dead. So make sure 'Arris doesn't cock it up; you know what 'e can be like at times. I know the cops are watching me but I'll be up West to distract 'em; you can go over to Cedars and pick up this bloke during tonight. Get 'im to Hornchurch and let fings cool down for two days. Make sure you're not being watched then dump the body.

'No problem.'

'Now bugger off, is 'Arris with you?'

'Yes he's in the Dragon. I'll pick him up in about an hour after you've left; then we'll know the coast'll be clear.'

Hindley picked up his coat and moved towards the door. He stopped as he opened it,

'Dolby, if you're caught and grass me up, so help me God I'll make sure you're a dead man, just remember that. Let me know when it's all over. There'll be a ton in this for you and 'Arris.'

Hindley headed to the underground station. Despite a number of people out window-shopping, he easily spotted his tail. The man in the cloth cap had been with him for a few days.

***

Frank was being kept in a small bedroom and handcuffed to the frame of a bed. If the men were in the house they would release him so he could eat or use the toilet. However, when he was on his own, they would leave a bucket and old newspaper together with scraps of food.

He hoped their guard would drop sufficiently enough to enable him to escape, but he would have to be patient.

He was worried for Joan, George and Lizzie. Ingleby would ensure they remained safe, but Joan, normally calm and resolute during his time working undercover, would still be concerned when she hears he's been exposed.

Frank was sure Ingleby would start a search for him and simply hoped he would be found in time. He doubted Donaldson would do anything other than have him killed. He was expendable and could only cause the Fascists even more damage if he stayed around much longer.

He knew the chances of escaping were slight, but he was determined to try - he had nothing to lose now.

***

After a short while, Dolby found Harris in the George and Dragon. He ordered himself a scotch and another pint for Harris. They sat at a table and Dolby explained the plan. As they left, neither noticed the man with a large scar on his face in the far corner reading the Evening News.

The two men walked the half-mile to Cedars Road. They stopped outside the house and looked round, making sure they were not being followed. Dolby unlocked the door and they entered. The man with the Evening News tucked under his arm came out of a dark doorway. He looked up and down the road and was disappointed not to see sign of Ingleby's promised tail.

He backtracked around the corner to a police telephone box. He undid the door with his key and dialled the special number for the armed unit. He spoke with Sergeant Davies who he had briefed earlier.

'Davies, this is Gosling, I need your squad to meet me at the police box in Water Lane, Stratford, as soon as possible.' Davies promised they would arrive in twenty minutes.

When Gosling arrived at the corner of Cedars Road, he spotted a black station wagon parked outside the house. The door to the house opened and a shaft of light shone from the hallway. A well-built man came out pulling a taller person with their head covered in a blanket. Another joined them and opened the car door, helping the bigger man push their captive inside.

The engine started and they pulled away. Gosling made a mental note of the car's number: CVX 478, which he kept repeating to himself as he ran round the corner to the police box. He called the number for Davies. A constable answered and confirmed Davies and his team had already left.'

'Put out a call to all London and Essex units,' Gosling ordered. 'Tell them to look out for and report any sighting of black station wagon CVX 478. Any sighting should be phoned through to this police box immediately. Is that clear?'

'Yes, sir, CVX 478, got it.'

Gosling cursed his luck. He had no option but to wait for Davies.

'Sorry,' he explained when Davies arrived, 'we're too late; they've gone. You stay here and stand your men down for now, but tell them to stand by in case someone reports seeing the car.'

***

Not wishing to draw any unwanted attention, Harris drove slowly through the light traffic. They travelled east along the Romford Road towards Ilford, down through Goodmayes and into Hornchurch. The house he was heading for was on Suttons Avenue. They pulled up outside Number 62 and Dolby made sure Frank was lying flat across the back seat. Harris unlocked the rear door, pulled the blanket off Shipley's face and hit him with a right haymaker, knocking him out. Dolby put the blanket over the prone body and they both carried Frank into the house.

***

Gosling and Davies waited for more than an hour at the police box, but no call came. Gosling became impatient.

'I'll wait in my office,' he announced. 'Let me have your notebook and I'll write down my number. You or your constable can ring me there in about half an hour if anything is reported. I'll catch a bus.'

***

Dolby and Harris stood over a still unconscious Frank in the kitchen. As he came round, he looked confused, not sure where he was.

'Ah,' said Harris, 'back in the land of the living. Here, take this, it's water.' He handed Frank a glass. Sipping the water slowly, Frank waited for his head to clear and to recall what had happened earlier. Suddenly he was pulled up onto a chair.

'Where am I now?' he asked.

'Essex. This is your short stay hotel; we do hope you like it.'

'So, you're Hindley's men, I take it. Doing his dirty work, I suppose?'

Neither man responded. Frank looked closely at both – he had met them before with Hindley at the marches and meetings; they were part of his protection. Now in their hands, Frank knew the ending was soon to be played out. He had no doubts about what now awaited him. Hindley was as evil as they come and knew only one way to deal with irritations.

He spoke softly to the men.

'Look, you two, you know who I am. Despite what you think, it will be impossible for you to escape the police. You'll be sent down with Hindley. He's poison. The police and intelligence forces will pick him up any day now and close down his operation. I know because I helped secure the evidence. What you're doing to me now means the net will close around you too. You're small fry but I can help you get out of this with only a short sentence if you confirm the evidence and help us nail Hindley and his senior men. If not, he'll take you with him. Do yourselves a favour: turn yourselves in to me and bring an end to it all.'

Harris looked at Dolby and walked over. Frank hoped he had successfully made his point, but Harris hit him with a backhand slap, knocking him off the chair. Blood poured from his nose and from a cut on his eyebrow caused by the man's ring.

Frank fell onto his back and wiped the blood from his face. The two men left the room and shut the door behind them.

***

Spending the whole of the next day in his office Gosling received no reported sightings of the station wagon but was updated on Hindley's movements which entailed a night spent at his club with today finding him at home with his family in Weybridge. Shipley's trail was worryingly cold. Finding the station wagon was now essential if Frank was to be rescued.

Evidence suggested that Hindley's previous victims had been left on the Essex Marshes near Rainham. Gosling arranged for officers to look out for the car there, but it was a large area to cover with any number of small roads. All units across the South East were on full alert. They needed a little luck or for Hindley's men to make a mistake.

Gosling spent another night on his camp bed.

***

Cycling along Suttons Avenue, PC Harrison was enjoying the warm summer morning as he made his way to Rush Green police station to sign off after his night duty. He would return home for a sleep after his breakfast in the canteen. Earlier he had been called to a house where a break in was reported in the early hours, but only loose change had been missing. He could write up his report over his breakfast.

This had been his beat for the past three years. He knew most of the people who lived here and was familiar with their comings and goings, nothing much changed. As he rode along, he saw a large vehicle with a cover over it parked between numbers 62 and 64, almost out of sight in the rear garden. Vehicles stood out, as there were so few; this unfamiliar one caught his attention.

He cycled on to the T-junction, but suddenly braked. Perhaps he should check the vehicle; it might have a connection with the earlier burglary.

Harrison propped his bicycle up against the wall next to the garden gate. He was about to knock at the front door, but instinct made him walk down the side of the house. He lifted the cover. It was a black station wagon and he looked at the number plate, CVX 478. That seemed familiar to him. Taking his notebook out of his breast pocket, he read through the various notes for the last week. There, from two days ago, was CVX 478. He remembered now that a call had been received to look out for it, although he didn't know why.

Returning to his bicycle he rode away from the house, looking up to see if there were any telephone wires. One ran to a builder's premises at the junction.

Workmen were loading lorries in the yard. One recognised him immediately.

'Good morning, Arthur, what d'you want?'

'I must use your phone; it's an emergency!'

'It's up in the office – mind the stairs, they're bloody rickety.'

Harrison rang through to his desk sergeant.

'Sarge, Harrison, I'm at Clacker's yard. There's a car in Suttons, CVX 478 – it's on our list.'

'Hang on,' said the Sergeant. He was away for almost a minute. 'Stay where you are, but make sure you can see the car or at least the house – armed officers are on their way. Be careful and don't be dragged into it.'

'Yes, Sarge.'

***

Gosling was at his desk when the phone rang. The car had been spotted in Hornchurch. He rang down to the main office to arrange for an unmarked car to pick him up outside, then called Davies. They agreed to meet at Rush Green Police Station as soon as possible. He grabbed his jacket from the hook behind the door and picked up the pistol in its holster from the desk.

In less than an hour he was with Davies. The desk sergeant briefed them on where the car was, the constable's name and his location.

'Tell your man to wait and we'll join him outside the builder's yard.'

Still in the builder's office, Harrison looked out of the window as he put the telephone down onto the receiver. He saw a well-built man come out of the house, look both ways along the road and return inside. The station wagon reversed out from the side of the house and was positioned as close as possible to the gate. With such a small garden and barely two yards to the door, the vehicle obscured the front of the house from Harrison's view. He ran down the stairs and out of the gates. Still not able to see far enough down the road, he crawled along behind a low garden wall until it ended at a small gate. Looking through its bars, he saw a second, smaller man appear from behind the car, also checking to see if the road was clear.

The man opened the rear double doors before returning to the house. Shortly after, both men re-appeared carrying a large bundle, which they pushed into the back of the car. Harrison moved for a better look. One man sat in the rear of the car and the other drove. They moved off slowly driving away from him. He was not sure what to do, but decided to head to the yard. He had only walked a few paces when three cars pulled up beside him containing armed, uniformed men. Gosling, in civilian clothes, wound down his window. Harrison leant over.

'They've just this minute driven off away towards Upminster,' he explained. He pointed in the direction the car had taken.

Gosling ran to the car behind. As he approached, Davies spread out a large map across its bonnet.

Gosling spoke first.

'We need to look at Rainham Marshes, but that's a big area.'

Davies did not look up from the map and was running his finger along several different routes.

'We have men there already, Commander, covering what they can. They are positioned here, here and here,' he said pointing at three places a little east of Rainham. 'Now, Shipley might be taken along all sorts of routes from here but, let's see, if you take your car that way and the other one goes that way, I'll head along here – that'll cover the most likely routes.' He folded the map and the men dispersed to their separate cars.

***

Frank lay on his side in the boot. However, the shelf above the back seat had been removed enabling the men to keep watch over him. His hands were still tied and he struggled to sit up.

'Look, there's no point to all this, call it a day,' he said. 'I told you I'll put in a word to help. My people'll be on your tail. Don't make it bad for yourselves or you'll end up dead. They'll be armed.'

Dolby leant over from the back seat and pushed a knife up into Frank's neck forcing his head back.

'Another peep out of you...'

The car lurched to one side throwing Frank backwards and away from the point of the knife as Harris turned off the main road and onto a dirt track lane following the sign to Wennington Marsh. In the distance, tall ships edged along the Thames and appeared to be sailing across the fields. The low-lying area was thick with hedgerows providing cover, but dust was being thrown up due to the dryness of the ground. Harris speeded up, but this only made it worse.

About a mile away on the main road, two officers sat in their car, scanning the flat landscape for signs of movement.

'Look, a dust cloud, someone's in a hurry, let's follow,' said the driver.

They alerted Gosling on the radio and gave their position.

Harris drove onto a smaller track close to the Thames. At the bottom of a slight incline the ground became boggy. He pulled over to one side and ran round to open the rear doors. With Dolby pushing from the inside, he pulled Frank out onto the ground. As Frank stumbled trying to stand Harris caught his arm and led him onto a path through tall grass interspersed with reeds. Harris held a knife to Frank's back and Dolby followed with a shotgun. The faint ring of the police car's bell carried to them on the breeze and became louder as it approached their position.

Frank stopped but Harris held the knife to his neck causing Frank to jerk his head back.

'Don't be so stupid! Leave me be and give yourself up.' Harris thrust Frank forward and he stumbled.

The police car pulled up next to the wagon and another drew up seconds later. Frank and his captors were a hundred yards further away.

'What we gonna do?' asked a breathless Dolby as he ran alongside Harris. Harris ignored him.

'Sod you! Leave him!' Dolby shouted as he suddenly veered to the right and crashed through the greenery in his bid to escape the pursuers.

'Come back here, you idiot, and use the gun,' Harris called after him but Dolby kept running.

Harris pushed Frank to the ground and knelt on one knee. He lifted the knife and plunged down towards Frank's chest. Frank managed to roll to one side and the blade caught his ribs a scything blow. He shouted out in pain. Harris was ready to try again, but, hearing shouts from not far away, he kicked out catching Frank's shin and ran off.

Within seconds, Gosling and Davies were at Frank's side with a constable right behind.

'Frank?' asked Gosling.

'I'm fine,' Frank said with a grimace.

'Look after him,' Gosling told the constable.

With Davies he continued on but after a short distance held up his hand and stopped, listening. Tall reeds rustled to their left. They ran in and there stood Harris, one hand in the air, the other holding the knife, pointing towards the ground.

'Don't kill me, don't kill me!'

'Get to your knees,' ordered Davies, as he pulled out his handcuffs. Two constables arrived to help.

'I'm off,' said Gosling, gun in hand.

He ploughed on through long grass following the trail Dolby had made. He came into a clearing and was confronted by Dolby pointing the shotgun. Gosling stood pointing his gun.

'Now what are you going to do?' Gosling enquired with a hint of sarcasm.

Dolby fired and Gosling followed a split second later. Dolby fell with his shirt splattered with his blood. Gosling had been hit in the face; he slumped onto his knees and fell forward. Dolby lay silently next to him.

Davies arrived, bent down and felt the men's necks. Both were dead. He sat for a moment shaking his head before picking up the two guns and returning to where the two officers were tending to Frank who, despite sitting up, looked pale. There was a red stain on his shirt above his belt, his shin was swollen and at an unusual angle.

'The wound's not too deep, but his leg's broken,' said the constable, standing up. 'What about the others?'

'Both their man and Commander Gosling are dead, I'm afraid.'

***

It was early evening. Hindley reached for a sandwich from the plate in the middle of the table as his wife poured the tea. His two daughters leant over to help themselves when the glass shattered in the wooden patio doors behind them. A policeman stood in front of them with a rifle. He said nothing but all four jumped up and the two girls screamed.

Ingleby walked through the shattered doors, 'David Arnold Hindley you are under arrest for murder – amongst other things. The officer here will caution you.'

***

A week later, Joan pushed Frank's wheelchair to the graveside. He bent down, picked up a handful of soil and threw it onto the coffin. The vicar stood and watched with his prayer book open in his hands. Mrs Gosling, all in black, stood on the other side of her husband's grave. She was alone with no other family there.

Joan wheeled Frank away, followed by Jack Ingleby.

'So this is how it could all end up?' she said to Ingleby. 'This is what I could be facing. I'm not sure I want Frank to return to that life; he came that close to being taken from me.' She stared at Gosling's grave.

'I know, Joan. I'm standing him down, letting him go. He knows that already,' Ingleby reassured her.

'It's a good pay off too, love,' said Frank cheerfully. 'It will set us up for a while and I'll look for work. I have a few irons in the fire already.'

Joan looked at Ingleby. She knew in her heart that this was not over, this relationship between her husband and this man. War clouds were gathering, despite what Mr Chamberlain had told the nation last year.

As if reading her thoughts Ingleby added,

'That is not to say Frank will not be a valuable asset for me with what might lie ahead for all of us. We all know what Hitler's ideas and ideals are. Mark my words, old thing, there will be another war before long and I can't guarantee that Frank will not be needed.'

Joan said nothing, but walked on ahead towards Ingleby's Bentley. Frank wheeled himself alongside Ingleby as they followed.

'I suggest you don't speak more of this to her for now, Jack. I must say though that I'd welcome the chance to work for you again.

12

Frank spent eight weeks in plaster to allow his broken shinbone to mend. During this time, the family were moved from Epping and provided with a bungalow on the edge of the small village of Roxwell, a few miles from Chelmsford. George was now in his final year at the Grammar School, but now lived at home instead of boarding; Lizzie had returned home from the Walmsley's. After his initial fortnight in hospital, Frank was thankful to be with Joan. His stab wound took time to heal, but was little more than a discomfort.

The pay-off from MI5 was substantial and he and Joan decided to buy a small car – a new Austin Seven and they fell in love with it immediately. It had soft leather seats and a front window, which opened outwards to provide a pleasant airflow on hot summer days; it was perfect for a family of four. Joan, a capable driver, took Frank out for a ride most days to relieve his boredom. There was no immediate necessity for him to find work, as the cash lump sum he had received would tie the family over for at least a year.

Although he said nothing to Joan, he suspected Ingleby would come knocking on his door again before too long.

***

Despite the prospect of war seemingly to have been averted when Prime Minster Chamberlain triumphantly returned from Munich a few months before waving the agreement signed by Herr Hitler, early 1939 saw the newspapers full of gloom predicting strife before the year was out.

Since the aborted assassination attempt, Frank had continued to maintain a close interest in Hitler's rise to power, now believing the British Government to be deluded. It appeared to him that Hitler still intended to dominate Europe – and the world - by whatever means possible. Germany's alliance with Russia was worrying. The Far East was unsettled, with China and Japan permanently at odds. Furthermore, Hitler had shown his hand during the civil war in Spain.

***

George was proving to be an accomplished linguist and was studying for his advanced exams in English, Latin and French before taking his place at Oxford in the autumn provided his grades were good enough. He was really taken with French and was now fluent, having spent more time with his pen friend's family in the past two years. They lived in Sedan – close to the border with southern Belgium.

Frank, with time on his hands at home, decided to improve his French too, from where he had left off with Josie Walmsley. He used the conversational phrasebook she had given him together with various books George used at home.

George received an invite from Jean-Luc to spend two weeks of his school Easter holiday in Sedan and included in that invite was another for the whole family to visit. Frank was keen to travel now that his plaster was long gone and the leg strengthened by the long walks he now took each day across the fields to the village. However, Joan faced a dilemma. Her mother and father were keen to have a Parmenter family holiday in a cottage near Great Yarmouth and had already booked a week. They compromised, with Frank agreeing a shorter trip with George and Joan taking Lizzie with her to Norfolk.

Four weeks later Frank and George took the boat train to Dover and a further train from Calais down the eastern border to Sedan. The Fontaine family owned a successful timber business that had been in the family for over a hundred years. They lived in a beautiful house on the outskirts of Sedan set in woodland overlooking the town.

Frank liked Thierry and Madeleine Fontaine, who were a similar age to him. He and George spoke French the whole time, even to each other. One evening, Thierry and Frank sat sipping a cognac on the terrace after dinner. The boys were in town watching the much-vaunted film, *The Adventures of Robin Hood,* starring Errol Flynn and Olivia de Havilland.

'So, what did you do in the war?' Frank asked.

'I missed the big battles at Mons and Verdun. Just as well because, if I hadn't, I probably wouldn't be here talking to you now. I was in the Pay Corps sorting out the men's money – nothing exciting and certainly nowhere near any action.'

'My first wife's husband was killed at Verdun,' said Frank. 'It must have been dreadful there, but the Somme and Passchendaele were ghastly too.'

'Jean-Luc told me you were in the Military Police. That must have been interesting?'

'Not really, apart from right at the end of the war with a deserter I captured and he was a sad case. We became friends and that's how I met Marie, my first wife. She had looked after him for about a year. We both attended the Court Martial to plead for clemency.'

'I know, George told us about it last year. Awful business.'

'So how about what's in the news; do you think there's a good chance of another war?'

'No doubt in my mind, Frank. The pact with Stalin won't last and there's more trouble out East.' Thierry thumped the table with his fist.

Frank was quiet for a moment.

'What about the Maginot Line? It's not far from here is it?' he asked.

'No, only a few kilometres, but it won't halt anything. Anyway, the Germans will simply march straight through Holland and Belgium before they even think about coming through here.'

'I agree. Some of us in Britain do also believe the Maginot will be of no consequence. I have experience of National Socialists and believe we should be frightened of them. Their forces are stronger than anything we have, certainly on land, and nothing will stop them – at least, not at first.'

'I'm worried about my business. I'm concerned the Germans if they come will want all my timber for whatever purpose and that'll be the end for the family after all these years.'

Thierry poured another glass.

'I tell you what Frank, I'll take you to the Maginot tomorrow and you can see what it's like. It's impressive yet useless in my opinion.'

A week later Frank and George left the Fontaines to return home, but they vowed to meet again next year, unless the escalating crisis with Germany became worse. Frank was left in no doubt the Maginot might serve a purpose following his visit there but agreed with Thierry that the Germans would almost certainly opt for seizure of the Low Countries should they decide to attack France as they had in 1914.

***

Soon after his return from France, Frank was tidying up in the front garden when a large car gently pulled up outside. Not many cars of this size were ever in the village and certainly not driven by a uniformed chauffeur with a passenger sitting behind. Curious, Frank walked out to the garden gate wiping his face with his handkerchief. The chauffeur opened the back door and out stepped Ingleby, smiling broadly as he came forward with hand extended.

'Glad to see you, old chap,' said Ingleby as they shook hands.

'Good grief, Jack; how are you? Follow me, come inside.'

'I'm not too bad but have this damned ulcer and it does give me trouble from time to time.'

'Would you like a drink? A cup of tea, maybe?'

'Water will be fine, thanks. My doctor's told me to drink plenty of water.'

Frank took a glass from the kitchen cupboard, filled it from the tap and handed it to Ingleby.

'Thanks. How are you, Frank? Fully recovered, I hope.'

'I'm very well, thank you, Jack. Yes, fully recovered. I've recently arrived back from a wonderful time in France with my son George and, as soon as summer's over, I'll be getting a job. Marconi in Chelmsford are looking for a new Head of Security and I had an interview before I travelled to France. The post would not be available until early September, but they've asked me to return for the final interview at the end of this week. They were impressed with my experience from the work in the war, the police force and with you. They hinted the job would be mine, but I'm not counting my chickens!'

'Tell me more about France.'

'The family we stayed with are business people and influential in that part of Eastern France. Being close to Germany they're worried, as they believe the French won't put up much of a fight should the Germans invade again.'

'They've every right to be concerned,' Ingleby confirmed. 'We're now extremely worried about Hitler. Those documents you copied were absolute proof that we must be on our guard about what could happen. The Government still has its head in the sand and won't listen to us. Only Churchill seems to be sitting up and taking notice. Most of the country isn't listening and he's *persona non grata* with many people. A few of us think he's right, though. Intelligence, accurate intelligence at that, shows Chamberlain has no idea about how serious this all is and clings to what Hitler said at Munich last year. But I believe it's a lie. Look what he's done with the non-aggression pact with Poland. Our spies in Berlin tell us he's about to invade Poland and it could happen before August is out.'

'Bloody hell, Jack, I didn't realise it was that bad.'

'You mark my words, old boy, we'll be at war again before the leaves are off the trees. If that happens, would you immediately be called up? All that time you spent with the Territorials and with us is bound to mean they'll want you.'

'That's probably true. I knew I'd be on a reserve list given I'm still young enough, but I was hoping nothing would happen until I was too old to be called up. Doesn't look like it after what you've just said.'

Ingleby was quiet and pensive, but added,

'You know what, Frank, if your French is as good as you say it is, we might be able to use you in the Service if the worst happens. What do you think about that?'

Frank blew out his cheeks and whistled,

'Phew! That's not what I was expecting.'

'The reason I came here today was partly to see how you were, but also to persuade you to come and work in my London office. Now I know you speak French, this puts a different complexion on things, old chap. Anyway, if you were to be called up if war breaks out, you might as well come and work with us. You're less likely to have your head blown off for a start.'

They both laughed. Joan came in through the kitchen door and immediately frowned when she saw Ingleby.

'Hello, Joan,' he said. 'Don't look so glum, old thing. Aren't you pleased to see me?'

'Sorry. Yes, Jack, I am. How are you? I do apologise, but it's just that every time I see you I suspect you will want my husband for something and that this occasion will be no different.' She half smiled.

'Well, you may be right and I do come with the offer of a job with me in London. Office based this time.'

'I seem to recall that's what you said last time and Frank nearly ended up dead down on Rainham Marshes!'

She turned and started putting away the crockery from the draining board. The two men watched, waiting for her to finish.

'Leave that now, love,' said Frank standing up. 'Come into the sitting room to be more comfortable.' Joan flashed an angry look at Frank as she brushed past him. She sat on the sofa with her arms crossed. Ingleby and Frank sat in the two armchairs.

Frank spoke first.

'Jack believes we'll be back at war soon, love. It could be within weeks. The word is Hitler's about to invade Poland and it won't be long before he comes our way. I'm bound to be called up, you know.'

Joan said nothing. She frowned again and smoothed her dress, not wishing to look up.

'I was just saying to Frank before you arrived,' Ingleby said soothingly, 'that it might suit him to come and work again with the Service. It would be much safer for him, as he would be kept well away from where the fighting is likely to be. You'd be happier with that too, wouldn't you?'

Joan fingered the pattern on her dress then looked up. Tears were welling in her eyes and she sniffed. Ingleby reached into his pocket, pulled out a pristine white handkerchief and passed it to her. She dabbed her cheek and eyes, blew her nose and handed it back with a nod of the head.

'I'm sorry to be a bit brutal with the truth, Joan, and it's a worrying time for all of us, but the fact of the matter is that Frank is a valuable asset. If he comes and joins me, he will not be in the normal call up. If he could say 'yes' to joining me pretty well straightaway, all that bother can be prevented.'

Frank leant over and held Joan's hand.

'Jack's right, you know, love. It would be better for us and I'd be in London, not in a god-forsaken water filled trench. I'd like to steer clear of that, thank you very much.'

'And, Joan, now I know Frank speaks French, we can possibly use him as a liaison with our contacts in France.'

Joan eventually spoke quietly and hesitatingly.

'I'm not sure about all this. I'd rather have Frank here and working in Chelmsford. He's already been for an interview, you know, and is hopeful of landing a good job. Hasn't he done enough for you already? It damn near killed him, after all.'

'But,' Frank interrupted, 'I would only be at an office desk in London and not out there being fired at.'

Ingleby stood up and picked up his hat from the table by his side.

'I can see you both need time to talk this over. But Joan, we need Frank to help us out. The work he could do for me would be just as safe as Head of Security at a local factory. I'll leave it with you, but will respect any decision you make. Frank, give me a telephone call when you can. In case you've forgotten the number, here's my card. Just one more thing, you will be able to keep your pay-off and resume on the same grade as before. You have no worries on that score, old chap.'

He kissed Joan on the cheek and shook Frank by the hand before heading out of the front door. The chauffeur held the car door open and Ingleby slid onto the back seat.

Frank waved and closed the front door, but Joan had already returned to the kitchen and was preparing their tea.

Frank pretended to read the book he had left open on the arm of the sitting room sofa earlier in the day. He stared blankly at the small print on the page. Nearly fifteen minutes passed and he had still not turned the page. His mind was racing as he tried to come to terms with what Ingleby had said.

Finally, he joined Joan in the kitchen. She had her back to him as she peeled potatoes. He put his arms around her waist from behind, but she remained stiff, unresponsive. He kissed the nape of her neck and he felt her body relax a little. She turned round with her eyes looking at the floor. Frank gently lifted her chin so their eyes met.

'Yes, you have to do it, sweetheart,' said Joan. 'Jack's right. I know you'd be miserable if you turned this down.'

Frank kissed her on the lips and they hugged each other tightly.

'I do love you, Mrs Shipley!'

'Very lovey-dovey!' George called out. He was standing in the doorway. Frank and Joan swiftly parted, a little embarrassed. Joan smoothed her apron and returned to her potatoes. Frank led George into the sitting room.

George, at eighteen, was as tall as Frank. Their time in France had brought them closer together and Frank saw so much of Marie in their son with his gentle, easy going nature and, most certainly, her smile.

They sat next to each other on the sofa. With war more than likely to be only months away, Frank feared for his son. He recalled what had happened in the last war when young men poured out of the universities as officers and straight, in many instances, to the Front. Most of them were never to return. Could this be what George had to look forward to? Frank shuddered at the prospect.

He explained to George what Ingleby had offered.

George was quiet for a few moments after his father had finished.

'Well, I agree, Dad, you need to go. It'll be safe in an office, but I know you better than most. Like Mum, I know you won't just sit behind a desk. That's not you, is it? They'll have you doing more dangerous things before too long.'

Frank said nothing as George smiled at him, but he knew his son was probably right.

***

One morning shortly after Ingleby's visit, Frank let himself in through the front door and joined Joan who was sitting at the table reading the paper.

'I've been down to The Hare and Hounds and telephoned Jack,' he explained. 'I'm off to London tomorrow to talk about the job he has in mind. Do you fancy a day out? I'm seeing him at nine-thirty and we could have the rest of the day together, perhaps take in a show. What do you say, love?'

'No, it's fine, sweetie. I'll have to stay here. We have the W.I. Fayre tomorrow afternoon and I need to be there. I'm running the tombola stall.'

'Damn, I'd forgotten about that, but I can't change the meeting now. I'll return home straightaway, as I don't fancy a day in London on my own. By the way, I've written to Marconi and told them I will not be proceeding with my application.'

Joan stood up, folded the paper and left it on the table. She opened a cupboard and picked up a saucepan. As she turned round, Frank could see she was upset. He put his arms round her and looked into her face.

'Come on, love, it's not all that bad. We don't know what they have in mind for me yet. Jack said it was a desk job and I'll be here whatever happens.'

'But what if you're not? You know what they're like; you could be sent anywhere, Timbuktu for all I know.' She cried and he hugged her tightly.

'As it's MI5, it should be based here because those in MI6 do the foreign stuff and it's not likely they'll want me to work abroad. As Jack is interested in the fact I speak French, I suppose it could possibly mean France or Belgium, if I go at all, but Jack has no plans to send me anywhere.'

Joan looked at him quizzically.

'Don't give me that old fashioned look,' he went on, smiling a little sheepishly. 'Look, we'll have to wait and see, but if he is correct and Hitler invades France, I'll soon be home anyway.'

'But then what?' Joan asked as she cuddled into him.

'Hitler would find it difficult to cross the Channel and we might be able to fight him off from here. My hunch is he won't even try. He needs the oil in the Balkans and more importantly in Russia. He's signed this pact with Stalin, but I bet you anything you like he'll move east and take on the Russians. That's why he's looking at Poland. He'll be in there before too long, you wait and see.'

Joan said nothing. She nodded, took out her handkerchief from her apron pocket and blew her nose. She pulled away from Frank, stood over the sink and filled the saucepan with water before adding the chopped cabbage. She lit the stove and left the cabbage to simmer.

13

A young woman sat at her desk outside Ingleby's office and welcomed Frank as he entered the room through the double oak panelled doors. She had dark hair tied in a bun, soft, blue eyes and a slightly turned up nose that gave her a youthful look. She was wearing a white silk blouse and tight business skirt, accentuating an hour glass figure. For a moment, Frank was lost for words. She reminded him of Marie when he first met her all those years ago and there was something familiar about her too that he could not quite put his finger on.

She gripped his hand tightly and shook it in a surprisingly masculine way, given how gently feminine she looked.

'Hello, I'm Lorna Parker and I work with Commander Ingleby. I'm, sort of, his Girl Friday, if you know what I mean.'

Frank nodded, although he was not really sure what she meant. She poured him a cup of tea without asking if he wanted one.

'One lump or two?' she asked poised with the sugar tongs above the bowl.

'Three, actually. Thanks. Have we met somewhere before?'

'Austria. The cigarette and the car, but I was younger then.' She laughed and passed him the cup and saucer.

'Of course,' said Frank. 'I knew there was something familiar about you.'

Lorna moved to the inner office door, knocked and opened it at the same time.

'Mr Shipley's here. Shall I show him in?'

'Oh, please do,' said Ingleby, getting to his feet.

She beckoned Frank forward. As he brushed past he caught the strong scent of jasmine.

'So good to see you again, old chap.' Ingleby shook Frank's hand and offered him the armchair in front of his desk.

'Clearly Joan is happier with the situation than when we last met,' he continued. 'These things are always difficult with the wives. By the way, I hear your lad has been offered a place at Oxford. You and Joan must be delighted.'

Frank was about to ask how he knew. However, Lorna came in and handed a cup of tea to Ingleby. She smiled at Frank as she passed.

Ingleby opened a green file marked 'Top Secret' from the pile on his desk and put on his reading glasses. He pulled out two sheets and read through them while Frank sipped his tea. He put his glasses into their case, clasped his hands in front of him and looked straight at Frank.

'I'm sure you're keen to know what I have in mind for you. It was to be that desk job, but things are moving fast and war will break out at any time. France is vulnerable, as we talked about at your house and I'm sure you saw that for yourself when you were over there. The Germans are much stronger this time and we feel France will easily fall. This puts our troops at risk, but they'll have to be there and do the best they can. I need agents in France and that's where you come in.'

'Joan was right,' said Frank, frowning a little. 'It was never likely to be a desk job, was it?'

'You know me too well, old boy! I'm sorry, but I didn't intend to mislead you and Joan. We had a job here for you, but when you told me you could speak French that all changed. If the French capitulate, we need to know those we can count on to carry the fight to the Germans if needs must. This is where you come in. Your experience on that Mosley job, makes you ideal to carry out what I have in mind.'

'Why are you involved, Jack, when MI5 only deals with security over here?'

'We're dealing with matters nearer to home; MI6 have their hands full out east in Eastern Europe, China and Japan.'

'If I do accept where, specifically, would you be sending me and when?'

'We've not sorted that out yet; it depends on whether you will accept the task. We must make sure you're happy to take it on. It was a big thing for you to infiltrate Mosley's people and I need to know you're up for this.'

The phone on the desk rang and Ingleby answered. He put his hand over the mouthpiece.

'Would you mind?' he said nodding towards the door. The outer office was empty and Frank sat in Lorna's chair. Would Joan be upset if he accepted? Possibly she would, but he felt excited about the plan, especially after the months of doing very little.

Frank was called back in.

'Sorry! Now, where were we?'

'I'm happy to take it on. I'll square it with Joan. She won't be happy, but she knows I'd want to do it. She'll come round.'

'Good man!'

'Have you decided where in France?'

'Well, it must be close to their eastern border. Why do you ask?'

'The friends we stayed with at Easter live near Sedan and not far from the Maginot Line. In fact, I visited it with our host, Thierry Fontaine. He runs a big timber company and is very anti-German. He's convinced, like you, they'll be coming through. I'm sure I could stay with him, but you might have to check him out. I'm sure it will be fine. I could even become a Frenchman in all but name if Thierry were to give me a job.'

'I like the sound of that. It seems perfect and I'll look into it.' Before he could say anything more, the door opened and Lorna came in with an envelope.

'Sorry, sir, but this is urgent and you need to see it right away.'

'That's fine, Lorna. Draw up a chair. I need to speak with you both anyway.'

She moved a chair from near the window and smiled as she sat next to Frank.

'Lorna is actually one of our operatives,' Ingleby continued. 'She just pretends to be my secretary and loves making tea. Like you, she speaks fluent

French – and German, too. She'll be there with you. You can pretend to be father and daughter if you like or, perhaps even better, husband and wife. It will give you much better cover if things turn nasty. We all have the habit of executing spies and the Germans, I'm sure, are no exception.'

Frank was surprised and looked at Lorna who winked. He flushed a little – not really sure of her.

'You might have to square this with your wife, Frank,' Ingleby continued, 'because it's better she knows that you'll be travelling and working with an attractive woman.

***

During the next ten days, all the necessary arrangements were put in place. Joan took the news very well and seemed unconcerned when Frank told her Lorna would be with him.

Ingleby ran the check on the Fontaines. It appeared Thierry had won the *Croix de Guerre* in the last war and had never been in the Pay Corps. His business was sound and he and his wife Madeleine were pillars of their local community. Frank wrote to them outlining the proposed visit without divulging too much, apart from the fact that he would have a colleague with him and that they would like to stay for three weeks.

Jean-Luc replied immediately. The family would be thrilled to see him again and, this time, with his friend.

Frank and Lorna received three days of training and instruction on what sort of activities they were expected to carry out in France, including how to record and pass on the information gathered. They also worked on their cover story. They were to be Thierry's cousin and his daughter, visiting the area to research a book on how France had recovered from the last war. They were to meet local activists and officials to assess who might be of value to Britain should France fall into German hands. It was apparent Frank and Lorna were not the only ones being trained. They were instructed, though, not to discuss their tasks with each other or exchange names in case it might lead to betrayal at a later date.

One day was spent on the Rainham Marshes sharpening up their shooting skills. Frank was reminded of the last time he was there and how close he came to losing his life. His TA work, countryside upbringing and previous training with MI5 made him one of the better shots, but not as accomplished as Lorna. She surprised the instructors and other agents with her prowess. Throughout the training days both indoors and out she had been friendly yet not as flirtatious as previously. She wore trousers with dark tops and her hair was tied back and covered by a beret when outdoors, but she had no make-up and, if it were not for her figure, could have passed as a man.

For their final briefing Ingleby invited Frank and Lorna to a Lyons' Corner House for lunch, instead of meeting at the office. He was not in his usual pinstripe, but a more fashionable two-piece suit with a colourful tie; Frank wore an open necked shirt and casual trousers. Lorna, on the other hand, was in a tight-fitting, dark blue dress, full make up and jewellery. Her hair was loose, reaching her shoulders and she looked stunning. She said she was due at the Ritz later, but did not say why. Throughout the briefing she returned to her most flirtatious. Even Ingleby seemed disconcerted by her.

'I cannot stress strongly enough,' Ingleby told them quietly, 'how important it is that you establish contact with as many local influential people as you can and assess who might collaborate and who might resist, should the situation arise. Frank, I know you have been down to the Maginot Line, but have another look. Ask around the locals to see what they think about it. If the threat of the invasion becomes real, I want you out fast. Do you understand?'

They both nodded. Ingleby continued.

'Our people will make contact and in this envelope are passwords and other vital information. Learn it all then burn the papers. Any questions?'

They had none and Frank stood to leave.

'Lorna, would you like a lift to the Ritz? I have the Bentley outside,' asked Ingleby.

'Oh, thank you that would be nice. I'll say cheerio, Frank, and see you soon.'

Frank walked to Liverpool Street station to catch the Chelmsford train looking forward to the rest of the weekend with the family.

Joan was unusually quiet on the Saturday. She always worried when Frank was working away, but at least this time she knew where he was. Lizzie seemed to expect her father to be away from home more than he was there and she said very little. George, on the other hand, was more concerned. He said his goodbyes that morning, when he left to see a friend in Manchester.

'Take it easy, Dad; come back here quickly when the balloon goes up. I'll see Mum's all right. I'll speak with Lizzie. She'll be fine, but don't get yourself shot, that's all.'

In the afternoon, Frank and Joan walked into the village and sat watching the cricket match on the village green. After the game limped to a draw, they joined the players in The Chequers for a drink. By nine thirty they were home and Lizzie was already in bed. Joan busied herself in the kitchen making sandwiches for Frank to take with him to London the next morning.

'Leave those,' Frank said, as he came up behind her and put his arms around her waist. Joan tensed briefly before relaxing a little as he kissed her neck. She spun round, put her arms around him and kissed him on his lips. She pulled away from him slightly and looked into his eyes. He smiled. She kissed him again, this time open mouthed and probing with her tongue. Frank responded and pushed her backwards towards the door. She broke away and pulled him to the bedroom.

An hour later they lay on the bed together. Joan cuddled into Frank resting her head on his chest.

'You will be careful out there, won't you?'

'We're not at war, you know, well not yet anyway. There's no need to worry. Jack wants us home if anything untoward happens. This is a nice little jaunt and it'll be good to see the Fontaines again. I'm sure Jean-Luc will write to George with news and you'll be kept up to date this time round.'

'I know,' said Joan as she rolled on top of him and kissed him again. 'But I still worry. Wives do.' She kissed his chest and moved up to his mouth. She could feel the hardening against the top of her legs.

'Come on, you'll be away for far too long and you have to make it up to me. Remember, no hanky panky while you're in France or my spies will tell on you!'

14

Lorna and Frank met up in a small hotel in Pimlico for an overnight stay before catching the boat train from Victoria station early the next morning. Once onboard the ferry at Dover, Frank was leaning on the ship's rail admiring the white cliffs as they were slowly left behind. Lorna joined him.

'Beautiful aren't they?' she said. 'It's amazing to think that this short stretch of water is our country's best defence from invasion. It's a pity someone invented planes or we'd be safe for ever.'

'Quite right,' said Frank, turning to face her. Lorna was wearing her normal working clothes with no make up and hair tied back, but remained strikingly attractive.

'Lorna, would you mind if I asked you something?' Frank continued, light-heartedly. 'We will be spending a lot of time together and you confuse me at times. I can understand you will normally dress for work wearing plain clothes and try to look most ordinary, but of course you don't. Other times you look quite different and all the men were talking about it during our training. One moment you seem to be flirting with any one of us but the next you are not. Quite frankly, I'd like an explanation.' He smiled but she giggled and tossed her head, brushing those hairs that had slipped from her headband away from her eyes.

'Don't worry, Frank, you're safe. All that posing and whatnot is just my way. The fact is I am not really interested in men - if you understand my meaning but keep it to yourself. I put on this act as a test, particularly for those I might work with. I always think it a useful guide. I seem to know where I stand by how they react. I must say you passed with flying colours. I know it all sounds a bit corny, but that's my way and it's stood the test over the years!'

Frank looked surprised.

'So, you mean you ... Bloody hell! What was all that when we were with Ingleby at the Corner House? You looked like a princess and you were off to the Ritz.'

'Just meeting a friend.' She looked quizzically at Frank. 'Yes, Frank, a girlfriend.'

He felt embarrassed. Lorna laughed.

'Oh dear. I'm sorry, Lorna, it's all a bit too much for an old man like me.'

'Don't worry about it. Anyway you're not old ...' she hesitated, and added in a low gravelly voice, 'but you're all man!' She laughed loudly, put her hands either side of his face and kissed him on the lips.

'There you go again. If I didn't know better, I might be getting excited.'

Lorna walked away.

'No, you wouldn't. You think too much of your wife and family. I'm a good judge of these things.'

Later in the day as their train headed across Northern France, they chatted about their pasts. Lorna asked Frank to fill in the parts of his life she didn't know about before it was her turn.

'I speak German fluently because my mother's German. She met my father out in Africa before the war when they were both working for their respective governments. Of course, when 1914 came along it was a bit difficult to say the least, but they both stayed out in South Africa for the duration and no one seemed to mind too much when they married. I was born there before they came home after the war.'

'It still must have been difficult for your mother to come here with the war having just ended.'

'I'm not sure. She's never said much about it, but they moved in such unusual social circles that perhaps people simply accepted these things. After all, our Royal Family is German.'

'What did your father do?'

'He had a hush-hush job in London, a bit like Ingleby's I'd say. I was at Benenden until I went up to Cambridge. I read Politics and managed a First. MI5 came knocking at my door, probably because of my father, but he's never confirmed or denied it. I've done a few minor bits of intelligence stuff, but nothing too exciting apart from that little exercise in Austria, where I was used because I spoke German.'

They reached the railway station in Sedan in the late evening. The only other person at the station was a man in a suit and trilby standing outside the ticket barrier. As Frank and Lorna walked past him he nodded and touched the rim of his hat in a semi-salute of recognition. Frank nodded and moved on. He assumed the man was from the Service and checking his arrival. As they left the station in a taxi, Frank saw him driven away in a black Citroen.

Frank and Lorna had brought a small selection of clothes and essentials. They had been told to buy more clothes when they arrived to look more like locals. As soon as they reached the Fontaines' house, Lorna handed over an envelope of francs to Thierry, but he insisted he wanted nothing.

Before dinner Lorna joined Madeleine in the kitchen. Thierry and Frank remained in the drawing room relaxing in the armchairs with a glass of chilled wine. Thierry leant forward and whispered,

'This is a surprise, my friend. We were expecting you and another man. She's a real beauty. Did you see how shocked Jean-Luc was? He's at that age when a woman like her stirs his emotions more than is good for him!'

'I'm sure he'll cope. She's a character too, you'll see.'

Madeleine supervised the cooking with the housekeeper and Lorna helped serve the meal. Frank explained the cover story they would use and agreed the finer details with the Fontaines.

Frank and Lorna spent their first day relaxing after their long journey. The housekeeper busied herself and said very little. The Fontaines both worked at their timber yard and were not due home until the early evening. Jean-Luc was still at school and in the middle of his summer exams. He had told them the previous evening that he hoped to attend college in Paris in the autumn. After a light lunch on the terrace, Frank and Lorna walked into the town to buy the clothes they needed. Lorna bought herself two dresses for social occasions. She wore one at dinner that evening to show Madeleine. Thierry and Jean-Luc were overwhelmed by how attractive she looked and could hardly speak. It was the first time Frank had seen her wearing full make up since she left for the Ritz. The dress was tight fitting and low cut, showing off her figure beautifully.

Madeleine laughed until she cried at the effect Lorna had on the men when she came into the room and how Thierry stumbled over his words.

The following day Frank and Lorna borrowed the Thierry's spare car to drive to the Maginot Line at La Ferté. They found a level of security much greater than they expected and certainly more than when Frank was there before. They were able to take long distance photographs and make notes about the defences, but nothing more.

'I tell you what,' Frank observed, 'there's not much we can tell London. They must have photographs and details already. It makes you wonder why we're here at all.'

'You're right. This getting to know the locals is a bit strange too. That agent we saw at the station the other night and any others out here could surely do it just as well.'

'The only difference is, Lorna, the locals will accept us more readily as they think we're French.'

Frank and Lorna had been briefed that the Service would make contact. The next day, the Citroen they had seen at the station pulled up outside the house during the early evening; although it had the same driver, the passenger was different. He came and knocked at the front door and spoke with Lorna in English passing her a letter signed by Ingleby confirming who he was. It said they were to provide him with what he asked for. He removed the film from their camera and handed over a new roll. He also gave them an updated list of locals she and Frank were to make contact with.

Frank wrote to Joan and the children that evening. He said very little apart from what the Fontaines were up to. As he was about to seal the envelope, Jean-Luc asked if he could put his regular letter to George in with it.

Frank and Lorna knew the information they were about to acquire about the locals could be very important in the months or years ahead, but their mission seemed like a pleasant holiday. Thierry introduced them to many of his friends and acquaintances around the town and at the yard, all of whom seemed willing to answer any questions. Many held forthright views and were decidedly anti-German; others were less so. The names the Service had provided were being ticked off one by one.

At almost every little meeting, in a bar or café or at the yard, Lorna's presence meant it was always easy to get the local men talking.

The man from the Service arrived every three days at the same time and collected their reports, but soon their three weeks were almost up. Having completed all that they had been asked to do, they now had two days to relax before catching the train and boat home. The beautiful hot sunny days had turned into a cool and wet July. On the first day they drove into Sedan and saw *Robin Hood,* which was showing for the second time. It was proving the hit of the year.

They watched the matinee performance and afterwards adjourned to a local bar. Lorna was in her normal trousers and jumper, but had her hair up and was wearing full make-up. They sat at a table by the front window. A rich aroma of freshly ground coffee filled the room as the coffee-making machine periodically blew steam into the already smoky atmosphere.

Frank leant across the table and spoke quietly in English.

'That smell, it does remind me of when I was a kid; it's beautiful.'

'Me too.'

'Can I say, Lorna, I think you look stunning.'

'Just making an effort for the locals.' She laughed, looked around and laughed again. The café was empty.

Frank swilled his coffee around the cup.

'Well, Lorna, it's been fun. Perhaps we can toast the future, whatever that might bring. We should say "To peace" I suppose, but that's not likely to last for long. What about – "To us and long life"?'

They touched glasses.

'I've really enjoyed our time out here,' said Lorna. 'Maybe we'll work together again some time. Good luck'.'

'Thanks and good luck to you too. But do you know, Lorna, there's something odd about being out here, don't you think? I think we've been sent out here on a dry run to prepare us for when the Germans do invade. It won't be the first time Ingleby's done that to us – remember Austria? We would be a perfect choice to be placed here as a French couple and be immediately accepted by the locals. That's why Ingleby sent us, I'm sure of it.'

'You're probably right,' Lorna said. 'They'll also be testing us out to see if we get on.'

'Well, that's been a success.'

'So,' said Lorna raising her cup towards Frank's, 'see you here, again, whenever that might be.'

***

Thierry and Madeleine had arranged a dinner party for the final evening and invited the town's Mayor and his wife. Lorna and Frank had been introduced to the Mayor at one of their more formal meetings. The atmosphere was relaxed and everyone enjoyed the meal, which had been prepared by the housekeeper, who, with her husband, helped serve each course and the couple were invited to stay after serving the coffee. Frank handed them a glass of wine each and proposed a toast thanking them for the excellent meal.

Thierry introduced them more fully.

'This is Gerard and his wife, Rosanna. Gerard was gassed in the war and his lungs were damaged, which is why he prefers working outdoors looking after the gardens – he's our handyman, too. I met him in the war and, knowing he lived nearby, offered him work. Rosanna joined us when they married.'

'If you don't mind, Thierry, I'd like to ask Gerard his views on what might happen to France,' Frank requested.

Thierry looked at Gerard and nodded. Gerard coughed and looked at each of the guests in turn, his eyes sharp and focussed.

'Hitler has one aim and one aim only. He wants us to eat dirt. He wants revenge for the Treaty after the Armistice and he'll not stop until he has us grovelling and begging for mercy. Our Government is as weak as I've ever known it and will cave in almost as soon as the first Germans set foot here. I tell you now the Germans will be here and goose-stepping down the *Champs Elysees* by this time next year, you mark my words. Our Government will seek peace and we'll all have to start learning German. Hitler will not bother with Britain. He'll do a deal with you and look to the east. He might be friendly with Stalin now, but he'll want to succeed where Napoleon failed; to sit in the Kremlin and order any Russians who show any resistance to be lined up and shot...' his voice trailed off.

For a few moments there was quiet before Thierry clapped lightly.

'I'm not so sure this should be a time for any rejoicing, Thierry,' said Frank curtly. 'Do you really want to live under the German jackboot? You spent more than four years fighting to stop that happening; now some of you believe you'll roll over and have your tummy tickled like a pussycat.'

'I'm not rejoicing, but applauding the way Gerard put over his point of view,' countered Thierry.

'Look, Frank,' the Mayor interrupted, 'you know what we lost last time and you too, almost a whole generation. Gerard is right, we have no stomach and when you return home you tell Mr Chamberlain what our man here has said. You British will be left on your own; your American friends will keep out of it for as long as they can, like the last time, or until they're threatened, which could be a long time off. The Germans will kick out Mussolini as soon as practical and come to an agreement with the Japanese, splitting up the east. We might as well accept that situation, save our lives and those of the next generation by accepting what the Germans can offer. You know what? We might just be better off.'

'Sorry, Mr Mayor,' argued Thierry, 'but we'll have to fight back. So Frank, Lorna, tell them back home what will happen here. Tell them to keep your men over there because the Channel will hold back the Germans. They'll try to blockade you and blow up the ships carrying the supplies of food and raw materials and bomb your towns and cities, but you will have help from the Americans. We'll eat away at the Germans here. I agree with Gerard that Hitler will turn against Russia but maybe, like Napoleon, he'll underestimate them and that will give you and the Americans the chance to fight back. Mr Mayor, you'll want to fight back, surely?'

The Mayor shook his head.

'Thierry, my old friend, we'll have to disagree on this, accepting the Germans will be the only way for us to move forward.'

Frank and Lorna looked at each other unsure what to say. Lorna spoke first,

'We hear all these stories about the Jews and other races already being persecuted. Do you want that to happen here? How soon before you French are picked on as Hitler tries to impose this so-called master race we hear about? In your colonies you have mostly black people and they'll be rounded up or made slave workers. Will you let this happen and not resist? Surely not?' She looked round the room.

Gerard spoke again.

'I'm sure what I said will happen, but that's not to say we won't resist. I don't think we want to dig trenches and fight and die like before. We will not stop the Germans and I believe we should let them take over then, like a cancer within, eat away at them. I'm sorry if you disagree.' He stood up. 'Come on Rosanna, we have things to do.'

Lorna and Frank moved to the terrace and stood looking out towards the lights of Sedan.

'Well that was a bit of an eye opener,' said Lorna. 'We must put that in our final report and perhaps Whitehall will do well to heed what was said.'

15

A letter from Ingleby arrived for Joan shortly after George and Lizzie had left to catch the bus into Chelmsford: a short note to say Frank should be home the following day. She could not wait to tell the children when they came home. George was coming to the end of his exams so was tetchy and getting on her nerves; Lizzie seemed to upset him all the time and she too was unusually grumpy. Joan knew it would be good for them to have their father home for a while.

Having made her own bed and cleaned the room, Joan opened the windows to make it smell fresh when Frank arrived, although she knew he would never notice. She had picked a bunch of sweet peas earlier and had placed them in a vase on the dressing table.

She found George's room in its normal chaotic state with books all over the bed from where he had been revising the night before. On his desk were screwed-up pieces of paper next to a dirty cup, half full of tea, but he had put his clothes away and straightened the bed. Joan picked up the books placing them neatly on the desk, but one toppled onto the floor. It was Virgil's *Aeneid.* A letter fell out and, as she picked it up, recognised Jean-Luc's distinctive handwriting.

The two pages were folded in half with writing on one side. She read through the first page and smiled at Jean-Luc's unusual grammar. On the second page, she was shocked to read of the beauty with Frank and how the two were pretending to be man and wife. She held her hand to her mouth and slumped onto the bed. The letter said no more than that. Perhaps Jean-Luc's grammar had misrepresented the real meaning. All sorts of things were passing through her mind. Surely Frank couldn't let her down now, not after all these years. What did George think of it? He had said nothing. Perhaps this explained the bad temper she had put down to his exams. She curled up on the bed.

Suddenly woken by a loud knock on the front door, Joan ran downstairs, smoothed her dress, tidied her hair in the mirror and opened the door. It was Des Brewer from the grocer's in the village with her weekly delivery of groceries. She looked as flustered as she felt.

'Sorry, Joan, did I wake you? You look very bleary eyed!'

'Just having a nap. You know how it is.'

'Is Frank still away? I'm sure you miss him.'

'He should return today, but the children are tiring me out. George has his exams and I'll be glad when they're over!'

'Yes, mine are like that too.' He picked up her order book for the following week and returned to his van.

Joan looked at the clock on the wall in the kitchen. It was nearly two o'clock and she had been asleep for almost three hours. She made herself a cup of tea before returning to the bedroom. She carefully returned the letter to the book, but not before she had read it again. Now she was annoyed, frustrated not to be able to take it out on Frank right at that moment. She returned to the kitchen slamming the bedroom door so hard the windows rattled throughout the house.

***

George and Lizzie were home by five thirty. Joan was a little short with them complaining about the untidiness of their rooms and not even asking George about his day's exam. She said nothing about their father coming home and busied herself preparing the evening meal as they left for their rooms.

At the dinner table she told them of their father's imminent return.

'You don't seem very excited, Mum. Is there something you're not telling us?' George asked.

'No, not really. I had a letter this morning; your father will be home any time now.'

George wanted to ask more but looked at his sister and shrugged as Joan left for the kitchen.

They heard their father's familiar, tuneless whistle as he came towards the front door. When he reached it, he whistled as if calling a dog. In response, Lizzie ran and opened the door. He held out his arms and she jumped at him to give him a hug. George came up behind them and shook his father's hand.

Joan stood quietly in the kitchen doorway with her arms folded. Frank gently eased the children away and reached out for her, but she kept her arms folded. He grabbed each shoulder and tried to kiss her on the lips. She turned her head to one side and said nothing. He kissed her cheek and let her go.

Behind his back, George gestured to Lizzie that they should return to their rooms.

'Joan, love, what on earth's the matter? What's happened?'

She said nothing.

'Joan, what's up, love? Are you not well?'

She stormed out of the back door and started off down the garden. Frank caught up with her and, grabbing her arm from behind, gently turned her round. She looked angry.

'Come on, what is it?'

She clenched her fists and hit him hard several times on his chest in quick succession, sobbing loudly.

'You'd better have a bloody good explanation about what you've been up to with that woman. I know all about it. I read a letter from the Fontaine boy to George about this Amazon with big breasts and that you and her were living as man and wife. How do you think that makes me feel? You lied to me!'

Stunned, Frank stepped back. Joan ran into the house and to their bedroom.

George appeared at the back door.

'I didn't show Mum that letter,' he explained. 'She must have found it when she was cleaning my room. I knew she'd be upset if she knew what was in it.'

'It's fine, son, it's all a misunderstanding. I'll explain later when I've spoken to your mother.'

When Frank tried the bedroom door, it was locked from the inside. 'Joan, love, open up I can explain; Jean-Luc has it all wrong, please let me in.'

There was no reply.

'Come on,' he continued, 'I don't want the children to hear all this. There is a very simple explanation. Open the door, please.'

The lock turned and Frank opened the door to see Joan standing at the window staring out blankly. He put his arms round her waist. She resisted. He stood to one side and she looked at him without turning her head. Her eyes were red, but she was no longer crying.

'This had better be good, Frank Shipley.'

He laughed nervously and he held her hand. Again she resisted, but he clung to it.

'Look, love, how can I put this? Lorna – she likes other women and not men, that's the God's honest truth, and Jack Ingleby will tell you if you like. We were working undercover and, in fact, supposed to be father and daughter and I don't know where the husband and wife bit came from. We had to make it look plausible. The ruse was for the benefit of the locals. We told them we were writing a book and needed their views on matters of a politically sensitive nature. We had to be convincing. We had separate rooms, of course, and, whilst Lorna is really attractive, she wouldn't fancy me at all. She turns heads everywhere she goes and uses it to secure what she wants from people and by that I mean information. You silly old thing – what did you think I would be up to?'

George appeared at the door looking concerned, Lizzie stood behind him. Joan smiled at him and cuddled into Frank.

'It's fine,' she said soothingly towards George. 'It's all a misunderstanding. When you next write to Jean-Luc you'd better tell him to be a bit more careful about what he puts in his letters and to check his facts.'

They had a laugh once Frank explained everything, although he kept the real nature of his trip from George and Lizzie. Frank opened a bottle of champagne brought from France and they finished it off before bedtime. In bed, Joan cuddled up to Frank.

'So this Lorna has quite a figure? How big are her breasts?' she asked. He put his hands out in front of him with his fingers spread as wide as he could.

'Oh, about this big!' They both giggled.

16

'Shush,' said Joan, 'it's the Prime Minister.' She leant over and turned the knob on the wireless, so they could all hear.

Joan sat leaning forward, inches from the set. Frank was equally close on the other side whilst Lizzie and George stood in the middle of the room staring at the set.

Mr Chamberlain's sombre voice began,

'I am speaking to you from the Cabinet Room at Ten Downing Street. This morning the British Ambassador in Berlin handed the German Government a final note stating that unless we heard from them by eleven o'clock that they were prepared at once to withdraw their troops from Poland, a state of war would exist between us. I have to tell you now that no such undertaking has been received, and that, consequently, this country is at war with Germany.'

'Bugger,' said George and immediately apologised as the others went 'shush'.

'You can imagine what a bitter blow it is to me that all my long struggle to win peace has failed. Yet I cannot believe that there is anything more or anything different that I could have done and that would have been more successful. Up to the very last it would have been quite possible to have arranged a peaceful and honourable settlement between Germany and Poland.'

'But you cocked it up, you fool!' said George, shouting and pointing at the wireless.

As Chamberlain continued Frank and Lizzie listened intently. George followed Joan to the kitchen.

'Well that's it, Mum. That'll mess me up for Oxford, if I am called up.'

'You won't be, at least not for a while. It won't be like the last one.'

'What about Dad? That Ingleby bloke'll want him for something dangerous, won't he?'

'Probably but we'll have to wait and see. Hitler might keep heading east and we'll do very little. It might all fizzle out.'

'Fat chance, Mum. I'll tell you that for nothing.'

Joan and George returned to the living room. Chamberlain was still talking.

'Now may God bless you all and may He defend the right. For it is evil things that we shall be fighting against, brute force, bad faith, injustice, oppression and persecution. And against them I am certain that the right will prevail.'

Frank stood up and turned off the wireless.

'Well, that's it,' he said. 'So much for "Peace in Our Time". Another damned dose of the Germans, and we haven't recovered from the last lot properly yet. That's it for Chamberlain; he'll have resign now after that farce in Munich, when some of us knew Hitler was a liar. Why didn't the Government think so too?'

Downcast, he sat down in the armchair by the window. Lizzie came over,

'Dad, does that mean you'll have to fight? Will George have to as well?'

'I'm not so sure about George, but I'm officially a reservist and could be one of the first called up, unless my other work takes precedence.'

'Will you go to Poland?' Lizzie added. 'That's a long way, isn't it?'

George joined in before his father could answer,

'No, he'll be sent to France to face the Germans when they invade to the west. It'll only be a matter of time before they do, won't it, Dad?'

'Well ...' Frank hesitated. 'I suppose you're right and, from what I found out when I was in France recently, we could soon be all on our own.'

'Will we be gassed? That's all the talk, isn't it?' Joan added.

Frank stood up and looked at the sky through the window.

'I wouldn't be surprised if that sky is full of planes within a month and it'll be the *Luftwaffe.* They'll be dropping bombs probably with gas in them.'

'But we won't be bombed here, surely?' asked George.

'It could well happen, son. Chelmsford is full of factories and Hoffmans make ball bearings. They are put into tanks, planes and all sorts of military equipment and as a result the factory will be a prime target, so we could be affected.'

***

After the momentous announcement, the nation panicked for the next few days. The air raid sirens sounded and people expected German bombers to arrive at any second, but they were all false alarms. Various restrictions were introduced immediately and Frank received a letter from Ingleby asking him to report to the London office.

When he arrived there, he found Lorna in her usual sweater and trousers. She gave him a kiss.

'Well, here sooner than we anticipated,' said Frank. 'Any idea what the boss has in mind?'

'Not a clue. Did you hear Chamberlain's speech? Brilliant wasn't it, but that's the end for him, don't you think? How have Joan and the children taken it?'

'They're fine. Well, a bit apprehensive, if I'm honest. You're right about Chamberlain, maybe Churchill's time might come again; he's been proved right.'

More than a dozen agents were there that morning and Frank recognised many of them from the training before their French trip a few months ago.

Ingleby and another sat in front of the group in the basement briefing room. The other man said nothing throughout, but Ingleby's demeanour towards him suggested he was more senior.

The intelligence secured out in France and from what had been picked up from elsewhere during recent months, suggested an invasion of France was almost certain. Frank and Lorna were to return to the Fontaines, who had already been briefed. More detailed and written instructions would be issued shortly.

When the briefing was over, Lorna and Frank had a drink in the bar at the Great Eastern Hotel near Liverpool Street station.

'I'm worried, Frank, about this war. I'm not sure how I'll manage with the real thing. You've been through it before and you'll cope better than me. Dealing with routine intelligence gathering is one thing, but working in warlike situations must be quite another.'

'You'll be fine and I didn't see any frontline action before, if you recall. Anyway, this war will be different with no trenches. It will be a question of occupation if the Germans come as we expect. Then it will be a case of gnawing away at them and that might be our job.'

'I'm not sure that's cheered me up much,' said Lorna, as she stood up to leave.

'Don't worry, Lorna, you've been well trained, you're very capable and you'll cope.' Frank looked at his watch. 'Right, I'm off, I'll see you later in the week.' He kissed her lightly on the cheek and they left together.

***

Frank had two days at home before reporting to London to receive the final instructions. Joan was apprehensive and concerned about what might happen. The last war was still a painful memory for her, having lost her brother. George was on edge, but his exams were over and he was hopeful he would make Oxford. He spent most of his time in his room, reading. Lizzie was at work all day and seemed unconcerned her father would be away again.

Frank said nothing about where he was travelling to this time, not even to Joan, although he guessed she knew.

When it was time for Frank to leave, George put his arms round his father.

'Take care, Dad, come back in one piece won't you? Try and write to us. Mum thinks it might be France, so watch out for the Jerries!'

'And you, son. Enjoy Oxford. I'm sure you'll make it there, but don't fall over yourself to join up when you do. There'll be plenty of time later.'

Frank let Joan drive him to Chelmsford railway station, but neither spoke during the fifteen-minute journey. Pulling up on the forecourt, Joan switched off the engine and put her arms around him. He held her tightly, put his hands to her cheeks and kissed her fully on the lips.

'Come on, love,' said Frank, kissing away the tears on her cheeks. 'I can look after myself. Jack Ingleby is keen for his people in the field to keep in contact with their families and I'll write when I can.'

'Just be careful, that's all. I do love you.' Joan lent forward, kissed Frank's forehead and his lips, 'I do you love you so much.'

'And I love you too, more than ever,' said Frank, holding Joan's hands. 'I should tell you that more often because it's at times like this when I realise how deep that love is, even after all these years.'

'I know that. It's always clear to me and you don't need to say it.'

They kissed again before Frank went to the boot to collect his kitbag. Joan came round the car to join him and he dropped the kitbag. She hugged him and kissed him lightly on the cheek. He lifted her off her feet and spun her round before putting her on the ground.

Joan looked at her watch. 'Go on,' she said, 'or you'll miss your train.'

''Bye, love. It might be difficult to get a message to you, but I'll try. Keep an eye on the kids but I think George will be fine. Lizzie has gone quiet in the past few days and may be more worried than she's showing.'

He put the kitbag over his shoulder and kissed the top of her head. The station was full of men mostly in uniform with families seeing them off. In the ticket hall he stopped at the door and waved back at Joan. She gave a limp wave and returned to the car. She sat for more than ten minutes hugging herself as if she was cold. She jumped when there was a tap on her window. It was Lizzie.

'I expect you could do with some company. I've been shopping and saw the car. Has Dad left?'

'Well, he's up on the platform.'

'He'll be fine, won't he? I mean, if he's somewhere dangerous?'

'Of course he will, sweetie. He'll be back here before you know it, safe and sound. Do you want a lift to work?' Lizzie opened the passenger door.

Brandishing his travel permit, Frank pushed his way through the throng to the ticket barrier. The police were trying to keep order and Frank spotted his old colleague, Stan Hebden, barking out orders. He saw Frank and came over.

'Where are they sending you, Frank?' He was not really expecting an answer.

Frank grinned.

'I'm not sure we should be discussing such things in public,' he said, pulling Stan to one side. 'Actually, Stan, I'm off to France for a bit of covert work, but I might have to hot foot it back here a bit sharpish if Jerry breaks through'

'Well, good luck, mate. Rather you than me. I'll be stuck here this time, but I'll be thinking of you. I'll keep an eye on Joan for you – and the kids, of course, especially if something happens ... you know.'

Frank gave him a playful punch on the shoulder,

'Thanks. I appreciate that. If I ever have any leave, I'll drop in to see you.'

He ran up the stairs and onto the crowded platform where more chaos and confusion reigned. However, within the hour he was with Lorna in the briefing room at Ingleby's offices.

***

Frank and Lorna's cover story in Sedan remained that they were father and daughter, but this time they would be employed by the Fontaines in their timber yard. Ingleby provided them with all the necessary papers to prove who they were plus a convincing background story.

Ingleby wanted them settled into the local community as soon as possible. They were only to become active should the Germans invade, but if that did not happen within the year they would be pulled out and the plan shelved.

***

During the early winter months there were many false alarms of an invasion through the Maginot Line, but all remained quiet. Lorna and Frank were even more convinced the Germans would strike in the north east via the Low Countries, as in 1914, and also to the south of the Maginot with its heavily forested area. In London, before they left, they had been told the forest was too dense for German tanks to penetrate. They were not convinced when they saw it for themselves and had now passed a message to Ingleby suggesting this area remained vulnerable and its defences should be strengthened.

Apart from occasional days gathering this information and intelligence, the pair integrated themselves into the community. Lorna worked in Thierry's office, taking over from Madeleine, who had decided she would like a rest from the business, whilst Frank was acting as the yard's foreman.

With Christmas approaching and with London's blessing, Frank and Lorna took a week's leave until the twenty-eighth which Frank spent with the family whilst Lorna travelled to London to be with friends.

George had already returned from university for Christmas. Lizzie stayed for Christmas Day and Boxing Day. On Christmas Day Frank and George cycled into Chelmsford to watch the local football team in a friendly match. Over three thousand were there, relieved to be able to watch a game. Frank again ran into Stan Hebden who was on duty patrolling the perimeter of the pitch in front of the terraces. Stan stopped to have a chat, asking quietly,

'Everything fine over there?'

'All quiet on the western front, Stan!'

'When are you due to return?'

'By next week.'

'Well, keep your head down!'

Joan was happy. They were all together, even if only for a few days. George had received a Christmas card and note from Jean-Luc mentioning that they enjoyed Frank staying with them again. On Frank's last night they spent the evening in The Hare and Hounds. The locals were keen to learn from him where he had been, but he gave them only the briefest details. Frank not being in uniform intrigued many, but they said nothing to his face.

It was as if the country was not at war at all. The newspapers were calling it the 'phoney war' or, perhaps more likely, the lull before a storm. No one was certain what was likely to happen next. Hitler was preoccupied with Poland and Czechoslovakia and concentrating his efforts there. The stories coming out of the east about the murder and torture of civilians, particularly the Jews, were so frightening as not to be believed at times.

When Frank left, there were tearful goodbyes. He travelled straight to Folkestone by train. Ingleby had not wanted to see him, being satisfied with the information sent to date and, in a recent letter, suggested Frank need only report anything of major significance.

***

One morning in January, as Frank parked a lorry in the Fontaine's yard after making a delivery, Lorna called him into Thierry's office to see a visitor.

Dusting himself down, he headed in. He was surprised to find Ingleby sipping a cognac with Thierry; Lorna was now sitting at her desk. Thierry, knowing they would wish to be alone, left immediately.

After the initial pleasantries, Ingleby spoke earnestly,

'Frank, old boy, I need to move you to Brussels. Lorna, you are to stay here and carry on as normal. Frank, we need someone at our embassy that can handle a gun, work covertly and speaks French. I can't think of anyone better than you, old chap. I want you to leave for there today.'

Momentarily, Ingleby hesitated. He turned to Lorna.

'Lorna, old thing, I suggest you leave us now, as it's probably better you don't know what Frank will be up to. No real reason why you shouldn't know, but just in case you let slip to the wrong person, I'll keep you in the dark. However, you can tell everyone here that Frank's had to travel home, as his father's very ill. Do you understand?'

Lorna nodded and smiled. She picked up her handbag from the table and left. Once she had shut the door, Ingleby continued.

'We will give you a new British identity, Frank. In fact, you are Wilson once again. I've drawn up the documents for you and some notes, which I want you to digest and then destroy. Essentially you will be a translator charged with working with our top man there, Sir Roger Keyes, and other senior figures. Only Sir Roger will know who you really are. You will be meeting with senior Belgian government officials on a regular basis and I want you to dig around their staff. Sir Roger is our Government's one link with the King of Belgium. We believe it likely the

Belgians will do a deal with Hitler and allow his forces to come through in return for non-aggression against the Belgian people.'

'Doesn't being neutral mean you can't do that?' enquired Frank.

'Well, this is war now and they want to protect themselves. They are weak and under pressure from their people not to allow the killing of the civilian population as happened in 1914. The Dutch will crumble just as easily and, as you know, we're convinced the French will be a push over this time around. Read my notes; they give you an exact idea of what you're looking for and how you report directly to Sir Roger. The basic premise is that we will want to move our troops into Belgium as soon as we know the Belgians are allowing the Germans through or the Germans are doing it anyway. Sit here, old boy, have a read through before doing the usual with them.'

Ingleby left, but through the window Frank saw him put an arm around Lorna and talk to her earnestly as they crossed the yard.

Frank read the notes twice through and then tossed them onto the open fire in the corner of the office. He found Lorna alone in the yard.

'Lorna, could you do me a favour? I would like to let my wife know where I will be. I know it's not the done thing, but I could send a message to her via Jean-Luc, assuming his letters to my son are getting through. If I drop her a note, could you ask Jean-Luc to slip it in his next letter?'

'Of course.'

'Thanks. I'll write it when I collect my things and leave it under your pillow.'

'Take care, Frank. Do come back here safe and sound, won't you?'

At the house, Frank wrote his note and packed what he needed. He returned to the yard where Ingleby was waiting. A car took them to the railway station where they both caught the train to Lille. Frank changed platforms and caught the next train to Brussels, with Ingleby continuing to the coast to pick up the ferry to Dover.

17

On arriving in Brussels, Frank pushed through the throng of travellers crowding the railway station concourse to find the nearest telephone. The number provided by Ingleby went straight through to the ambassador's office. Within half an hour Frank was collected by a junior official in a taxi which took them to the rear annexe of the embassy where Frank was shown to his quarters. There he was served with a light supper and handed a personal handwritten note from Sir Roger Keyes requesting Frank be ready for a meeting at nine the next morning.

Sir Roger immediately impressed Frank when they met alone in a private room. He was statesmanlike but with an affability not often found in senior civil servants. They chatted about the current state of affairs before Sir Roger explained what he wanted from Frank.

'You come well recommended, Shipley, and we have an important job to do here for our Government. We are five months into this war and nothing much has happened. We believe the Germans are on the point of releasing their troops over their borders and I am sure you are aware of this from your time at Sedan. I really do believe the Germans will launch their offensive northeast from here. We have heard rumours that the Belgians have captured German plans following a plane crash earlier this month. We think the Germans know the Belgians have it and may have postponed the start date of their offensive as a result. We are desperate to have our armies in Belgium to be in a position to halt the Germans, but we need the Belgian King to invite us in. What I want you to do is snoop around. I understand your French is first class – meaning you will be able to converse with the Belgians better than anyone else. Do you speak Flemish?'

'A little and I understand it pretty well.'

'Good,' said Sir Roger, 'because some of them here speak it and you'll need to pick up what they're saying. I'm told you have a gift for mixing with locals and know how to tap into them.'

'Well, I had some success in my military police days in the last war and a bit since.'

'I heard you successfully infiltrated Mosley's people a few years ago?'

'That's correct.'

'Good man. Well what I want you to do here is to mix with the Belgian officials. Find out where they socialise, have a drink with them and get to know them. My people here will provide you with all the information and help you might need. It is vitally important we find out what we can about any German plan and do report to me each day. Now, do you have you any questions?'

'No, sir, I understand what I need to do, but what happens if and when the Germans move forward. I mean ... to us here in Brussels?'

Sir Roger laughed. 'We leave here as quickly as we can. If that happens or should I say when that happens, Ingleby wants you to return to where you came from in France and carry on with your work there. I would be surprised if the Germans wait much longer and I expect you'll have to return pretty soon. If you come with me, I'll introduce you to my secretary, George Anderson, who will be your liaison but if you need to come directly to me do so by all means. George will introduce you to other staff able to provide the back-up you need.'

***

Joan was clearing leaves from the front garden when the postman cycled up and stood by the gate.

'Just the one today, Mrs S. It's from abroad, perhaps from Mr Shipley?'

Joan reached for the letter.

'Could be,' she said, before recognising Jean-Luc's handwriting.

'Looks like rain again,' added the postman, the weather being his normal, single topic of conversation apart from the letters. As he moved on to the house next door, Joan slipped the letter addressed to George into her apron pocket and continued raking the leaves from the lawn.

George opened the letter when he arrived home at the weekend.

'Mum, there's a note in here from Dad.' He handed her the small sheet of writing paper.

'Dad's in Brussels,' she told George. 'That's all it says. I suppose he can't say more. I wonder why he's there?'

'That's a bit close to Germany, Mum. I hope he can escape quickly enough when the Germans come over the border.'

'Perhaps that's why he's told us where he is. He couldn't say where he was before although he knew we knew it was France.'

'And he was with that woman again; Jean-Luc mentions it in his letter.'

'Really. That's interesting.' She smiled.

'Now then, Mum, we've been through all that before.'

'I know. I trust him and you know that. I just worry about him, like all wives do.'

'He won't fight though, Mum, with him not in the Forces and if it's too dangerous he'll be sent home, surely?'

'I would like to think so, George, but it depends on what he's been sent to do.'

***

The evening after his meeting with Sir Roger and following a lengthy briefing from Anderson and chats with younger, more junior staff aware only that Frank was on a fact-finding mission for the Foreign Office, Frank joined some of these staff members in a bar also popular with those from the Belgian Government offices situated in the same quarter of the city.

The talk was all about the war and what might happen. The Belgians were cagey at first, but, as the amount of alcohol consumed rose, tongues began to loosen. Aware of the strength of the local beer Frank drank sparingly.

Most of what he heard was little more than gossip with no meaningful intelligence, leaving very little to be reported back.

As his first week there wore on Frank spent each night in the same bar. He made sure he sat with the Belgians whose behaviour became more raucous as each evening unfolded. He engaged them with stories of his service in the Great War, much of which he made up, but he was soon accepted as part of their group and no one quizzed him about his work at the embassy.

Invariably he was one of the last to leave with the Belgians normally outstaying their British counterparts well into the night. On his sixth evening there he was left with three drunken locals all of whom he knew held relatively senior positions in their government service. They were singing bawdy Flemish folk songs much of which Frank could not understand. One swayed to his feet.

'Another round of drinks?' He didn't wait for an answer, but headed unsteadily to the bar.

Frank took his chance with the two Belgians left at the table.

'So what's this about you having the German plans after a plane crash?'

It was as if he had fired a shot, the Belgians looked surprised. The man at the bar returned and spoke to the others in Flemish.

'What plane crash?' one asked, reverting to French.

'Oh, we heard two Germans were lost, ran out of fuel and crash-landed to the east. They had top-secret plans about the invasion and you've been using this information to do a deal with the Germans.'

'You have that wrong, my friend; you are mistaken,' the man said hesitatingly and looked at his watch. 'Is that the time? Come on you two, we're off.' The three shook hands leaving Frank alone to finish his beer.

'I think that told me all I need to know,' he said to himself, as he lifted his glass in a congratulatory salute.

He sought out Anderson before seven the next morning. Sir Roger was soon in possession of these facts and talking with London.

Frank continued to spend each evening in the same bar. The Belgians kept their distance at first but soon, as if the whole matter had been forgotten, they socialised as before but nothing more was said about the German plans until after one particularly heavy drinking session Frank helped one of the Belgians to a taxi. The man could barely stand and was slurring his words.

Frank opened the taxi door. 'Come on, Nicolas, in you go!'

'Thank you Frank, my friend, you are too kind, a real English gentlemen.' He slipped to the ground and giggled. Frank hoisted him up onto the taxi's back seat.

'I salute you,' the Belgian slurred. 'You are my best friend and, do you know what Frank, do you know, you are very clever knowing about the crash. You know something else? I have many stories I can tell you. You see – you see my friend, I don't like what my people are doing and, when we can, we must have a talk.' He collapsed back on the seat. Frank shut the door and gave the driver enough cash for any fare plus a tip.

Seizing on this fortuitous development Frank contacted Nicolas the following day. It had not been a drunken boast and, true to his word, he confirmed he was happy to provide information to help the British. Only snippets of relevant intelligence passed between them until one evening in early April, Frank received a call from Nicolas at his office at the embassy, suggesting a meeting in a local park the next morning.

As they walked along the edge of the park, Nicolas explained how he was aware from a contact in Berlin of German plans to invade Norway and Denmark in the next few days.

After they had split up, Frank returned to the embassy and reported to Anderson who ran round to the Royal Palace where Sir Roger was attending a formal lunch. He in turn rushed to his office to alert London.

The Germans executed their plans in Scandinavia making the Belgian staff nervous about what might develop from here. If the Belgian government was using the captured plans to broker a deal with the German, nothing had materialised or at least been announced.

The evenings in the bar became more measured and sober with a group of young Dutch officials now mixing with Frank and the Belgians. Discussions and arguments over what might happen became their focus rather than the beer. With Holland and Belgium still maintaining embassies in Berlin, a constant flow of information and intelligence came from there. The group communicated in French allowing Frank to be a party to all that passed between these two neutral governments, the Dutch seemingly unaware Frank was indeed British. What was plain to Frank was that they all knew the writing was on the wall and it was only a question of time before the Germans made their move.

Nicolas still passed what he could to Frank; never in the bar but in the park opposite the Royal Palace where they would meet for a light lunch in a café on a regular basis. He fully expected the Germans to sweep through at any time and knew Britain and France would need all possible help.

At the beginning of May, Frank received an unexpected telephone call from Nicolas suggesting they meet up not at the café but at the bar in mid-morning. When Frank arrived Nicolas was already waiting at a quiet table in a corner. They shook hands and Nicolas looked round to make sure no one could hear, before saying softly,

'I've had a call from one of the chaps at the Dutch Embassy. It's pandemonium there. They've received intelligence that the Germans will invade Holland tomorrow. The troops will move on two fronts, sweeping to the south as well. If they are coming this way, you might want to leave Brussels pretty soon.'

Frank was not surprised.

'Nicolas, I do appreciate this. We all knew it would only be a question of time. Now it's here, it's unsettling. Are you staying or leaving?'

'I have to stay; I owe it to my country but would prefer to leave with you. I'm not putting up a fight when the Germans arrive here and I doubt many others will either. Now, be off and return to your embassy to pass this on. I hope all goes well and, perhaps, we can enjoy a beer in London when all this is over.'

'Indeed we must, said Frank, 'and thanks for this and the other information over the past month or so; it's been a great help. Well, goodbye, and I'll hold you to meeting for that beer.'

They stood up, hugged each other, and left separately.

Frank stood next to Sir Roger as he spoke on the telephone. When he put the receiver down he turned to Frank.

'Splendid work! The Prime Minister has asked me to pass on his thanks. He's onto his commanders in the field as we speak. They're spread all over the place, but at least they'll now be more prepared, thanks to your contacts. Let's hope it makes a real difference. I fear it might not.'

The following morning Anderson called Frank into his office.

'I want you to gather up what you can carry of your belongings and return to France. The rest of your stuff will be returned home to your family with a note that you have been transferred. We will not be able to tell them where I'm afraid, but they might guess if they knew you had been in France before you came here.'

Within two hours Frank was on his way to Sedan. Everyone else seemed to be on the move and the train was packed. It was not until he caught a local train that he had a seat.

18

'Frank, what a surprise,' exclaimed Madeleine Fontaine, when she found Frank in her drawing room reading a newspaper.

'Madeleine. So good to see you.' He placed the paper on the table and stood up to kiss her on both cheeks.

'You're back sooner than you thought.'

'I had to depart Brussels in a hurry with the invasion imminent. I'm not sure if France is under threat yet, but Belgium and Holland most certainly are,' he explained. 'Are Thierry and Lorna due any time?'

'They'll be late as they have a meeting somewhere to the north but I'll arrange supper and you can tell me what you can about Belgium and what's happening.'

It was almost midnight before Lorna and Thierry arrived home. They were surprised to find Frank, fully expecting him to have been shipped back to England once they heard of the developments in Belgium. All four sat to hear Frank's story of his time away.

'Since you've been there, Frank,' Lorna explained, 'I've had another recce of the Maginot. Nothing much has changed despite our warnings to London. Yes, the Line is fine but beyond it, little else. I'd be surprised if the Germans aren't coming through there before too long but I've passed on another report to Ingleby.'

Their mood was sombre as they headed off to bed.

'It looks like our real work is about to start,' said Frank, as they reached the stairs. 'The Germans'll rip through here so I don't expect much fighting nearby, but there may be more of a stand to the north. The British will be stretched, as they'll be concentrated up by the Dutch and Belgium borders. From what we know the Germans will be far too strong for the thin defence line we have.'

'Well, Frank, we've done what we can for London,' said Lorna, 'and you're right, surely the defence will form around Paris and on a line to the coast from there.' They paused at the top of the stairs.

'Let's sleep on this and in the morning you and I had better sit down and talk through our strategy,' said Frank.

'Fine and it's good to have you back Frank. I'll say goodnight then.' With that she kissed him fully on his lips and opened her bedroom door.

***

By mid-afternoon the next day the Germans had arrived in Sedan, immediately setting up a temporary command post nearby. Many of the locals had left by any means possible once news filtered through that the Germans had indeed pushed through the forested area south of the Maginot. German soldiers were in the streets moving from house to house ensuring no French troops remained. The Mayor came out to meet one group of Germans and handed their officer a note, containing a plea for them to treat the locals with appropriate humanity and respect. The Mayor was clearly following through his idea of conciliation.

Other German troops randomly stopped locals to check their identities with unexpected politeness.

Frank and Lorna, now living in an old lodge to the main house, dined that evening with the Fontaines. They all agreed their cover story discussed earlier in the day with the Fontaines and ensured their papers were in order. Thierry remained fearful about his business but Frank did what he could to persuade him to go along with the Germans; there was little to be gained, he explained to Thierry, by working against them.

This was soon put to the test when the following afternoon a squad of Germans arrived at the yard. An officer came into the office with an unarmed junior. Behind them a soldier stood in the doorway, his rifle at the ready. Frank stood up from the desk where he was pretending to sift through papers, but Lorna remained seated at her typewriter. Thierry stood by a window looking out onto the yard but remained silent. The Germans' uniforms were dirty, their faces grubby streaked where rivulets of sweat had run down their cheeks.

The officer spoke sharply in German. Lorna knew exactly what he was saying, but said nothing. His junior translated into French. They required a list of employees and the name and address of the yard's owner. Lorna opened a filing cabinet, sifted through a file and handed over a typed list not mentioning the owner was standing only feet away. The officer checked the list, seemed satisfied and put it in his pocket. They left to join their men resting on boxes in the yard. After a short break they marched off with Thierry, Lorna and Frank watching on.

'They look pretty fearsome don't they?' remarked Lorna. 'Well-honed fighting men, professional, and a force to be reckoned with, that's for sure. I'm not sure our boys and the French will be much of a match for them.'

Frank nodded, saying,

'You're right, but at least, Thierry, they didn't ask about your timber.'

'They will.'

'For sure they'll leave some troops here despite their push north,' said Lorna. 'It's strategically well placed, so you'll probably be proved right.' She put on her cardigan, picked up her handbag and moved towards the door. Frank followed with his briefcase leaving Thierry to lock up. Outside in the yard all was quiet. Thierry walked slowly towards the gate then stood momentarily and looked around before re-joining them without saying a word.

Their collective mood remained no better as the four again had dinner together, this time listening to the wireless and the latest news. It did not sound good with unconfirmed reports of a fast moving German offensive moving unchecked rapidly northwards. There were also rumours of atrocities against the civilian population in both Holland and Belgium and Frank worried for those he had left behind to their fate.

'Perhaps the Mayor and those pro-German people around here might change their views when they hear this,' said Lorna.

'As far as we can,' Frank suggested, 'and in these early days at least, we should make sure local hotheads don't start shooting at the Germans or they might take it out on us as well. We must pass the word.'

***

The following day Thierry, Lorna and Frank arrived at the yard a little after seven o'clock, but they were not the first ones there. The German officer, his interpreter and six other men were standing by the locked gates. They all stood to attention as the three approached.

'We need wood,' said the interpreter, 'and we will pay you the normal price. In time we will need more, as the intention is to base a permanent command post near here. The men have a lorry parked nearby and we'll take what we want.'

This seemed an order and not a matter for discussion. Thierry started to protest, but Frank pushed him forward to release the padlock and the Germans helped him open the two large gates. One of the soldiers jogged off along the road outside the yard and returned minutes later with a lorry. For the next hour, the Germans loaded as much wood as they could onto the truck. Thierry's men soon arrived to help.

The German officer supervised what was happening and occasionally barked out orders to his men.

Lorna returned to the office with Thierry while Frank engaged the interpreter with small talk as he helped him with the planks of sawn wood. His name was Luther Glock, only twenty-two and from Hamburg. He had learnt French from his days on a cruise liner out of Le Havre. The men were from the 10th Panzer Division, but their chat was brought to an abrupt end when the officer ordered Glock to prepare to drive the lorry.

It was clear the Germans were now in Sedan to stay. All that morning, as with the previous night, gunfire and shellfire could be heard to the north and west. The wireless carried reports of French defensive blockhouses having fallen near Bellevue about two miles to the west and the Germans having struck out to the north through the Gaulier gap where no fortifications were in place. They appeared to be moving forward so quickly it would only be a matter of time before the French were completely overrun. This meant the British to the north would be trapped in a small pocket around the channel ports between Calais and the border with Belgium.

Frank excused himself once the Germans had left, having arranged to meet with his liaison contact in order to send a message to London. The man arrived at the Fontaines' with a radio and a message from Ingleby. Frank was to continue to pass any intelligence but now without the go-between and to use the radio himself instead.

After dinner Frank sat with Thierry and Lorna.

'We need to start thinking about the precise role we've been sent here for,' Frank suggested. 'Let's draw up a list of those we know will support us. We need to check them again because they might have a different view now the Germans are here. Those who said they would prefer not to help might also have changed their minds. In the coming days we'll need to approach them all if we can.'

They started the list but Frank detected a change in Thierry. He was quiet and withdrawn, perhaps because of the yard and what the Germans might want. Frank expected much of France would feel the same perhaps wanting the war in their country soon over with little stomach for a fight or to resist any occupation. Also, if the French government surrendered and the British forces became trapped, would it be the end of the war? For Sedan, now under German occupation, it might be. Would Britain seek a deal with Hitler or fight on? It seemed certain France, Belgium and Holland would fully be in German hands before too long.

***

Two days later, when Lorna and Frank arrived at the yard, Glock was waiting by the gate. He had a message. Two lorries would arrive in about an hour to pick up more timber. Before leaving he handed over an envelope stuffed with francs as payment for the timber taken previously and for the next load.

In the office they found Thierry at his desk. He seemed pre-occupied and was sweating, although it was a cool day.

'What's wrong?' Frank asked. 'You're sweating, are you ill?'

Thierry looked up.

'I'm fine,' he snapped back.

'The Germans are coming for more wood later,' Frank continued, 'but they've given us more than enough money.' Lorna showed him the envelope. Thierry threw his arms up in frustration.

Lorna sat at her desk and typed an invoice. Frank had brought in the radio the day before and hidden it behind a loose wall panel. He checked outside to ensure no Germans were nearby before retrieving the radio and trying to contact London. It was nearly an hour before he was able to transmit his message through to one of Ingleby's operators. He told of the latest troop movements and the current situation in and around the town.

Frank was walking in the yard when a large lorry came through the gates followed by a smaller one, both with armed Germans sitting facing each other along each side. As they stopped, their officer leapt down. A few soldiers followed and walked towards the timber whilst two stood on the back of the lorry with their guns trained on Thierry's men in the yard. The bigger lorry had parked right up close to the sawn tree trunks. Luther Glock was one of the armed guards. The officer barked out his orders and the men managed to roll the trunks to the pulley system the yard used to load the wood. They tied the ropes round the first trunk and were about to hoist it onto the lorry when three armed men in civilian clothes appeared on top of the woodpile in front of them. Two of them fired into the Germans who starting falling to the ground. Glock and the other armed German returned fire, but the third gunman immediately shot them. The officer went for his revolver and had barely pulled it from its holster when he fell with a wound to his upper chest. With all the Germans down, the three Frenchmen ran to the gates. A light grey Citroen picked them up and drove off at speed with one of the doors still flapping open.

Frank had ducked beneath one of the lorries. Once he saw the car drive away, he ran over to the officer, but he was dead. Glock was still alive with a wound to his abdomen and two of the remaining Germans were moaning, but the rest were quiet.

Lorna ran out of the office to join Frank. Thierry slowly followed carrying a gun. Lorna attended to Glock who was in a bad way with blood gushing from his wound. She removed her cardigan and was holding it against him trying to stem the flow of the blood.

Thierry looked calm as he walked over. Frank stood up and shouted at him,

'You knew about this, didn't you, that's why you were off hand earlier. Do you realise what you've done?' Thierry said nothing.

'How did you know the Germans were coming here today?' Frank continued. 'I only found out this morning.'

Thierry again said nothing and, before either Frank or Lorna could stop him, fired straight into Glock's head killing him outright. He moved quickly and shot the two remaining Germans still alive. Frank tried to stop him, but Thierry waved the gun threateningly.

'You stupid, bloody fool!' Frank shouted. Thierry simply turned away and returned to his office as if nothing had happened. Frank followed, but a stunned Lorna sat on the tree trunk still swinging from the pulley.

In the office, Thierry opened the safe, wrapped the gun in an oily rag and placed it on the shelf, before re-locking the door.

'The whole bloody German army'll be here any minute,' shouted Frank. 'Why did you want to involve yourself in something like this after all that we'd agreed? This is no way to go about things. There'll be reprisals and you've allowed those local fools to put all of us in the town at risk.'

Thierry looked up.

'I couldn't stop them,' he said. 'They saw no point in waiting until it's all over and they wanted to start the fight now. Many of us have old scores to settle and we will not stand idly by.'

'London will not like this, you know. Did you have to come and shoot those injured men like that? It's barbaric.'

'They'd do it to us, Frank. And do you know what, I don't care what's happened. Look, my friend, this is not England. We're fighting to save our land, our livelihoods and you are not – there's quite a difference.'

'But you might have waited or, at least, told me about this last night. Why your sudden change of heart? The Germans are trigger-happy and will not take this lying down. Like I said, you can expect reprisals and we are in the thick of it.'

Thierry was adamant.

'None of them are left to say what happened, that's why I shot the injured. We can say the gunmen appeared and were nothing to do with us. The Germans will never find out.'

Lorna rushed in through the door.

'Germans have arrived outside and they're not very happy. They must have heard the shots and came straight over from the main square. The man in the leather coat looks like a high ranking officer.'

They all looked out of the window. Frank recognised the insignia of the uniform under the coat as being that of a Colonel. The officer was shouting at his men who were moving from body to body, but at each one they shook their heads. Lorna was able to translate what the Colonel was saying. He wanted the bodies put onto the troop lorry and taken away. He turned and looked up at the office and all three pulled away from the window with Thierry and Lorna returning to their desks. Frank opened the door and the Colonel walked towards him, speaking in French.

'What in God's name has happened here?'

Frank feigned shock.

'Three men came, shot your men and ran off as quickly as they'd arrived. They were in uniform,' he lied.

'French or British?'

'Oh, definitely British, I'd say, they were wearing their khaki.'

'They'll pay for this, but we understood no British were left. They must have been hiding out in the town; perhaps they're still here.'

Frank could see where this was leading and now wished he had not lied. He had hoped his explanation would persuade the Colonel this ambush was simply a case of soldiers carrying out their orders, and as a consequence allowing the local people to escape any reprisals. Now he was not sure it would.

As they were speaking, more of the yard's workers arrived. The Colonel barked out an order to his men in German, pointed at the workers and Frank. The soldiers cocked their guns and circled the men. The Colonel drew his handgun and beckoned for Frank to join the others.

'Who else is in the office?' he asked.

'A typist and another.'

The Colonel pointed his gun at one of his men before waving it in the direction of the office. The soldier returned with Thierry and Lorna. As she passed Frank, Lorna whispered in French, 'Secret Police', nodding towards the Colonel. Frank raised his eyebrows in surprise and frowned.

Together with the five men from the yard, the three were ordered up onto one of the lorries. Once settled Thierry explained to his men what had happened earlier leaving out one or two of the more important points and repeating the version Frank had given to the German officer.

By the time the lorry edged through the yard's gates, a large crowd had gathered outside, keen to know what had happened.

The lorry containing the dead bodies followed. Progress was slow as the locals crowded round and the Colonel shouted at the driver to stop. He stood on the running board and addressed the crowd in French,

'There has been a monstrous atrocity against the German Army with an attack on my men by British soldiers being sheltered by the town. I can tell you now that, if the perpetrators of this attack on my men are not handed over to us by this time tomorrow, your people on this lorry will be shot. You have twenty-four hours. I shall be in the Mayor's office when you have the information of where these men are or if you wish to hand them over. We did not wish to harm the civilian population, but actions like this will leave us no choice.'

He returned to the cab and told the driver to drive off. The crowd were stunned and bewildered.

Lorna tried to comfort the frightened workers on the lorry. Thierry looked calm and looked up when Frank kicked his foot,

'I told you this would happen,' Frank whispered.

'I've already told you why it happened,' Thierry said, angrily, 'you can't talk, anyway. Why mislead the Germans about these non-existent British?'

'They would have found another way of taking out their revenge on us whether I said they were British or French,' said Frank. It was now important to have the workers taken out of danger, but he, Thierry and Lorna would have to take their chances.

Their lorry arrived at the main council building in the central square where the Germans had set up their temporary headquarters. As Frank stepped down he spoke to the Colonel.

'Look, Colonel, it was awful what happened to your men, but what if the British are now clean away? You can't be sure anyone here is protecting them. The British might be a group separated from the rest and they took a chance. At least, release my daughter; she's an innocent typist. Keep me but release the other men. You don't need to keep us all, surely?'

The Colonel spoke impassively.

'We shall see what happens in the next twenty-four hours.' He turned and walked away.

A bright red, white and black flag with its prominent swastika hung from the flagpole on the front of the building. To the right of the entrance, the French tricolour lay screwed up against a pile of empty boxes on the floor.

Frank and the others were taken into a small back room. As they crowded inside, a single armed soldier joined them. He locked the door behind him, turned on the one light and closed the shutters. He stood guard at the door only opening it when food and drink arrived. The guard was changed each hour.

The group sat on the floor leaning against the walls. Occasionally, they were all escorted to the toilets at the far end of the building, enabling them to stretch their legs at the same time. Frank tried to reassure the men, but this did little to lift their spirits. They talked of escape yet found it hard to see what they could do without getting themselves shot.

Lorna and Frank sat together, but Thierry was alone in one corner with his knees up to his chin where he rested his head with his eyes shut. Lorna spoke quietly to Frank in French.

'What do you think will happen?' she asked.

'I really don't know. They mean business and I wouldn't put it past them to shoot us.'

Lorna looked shocked.

'Really? But it's early days. Do they really want to alienate the locals like that?'

Frank leant over and whispered close to Lorna's ear,

'The men here may know who did the shooting. Thierry knows for sure and could save our necks.'

'I don't rate our chances,' said Lorna, unconvinced. 'We must try something rather than wait to be shot.'

'You're right. I'll think about it. We might just have to make a run for it and take our chances, especially if we're to be shot anyway.'

Nothing was said for a while. After the silence, Frank tried to lift her mood.

'If you could be anywhere else right now, Lorna, where would that be?'

Lorna looked surprised and hesitated.

'Driving in my Bentley along a country road in the Cotswolds on a beautiful sunny day with a pub just around the next corner. What about you?'

'Well, I – hang on, a Bentley? Not a blue one?'

'Ah - ...' Lorna looked embarrassed. 'I've let the cat out of the bag, haven't I? Damn!'

'You and Jack? But you said you preferred - ...'

'A double lie, I'm afraid Frank, or is it a bluff? Yes, Jack and I are husband and wife, but few people know that. We haven't even told our parents, so keep it to yourself, please. I'll tell you more when we get out of this.'

'Well, I'm blowed, you sly old thing. That day at Lyons' – you and Jack left for the Ritz together.'

'Yes, that's right.'

'Well, well. I won't ask anymore. It wouldn't be right.'

Lorna held his hand and squeezed it.

***

It was an uncomfortable night spent attempting sleep on the hard cell floor. Not long after their frugal breakfast they were ordered to be ready to move, then escorted into the foyer by armed guards and told to wait. The Colonel arrived shortly after. He stood on the stairs looking at them.

'No one has yet owned up to the killings and, as a consequence, you are being taken from here to the churchyard to be put on display for one hour. If no one comes forward, you will all be shot to teach everyone a lesson they will never forget. This soldier here will lead the way and my men will be along the street. Try to escape and you'll be shot immediately. Right, outside!'

Frank called out, 'About what I said yesterday, Colonel? Keep me and this man, but release the girl and the rest.' He pulled Thierry towards him.

The Colonel said nothing and the group were led towards the front doors. As they were halted at the top of the steps leading down to the square, Frank pretended to tie his shoelace. He tapped Lorna on the leg and whispered up to her,

'When we walk to the church we'll pass Manins, the grocer's shop. We could run through it and out the back door towards the woods, it might be our only chance.'

They moved out into the square. Frank stood closely behind Lorna and whispered,

'When we're opposite the grocer's door we'll make a dash for it so edge to that side of the road, to give us more of a chance. Don't stop for anything and follow me.'

Lorna said nothing, but tried to visualise the shop and what was behind it. She could see what Frank meant.

A large crowd had gathered. Frank recognised a few, including the Fontaine family. The Germans formed a line stretching along the road as it rose up the hill to the church. The Colonel was standing on a jeep, waiting in the middle of the road. As the throng approached, he held up his hand and they all stopped. Behind him, by the church gates, a machine gun stood mounted on a truck with two men crouching, ready to fire.

'This is your last chance to hand over the culprits or tell me where they are. Failure to do so will mean the executions will start in one hour.'

No one moved or said anything. The only sound came from women and children crying. The Colonel sat down as the jeep moved alongside the machine gun. Frank and the others were ushered forward.

Manins was some thirty yards along the right hand side of the road. Frank and Lorna moved out to their right without the Germans noticing. Frank was slightly ahead and he frowned when he saw two women standing in the shop doorway blocking the entrance.

As soon as he was opposite the door, he veered off to his right. He used all his size and strength to barge past the two women. One moved out of his way, but the other was knocked over and fell in front of him. He stepped on her back and leapt forward towards the open side door. Lorna followed, pushing past the first woman who cursed. Lorna stepped on the back of the prostrate woman as Frank had done, but unfortunately for her, the woman lifted her head at the wrong moment, catching Lorna's leg. She fell forward onto one knee and put out her arms to break the fall. She hit the ground hard and winced as her wrist twisted with a loud crack. She slid along the tiled floor, smacked her shoulder into a doorframe causing her to call out in pain before she slowly stood up. Frank hesitated in the back garden on hearing her shout before continuing towards the woods.

As Lorna leant against the counter, a German appeared at the shop door. He fired with the loud report echoing around the confines of the small shop. The bullet travelled straight through Lorna's left breast and out of her back, shattering the mirror behind the shop's counter. She fell out through the side door as the blast hit her and spun around in the alleyway before slumping onto the path with the soldier standing above her. She looked up appealingly, but he fired again into her forehead and a splatter of skull flew up the brick wall behind her.

Frank heard the first shot and stopped. Looking round he saw the German shoot for the second time. He grimaced, turned and ran.

In the road there was uproar. Thierry and the other prisoners ran down the hill towards the square and mixed with the crowd. Within seconds the machine gun started firing wildly. Several people fell as the bullets raked through them. Thierry stopped at the entrance to the square and stood with his arms raised,

'Stop this, stop this!' he shouted. Momentarily the machine gun was quiet. He started up the hill, but the gun opened up again. The bullets strafed across his chest and he fell. Some bystanders were hit by ricochets and also fell to the ground. Others turned and ran.

Madeleine was kneeling by Thierry, but he was already dead. She fell forward to lie across his back. Jean-Luc stood above them shaking uncontrollably.

It had all happened so quickly, but now it was eerily quiet. Locals sat on the kerbstones with their heads in their hands, not quite believing what they had just witnessed. Families stood over, or knelt next to, those shot and the silence was broken with their wailing. The Germans remained watching over the crowd, but a few had run through the shop to follow Frank.

Frank reached the edge of the wood. He turned hoping to see the Germans had given up the chase, satisfied they had made their point with the killing of Lorna and possibly others. He crouched and looked back. Soldiers had climbed over the fence at the end of the grocer's long backyard and were starting up the hill towards him. Suddenly a shout came from inside the shop and the men stopped; they were being called back. One fired two random shots towards the wood before joining the others. Frank could see the Colonel standing above Lorna's body. Poor Lorna, dead in the doorway: a young, wasted life, not killed in the line of duty, merely a victim of circumstance. He cursed Thierry for his stupidity. What of Ingleby in London, waiting for news?

19

Frank made good progress heading northwards, his aim to catch up with the Allies. The sound of artillery fire had long since ceased and he had no idea how far they might have retreated. He would keep on the move and look out for transport. The rail line was nearby, but perhaps the trains had stopped now the invasion had started; he could not recall hearing any that day. Maybe he could steal a car, but that might expose him to more scrutiny should he be stopped by the Germans; perhaps a bicycle would be a better option. He walked on at a brisk pace and soon picked up the main road. Ahead was a hamlet of houses about half a mile away.

***

Still wearing his pyjamas, George, home from university for a few days private study, came into the kitchen where his mother was cleaning the floor.

'Mind your feet, stay there until it's dry,' she told him. He stopped in the doorway.

'Mum, have you heard the news? The Germans have invaded France.'

Joan leant on her mop.

'Yes, I heard it on the seven o'clock news,' she said, 'but didn't want to wake you. I told you this had to come soon. This phoney war's dragged on for far too long. I don't know why Hitler has waited all this time, do you?'

'Well, the invasion was bound to happen sooner rather than later. I wonder where Dad is?'

'That last letter said Brussels, but he must have left there. At least I hope so. Perhaps he returned to be with the Fontaines.'

'I hope he didn't, Mum. They've just said on the radio that the Sedan area is already in German hands.'

Joan stepped back and held onto the sink. George tiptoed across the wet floor to stand by her side, not sure what to do.

'Mum, don't worry. He'll have been taken out of there, if he was there at all. He could be on his way home for all we know. It'll be total confusion with not much information coming out.'

She looked at George and put an arm round his shoulders.

'Your Dad can't tell me much of what he does and you know that, but I've a hunch he and that Lorna were sent with the sole purpose of remaining with the Fontaines, even after the Germans arrive. That is when their work starts properly. That could mean he'll be needed for a long time, so it's unlikely he'll be coming home – at least not for quite a while.'

George looked shocked.

'That hadn't crossed my mind, of course he'll have to stay. Mum, you seem to be taking this very calmly, yet you must be worried.'

'Oh, son, believe me I am. I have become used to the dangerous work he does, but this is different. We have to accept he might not return. He's just like any one of our men over there; they are all in danger of being killed, wounded or captured. I've been through this before in the Great War and, as you know, lost my brother.'

'Yes, of course, but Dad's resourceful and I'm sure he'll be fine. Do you think that Jack Ingleby fellow will let us have any news?'

'I'm not sure he can, but I do have a telephone number for him. I'll wait and see what the news is from France before I do anything. Jack did keep me posted in the past; although I'm not sure he should have done so.'

***

The first house was empty. At the next, the door opened a little after Frank's second knock, a face shrouded in the darkness of the hallway asked enquiringly, 'Hello?'

'Hello, sorry, but I'm on the run from the Germans,' Frank explained. The door closed a little. 'There's been a shooting of civilians in the town. I managed to escape.'

The door opened wider and an old man's face appeared.

'A shooting, you say?' he asked.

After Frank briefly explained what had happened in Sedan, he was invited inside. The man's wife came through from the kitchen.

'We've met the Fontaines,' said the man. 'Good people. I know a number of men who've worked at their yard. It sounds a terrible thing and that poor woman, but at least you're safe.'

'Yes ... it was quite awful,' said Frank, his voice trembling a little. 'If possible I'd like your help. Would you by any chance have a bicycle I could use? I can't pay you anything as the Germans confiscated all my money, but I would like to reach our lines as quickly as possible.'

'Of course,' said the man standing up. 'I've an old one. It's spare and you're welcome to it, but you'll need something warmer than what you're wearing. Wait here.'

He left the room. His wife smiled and followed. The man returned with an old jacket.

'Here, you'll need this to keep you dry and warm. You're welcome to it. The cycle is in the shed at the back. Would you like any food and drink?'

'No, I'm fine; I'd like to get on my way.'

The man opened the drawer of a sideboard. He rummaged around and pulled out a wad of francs, peeled off a few and handed them over.

'I can't possibly take that.'

'Please do. Treat it as my contribution to the war effort; it's likely to be the only one I'll make.'

His wife returned and handed Frank a glass of red wine. She also held a bag containing bread and cheese, which she placed in the jacket pocket.

'That's very kind of you,' said Frank as he gulped down the wine and handed back the glass. He gave her a light kiss on both cheeks, but again she said nothing.

Frank was taken through the kitchen, out of the back door and into the garden shed. A rusty old bicycle lay on the floor, but the brakes worked and it had decent tyres.

'Well, I wish you luck,' said the man wheeling out the bicycle. 'My advice is head towards the smoke in the distance, but keep going north. It seems the Germans are moving very fast and you need to get a move on. Quickly.'

Frank gingerly sat on the worn saddle and wobbled off along the side of the house. The couple laughed as he fought for balance, but with a wave he pedalled off. The man looked at his wife and shook his head.

***

Ingleby stood looking out at the sky from his London office. It was grey and overcast. It had rained all morning, but had now stopped. A few people were in the street and scurried about their business. They looked as grey as the weather.

He returned to his desk, picked up the handwritten note and read it for the umpteenth time. It was from the communications section and a message received overnight from the agent working with Lorna and Frank.

It told of the shooting and confirmed Thierry Fontaine and Lorna were definitely dead, but that Frank's whereabouts were currently unknown and he might have escaped. The agent was confident the Germans were no longer looking for him. Ingleby hoped so.

Ingleby screwed up the message, held it tightly in his hand and tapped it repeatedly against his chin. He and Lorna had been together for nearly twenty years. She had been a teenager when they first met, but now she was dead and he felt responsible although he knew she died doing something she enjoyed. He had tried to discourage her, but she had insisted.

He would have to let Lorna's family know of her death and that would be difficult. Should he tell them of his relationship with their daughter or simply send the more traditional official letter? His other problem was what to tell Joan, or whether he should tell her anything at this stage. He felt he should see her in person, but all he could say was that Frank's fate was as yet unknown. He would wait. He picked up a pen from the inkpot and took out a piece of notepaper from his desk drawer. He drafted a letter for his secretary to type and send to Lorna's family.

***

For the rest of the day, Frank cycled along a series of minor roads, always making sure he was heading roughly north. His progress was steady. As the night set in, he came into a small village and was able to use the Frenchman's francs to obtain a meal with overnight lodging at the small inn in the main street. The owner was surprised to see anyone travelling, with all that was happening, but did not ask any awkward questions.

During the night Frank was woken by a deafening noise. The whole building shook and, when he looked out of the upstairs' window, he saw armoured trucks passing with soldiers aboard. Without any street lighting, he was not able to identify their uniforms or any insignia on the trucks as they were travelling so fast, but he guessed they were Germans.

After breakfast he set off again. He heard a rumbling noise behind him as he moved into the open countryside. The unmistakable shape of a tank was heading towards him, throwing up dust from the road.

He pulled over. Ahead was a wooden barred gate to a field with a herd of dairy cows standing idly the other side, munching on the grass. He wheeled the bicycle over to the gate and opened it. The cows cowered away.

The tank was close and to its side a motorbike with a sidecar carried an officer. Frank caught his breath not wanting them to stop. He walked to the nearest cow and stroked the side of its neck as if it was an old friend. The noise of the tank was deafening and the frightened cows moved away. Frank moved with them. The motorbike pulled up, the officer stood up and looked straight at Frank, who gave a half wave and half salute. The officer lifted his goggles to see better, pulled them down again and beckoned the rider to move on.

A relieved Frank slapped the cow on its rear end in triumph. No doubt the officer had decided this was nothing more than a local cowman attending his herd and not worthy of any precious time.

A convoy of heavily armed troop carriers interspersed with more tanks took more than a minute to roar by. Many of the soldiers turned and looked at Frank as they passed, but soon they were gone and the cloud of dust began to clear. With the cows now at the other end of the field, Frank shut the gate and cycled after the cloud. As soon as he reached the next road junction he took a different road.

During the next hour or so a constant stream of conveys passed by on the road he had left. By late morning he could see not only the dust clouds ahead, but also much darker smoke rising. This suggested the fighting was not far away.

He rested a while to plan what to do. If the fighting was close, he knew there was no point in passing through the German advance and he would somehow have to work his way round to the east or west to reach the Allied retreat.

Moving west, he came upon a village where he used the last of his francs to buy bread, cheese and a bottle of beer. Sleeping rough would now be his only option until he reached the Allied troops.

***

Ingleby was dozing at his desk when his secretary knocked on his office door. She brought in a cup of tea and a slice of toast coated in butter along with note from the communications room. It was a transcript of another message from the agent in France. He confirmed Frank had not been killed during the shooting incident and had escaped into the countryside.

'Excellent news about Major Shipley?' asked the secretary.

'So far so good; he'll probably lie low then try to make his way to here. It won't be easy, but he's a resourceful chap.'

'Don't you want him to stay and carry on with his mission?'

'No, having been compromised, it's better he returns. We'll find other work for him when things have settled down.'

'Is there a reply to France?'

'No, we'll leave it, thanks.' Ingleby screwed up the piece of paper and threw it across the room, but missed the waste bin. The secretary tidied it up as she left.

He had still not made up his mind about visiting Joan, but this latest news meant there was no immediate need to do so and it was against protocol anyway. Perhaps there was another way. What of Lorna's parents? They would have received his letter that morning and, although they did not know it, would be sharing his grief.

***

Once he had finished the food, Frank left the village and pedalled slowly along the winding lane towards a more wooded area to the north. The stop had stiffened up his legs a little and his bottom now felt very sore from the chafing of the old saddle. It was time to find another mode of transport, preferably quicker and more comfortable.

The weather remained fine and typical of late spring. The pleasant woodland area gave way to open, undulating farmland. The gentle landscape made cycling easier, but Frank began to feel twinges of cramp in his calves and had to resort to keeping his bottom off the saddle for long periods, his skin red raw. He passed through a number of small villages and hamlets until ahead of him lay a larger town, sitting pleasantly in a hollow. Alongside a stream he pulled over and washed his face and hands. Resting on the grassy bank he exposed his bottom to the air and used his handkerchief to dab on cold water, but it stung uncomfortably.

As he approached the town, he saw a plume of white smoke billowing upwards from behind the church in the middle of the town. It was not a bonfire and was too white to be the result of any shelling. Also, there was no evidence during the day of the main invasion force having come this way.

He decided to head towards the church. As he approached, he heard the familiar chugging sound of a steam engine. A sign directed him to the railway station and, at the end of this road, he could see the trucks of a goods train parked in a siding. White smoke rose from the engine's funnel. He left the bicycle up against the railings around the churchyard. Not finding anyone on the engine's platform, he walked along the wagons. Two men were sitting on the tailgate of the last wagon and looked up as he approached. One was wearing the traditional boiler suit of a driver and the other wore a rather shabby jacket with red piping, a shirt and tie. Both were smoking.

'Could you tell me where you're making for?' asked Frank. The man in the jacket, the guard, stood up.

'Who are you?' he asked.

Frank ignored the request and spoke to the driver. 'Where are you heading for?'

Before the guard could interrupt, the driver stood up.

'We don't know,' he confirmed, 'but we've heard it might eventually be Lille. A German infantry group, who hopped on for a lift about fifty miles back, commandeered us, but they got off here. Most of them left on foot, so only a few still remain in the town.'

The guard rose to his feet and came over.

'So who are you?'

Frank explained he was a French agent working for the British and that it would not be safe for him to fall into the hands of the Germans.

The two men looked at each other before the guard added,

'That must be true because it's so ridiculous, you'd be stupid to make it up!'

The driver looked more serious,

'Your accent, it's not from round here, is it?'

Frank laughed it off. 'No,' he said. 'I've been living in England for a while, you can probably tell.'

'We were told to wait here,' the driver continued, 'but to be ready to move at a moment's notice. We've been here for hours. One German soldier spoke French and he's supposed to be liaising with us, but he's not been here since lunchtime. I left my fireman up front in the engine to keep it ticking over and now we're sat here waiting; he's having a nap right now. The German believes we'll follow the advance when it's safe to do so with a view to picking up the injured, the dead or any prisoners.'

'Would you be able to turn a blind eye if I slipped into one of these wagons when it's time to move off and cadged a lift? I'd get off once we approach where the Germans might be, so you won't need to worry and, of course, to them I'm simply a Frenchman and they wouldn't be that suspicious anyway.'

The two men looked at each other and the guard nodded towards the driver and shrugged as if to say 'Well?'

'Fine,' the driver said. 'We know nothing, if we're asked, and you are on your own. Agreed?'

'That's fine,' said Frank.

Suddenly, a jeep headed their way. Before it came into view, Frank ran around behind the guard's wagon. He struggled to open the door of the next wagon, but once he had, jumped up inside and pulled the door almost shut, leaving a small gap to see out.

The jeep containing two Germans pulled up and one spoke to the engine driver in perfect French. The train was to head for a place called Promone and to wait there for further orders. After the Germans had left, Frank heard the driver walk off along the track. The guard came to the wagon from where Frank was looking out.

'Did you hear that?' he asked Frank.

'Yes, Promone. Where's that?'

'On the way to Lille. It's about a hundred and twenty kilometres from here. Are you staying there or joining me?'

'I'd like to remain in here and catch up on my sleep.'

'You should try next door, there's a pile of straw bales and you'll be more comfortable.'

Frank jumped down and pulled open the door of the next wagon. He called out to the guard,

'Wake me up when you near this Promone place, won't you?'

'Fine, we've been told to travel slowly and it could take us all night to reach there.'

Frank climbed up and pushed the door open wider. The bright light lit up the gloomy wooden walls showing the bales pushed into one corner. His eyes adjusted to the change. He recoiled in surprise. Sitting in the far right hand corner was a British soldier. Frank swore in French and then spoke in English.

'What in God's name are you doing here?'

The man had a blackened face as if camouflaged, and his uniform was muddy and torn. He appeared unarmed.

'You're British – not French?'

Frank recognised the distinctly northern accent, he suspected Manchester.

He explained who he was and briefly how he came to be there. The soldier looked at him as if he was not sure whether to believe him or not, but could think of no good reason why Frank would want to lie to him.

'So how did you come to be here?' Frank asked

'I was with the South Lancs. We were sent miles to the south of here, but were completely overrun and fled in all directions. On the second night I was still on my own and I came upon this train in a siding being coupled up. I climbed aboard, hoping it would take me to the north where I could take my chances on foot, cross-country to the coast.'

'That was a smart move. The Germans are moving pretty fast and there's not much time.'

Both remained quiet before the soldier asked,

'So if you're not proper army, what rank are you?'

'Major.'

The man looked surprised.

'Don't worry,' added Frank. 'It doesn't mean that much and you can call me Frank, Frank Shipley. And who are you?'

'Tom Bramhill - Private.'

'That name sounds familiar. Isn't there a cricketer with that name?'

'Yes, that's me and I also play Rugby League.'

'That's right, Lancashire and Warrington, if my memory serves.'

'Very good! I'm impressed! A bit of a sportsman, are you?'

'Used to be.'

Tom opened the door a little to let in more light, but it was now dark outside and made little difference. He shared his small amount of food with Frank as the train started off at a snail's pace. They both dozed before Frank was shaken awake.

'We've stopped,' said Tom, quietly. 'We might have to get off.'

He put his head out of the door. It was now light.

'Damn! Germans up at the engine.' Frank crawled to the door and looked out with one eye with his head below Tom's.

'We can't jump down now,' said Frank, 'they'll see us. If they catch us, I might get away with it as they'll think I'm French, but you won't. Let's stay here, keep a look out and hope they move away.'

'They're coming along looking into each wagon,' Tom suddenly announced, moving away from the door. 'What can we do?'

Frank slowly slid the door shut making sure it made little noise. He whispered to Tom,

'Look, stand in the corner on this side where the door is, put your hands in your crotch and face the wall. It's that dark in here they might not look right into the corners. I doubt they're looking for people, probably sizing up what they can put in here and what might be in here already. As soon as they start to open the door, do what I just said.'

Tom nodded and they waited nervously for the Germans to arrive. They could hear the crunch on the stones outside and turned to squeeze themselves tightly into the corners as the door opened a little. Frank had been right; the Germans were only making a cursory check. The door closed and the Germans moved off.

Although Frank couldn't see him, he heard Tom sigh with relief. As they sat on the straw, the guard called from outside and Frank pulled open the door.

'They've gone, but I think you'd better leave; this is about as far as we're going. The fighting is not far from here, can you hear that?'

There was occasional artillery fire and the chatter of a machine gun, but it was way off to the northwest.

'We're about four kilometres from Lille,' the guard added. 'I would avoid heading towards the noise. It looks like it might be better to circle round to the east and miss the town that way. It might be your best chance.'

'Thanks,' said Frank, 'by the way I've found a friend.' Tom appeared at his shoulder and nodded.

'You'd better leave,' said the guard. 'If the Germans see you with me, I'll be in trouble.' He turned and ran off towards the engine.

***

Shutting the front door, George called out,

'Mum, I'm home. I'm off to my room.' He waited but there was no reply. 'Mum?' He called louder. Still nothing. She was not in the living room or the kitchen. Through the open back door he could see her sitting on the old wooden bench at the side of the lawn.

'Mum?' he called. Joan stood up and turned round. George could see she was upset. She held out a piece of paper. It was a letter, but instead of reading it he put his arms around her and held her tight.

'What on earth has happened? Is it Dad?'

She tried to speak, but shook her head as George took the letter. It was from a Mr Parker.

Dear Mrs Shipley,

Very sadly I have learnt of the death of our beloved daughter, Lorna, who was killed in action near Sedan during the German advance. However, the man with her has escaped as far as is known. I remember Lorna telling me she was working out there with a Major Shipley. I found his address amongst her things and thought I would write to pass on what I know. I hope this is good news for you and your family.

Your most obedient servant Nigel Parker

George pulled back, held Joan at arm's length and looked into her eyes,

'That's not so bad. Well, it is for the woman but it looks like Dad's alive.'

Joan said nothing and looked at the ground; George put his arm around her.

'Come on, cheer up. Come inside and I'll make you a cup of tea. It could be worse.'

Inside the kitchen George read the letter again.

'Mum, have you noticed there's no address, so we can't write to commiserate and thank him. That's a bit odd, don't you think? Perhaps he's not allowed to tell us.'

Joan glanced at the letter and shook her head.

***

Ingleby arrived late in his office after being held up again on the Underground. His secretary was busy typing. He hung his trilby and mackintosh on the hat stand.

'Good morning, how are we today? Did that letter go off last night to Mrs Shipley?' he enquired.

'Yes, sir, it did.'

Lorna's file was lying open on his desk. Next to it was a carbon copy of a letter from a Mr Parker to Joan Shipley, but underneath was another carbon - of a letter to Lorna's father and mother. Ingleby smiled and closed the file - pleased with his idea.

20

For several hours Frank and Tom walked briskly in the general direction of the northeast. The noise from the fighting continued to reach them on the wind, but was a long way to their left.

That night they slept rough in an isolated barn at the edge of a field of sprouting vegetables and a short distance from the road. Tom still had a few francs and Frank had used some to purchase a tin of meat and a jar of pickle from a village store during the day. No one questioned him about his sudden appearance, perhaps assuming he was another Frenchman avoiding the fast moving German advance.

They made good progress the next day. In the late afternoon, they rested beside the road beneath an apple tree. Its early fruit had a tinge of red and Tom reached up to pick two. They were barely ripe, but edible. Frank gave Tom a leg up to the lowest branch and he picked a few more

'How much money have you left?' Frank asked.

'About two francs, that's all.'

'I suggest we find a more comfortable bed for the night and some food in the next village. We may have to rely on charity, but I'm sure it'll be fine. Let's rest here for a while and wait until it's dark.'

Frank was dozing off in the warmth of the early May evening when Tom shook him awake. He stood over Frank with his finger pushed against his lips.

'There's a small group coming towards us on the road,' he whispered, 'and, by the sound of it, they're soldiers on the march.'

Frank rolled over to look. He could hear the unmistakable noise of hobnail on tarmac, but could see no one due to the bend in the road. He beckoned to Tom and pointed at the ditch behind a hedge to their right. It looked dry and was full of nettles. Frank slid in through a gap in the hedge gasping as his hands were stung. Tom followed.

The footsteps came closer. Frank peered through the gap in the hedge.

He could see a small group of men in British army uniform about fifty yards away. He mouthed 'British!' Tom immediately eased himself out of the ditch, making a loud rustling noise. The soldiers must have heard it as the footsteps came to a halt and Tom heard a rifle being cocked.

'We're British soldiers; don't shoot we're coming out,' shouted Tom, standing up with his hands above his head. Frank scrambled out of the ditch to join him.

'Who the bloody hell are you?' said the soldier with the rifle, lowering it as he saw Tom's uniform.

'Private Thomas Bramhill of the South Lancs. Who are you from?'

'You won't believe this; I'm from the East Lancs - Captain Dawson.'

Frank emerged from behind Tom.

'It's fine,' said Tom to the officer, 'he's with me and he's British like us. He's a sort of Major.'

Dawson moved towards them, 'What do you mean 'a sort of Major'?'

Frank came forward,

'I've been working with Intelligence south of here, near Sedan, with another agent, but we were caught up in what became something of a massacre. She was killed, but I escaped.'

'She?' said Dawson, surprised.

'We'd been posing as French locals, father and daughter. Here to set up a resistance network assuming the worst happens, which looks like it has. I met Tom here when we both hitched a lift on the same train.'

'I've questioned him and he's genuine,' added Tom. 'He was in the last lot out here in France and Belgium.'

'You mentioned an atrocity,' said Dawson to Frank. 'We heard about it last night. Locals were shot after some Germans had been murdered.'

'That's the one,' Frank confirmed, 'I managed to escape by the skin of my teeth. Where have you come from?'

'God knows. It's been a bloody cock up all round,' said Dawson. 'No one expected the Germans to come through the forest and skirt the Maginot because their tanks wouldn't cope – or that's what the top brass thought. Well, they were wrong.'

Frank felt annoyed the warnings he and Lorna had passed on had seemingly been ignored. Dawson continued,

'We were sent south in a desperate attempt to stop them. They were moving so damn fast they sped past us, but it was only their tanks. Their infantry were way behind, but they eventually ran into us and we were badly mauled. In the end we scattered, with everyone for himself, but a few of my lads were still with me and we joined up with remnants of other units. We finally split up into smaller groups to make our way to the coast. Near Sedan we commandeered a lorry and reached near here before it ran out of fuel. We met a group who had received a message to head towards a place called Poperinghe and from there north to the coast. That's the area likely to be the last the Germans will reach and there's a corridor through to it at present. It's likely to be our only chance of avoiding capture or worse.'

'We'd better not hang around,' said Frank. 'I reckon it's about eight miles to Poperinghe. I was there in 1918 and know a little about the area.'

'We're all tired,' said Dawson, 'but I'm sure we can make it there. Lead on.'

'No, you carry on in charge; you have the proper rank.'

Dawson called his men together and introduced Frank and Tom. He asked for one last effort from them for the push to Poperinghe where they should be able to have a more prolonged rest. They all set off at a brisk marching pace with Frank and Tom at the rear.

As they neared Poperinghe, they saw more and more soldiers on the roads. Many were injured and being helped along by their comrades. Others had blood soaked bandages around their heads and legs. Some used improvised crutches to help them along. Carts carried injured and exhausted men, but with no horses to pull them, the fitter men did the job instead.

Abandoned vehicles littered the side of the road. Many of them were burnt out wrecks set on fire with what little fuel they had left to stop them falling into German hands. From time to time, the German artillery landed shells nearby. The loudness of the firing suggested they were close, perhaps a mile or two away.

In the town, Dawson and Frank left the men resting and headed towards an improvised command post made out of a tarpaulin stretched between two abandoned lorries. Beneath it were two officers poring over a map. Dawson introduced himself and explained who Frank was. The Colonel was interested to hear from Frank exactly what had happened in Sedan and took him to one side.

'Shipley,' he explained, 'you had better get into a uniform, as it will be better for you should you get captured. The Germans will at least honour the code if they think you are a soldier, even if you're not. What rank are you?'

'Major, sir.'

'Well, you'll find bodies at the Town Hall and you can take your pick of a uniform from one of them, but be respectful, mind. When you've sorted that out, you had all better head out of here. We've been told to make for Dunkirk.'

The Colonel looked at the map, pointed to Poperinghe and the port of Dunkirk.

'Look at this corridor on the map here,' he continued, 'all I can say to you is, get up it as quickly as you can. Small units have been told to stay and fight off the Germans - bloody brave chaps - and that's supposed to give us the best chance of getting away. We've been told Winston Churchill is now in charge and he's organising ships to take us home. It's all a question of time. I think the Germans will move too quickly for us, but we have to take a chance. Off you go and good luck.'

Tom and Frank headed off to the Town Hall. Dawson returned to the other men now stretched out around the town square, most were sleeping.

'This place has hardly changed since I was last here,' said Frank as they walked along the main street. 'It was for a deserter's Court Martial. He was from the East Lancs. A chap called Eddie Wilson, a promising footballer. Ever heard of him?'

'No. A bit before my time, Frank.'

'Of course. Ah, look, here's the Town Hall. They climbed the flight of steps, walked through the foyer and into the room at the rear. The bodies were laid out neatly on trestle tables. Frank hesitated.

'What's the matter?' asked Tom.

'This is where Wilson's cell was. It's been changed from how it was, with the walls knocked down to make this one big room.' Frank moved forward and walked alongside the three tables. He counted sixteen bodies; some were in a gruesome state with the uniforms all torn and splattered with mud and blood. He came to the body of a Captain without a mark on him and he appeared to be asleep. His face was pale as if the lifeblood had simply drained out.

They carefully removed the uniform and dressed the body in Frank's civilian clothes ensuring the identity tag remained visible. Once finished, they took a step back, came to attention and saluted.

'To think, Frank, all these poor buggers here, and those we saw along the road, have family at home fretting about them, hoping for the best ...'

Frank had an image of Joan and the children. What would they be thinking and feeling right now? He was not sure they would even know he was in France.

Frank led Tom out through the door, into a courtyard and stopped to look round. He recalled this as the exercise area for prisoners and ran his palm along the wall.

'Look at this, Tom; feel those holes. Bullets made them. This is where the executions were carried out and Wilson was one of them.' He stared at the wall, shaking his head before following Tom out into the street. They headed towards the command post where they found Dawson sitting on the tailgate, eating.

'I've managed to scrounge some rations. Here.' He handed them two open tins of bully beef. 'You'll have to use your fingers, but it tastes good.'

Frank sat next to the Captain. Charlie Dawson was barely out of his teens and not much older than son George. He was now leading men to fight for King and country, when he looked as though he should still be at school. He had explained that after Manchester Grammar School he had been to Leeds University followed by Sandhurst. He had just completed the officer training when war was declared and was following in his father's footsteps. A father killed at Cambrai when he was a baby, burnt up in a tank.

After finishing their food, Dawson and Frank returned to speak with the Colonel.

'Colonel, is there any transport we could take?' asked Dawson. 'It would help us enormously.'

The Colonel laughed,

'You must be joking, that's long since gone, I'm afraid, and Shanks' pony is all you have. You can take one rifle with you; we need everything else to try and hold up the Germans.'

'Are you staying?' asked Frank.

'For as long as we can. Hopefully, we can follow and protect your rear.'

'But that means you will almost certainly be captured, or worse.'

'Yes, I know. Now, be on your way.'

Frank hesitated for a moment,

'Sir, I know communications are difficult, but it's important this man knows where I am and what I'm doing.' He handed the Colonel a piece of paper with Ingleby's details and a message in code, 'Perhaps you could possibly get this to him. It tells him I've passed through here and am trying to get home. It would be very helpful – he is the senior intelligence officer I've been working for.'

The Colonel looked blankly at the writing,

'I'll do my best – you have my word. I'll ask my radio operator to try and send it, but communication has been hit and miss.'

Frank saluted and left, comforted that if the message reached London, at least Joan might be told where he was captured or killed, particularly if she still expected him to be in Brussels.

***

Dawson rallied his weary men and briefed them before they set off towards the northwest. They soon came upon a group of locals on the road carrying all they could manage. Some wheeled bicycles laden with sacks of belongings on the handlebars and saddles, whilst others had prams stacked with items, as well as their babies. An elderly couple struggled with a handcart.

Frank spoke with one of the women as they passed,

'Where are you heading for?' he asked.

'We're trying to reach Paris.'

'I hope you make it but if I were you I'd keep heading west. The Germans will want Paris and you might be safer well to the other side.'

She waved as Frank moved off, but as he re-joined the others three planes swept towards them from the west. The soldiers dived onto the grass verge by the side of the road. The lead plane fired its cannons from about a hundred yards away and the bullets spat up the ground towards them. Frank looked up and could see the line would miss them. It passed to his left. The second plane failed to fire at all, but the third had its line spot on.

'Move further to your right,' shouted Frank, as he dived into a ditch. The others did likewise, but one of the men was too slow. The line of bullets hit his legs as he dived. He screamed out in pain.

All three planes were now well past and firing again, straight into the locals further back along the road. Debris was thrown into the air from two explosions.

'Bloody hell!' shouted Frank. He grabbed Tom's arm and pulled him up. 'Come on Tom!' Tom hesitated, more concerned for the badly injured man next to him. Frank pulled him again. Dawson came over and knelt by the man, whose trousers were blood stained and scorched. The bullets had shattered both thighbones.

Frank and Tom sprinted off towards the columns of smoke left by the explosions along the road. When they arrived the scene was one of utter devastation. Dead bodies were scattered everywhere together with body parts with pieces of clothing hanging from them. A baby cried and Tom picked it up. The body of a young woman, probably the child's mother, was a yard away.

A man with a wizened face sat cradling an old woman's head with her lifeless body stretched across his legs. Frank asked him if he was injured, but all the man could say was 'Why? Why?' Another woman walked round in a dazed state. Frank led her to a large, fallen branch. She appeared uninjured. As he spoke to her, he heard the sound of another plane. This one was flying much higher than the others and dived towards them with a high pitched whine. Frank pushed the woman to the ground and fell on top, shielding her. As the plane levelled out, it fired along the middle of the road and the bullet line travelled straight through the old man and his dead wife. Both bodies were thrown up into the air and fell to the road.

The woman with Frank trembled as he held her to him. She was now all that was left of the whole group, apart from the baby. Tom had the little boy in his arms. After a few minutes quiet, Frank helped the woman to her feet. She asked Tom for the baby.

'She's my granddaughter,' she explained to Frank. She walked over to the body of its mother and knelt beside her. She tipped the baby forward, so its head touched the mother's. She handed the baby to Tom and fell onto the body, weeping. After a few minutes, Frank gently lifted the woman away.

She started to head off back towards Poperinghe with the baby in her arms. Frank stopped her.

'Are you sure you want to return to where the fighting is?'

'I might as well and if the Germans shoot me, so be it, but this child will be better off back there now. You carry on.'

She slowly walked off as Frank left to re-join the others.

'The baby's mother is dead over there,' said Frank to Tom, pointing. 'The grandmother's going back and leaving her daughter to rot.'

'That's war for you. Perhaps she didn't want us to be held up knowing we'd offer help.'

'Sad, so sad.'

They jogged back to Dawson who was helping his injured man whilst the others watched. No one else had been injured in the attack. Frank knelt beside Dawson and felt the man's neck for a pulse, but the skin felt cold to the touch.

'He's dead!'

Dawson stood up.

'But he can't be, he spoke to me just after you left. He can't have died because of the bullets in his legs, surely?'

Frank called to Tom,

'Give us a hand here, Tom.' Tom moved forward and together they lifted the body to a sitting position. Frank looked at the man's back and a hole in the tunic where a bullet had passed through. He looked at his front and another small hole where the bullet had exited. Too busy dealing with his legs, none of them had noticed this other wound.

Frank looked up.

'Well bugger me!' said Dawson.

Tom and Frank placed the body face down in the bottom of the ditch whilst Dawson gathered himself. For a few moments, all stood staring at the body. Eventually Dawson spoke.

'He was a gentle man, a decent sort and a good soldier. No family that I know of. We'll have to leave him here like this. We've no way of burying him. Do you think we should at least cover him over with branches, or something like that?'

Tom looked at Frank.

'We should leave him like this,' said Frank. 'The Germans will be through here before you know it and they were pretty good in the last war at burying the dead. Best to leave him with his tag, so they can find him and know who he is.'

They moved off.

'So what happened back there?' asked Dawson.

Tom filled him in with the details.

'You must have witnessed that type of horror in the last war, Frank?' asked Dawson.

'Not really. Being a military policeman, I only saw the other side of the war and more the result of the action rather than the action itself. I did see badly injured men, many maimed for life, and dead bodies on stretchers, but also many broken men with their minds wrecked completely. I hope we've learnt our lesson and deal with these things much better this time round.'

Dawson put his arm round Frank,

'Let's hope so, but I'm sure you didn't see civilians killed like this. Hitler's army are a different kettle of fish and nothing will stand in their way. I'm really worried for those at home once the Germans have a foothold around here because they'll send over the bombers and use gas and all sorts. If most of our men in France remain stuck over here and don't return home, I would not be surprised if our government made a deal with Hitler.'

Leaving his comments to sink in, Dawson walked on ahead.

'Do you think he's right about the gas, Frank?' Tom eventually asked.

'Wouldn't be surprised at all; that's why we were all given masks. Not so sure about a deal with Hitler though. If Churchill has now taken over like we've heard, he'll stand up and fight; he bloody hates the Germans. If the Germans and the Russians remain friends, we've no chance, but if Hitler opts to take on the Russians we might get away with it. After all, the Channel is a bloody great tank trap. But what's important is that as many of us as possible out here actually reach England. I've a nasty feeling we'll be trapped, leaving us no option but to surrender or choose to fight to the last. A bit worrying isn't it?'

Tom pursed his lips, taking it in. Dawson called a halt and the men rested on a grassy bank at a small crossroads. Dawson opened a packet of biscuits picked up in Poperinghe and offered one to Frank as he sat next to him.

'We should have a rest now that it's dark,' said Dawson, 'and move off in a couple of hours, unless Jerry turns up. We need sleep.

Tom and Frank looked at each other and both frowned.

'Captain,' said Tom, 'we must keep going or we'll have no chance whatsoever. Everyone was saying in the town our only chance is to reach the coast and hope for the best. The sooner we're there, the better off we'll be. We must give ourselves the best chance we can and there's no time for sleep.'

Dawson looked at Frank enquiringly.

'He's right, Captain. We have to push ourselves, but let's take half an hour break, eat what we have left and march through the night. The Germans might well stop now it's dark. They probably think they've plenty of time tomorrow to tighten the noose.'

They shared out the food and, after a few minutes, Dawson spoke again.

'I feel I need to sleep, I'm done in – you continue if you like. I'll make my own way and catch up with you at the coast.'

Frank looked at Tom and moved his head to one side as if telling Tom to move away. Tom stood up, crossed the road and sat on the verge opposite.

Frank moved closer to Dawson.

'Charlie, we're not leaving you here. You can take this as an order if you like, but you have to make one last effort – it might be your only chance. The Germans might not stop for the night at all and then you'd have no chance. We'll give it a little while before we must move off, do you understand?'

Dawson said nothing and lay on the grass. Frank joined Tom.

'We'd better keep an eye on the Captain,' Frank whispered. 'He's travelled further and for longer than we have and he's all in. His spirit's wilted and we need to encourage him as best we can.'

Tom nodded and ate the remaining piece of biscuit before he, too, stretched out on the grass. The rest of Dawson's men had decided to move on, leaving the three of them behind.

21

As George came into the living room, he could hear Alvar Liddell's voice on the radio. Joan waved him to be quiet and to sit down. Lizzie was sitting next to her and they were leaning forward towards the wireless. Joan turned up the volume a little. They all sat in silence for several minutes as Liddell brought the grim news of the wholesale retreat of the men in France and Belgium.

'That sounded a bit grim, Mum,' Lizzie eventually said.

'What did I miss, Mum?' George said, as he sat next to Joan on the settee.

'Well, there's talk of Churchill organising every sort of boat to lift the men off the beaches. He has the Navy out there, but they'll need the smaller boats to come nearer to the shore so the men can wade out to them. A call's been made to all boat owners to help out. They're talking about riverboats, fishing boats, the lot. Let's hope your father's near the coast.'

'Don't worry, Mum. You know he can look after himself. I'm sure he'll be here before you know it.'

Joan followed Lizzie to the kitchen. She put her arm across Lizzie's shoulder. Lizzie turned and cuddled into Joan. Nothing was said. A police car pulled up outside and it was Stan Hebden.

'I came to see how you were getting on,' Stan explained once Joan invited him into the sitting room. 'Frank told me when I saw him at the station and then at the football match that he was in France. Did you know that?'

'Yes we did, but he was in Brussels when the Germans went on the move,' said Joan. 'We've had news that he might be in France and is probably on the run. We believe he might stay there as that's what he's been trained for.'

'I guessed it was something like that, Joan, and I did promise Frank I'd keep an eye on you. How are you all coping?'

'Not too bad, thanks, and it's kind of you to come over.'

'It's the least I can do. The news was grim earlier but now there's some hope. Still, Frank might not be trying to get back, as you say.'

'In some ways,' added Joan, 'I hope he is staying behind because those on the beach could be at the mercy of the Germans. If Frank's still in the place in France he was previously, he may well be safer. The trouble is we just don't know; like every other family with men out there.'

'Right, well let's hope he is safe. Do let me know if you hear anything or if you want any help of any kind. You know what I mean?' Stan asked, pointedly.

'Thanks, Stan, we do appreciate it.'

'Oh, by the way, we in the police have been told it is likely families will receive an official telegram from the War Office with the message that their loved one is 'missing' – one will be issued for all out there, so don't be too upset if you get one, although with Frank in intelligence that might not apply. Either way you're not to worry.'

'I know and thanks, Stan. Frank's people said they'd vow to keep us informed, but it must be difficult to get word back with all the confusion.'

***

As Ingleby entered the communications room, one of the operators, wearing headphones called him over and held up a message note.

'Sir, I've just received this brief message for you from the military and it's in code. Do you want me to decipher it?'

'No, it's fine. I can do short ones myself. Thanks.'

Ingleby took the note and read the scribble before handing it back, smiling.

'It's from Shipley and he's on his way to the coast.' Ingleby scanned his large map of Northern France and Belgium and looked for Poperinghe. He measured the distance from Poperinghe to the coast using the gap between his thumb and index finger, before moving to the scale measurement at the bottom of the map. He estimated about twenty-five miles.

***

Whilst the three men rested for almost an hour, several disparate groups of soldiers passed by, all looking bedraggled and exhausted. They confirmed that

Poperinghe was now in German hands. What had happened to the Colonel and his men, left behind there? What fate had befallen the grandmother with the baby? Frank felt for them.

The road behind them now appeared clear. Dawson was still asleep and Tom was stretched out with his hands behind his head.

'I'm climbing up the hill here to see if I can see any Germans,' said Frank. 'Wake up the Captain and start walking; I'll catch you up.'

It was a gentle slope up to the wooded crest of the rising ground. From the top Frank had a view of several miles and there was enough moonlight to scan the fields in front of him. At first he could see nothing before a cloud of dust appeared on the furthermost hill. Could it be British troops from Poperinghe, or was it the Germans? When tanks appeared over the hill and spread out in a line almost a mile in width, he knew they were most definitely German panzers.

Frank ran diagonally across a field of sprouting corn to catch up with the others. They heard him call out and stopped. When he reached them he stood breathless with his hands on his hips and gulping in air.

Tom rested his hand on Frank's shoulder.

'Well, did you see anything?'

Frank held his hand up as if to say, 'wait a minute' and Dawson handed him a water bottle. After a mouthful he gasped,

'God, I'm out of condition! The German tanks are about three to four miles away and moving fast, they're fanned out across the fields and not simply keeping to the roads. There's no infantry as far as I could see and this bears out what you said, Captain. If the tanks supported by artillery are the spearhead, it might be a good thing. If they wait for infantry support, it might buy us valuable time.'

'We'd better move on quickly to make the most of it,' said Dawson.

They jogged off and eventually caught up with the group who had passed by earlier. Having given them the news about the German advance, Dawson offered to take charge of this larger body of about thirty men. No one objected and they continued at a good pace, but after more than hour, the men were flagging and desperate for rest. It was now dark. Dawson was feeling as bad as anyone. He stopped to let the rest of men pass and waited for Frank, who was at the rear.

Before Dawson could say anything, Frank spoke,

'We should stop, Charlie, and hope the Germans have. I can't see any lights behind us. There's no moonlight now with this cloud cover, perhaps they are definitely waiting for their main force.'

'I was thinking the same. Pull over men!' Dawson shouted. They didn't need telling twice and fell onto the grass beside the road.

Frank climbed on top of a dry-stone wall to look over the hedgerows.

'Can you see anything?' asked Dawson.

'Just smoke with the occasional flash of flame and it's probably shelling. It seems to be coming from the east and, if what we heard is right, the Germans are circling round us.'

Dawson went over to talk to the rest.

'Men, we think the Germans have slowed behind us, but they're shelling up ahead, not close to here at present but it looks like we have no time to lose. Our only hope is the coast and, although we're all tired, we must keep going. Take another fifteen minutes then we must set off again.'

Later during the night, other French and British soldiers joined them at every road junction with some from across the fields. This larger column headed towards the black smoke rising in the distance.

By first light, many had decided to stop and rest by the roadside, but others struggled on. Dawson was completely done in. Frank and Tom took turns to give him support by letting him put his arm across their shoulders. Progress slowed to little more than a crawl. All they had left to nourish them was putrid water secured from ditches and were desperate for food and a decent drink. Ahead, they could see the outskirts of a large town. Shortly after, they came upon a broken concrete post and next to it a 'Dunkerque' sign lying in the road. A hundred yards beyond that stood a sandbagged machine gun post occupied by a fully armed unit. A Lieutenant there shouted over,

'Keep to this road and don't stop. You'll eventually reach the beach.'

They waved and moved on.

***

Not long after they had passed the machine gun post, Dawson stopped.

'I'm sorry,' he said, wearily. 'I've had it. Leave me. You go on, I'm holding you back.' Suddenly, he collapsed, but Tom caught him before he hit the ground.

'Let's put him over there,' said Tom pointing to a pile of rubble where a house once stood. They laid him on the ground as gently as they could.

Dawson reached for his water bottle attached to his belt. Frank took it from him and shook it. He opened it, put the spout to Dawson's mouth and gently poured the water onto the dry and cracked lips. Dawson licked the moisture but closed his eyes again.

'Charlie, come on,' encouraged Frank. 'There's only a short distance left now, let's have one last effort.'

Dawson shook his head which then drooped forward and to one side. He was unconscious again. Tom knelt, took hold of Dawson's arm and pulled him up into a sitting position.

'Come on, Frank, help lift him up onto my back and I'll carry him. It'll help my training for the new cricket season.'

Frank laughed and lifted Dawson, who was now in a crouched position. Tom stood in front with his back to him. Frank helped him force the Captain's legs apart. Tom moved backwards between them and, with a grunt, lifted Dawson up into a piggyback. Balancing himself, he manoeuvred Dawson's body as comfortably as he could and started off. Frank picked up the water bottle and shook it again. It was now empty and he tossed it away onto the rubble, but thought better of it and retrieved it in case if they found any fresh water up ahead.

Tom was coping well with his passenger. The Captain was not heavily built and Tom had strong shoulders, built up over his time at Warrington playing rugby and bowling for Lancashire Seconds for most of the past three summers. 1940 was to have been his breakthrough year for the county side, but that was now all on hold. Simple survival was now all that mattered.

Dunkirk was badly battered from the shelling with only a few buildings undamaged. Very few locals remained, but soldiers were everywhere with most, including the French in their separate groups, heading towards the beach. They were a mix from all different parts of the services, their faces mostly dirty and their hair matted; very few wore hats or helmets. No one seemed to have a weapon. All the injured, many on stretchers, had been left together outside a shop, now being used as a temporary aid post.

In the middle of all this chaos, Frank saw a bristling Sergeant Major still looking immaculate amongst the rabble of soldiers. He stood in the middle of a crossroads that only a few weeks before would have been a busy junction. Now it was strewn with bricks and concrete with a large shell hole, to the right of which the Sergeant Major continuously barked out the same order.

'French to that road there,' he said pointing. 'British to the right and head for the beach to await further orders.'

Tom walked past still carrying the Captain and the Sergeant Major came over,

'What's wrong with 'im?' he barked.

'Don't know, Sarge, he collapsed earlier.'

'Bloody officers, as weak as my wife's tea.'

'How much further is the beach?' asked Tom.

'You've only a couple of hundred yards more, son. Well done, now move along, there's a good lad.'

Frank was a few yards behind and, seeing his uniform, the Sergeant Major gave an exaggerated salute that Frank routinely acknowledged.

'What's the latest, Sergeant Major, do you know anything of what's happening?'

'It's bloody chaos, sir, if you'll excuse my French. These big ships are offshore and they look like the Navy, but they've stopped. We've heard they might send the smaller ships to the mole that juts out into the sea. The waiting men are sitting ducks for the Jerry planes and many have bought it already. Bloody awful, at times it is. You wait until you see the beach, seen nothing like it in all me life.'

He turned away and shouted at another group of French soldiers who gesticulated indignantly.

'Who are you with, sir, you know, regiment and that?'

'Ah, don't be fooled by the uniform, it belonged to someone else. I was over here working with Intelligence and became caught up in all this. What about you?'

'I'm Essex, but attached to the Royal Engineers. I was called up as a reservist. I was out here in the last war.'

'So was I. It looks like this might be over before Christmas the way things are developing. Mind you, we said that in 1914.'

'You're ...' the Sergeant Major broke away shouting this time at British soldiers,

'Keep going that way.' He pointed them towards the beach before turning back to Frank. 'Sorry sir. Yes, you're probably right.'

'Well, I hope you come through this and we all get away.' Frank moved off, but turned and asked,

'By the way, what's your name?'

'Pettit, sir.'

'And where do your family live?'

'Chelmsford, we run a sweet shop. If you're in that neck of the woods, tell 'em you saw me, in case I don't make it. You can't miss the shop in the middle of the town.'

'You'll reach home if I do. I live in Roxwell and used to be a policeman in Chelmsford. I know your shop. Small world, isn't it? We ought to meet up for a drink. Perhaps I'll see you in The Saracen's Head in a couple of weeks.'

'I hope so, sir, but I prefer The Royal Steamer, if you don't mind.' They both laughed.

Frank returned to Tom struggling with Dawson. As Frank tried to help, a large explosion threw up pieces of the road less than fifty yards ahead.

The force of the blast knocked them to the ground causing Dawson to wake up.

'What the –?' he asked.

'Artillery shells and from the south at a guess because they're not from any planes.' They all looked up at the sky. Two more explosions followed a little further away.

'Things are about to become mighty uncomfortable,' added Frank.

Tom stood with Dawson's arm around his shoulder and Frank supported the other arm to enable Dawson to swing between them with his toes just scraping the ground. The shelling stopped as they moved off towards the sea. The road reached the sand dunes skirting the beach and turned right to follow the line of the sea, but a well-worn path weaved through the dunes and they followed that.

At the top of a rise in the sand, the whole of the beach was in view.

'Good grief!' shouted Tom as he released Dawson's arm. The Captain, now fully conscious, sank to his knees.

'Can you believe that?' muttered Frank as he tried to lift Dawson to his feet, but was waved away.

Before them was a sight so startling it was almost like a mirage. As far as the eye could see thousands of men were crowded to the right and left along the beach, sitting in small groups. With the tide in, the beach had become much smaller and the men more cramped together.

Burnt out wrecks of army vehicles were now half submerged in the waves. At the top of the beach were makeshift graves with improvised crosses stuck in the sand. A few men were digging new graves next to a pile of bodies.

'There must be more than a hundred thousand men here,' said Dawson.

'At least that, probably nearer two hundred,' added Frank.

'Where in God's name have they all come from?' said Dawson rising to his feet and brushing the sand from his trousers. 'How on earth will we get away from here, with this many? Look at the French over there.'

The other two looked to their left. A large group of men in distinctive blue uniforms sat around or stretched out asleep resting their heads on other's bodies, instead of in the sand.

Tom scanned the horizon.

'Look out there, they look like battleships or cruisers.'

Frank and the Dawson shielded their eyes against the bright sunshine.

'Well, we were told they would come,' said Dawson, 'but I don't see how on earth they'll reach us. It'll take a week to clear these beaches and the Germans'll probably be here by tomorrow.' He looked despondent.

A Major, sitting in front of them, stood up and came over. As he approached, they all stood more upright and saluted.

'At ease men, there's no such ceremony here, we're all in the same boat.' He laughed as he realised what he had said. 'Well, we're not in any boat yet, of course.'

The other three smiled.

'How far away are the Germans from here?' asked the Major. 'Did you see them?'

'I doubt they're more than five miles away,' said Frank, 'and moving fast. Have you any idea if the ships are coming in? It'll take forever to lift all these men off this beach; we don't stand a chance do we?'

'It would seem we might not,' said the Major, 'but all I know is a large number of our troops have been ordered to stay and form a defence around Dunkirk. In reality, fight to the last man, poor blighters, but that might all be a waste of time, unless somehow we can get out to those ships. We just hope we are given the chance.'

'Aren't we sitting ducks here, sir?' asked Tom.

'Yes, we are and we're losing men every day up and down the beach. The Stukas strafe us continually, but, now the Navy's arrived, perhaps they'll target them rather than us. We can only hope.'

'Any advice for us?' Dawson asked.

'Yes, stay up here in the dunes because, once the bloody *Luftwaffe* start bombing, you'll want as much protection as you can. Also, the sand in the dunes softens the effect of the explosion and the missiles have been known to bury themselves and not explode at all. Many of the men bury their heads in the sand when these Stukas come over. They have these siren things on their wings and are bloody deafening. With your head in the sand it might also not be blown off.'

'Sounds wonderful!' said Frank ironically. 'Is there any food at all? I can smell cooking.'

'It's only what the men have brought with them and some have tried fishing in the shallows when the tide's been in, but the fish appear to have gone AWOL. We have food over here and can spare a little for you. It's not much, but you're welcome to it. It only needs to last for a day or so because, after that, we'll either be on one of those ships or eating *sauerkraut.'*

As the Major led them to his group the familiar screeching sound of German planes headed in their direction. Like flies rising off a carcass, men on the beach rose and headed to the dunes. Five Stukas came along the shoreline, low. The noise was deafening. Frank put hands over his ears as he fell with the others to the ground. The first two planes fired several rounds towards the fleeing men and the other three planes dropped their bombs along the beach. Only one landed in amongst the men, but this left at least a dozen causalities prostrate on the sand.

Just as fast as the planes arrived, they were gone again. The Major stood up,

'You'll become used to that,' he explained. 'It happens two or three times a day. The dead then have to be buried and the injured patched up as best we can. Many won't make it, I'm afraid. As I said, we really want the air attacks to be directed at those ships out there, but the trouble with that is the ships could turn tail and head home without us.'

'I bloody hope not!' said Tom.

'Rest with my chaps here,' the Major continued. 'Have some food. It won't be much but it'll help and we do have water.'

A Corporal brought a small tin with 'Scotch Mutton' stamped on its lid. It was open and he gave them a penknife to scoop out the jellied meat. Each of them took a chunk and it was soon gone. They swigged from a water bottle to wash down the mutton, but the salty meat only served to make them feel even thirstier and just as hungry.

22

Johnny Stevenson knew he was late and would incur the wrath of Captain Sawbarn – and not for the first time. He freewheeled down the slipway and along the small quay. He leant his bicycle against a 'for hire' sign and ran up the gangway to the deck. Unusually, no one was working there. The door to the small wooden office on the quay opened and the Captain appeared,

'Come with me to the store shed, Johnny,' he shouted over. 'I need to speak to you and the crew; they're already there.'

Johnny ran down the gangway and followed Sawbarn to join the other five members of the Southend Arcadian crew in the store further along the quay. Inside, Sawbarn stood in front of his men and pulled a letter from his pocket.

'You've all heard about our boys stuck on or near the beaches in France,' he announced, waving a piece of paper, 'Well, we have to get them off and the Navy needs ships like Arcadian to sail in closer to the beaches and use our small lifeboat if we have to. An Admiralty man'll turn up this morning and tell us what he expects.' He strained his eyes to read from the letter in his hand. 'It's a Lieutenant Horton and he'll command us, although I'll do the usual when we're at sea. Now, I can't make you come, but you might want to do your bit as, apart from Johnny, you're past active service and Johnny'll have to wait at least a year or more. I'll give you all an hour to go home and think about it. Talk to your families if you can. Johnny, you'll have to ask your mother to write a note to give you permission and, by the time you all return, this Horton chap'll be here and we'll be leaving. Off you go. You'll be away for a few days.'

Johnny was excited. He had worked on Arcadian in his summer holidays for the last three years. He had decided to stay on and work as part of the full time crew until his eighteenth birthday when he would join up, but this could not come soon enough, so he felt delighted to have this earlier opportunity to do something for his country. He cycled home as fast as he could. He was already nearly six feet tall, with strong shoulders built up from his swimming prowess at junior county level. He also enjoyed athletics and was a strong miler. He was not short of female admirers in the town, with his tightly curled black hair, worn quite long compared with most.

When he arrived home he was disappointed his mother was not there. He continued on into the town centre to look for her. The RAF had already posted his father to India the year before. Shoeburyness was never that busy at the best of times and he soon found his mother in The Maypole buying groceries. He blurted out what the Captain had said.

'I'm not sure, Johnny, what with your father being away. They can't make you, can they? You're far too young and it'll be dangerous. The captain'll have plenty without you.'

'But Mum, they're all old fogies. When we near the beaches, we'll need swimmers and maybe rowers. Those old boys will be useless for that. Come on, Mum, please!'

All the way to their house, Johnny pleaded with her and he could tell she was softening.

'Dad would want me to. They said on the radio last night that there's thousands trapped. Mum, they need our help. I can be valuable what with my age and everything; you must see that?'

'Your Dad might have agreed, but you know how I worry. One's bad enough and now there would be you too.' She hesitated. Johnny pleaded with his eyes.

'All right, you can go, but for goodness sake be careful.'

Johnny found a piece of paper and a pencil. Mrs Stevenson wrote a few appropriate words and signed it. She gave him one final hug and a kiss. He felt a little embarrassed, but knew how much she cared.

Within minutes, Johnny was on the quay. All the crew were there and keen to get underway. An officer in naval uniform stood next to Sawbarn. They were supervising the loading of medical supplies from an open truck.

Johnny sought out Sawbarn.

'This is from me mum.' He handed over the note and went to join the rest of the crew. Sawbarn stuffed the note in his pocket without looking at it and called Johnny back,

'One moment, Johnny, this is Lieutenant Horton who I mentioned earlier. You must call him, sir. Right?'

'Sir,' said Johnny, acknowledging Horton with a half salute.

'Johnny,' said Horton, saluting in return and smiling.

Within fifteen minutes Arcadian was underway. The smoke billowed from her twin funnels as she chugged out along the Thames Estuary, heading towards the northeast corner of Kent. For fifteen years this little steamer had ferried holidaymakers on day trips around the mouth of Estuary, stopping off at Southend, Sheerness, Margate and other places along the Essex and Kent coastlines. Whilst 1939 had been one of the boat's busiest years, in 1940 there had been little demand. The Thames Estuary was on the flight path into London for the German bombers and somewhere best to avoid, certainly when it came to holidays. Arcadian had, instead, been used for ferrying various war materials from the Port of London and, in particular, concrete slabs for building coastal invasion defences and pillboxes.

Sawbarn was at the helm, whistling. At last he had duties to break the tedium of those regular trips along the Thames, day after day. Now he felt he was taking his little boat on her greatest adventure. Horton was standing next to him.

'Do you know what, Lieutenant?' said Sawbarn, wistfully. 'This is what it must have been like joining up with the bloody Spanish Armada, except we're sailing the other way.'

'Well, almost!' Horton laughed. 'It might look like it, when we meet up with the other boats.'

As they rounded the northeast headland of Kent, Johnny could see Margate pier and, behind that, Dreamland Park where he had spent many happy hours during past family holidays. With money tight for his parents, a short trip on the Royal Sovereign across the Thames Estuary was all they could afford, but a week staying at the same hotel in Cliftonville had provided the best times of Johnny's early years. From this distance, and on such a cloudy, damp day, Margate now looked forlorn and drab. The beach was empty and with the tide out the sand was covered with seaweed making it look more like a field of vegetables than a sandy beach where he and his dad had played endless games of cricket. The Dreamland amusement park was closed with the Army rumoured to be moving in. For Johnny it might never be the same there again.

Once round the headland, they were into a strong south-westerly. The small steamer was buffeted by the waves with its three feet of draft not providing much stability.

Lieutenant Horton, looking pale, left the bridge for his bunk. Johnny felt a twinge of seasickness after he saw two of the crew leaning over the rail to deposit their last meal into the waves. Sawbarn shouted at them,

'Call yourselves sailors? This is just a slight swell. Wait until we're out another few miles.'

Out of the murk ahead, three small boats appeared. All Arcadian's crew stood by the rail and watched them sail past. They were full of soldiers, but not one of them acknowledged Arcadian's men. The only sound was the throb of the ships' engines. Each captain saluted towards Sawbarn, but that was all. Johnny had to turn away. Many of the men were badly injured; the rest looked beaten, their eyes sunken and dark.

Another boat appeared full of Frenchmen who waved in unison as Arcadian motored by. Towards France, Johnny could see the Navy's big ships moving slowly, but soon realised they were just circling. Their guns fired intermittently towards the coast with the smaller guns directing their fire at the frequent planes flying overhead. Even from this distance, Arcadian's crew could hear the noisy whine from the planes as they swooped on the fleet before firing at will. Too often the ships were being hit and many had smoke billowing from their decks.

The sea was now much calmer. Horton returned to the bridge and asked Sawbarn to heave to now they were ten miles off the French coast. Horton proceeded to speak constantly into the wireless he had brought with him and

Johnny could hear the crackle of the reply, but not make out what was being said.

As they waited, the crew watched more of the skirmishing between the large ships and the menacing planes.

'If it was not so worrying, it would actually be entertaining,' said Horton to Sawbarn.

The action came a little closer. A small steamer, similar in size to Arcadian, came towards them. It was about a mile away when a lone Stuka fired on her. Johnny and the rest of the crew raced to their bow. They could see men lining the steamer's rails looking upwards, but then the boat blew up. The plane pulled away avoiding the blast and headed straight towards Arcadian. Her crew threw themselves to the deck. After another explosion well to their left, the plane banked before heading off towards the French coast. When they looked over the rail, there was no sign of the steamer, just debris floating on the sea.

The Lieutenant ordered Sawbarn to look for any survivors. Nothing but flotsam was being pitched about on the swell along with a large black patch of oil. Bodies and parts of bodies were floating over a wider area, but Arcadian's crew could not find a single survivor despite a search lasting for over an hour. Eventually, the Lieutenant told his men to have a hot drink and a snack. As the crew arrived in the mess, the cook already had the tea and cakes set out on the small table. The men, tired from their work, collapsed into the chairs. No one said a word.

Johnny looked round at the older men. Some were in action in the last war and the sights they had witnessed today might have been similar to what they'd seen before, but they still looked shocked. The weather-beaten faces looked pale as they sat and drank their mugs of tea.

***

Joan returned home from picking up a few items from the village and was emptying her shopping bag. Lizzie appeared through the door from the garden and without saying a word helped her mother put away the various items. Joan glanced out of the front window and saw the telegram boy pull up by the gate.

He stood his bicycle against the hedge, opened the squeaky catch and came towards the front door.

Joan felt a sickening feeling in her stomach and she gasped out loud,

'Oh God, no!'

Lizzie turned around and was about to say, 'What is it?' but her mother was already in the hall and opening the door.

'Hello Harry, how's your mother? Has she heard from your father lately?' she said, nervously hiding her concern.

'She's fine, thanks, Mrs Shipley, and we had a letter from him just the other day. He's on a minesweeper somewhere.'

The boy said nothing more, but smiled, handed over the telegram and left.

'Give your mother my best wishes and tell her I'll see her at the W.I. on Wednesday,' Joan shouted after him and he waved his hand in acknowledgement.

Joan stood at the door watching him disappear from view. Her hands were shaking and her mouth had gone dry. She looked at the small envelope, not daring to open it. Lizzie was now at her side, but said nothing. Joan noticed that this looked like an ordinary telegram and not what she imagined one would look like if it had come from the War Office or the Military or whoever sent the dreaded things.

She used her forefinger to slit the envelope. Lizzie caught hold of her mother's elbow and squeezed. Joan stopped for a moment, still not really wanting to open it. Finally, she pulled out the small piece of paper and read the few words.

FRANK ON WAY TO FRENCH COAST STOP MORE NEWS TO FOLLOW STOP INGLEBY

She held the paper to her chest, but was still trembling.

'I imagined that was to tell us your father was...'

'Yes I know. I felt the same and wouldn't want to experience that again.'

They both smiled a little nervously. George came through from his bedroom looking as if he had just woken up.

'What's up? Who was that at the door?'

Joan passed him the telegram from the pocket of her apron.

'Well, that's good news isn't it, Mum?'

'That news has to be a few days old,' said Lizzie, 'but, at least, we know he's alive and he must have reached those beaches where all the other men are.'

Joan stood in front of Frank's photograph on the mantelpiece.

'Anything could have happened since that message was sent from France,' said Joan glumly, with her back to the children. 'The news this morning is that the men are coming off the beaches and piling into small boats. It will take days to have them all off. The Germans are still advancing and very close to the coast by all accounts. Who knows what's happening right now. We'll just have to hope for the best, won't we?'

***

Dawson took Frank to one side as they stood at the edge of the beach where the dunes started.

'I'm sorry I simply flaked out back there in the town. It hit me totally without warning and I just don't know what came over me.'

'Don't worry about it, Charlie, you've been on the move for days without much sleep, food or even a hot drink and you're bound to suffer; it affects us all in different ways. Why not get your head down and sleep. You'll feel better in the morning. Tomorrow we'll have to find out when we might be able to leave, but it's bloody chaos out there.' He pointed towards the crowded beach. 'God knows if it'll ever happen.'

They walked down to the shallows. The tide was on its way out and small boats coming in against it would have difficulty, even if the men could walk out a reasonable distance.

'Have you any young lady at home waiting for you, Charlie?'

'Not really – just my mother. I've not had much time for girls. One or two at university but nothing serious. What about you?'

Frank told him about Marie, Joan and the children.

'It must be awful for those at home,' Frank added. 'Look at the last war. Your family experienced it with your father, as did millions of others. Closer to home, I have to face my boss when I arrive in England. That woman agent I told you about was married to him. No one knew and I only found out by accident. This chap might have received word of her death, I don't know. But it might be down to me to tell him and I'm not looking forward to it; not one little bit. He has had heart attacks in the past and this news won't help his condition, will it?'

'You receive training for dealing with that sort of news nowadays at Sandhurst and what to put in letters. Did you have anything like that in the last war?'

'No, Charlie. I was an NCO and, as far as I know, the officers received nothing like that. Have you many letters to write when we return? There's that chap back on the road for one.'

'I have three, but possibly more of my original squad are dead. I have no idea what's happened to them or where they are and I suppose, like us, they'll be posted missing. I keep those I know about in this little black book.' Dawson pulled a leather bound pocket book from his tunic. 'I've written a little bit about each and how they died. If anything happens to me, make sure you pass this on, won't you.'

'I will, Charlie, but we'll be fine now, you'll see.'

'Don't worry too much about telling your boss. He must have known his wife would be in danger of being killed, especially if she were an agent in a foreign country. Spies are shot – no questions asked, surely?'

'Yes, I know. We have other agents out here and they should have passed on the news when they heard of the atrocity. I do feel partly responsible because my French friend dropped us in the mire but then ... that's war.'

They were now with Tom. Dawson sat next to him,

'Thanks for carrying me, Tom; it was very kind of you. Good job I've lost weight since I've been out here, otherwise you would have found it more of a struggle. No doubt all that power work you must do for your rugby and cricket has strengthened you up. But thanks again.' Dawson held out his hand and Tom shook it.

Frank stood above them and looked along the beach. It was a warm evening for late May, but it would become colder later. A group to his left had a lit a fire and called him over. Frank tapped Tom on the shoulder and beckoned him to follow. They left Dawson curled up on the sand, fast asleep.

All along the beach similar small fires glowed in the gathering darkness. Men sat round in their groups, their faces occasionally lit up by a sudden flame. Some were singing softly, not joyful songs but sombre ones: to his left Frank could hear 'Abide With Me'. It was a surreal image and seemed out of place with the war close by.

As Tom and Frank settled on the sand, they could see the Major working his way towards them, talking to each group in turn.

'I want you all to make sure you split into even smaller groups and spread yourselves more thinly along the beach,' he told Frank. 'This will present less of a target for the planes and from any shelling from inland. I know many will ignore what I say, but I'd like you to have the men do what I ask, it makes sense. We're not putting any more men out along the mole because it's too dangerous and they've been too much of an easy target. Everyone from now on will have to be taken from the beach. There's a meeting of all the officers over by that burnt out jeep at 0600.'

Frank slept fitfully and woke up Dawson just ahead of the meeting. They joined a large group of officers on the edge of the dunes. Colonel Addison stood on the jeep and addressed them all.

'I cannot stress strongly enough,' he said, quietly, 'the importance of taking these men home – well, as many as possible. It could be vital for the country enabling us to re-group, return stronger and prepared. The German advance has inexplicably slowed. It is too early to say if it's because of the bravery and resistance from those men left behind to fight it out or for another reason. Perhaps Jerry's waiting for their infantry, as many of you suspect. Our boys on the edge of the town will give them hell, that's for sure, and we have to make the most of it here on the beach. Good luck and I hope to see you all in Blighty!'

Frank returned to his group and lay on his side, propping himself up on one elbow. He stared at the sand and sifted some through his fingers. Dawson was now asleep next to him. Frank worried for Joan and how she was now feeling, probably like any of the wives and mothers of the men spread out before him. He hoped George and Lizzie would be strong for her if he failed to make it home. Perhaps he should stay and continue the work he had been sent here to carry out. What would Ingleby want? Of course, he would be of no use if in German hands or in a prison camp on the other side of Europe. Perhaps he should have stayed around Sedan and waited for things to calm down after the shooting and carried on organising the resistance. Inwardly he knew he should try for home, perhaps to return to France when everything was somewhat clearer. Falling onto the sand, he shut his eyes. He was woken by the sound of approaching aircraft. The tide had come in and the beach looked more crowded than before,

'So much for spreading the men out as the Colonel wanted!' Frank said to Dawson.

The three planes swooped with their awful noise and opened fire, the bullets kicking up the sand along the beach in a straight line. Most men held their nerve and simply moved out of the way of the line of bullets, but others ran for the extra protection of the dunes. Due to the crowding, the men could do little in some places to avoid the bullets. Many were hit and their screams could be heard above the noise of the planes.

The wounded were attended to and the dead carried to where men were already digging a mass grave using shovels or their bare hands in the fine sand. Frank counted seventeen bodies dropped into the small trench and covered with sand. Crosses, already prepared, were pushed into the sand. A padre spoke a few words and made the sign of the cross before collecting the names of the dead for passing to Colonel Addison.

Frank's group sat in a circle and pooled their food and drink before sharing it out. They had plenty of water, but little to satisfy their hunger. Suddenly, they heard another attack coming from the east and out of the sun. The men shielded their eyes to see how many planes this time, but it was difficult to make out anything. Sand was being thrown up as explosions came along the beach towards them.

Tom, Frank and Dawson stood up and headed further up into the dunes. Dawson tripped and fell, ten yards behind the other two. Sand flew in the air from an explosion behind him. Tom and Frank were thrown off their feet by the force of the blast. As they recovered their senses they looked for Dawson. He had been blown several yards from where he had tripped, but his body was motionless. Frank ran over.

'Charlie! Charlie?'

He rolled Dawson over. The Captain's eyes were fixed and staring. Frank knelt and felt for a pulse. Tom crawled over to help, but Frank said,

'He's dead.' He closed Dawson's eyes.

Tom collected two shovels and threw one at Frank. Without a word between them, they dug a shallow grave. Frank took the black book from Dawson's tunic pocket before they lowered him into the hole. Tom found a piece of chalk and a large piece of wood. He wrote out Dawson's rank and name then stuck the wood into the sand next to the grave.

Later, Frank passed the book and the rest of Dawson's possessions to the Colonel. When the padre came by, they asked him to bless the grave. He told them the last bombing had killed more than a dozen men on this part of the beach alone and fifty or so had been seriously injured.

***

Johnny managed to sleep during the night ahead of his two-hour watch at dawn. As a weak sun rose behind Arcadian, Lieutenant Horton came up from his quarters and looked out towards the French coast. The *Luftwaffe* had taken the rest of the night off due to the low cloud cover.

Horton stood on the bridge next to Johnny and spoke into the wireless set. He asked for the day's orders. Johnny could not hear the reply as Horton was wearing headphones. Removing them, Horton turned to Johnny.

'We're moving in today. Please ask the Captain to assemble the crew.'

Minutes later, Horton stood on deck to address the men.

'Today is our big day – we're going in. You see that large battleship to the right?' All the men turned and looked at the large grey shape. 'Well,' Horton continued, 'I'm receiving my orders from her. The big ships cannot sail anywhere near the shore; consequently, they are relying on us to move in closer, pick up as many as we can and return home. They will, however, provide fire support.' He paused as several large explosions took place towards the shore. The planes responsible headed towards them but suddenly spiralled away, heading off to the west. Horton spoke again,

'It looks like those poor devils on the beach have copped another load. They really are sitting ducks. The Navy believe we've two days and no more. With the tide now receding, even we cannot get that close to the shore, which means we'll have to send in our lifeboat. Johnny, you're by far the fittest and I want you to go in on your own. That way we can crowd as many of the men into the boat as possible. Can you handle that?'

'I'm sure I can, sir. I've rowed before and know how to manoeuvre a small boat. Would it not be easier if I leave at the point the tide turns? The Captain will be able to edge closer in, the tide'll help me drift in and the soldiers can help me row out against it.'

Horton looked at Sawbarn who nodded.

'Good idea, son,' said Horton. 'We'll head off now to the reference point I've been given. Captain, what time will the tide start in?'

Sawbarn scratched his chin, 'About 1400.'

'So, men, at 1400 we'll be ready for action.' Horton briefed the crew about where they should put the men as they came aboard and particularly the injured. The cook was given the responsibility of looking after the injured in the galley area of which one of the crew said, 'They'll be fine as long as he doesn't give them any of his food.'

Horton joined in the laughter.

'Right,' he said, seriously, 'those not on watch must rest; it could be a while before you have another chance. We'll rotate the watch every two hours, but once we have the men aboard it'll be all hands on deck.'

By 1300 they were in position; they would move in a little closer at 1400 and send Johnny off. The lifeboat was designed to hold no more than eight people, but now would be expected to carry nearly twice that number.

***

Tom had become morose after they buried Dawson. He sat leaning against a tuft of thick, tall grass in the dunes staring at his feet and idly played with the sand. Frank decided to leave him in his own world. Later he found him asleep.

Frank had been considering whether to reveal his true identity to Colonel Addison. If the Colonel made it home and he did not at least Ingleby would receive word, yet without knowing if Frank were alive or dead. Frank found Addison drinking a cup of tea in his makeshift command post and told him the story of his past few months.

'I know Commander Ingleby,' said Addison. 'We spent time training together in the early thirties. I heard he was with Intelligence. Always going places he was. You've been through a nasty business losing your partner like that, let down ... but that's the nature of your sort of work, I guess, with so many imponderables and improbables and you can't trust anyone.'

'Yes, that's true. I've learnt that very, very quickly!'

'Now that I know your true rank and background,' Addison continued, 'there's something I want you to do for me. I've just heard our sector is targeted for evacuation from the beach tomorrow, God willing, and I want you to remain here to the last to ensure an orderly evacuation. I shall be leaving early on, not through choice, but because it's an order. Should the worst happen and you're captured, you've been trained to deal with difficult situations. You'll cope better than most and you'll have the wherewithal to survive or perhaps escape. Sorry, but I hope you understand!'

Frank smiled at the backhanded compliment, but could see the logic. Later, Addison outlined the plan of evacuation to all the other officers, including the

French. He revealed Frank's true rank, but nothing more. He told each officer to take charge of a group. Frank was to coordinate the evacuation, with his group the last to leave.

Once the briefing was over, Frank returned to where Tom still slept. Just as the light faded completely, a large group of men swarmed onto the beach, bursting through the dunes and tripping over the men sleeping there.

Frank immediately recognised a familiar face it was the Sergeant Major they'd encountered in the town at the crossroads. Frank called out,

'Sergeant Major Pettit ... what are you doing here?'

Pettit walked over and saluted.

'The Germans have come to a complete halt outside the town. An officer told us to come down onto the beach, as we had no German advance to stop.'

He looked over Frank's shoulder at the beach.

'I guess we'll stand a better chance here, although this doesn't look like much fun either. Are we likely to get off?'

'We're hoping to leave tomorrow. You were right in what you told us in the town, small boats are coming inshore to pick us up and take us out to the larger ships further out to sea, but we're constantly being strafed. No sign of the R.A.F., perhaps they're engaged elsewhere. In the last hour or so, the Germans have been shelling us from those static positions they've taken up outside the town. That's probably their plan; shell us into submission and pick us off rather than lose too many troops trying to reach us.'

Frank sat down. Pettit's men were now in a group behind him.

'Sergeant Major, tell your men to find space here and join us, but it might mean you're last off. Where are your officers? I'd better make myself known.'

'They've stayed behind and put me in charge of these boys. Bloody brave them officers ... or stupid, depending on your point of view.'

Frank shrugged in agreement.

Pettit continued, 'Are your two friends still here with you?'

'No, the Captain bought it in an air attack. Tom Bramhill's a bit upset and I've left him to sleep it off. He's over there,' said Frank pointing at the curled up body, half buried in the sand.

'I'm sorry to hear that, what a bugger!' Both men fell quiet until Pettit changed the subject.

'We managed to bring some food with us and I'll ask my lads to distribute it amongst the men around here.'

Frank stood up and tapped Pettit on his shoulder.

'Good man.'

He ambled to the water's edge, alone. Two miles or so along the beach men were wading out to the small boats, many only rowing boats. With no recent air strikes, it was the right time to be leaving. He was running through in his mind what needed to be done the next day. The men would have to be orderly, but they were desperate and might be difficult to control. He would need strong leaders like Pettit to help and, in order to give everyone the best chance he decided he would stop the men wading out haphazardly to the nearest boat.

For the rest of the day all remained quiet and the men settled down to another cold night in the dunes.

A watery sun appeared to the east, Frank stood in the shallows washing his face. A heavy mist hung low over this part of the beach reducing the visibility to no more than a hundred yards close to the ground. If it did not lift, no one was going anywhere, but with the sun rising he hoped the mist might be burnt away. Beyond the gloom booming anti-aircraft guns started firing followed by the chatter of aircraft cannons. The attack sounded unrelenting and Frank recoiled when one large explosion sent flames soaring above the mist. It was a long way off, but he assumed it was a direct hit on one of the ships.

The mist began to lift as a breeze sprung up. Frank stood in amazement at the sight out to sea. Across the near horizon was a flotilla of small craft heading straight towards him.

He ran up the beach shouting out the news. Slowly the sleeping men rose to their feet and moved to the water's edge. Officers were shouting at them to organise themselves into small groups. Frank's formed up like the rest, despite expecting to be the last to leave.

Men further along the beach broke ranks and ran out into the sea towards the incoming boats. An officer shouted for them to stop, but few took any notice. He fired his pistol over their heads and those in the water stopped and returned to the beach.

Frank was handing out orders when several Stukas dived down from immediately above them. The whine of their sirens sounded even louder in the morning quiet.

The men ran for the cover of the dunes, but some fell to the damp sand, burying their heads and as much of their bodies as they could. As the planes levelled out, Frank and Pettit stood still and watched the line of bullets moving along the beach, spitting up the sand well to their left. All but one of the planes turned out to sea and began firing at the men still in the shallows. They continued on towards a large cruiser at the rear of the flotilla. It received a direct hit. Although it was a good way out at sea, those on the shore could see its crew jumping over the side of the ship. The one remaining plane near the beach swept down firing on those men in the sea. Many fell and the receding tide soon became stained a rich red.

This plane was now heading straight towards Frank and Pettit. They sprinted up the beach and dived for cover in the dunes a few yards from Tom. Frank, face down, heard a whistling noise and a thud to his left. Ahead of him was an explosion and he was showered with sand. Shrapnel landed around him. For a moment he was deafened, but a quick blow of his nose whilst holding his nostrils made his ears pop.

Pettit tapped Frank's shoulder and pointed to his right. There sticking out of the sand only yards away were the points of a bomb's tail fin. Gingerly they moved away on their hands and knees, nudging the men they passed and telling them to move.

A sapper drew up on a motorcycle, one of the few vehicles still working on the beach, saluted and laughed,

'You've been lucky, sir,' he told Frank. 'It shouldn't explode, but I suggest you don't touch it; we'll deal with it. It happens all the time – it's the sand.'

'Well, if you don't mind we'll leave you and your mates to it, thanks.' Frank joined the men washing the sand from their hair and faces at the water's edge, but there was no Tom. Frank ran to the dunes, carefully avoiding the bomb and there found Tom, motionless. Frank knelt beside him and called out for Pettit.

'He's injured!' Blood was oozing through a black scorch hole at the back of Tom's trousers. Pettit pulled a penknife from his pocket and cut the thick material, exposing the wound. It was a neat hole with a little burning around its edge and about two inches above the knee.

'Let's turn him over,' said Pettit. 'Gently now.'

Tom stirred and opened his eyes, grimacing as he was turned onto his back. Pettit slit the material further to expose the front of the thigh with an exit hole, but no burning.

'It's gone clean through,' said Frank. 'You'll be fine Tom. You'll still be able to open the bowling from the Stretford End at Old Trafford next season.' Tom managed a smile.

Pettit called for a medic, who applied a field dressing to the wound and handed Tom a small brown packet.

'Put that on in about two hours,' he explained, 'like I've just done. You'll be fine. The sea'll wash the wound clean, so you might want to put the powder on when you are on a boat. I'll also leave this tourniquet to use if the bleeding starts up again, but only use it if it bleeds really badly. See an M.O. when you're in England and have it checked.' He patted Tom on the back and left.

Pettit took the tourniquet and tied it lightly on the top of Tom's thigh saying,

'It'll be safe there and you can tighten it when you like rather than fumble in your pocket for it when you're in the sea or on one of the boats.'

Tom gave a weak smile,

'Thanks ... both of you.'

***

The morning passed by without incident as the crew on Arcadian waited for the tide to turn. The *Luftwaffe* was active throughout, but mainly in the distance and was concentrating more on the larger vessels; occasionally they strafed the shoreline. It was fascinating for the crew to watch the evacuation unfolding before them with small craft scurrying from the shore to their mother ship or simply sailing off towards the Kent coast. Sawbarn's old telescope and Horton's army field glasses were passed to each of the crew to have a clearer look. Johnny took his turn and concentrated on the men wading in the water. He hoped he could row far enough in to help them, as they would find wading out more difficult once the tide was in.

To Johnny, it was like watching one of those grainy films at the cinema about the last war. Through Horton's high quality glasses and from the distance he was out to sea, it looked unreal. It intrigued him how orderly the soldiers stood waiting for their turn to be lifted off the beach or told to wade out. They stood in tight-knit groups, but suddenly dispersed when the air attacks came. Sporadically, they were shelled from inland to add to their misery, but largely appeared well disciplined. Johnny trained the glasses to the right. He spotted men in different coloured uniforms; French, he assumed. In comparison, they looked in disarray. He could see one rather portly French officer berating his charges as they ignored his orders. He stood on the water's edge jumping up and down, brandishing his pistol and pointing it at the men, but he never fired.

As the French soldiers reached one boat, Johnny was shocked to see some throwing others off just to make sure they kept their place.

Soon after, Horton briefed Johnny on what to do when close to the shore.

'We've put the extra oars in the bottom of the lifeboat. I'm not sure the boat is stable enough to take any more than a dozen. You make the decision on the first trip based on what the swell is like. Have the men help row against the tide. Don't tire yourself out because you'll need to do several trips.'

Whilst at first light it had been misty and calm, the wind was now much stronger and the sea choppy. Arcadian bobbed up and down while she waited. A little after two o'clock Horton ordered Sawbarn to edge as close as he dare to the shore. The lifeboat was lowered with Johnny in position. Sawbarn knew this part of the Channel well from his days on the ferries and moved in much closer than Horton would have dared.

Horton leant over the side to give Johnny his final instructions.

'Remember, try a dozen at first and see what that's like. You need to return here as quickly as you can, but only do the steering on the return journey to save your strength and let the men do the work. You might need at least four trips; we can probably manage as many as fifty. Good luck, son.'

As Johnny picked up the oars, a plane came towards him and fired its cannons. He fell forward onto the floor as the bullets hit the sea several yards away. Once the plane had passed, Johnny sat up, smiled and began to row. As he eased away from Arcadian, he heard the whiz of shells passing overhead. The shelling was random and speculative coming from so far inland. But the small boats were now being targeted and Johnny knew time was precious not just for the men on the beach but also for those already on the larger vessels.

The sea had a considerable swell making Johnny's job more difficult. He was pitching all over the place, but the inrushing tide was pushing him towards the shore. He stopped rowing to make sure he steered as straight a course as he could.

Sawbarn stood next to Horton watching.

'Although that lad's strong, Lieutenant, it's a lot to ask him to do all of this on his own. You might have to take over.'

'We'll keep an eye on him and I will if he becomes too tired or can't cope. For now I'm staying here and will watch him every inch of the way through these glasses. I'm sure he'll do fine.'

Johnny edged towards the shore and the swell dropped. Around him were similar sized boats full of men, heading out to sea. One capsized under the weight and the men struggled to right it. He felt like helping, but knew he had to push on. In front of him, the waves were beginning to gather before rushing onto the beach and they were pulling him along. Two bodies passed on his starboard side each with a bullet wound to the head.

Another shell exploded nearby and the shock wave from it had Johnny hanging on to the side of the boat for support. The spray thrown up fell and drenched him.

He soon reached men in the water. He leant over the side, holding out his hand.

'Get hold of this,' he shouted at the first man. 'That's it; I have you, now try and pull yourself up.' The young soldier rolled into the bottom of the boat. 'Thanks mate, thanks for coming out, but we thought you'd never bloody get here!'

'Sorry, I came as soon as I could, but it's hard work in this sea. Now, give us a hand will you?'

They pulled the next British soldier on board, followed by two Frenchman, who gabbled away to Johnny. He had no idea what they were saying but they did seem pleased. He picked up a further eight British soldiers and handed out the oars. They all rowed hard against the strong tide towards Arcadian. He looked at the men's faces. Every one of them looked tired, drawn and unshaven.

There were no problems on the first trip. The crew on Arcadian had helped the men as they clambered up the net on the side of the boat. Almost immediately, Johnny was on his way back to the shore. The whole of that first trip had lasted no more than forty minutes from start to finish.

The beautiful azure sky had arrived as the early morning mist had cleared, but now the sky began to fill with foreboding clouds. Heavy rain began to fall and the wind became even stronger. Johnny knew the number of trips anticipated by Horton might have to be curtailed and on his second trip he picked up sixteen men from the shallows. He could see a dwindling number on the beach, but still more than a hundred were left in this sector alone. With too many men in his boat and the swell tossing everyone around, two fell into the sea. Luckily, they were able to hold onto the boat and were towed to Arcadian.

The third trip went much the same with another sixteen men collected, but this time Johnny made sure four of them stayed in the water to be towed along and so putting less strain on the rowers.

On Arcadian the open areas were filling up as the men came on board. With no significant injuries being reported to the cook, he dispensed mugs of tea and a biscuit to each man. The rain became even heavier and Horton shouted from the deck to Johnny pitching in the sea below him,

'You'll have to make this the last one. Another full load will be enough and we'll have to leave. Are you able to cope or shall I take over?'

'No, I'll do it. Rowing in is quite easy and I don't do much coming back,' shouted Johnny above the noise of the wind, as he moved away.

Sawbarn arrived at Horton's side,

'That kid'll deserve a medal for this. You make sure you tell someone about this when we're home.'

'Don't you worry,' said Horton, 'I'll do the right thing.'

The rain eased a little as Horton looked towards the shore through his glasses. He could see a knot of men waiting. Another wave of planes came along the beach from the west. As they split up, one attacked the remaining group at the water's edge firing at will. Horton saw the men scatter and dive to the ground near the dunes, but two remained where they were. As that plane veered away another came in. He saw the two men suddenly run towards the top of the beach and dive into the sand to join the others. The plane dropped two bombs, but only one exploded.

Johnny was twenty yards from Arcadian when the plane swooped towards him and started firing. Instinctively, he fell over the side and into the sea. The bullets missed him but ripped through Arcadian, where two soldiers and a crewmember jumped over her side to avoid being hit. Screams came from the deck as the plane turned away and flew off to the east.

Johnny climbed back into his boat and pulled the three men on board. He steered towards Arcadian and reached up for the rope ladder draped over her side. He steadied himself and helped each man to start their climb, but one had a serious shoulder injury and found it difficult to grasp the rope. He was still standing on the rim of the lifeboat and blood from his wound dripped into the pool of water at Johnny's feet.

'Get a length of rope and sling it down here, I'll tie him and you can winch him up,' called Johnny to those on the deck, as he also balanced on the boat's rim. The man was in considerable pain with the bone in his upper arm completely shattered. Johnny quickly tied the rope around the man's waist and he was pulled up.

Johnny rowed away tired after his efforts and glad this was his last trip. The rain had now stopped but progress was slow in the swell. He edged towards the almost deserted section of beach with a glow of pride that, with luck, the men left there, and those now on Arcadian, would arrive home safely.

He headed towards this last remnant of the British Expeditionary Force, who emerged from the dunes and ran towards the lapping waves of the incoming tide. Behind them a plume of smoke hung above the grass, the result of more recent shelling. He waved; they responded and started to wade into the shallows.

Johnny looked around to see he was alone with only the Arcadian for company apart from those ships a mile or so out, marking time and waiting for their final delivery from the small boats floating towards them with their human cargo. He was the last hope for these men in front of him who shouted encouragement, but their words were mostly lost on the wind. With a strong cross wind now whipping up the waves Johnny had to tack meaning his progress slowed. His arms ached and it was all he could do to keep his boat moving forward.

***

'Do we know why the Germans have stopped?' Ingleby asked his assistant, who handed over a piece of paper.

'We had this message from our agent in Berlin, sir, and he says the order has been given directly by Hitler, himself. Why on earth would he want to do that?'

'Because he's a cunning bugger, that's why, old chap!' Ingleby grabbed the piece of paper as he spoke. 'I believe he wants peace with us and, despite signing those treaties with the Russians, he knows he'll have to take them on, maybe in a year or two, but take them on he will. He knows we won't accept a deal now and even less likely if he kills the men on the beaches or takes them prisoner, because that will make Churchill even more determined. Hitler'll let the men reach home and try to bomb or gas us into surrender having cut off our supply chain across the Atlantic. He knows the Americans have suffered too much in the past ten years in their own country and cannot afford the cost of a long distance war. By the end of this year, he'll expect us to opt for peace so he can turn his attention towards Moscow. He'll have the Japs consolidate through China and India and draw the Russians to their southern borders. I hope I'm wrong, but I think that's the man's plan.'

'Well, sir, there must be a reason to hold his men on the outskirts of Dunkirk and the other towns and, as usual, you're probably right.' Ingleby smiled at the compliment.

'Tell our man in Berlin to keep us posted,' he added, as he left the room.

***

Frank's group watched as the small pockets of men along the beach were picked up and taken away from the shore. The evacuation had remained orderly and disciplined, with the officers establishing control after the problems when the small boats first arrived.

Colonel Addison had left during the morning leaving Frank in charge of this sector for what everyone hoped was the last day. Following the previous attack, a few, like Tom, were injured, but not so badly as to be left behind. Frank found himself continually looking towards the path through the dunes, half expecting the Germans to arrive at any time. The beach looked desolate. Thousands might have left, but their rubbish remained, piled along the beach where the tide had taken much of it out to sea then brought it back. The abandoned vehicles were already beginning to rust. Rifles were piled high – useless without ammunition and too cumbersome for the men to take out to the boats. Two huge artillery guns lay on their side having been blown apart. Beyond the high tide mark rows of graves with their makeshift crosses created a surreal scene. Shell holes, full of water, littered the sand, reminding Frank of the battlefields from the last war.

Squally showers with occasional heavy bursts swept in from the sea. White-topped waves pitched and tossed the medium sized boats further out. One by one they turned and left, their work done. Just one remained. Frank remembered this had been the last to arrive and, with its bright colours, looked like a pleasure steamer.

Finally, Frank had only Pettit, Tom and eleven others left with him. The one remaining boat was still out there, but not moving. Frank's men stood at the water's edge with the surf breaking over their feet; they were oblivious to the driving rain. They scanned the sea between them and the steamer to see if a smaller boat was on its way, but visibility was too poor due to the low cloud and the rain. They were cursing their luck as it was beginning to look like they might be left behind, but Pettit encouraged them to have faith and to keep looking.

Frank sat watching from an overturned jeep as the rain eased to a light drizzle. Pettit came over and sat next to him. He took a packet of cigarettes from his breast pocket and offered one to Frank.

'No thanks, Sergeant Major, but please carry on.' Pettit lit up and blew the smoke away.

'What are our chances now, sir?'

'Well, I can't see anyone coming because of this low cloud and rain, but we can only hope. I expect the Germans to turn up at any moment and that would be it.'

'If we do end up in a P.O.W. camp where would that be, do you think?'

'Phew! That's hard to say – in Germany and out of the way, eastern Germany, possibly. I know they do have camps out there where they've put some Jews and others they don't like, but they'll have to build new ones for the thousands of our men captured already.' Pettit slowly shook his head.

'Have you family, sir?' he asked.

'Yes. I have a wife and two children all grown up now. Like I said, we live in Roxwell, but used to live in Chelmsford. What about you?'

'I have a wife and just the one child: a girl aged fourteen. It's amazing we've come across each other, I mean both from the same town, and here of all places. Do you think the wives know what's happening here? Is it the sort of thing the powers that be would keep quiet about?'

'No, I doubt it. I'll wager the news will be full of it. Morale at home will be low right now and, whilst this is hardly a victory for us, bringing all these men home will be quite something and the Government will want to use it positively.'

'If our men in the town retreat to here, do you think we should fight off the Germans when they turn up?

'I'm afraid the time for that has gone, Sergeant Major. Only a few working guns are left behind and, I suspect, precious little ammo. Surrender and accept imprisonment would be my advice; there's no point being killed for nothing. But I, for one, would see it as my duty to escape once in captivity. After all, this is what I've been trained to do. As for you and the rest of the men, just take your medicine and ride out the war for as long as it takes. Return to your families in one piece when it's all over.'

'But what about your family, sir, wouldn't they like you to see it out?'

'My wife knows what my job entails, well at least in part, working undercover, so she will accept it. I would imagine every other officer would see it his duty to escape, but the rest of the ranks should sit it out. It won't be pleasant and depends on what happens. If Hitler successfully invades us, we'll soon return home and probably all end up fighting the Russians. I'm convinced that is what he has in mind, but you'd better keep that to yourself.'

Pettit smiled and stood up, tossing his cigarette end onto the sand. He turned up his collar as the rain became heavy again and walked towards the men at the water's edge.

'Look there!' said one of the men as Pettit arrived. They all strained their eyes to see what he was pointing at. A small boat was edging towards them. It was being buffeted by the waves and blown by the wind. They could see a small figure manfully rowing, strongly fighting the drift of the boat. Occasionally, the rower looked up at the men in the shallows, who shouted and waved.

'Sodding hell, there's a young kid in it,' shouted Tom above the noise of the wind, rain and the waves. Four men waded out and dragged the boat into the shallowest water. The young rower jumped out and helped Pettit load Tom onto the boat. Frank ran into the water and grabbed the young man by the arm.

'What's your name, son?' he asked.

'Johnny. I'm with the Southend Arcadian. We've come out from Shoeburyness.'

'Well done, son, what a bloody fine job you're doing. I know Shoeburyness well,' Frank shouted back. 'Are we heading there now or have you more to pick up?'

'We're the last boat,' said Johnny. 'We're really too full already, but we have to take you, after all we couldn't leave just the few of you behind.'

Frank slapped Johnny on his back, 'You'll be given a medal for this.'

Johnny laughed as he climbed into the boat and handed out the oars to the strongest looking men crammed into the small space. He stood up above them,

'Right, everyone, I'll shout the stroke and you do the work, I'll steer us out to Arcadian. Ten minutes or so and you can have a nice cup of tea- ... well a cup of tea, at least.'

The men rowed as strongly as they could against the tide, but they were all finding it difficult to maintain the stroke as they were continually soaked by the waves crashing over them. Tom's wound began to seep again following the stretching of his leg when climbing into the boat. He tightened the tourniquet a little, mindful of what the medic had said, and dabbed the wound with the seawater sloshing around his feet. It stung and he swore loudly, but the pain slowly eased.

Johnny took an oar to help steer the boat but found it hard to keep any sort of straight line. Arcadian was closer, but he realised his earlier comment about reaching her in ten minutes was a little wide of the mark.

***

George pulled the Daily Sketch out of the letterbox and walked into the kitchen reading out loud. "German troops numbering more than three hundred thousand were being defied by the B.E.F. around Dunkirk and four-fifths of the B.E.F. have been saved," it says here Mum.'

'Let me have a look.'

She wiped her hands on her apron and took the paper from him. She turned the front page, 'There's a quote here from Mr Eden "More *than four-fifths of the BEF in Flanders, which the Germans claimed to have surrounded, have been saved. British troops have proved themselves superior to the Germans wherever they have met them. Stories of individual exploits are legion but the triumph is the triumph of an army. There is no braver epic in our annals*"'

She threw the paper onto the kitchen table. George picked it up and read the rest of the report then asked,

'Don't you believe Mr Eden, Mum?'

'Do you?' she said angrily.

'Part of it, Mum, but some of what he says is a load of bunkum. Triumph? Sounds like a defeat to me. Let's say we have about three hundred thousand or so men there like the Germans have; that means sixty thousand of our chaps are dead or captured, maybe wounded. That's not much of a triumph, is it? And the other two hundred and forty thousand who have been saved are coming home. It'll be a devil's own job to return to France and don't you think we'll be at Hitler's mercy?'

'I don't know, dear. As long as your father returns in one piece that's all I care about, and thousands of other wives and mothers will feel the same. Let's worry about that for now not what the Germans might or might not do. What if your father is one of the sixty thousand?'

'Let's hope he makes it home, Mum,' George said, glumly. 'He'll probably turn up in a couple of days as if nothing has happened. Trouble is, though, he'll probably be sent off somewhere else.'

He returned to his room and Joan shouted after him,

'What about your cereals and toast?' She received no answer.

A few minutes later George returned to finish his breakfast. Joan said nothing, but could see he had been crying.

***

It was slow progress in the small boat. Arcadian appeared to be moving away. Frank urged the men to row harder. Those without oars leant over the sides and used their hands to scoop the water.

Out of nowhere came a huge explosion to their right with a spout of water shooting up into the air; the shock wave knocked two sappers clean out of the boat. The other men helped haul them back on board.

'That was a bloody artillery shell!' shouted Pettit. As he spoke another landed even closer. The boat capsized completely and all the men were thrown into the water. Two men were trapped underneath. Frank and Johnny lifted one side of the boat and the two men swam out.

Three shouted that they couldn't swim and splashed about in a panic. Frank grabbed one, Pettit another.

'Calm down, calm down, relax!' shouted Pettit trying to hold his man's chin above the water, but the sea was so rough this proved difficult. The remaining non-swimmer had floated off out of sight – the only hope for him was to drift into the shore. Johnny and Tom managed to right the boat and they helped everyone aboard.

Frank finally counted round and found it was just the one man lost. They had now drifted towards and along the shore leaving them further from Arcadian than when they had started out.

On Arcadian, Horton watched this unfold and asked Sawbarn to move further in, trying to cut the gap between the two boats. He also knew that if Arcadian remained stationary, it was more exposed to the German artillery spotters who could now possibly be close to the beach.

As Arcadian headed towards Johnny's boat, a single plane emerged from across the sand dunes and roared towards them. It fired at both boats and the men in the lifeboat stood up, almost causing it to capsize. Some dived over the side and two were hit as they did so. They fell face down into the sea and drifted off.

From the front of the boat, Johnny urged the men still with him to sit down and keep rowing while those overboard climbed back on. Tom was steering, but his leg was bleeding from his efforts to pull men on board.

Johnny spotted Arcadian chugging towards them. He shouted to the other men and pointed. They all looked through the spray and a little cheer went up as they made out her bow cutting through the waves.

Three more artillery shells landed in quick succession around them. The small boat pitched so violently that Frank lost his balance and fell into the waves. Within seconds, he found himself drifting away from Johnny and the others. He tried to swim towards them, but all his strength had been sapped away and he allowed himself to drift aimlessly.

Johnny took over an oar and headed towards Frank, but, as hard as he tried, found it difficult to cut through the whirlpools created by the explosions. No one noticed the approaching plane and it fired again. Pettit was hit and had a wound to his shoulder. Two were dead.

The plane also fired on Arcadian and the men crowded there threw themselves to the deck. Fortunately, the bullets missed their target because Sawbarn had spotted the approaching plane and turned away from its path causing the firing line to pass them by. The men looked up to the bridge and cheered. He acknowledged with a wave.

The change of course left Arcadian only yards from Frank. Horton asked the Captain to bring the boat around. Two of the crew scrambled down the netting and reached out. One grabbed Frank's arm and nearly pulled it out of its socket as they hauled him upwards. The other man grabbed the other shoulder and, exhausted, Frank grasped the rope of the netting. He was so tired he could hardly move, but eventually fell over the side of the boat and collapsed onto the deck. Plenty of hands sat him upright. He coughed and brought up much of the seawater he had swallowed.

As soon as he caught his breath, he looked out towards where the others still struggled with the small boat, but they were now much nearer and the sea seemed calmer.

Pettit was finding it difficult to row because of his injured shoulder and was only using one hand. Johnny told him to take over the steering and urged the others to make one final effort. They eventually came alongside Arcadian. The two crewmen who had helped Frank were still on the rope netting. Ignoring his tiredness, Frank dropped over the side and down the rope ladder. He stood with one hand holding the rope and his other outstretched ready to help Johnny and the rest once they were close enough.

'Right, let the injured off first,' shouted Johnny. He took an oar from Tom and helped paddle to maintain position. He was thrown a line from Arcadian and tied it to the iron ring at the bow.

Pettit and Tom were being helped onto Arcadian. Frank jumped into the small boat to help the remaining men onto the netting and ladder. The small boat lurched suddenly and Frank was swung round, but managed to grasp the rope. The momentum swung him against the side of Arcadian winding him in the process. He dangled there for nearly a minute to regain his breath.

All those on the netting were thrown into the sea, but were immediately able to scramble up again.

Frank dropped down off the rope to re-join Johnny. The small boat was pitching and hitting the side of Arcadian. They both had trouble keeping their balance as they reached up for an outstretched hand above them.

'After you,' said Johnny and he stood back to let Frank step forward. Two hands yanked Frank from the boat and he climbed up the netting.

Johnny stood right on the rim of the boat and was about to jump onto the netting when another surge swung him and the boat round. He fell backwards and smashed his head on the side of Arcadian. He dropped unconscious into the sea with blood pouring from a gash on his head.

Frank was now at the top of the net. Turning round he could see Johnny face down in the water and drifting away. Frank was about to jump in to help him when an explosion close by showered him with water and the blast pinned him to the side of Arcadian. When he looked again Johnny was not there. Above him, he heard Horton shout at Sawbarn to turn and head for home.

Another shell landed right on the lifeboat. Wood spewed into the air and sharp slivers landed on Frank and the men on the deck above him. Frank scrambled over Arcadian's side and onto the deck. He knew Horton had little choice but to leave without Johnny with Arcadian in such danger. Still, many of the men on the rails booed and shouted at Horton for not staying.

Tom joined Frank.

'Are you all right?' he asked.

'Just about, can you see the young kid?'

Tom pointed. Frank strained his eyes and could just make out something floating in the slight swell. Arcadian was now at full steam. The object bobbed and turned over. They could clearly see Johnny's face, but it looked lifeless. The shelling had now stopped.

'The poor kid doesn't deserve that.' Frank said, mournfully. He's younger than my son and not even old enough to serve his country, but it looks like he's died trying to protect it'.

'You're right there ... bloody hell, did you see that. I saw the lad's head lift up and turn round.'

'Are you sure, Tom? It's not your imagination?'

'Look!'

'I can't see anything,' Frank shielded his eyes.

'No ... no ... damn! I can't see him now, but sure I even saw his eyes open.'

'Well,' said Frank, 'if he's alive he'll be able to drift into shore and be picked up by the Germans.'

Frank helped Tom and Pettit towards the treatment room in the galley before returning to the deck to help the others. Of those who had left the beach with him, only six had reached Arcadian. After taking a few minutes rest sitting on the deck, Frank re-joined the cook and they bandaged Pettit's shoulder. It was not a bad wound, but Pettit winced each time they touched his arm.

'What happened to the men in the boat?" Pettit asked Frank.

'Eight didn't make it and nor did the young lad, but we think he may be drifting into shore. We had to leave him, as it was too dangerous with the shelling to hang around.'

'That lad deserves more than just our thanks for bringing us out to here what with the sea being so rough and him being under fire for much of the time.'

'I know. He made umpteen trips from here to the beach. I'll make sure the right people know what he did. I just hope he makes it and we find out the Germans have him, but it will be interesting to see what they do with him. He can only be a schoolboy and not in the forces, so perhaps they'll send him home.'

Horton appeared in the doorway,

'Ah, Captain,' he said to Frank, 'there you are. Could I have a word outside?'

They stood in the small area between the galley and the steps up to the deck.

'I am Lieutenant Horton from the Royal Navy and who are you sir?'

'Frank, Frank Shipley, I'm not actually a Captain. I just, sort of, borrowed this uniform. I'm actually a Major, but I work for the Intelligence Services.'

'Really!' he said, surprised, "you'll have to tell me more about that later."

'Right. Where are we heading for?"

'Shoeburyness – if we're lucky. This boat works out of there. We commandeered her and the crew as with hundreds of small craft. You must have seen them toing and froing to the beach. Were you the last ones off?'

'Probably,' answered Frank, 'and certainly on our part of the beach, men still remain in the town trying to hold back the Germans. We can't make out why the Germans stopped and gave us this chance. Sure, they attacked from the air and shelled us, but they're massed to the south and have been there for days. Curious. By the way, remind me of the name of the kid back there.'

'Johnny Stevenson, but I think he's bought it don't you? I feel bad about leaving him, but we couldn't wait any longer. We're so jam-packed on here it was too great a risk to stay.'

'We're pretty sure he's alive and there's no need to be hard on yourself. You did the right thing and let's hope we hear about him. So how long before we reach Essex?'

The Lieutenant blew out his cheeks,

'Well over a day and a half, I'd say. With so many aboard, we can only travel slowly. We don't want to sink having taken all this trouble to get you here.'

"Quite right and thanks for coming for us, many very grateful men are both here and on the other boats." He shook Horton's hand and they both smiled.

'The cook will give you food and drink, Major. Later, come to my quarters, such as they are, and you can sleep there. I'm sure you could do with it.' He climbed the steps to the deck and Frank returned to the galley.

Frank decided to stay with Pettit. Tom came in. His wound had stopped bleeding, but looked messy despite having been washed clean by the salt water. It was now dry. The cook followed holding a thick bandage, opened one of the cupboards and took out a small bottle of brandy. He poured a little onto a cloth and dabbed the wound. Tom jumped.

"'Bloody hell – that stings!'

The cook spread his arms out in mock surrender. Tom made as if to kick him.

Frank wound the bandage round the top of Tom's leg. He turned to Pettit sitting on the table next to Tom,

'Sergeant Major, I've been told by the skipper that we're heading towards Shoeburyness in Essex. You'll know it, of course, and it's not far from home. You could be with your family tomorrow.'

Pettit was not so hopeful.

'Sir, this is the British army we are talking about here. It will never be that simple.'

'I'd prefer to be sent straight home up north,' said Tom.'

'Not before you've had that leg properly sorted, you won't.' said Frank. 'And you, Sergeant Major, will need to keep an eye on that shoulder, although it doesn't look too bad.'

Pettit eased himself onto the floor and, when the cook wasn't looking, picked up the brandy bottle. He held it behind his back, waited for the cook to leave, took a swig and passed it to Frank.

'Why I know I will not be home with the family that quickly,' said Pettit, 'is because, when we were in Dunkirk, we were told we had to report to Southampton and that's a bloody long way from Shoeburyness. To be fair, though, they won't know where anyone is in all this chaos or what men are alive and home and who are still stuck over in France. They will need to record everything and it will take ages for them to find out about everyone. It'll be awful for the families of those dead or captured and every family with men in France are bound to fear the worst.'

Frank was not sure if the order to make for Southampton would apply to him or not and doubted anyone from Intelligence would be at a place like Shoeburyness to tell him what to do. He hoped he could head straight home by train, bus or even cadge a lift. He knew he would walk if he had to.

Frank left Pettit and Tom to rest and reported to Horton to explain more about his circumstances. After that he slept soundly on Horton's bunk.

By late the following afternoon, they were all sitting on deck. Someone shouted.

'Look, there's Southend Pier!'

It was the first recognisable landmark and shouts of joy echoed around the boat. Sawbarn sounded the ship's horn when he heard the shouts and this brought up a cheer from the men.

Boats galore filled the Thames Estuary. Many were motorboats not much larger than the lifeboat left behind by Arcadian.

Frank stood on the rail with Tom and slapped him on the back,

'Won't be long now, Tom!'

23

Word soon spread that Arcadian had been sighted off Shoeburyness and the quayside filled up with the crew's families eagerly awaiting its return. She bobbed towards her berth with her deck crammed with soldiers, smiling and waving. Another cheer went up as the engines stopped. Those waiting searched anxiously for the face of their loved one amongst the crew who were busily securing the boat. Frank stood with Horton on the bridge.

'Well, we made it, Lieutenant. Who'd have imagined it? Not many of us on that beach a few days ago and that's for sure.'

Three smartly dressed soldiers moved to the end of the gangway as it was lowered to the quay. One held a clipboard with a pencil tied to a piece of string whilst a sergeant stood looking over his shoulder. An officer stood to one side. The sergeant shouted to the soldiers on the boat.

'When you come off, give your name, rank and serial number to the Private here and I'll tell you where you have to report to. At that place you will be given further orders followed by two weeks' leave.'

Compared with the neatly turned out soldiers on the quay, the men on the gangway looked dishevelled, tired and demoralised. Their relief and excitement was beginning to pass. Those with injuries were helped down and taken to stretchers to be assessed by two nurses. A doctor attended to the more seriously injured and two orderlies carried these to a waiting ambulance.

"They don't look like "triumphant men", do they?' said Horton to Frank. 'That's what Mr Eden's calling them, so I've been told. But at least they're here and not over there. I spoke with the Admiralty on the radio and they say as many as three hundred thousand might have been saved including many French. We're all glad we're safe, but it's been a defeat and the men's faces show it, don't they?"

"Absolutely,' said Frank, moving away. 'Would you come and give me a hand with my two friends and make sure all the stretcher cases have been taken from the galley?"

They met Tom coming up the stairs with Pettit behind. Horton led them to the deck and Frank dropped down to the galley where he found the cook tidying up on his own.

On the quay, two more nurses were assessing the men as they stepped from the gangway. They gave each man a number between one and five depending on the extent of his injury with the instruction to wait by the office door. Tom was a more serious four and Pettit just a two.

A lone man dressed in a trilby hat and a coat stood in the harbourmaster's office doorway. He scanned the faces as the men edged down the gangway towards him.

Frank stood next to Sawbarn looking at the crew's families below.

'Which one is waiting for young Stevenson, do you happen to know?' Frank asked.

Sawbarn scanned the group and saw Mrs Stevenson in her familiar red cardigan; he pointed her out.

With the last group of uninjured soldiers waiting their turn to be recorded, Frank joined the end of the queue. He was next in line to provide his details when the man in the trilby moved out of the doorway and headed to the gangway. He reached into his pocket, took out his warrant card and showed it to the officer without speaking and then moved towards the private and sergeant still holding the card. He pointed at Frank and said,

'That's fine, men, this one belongs with me. There's no need for him to give his name; he's leaving with me.'

They both looked at the officer who nodded and they let Frank pass.

Frank recognised Jack Ingleby under the hat. As they walked away together, Frank could see Ingleby looked pale and drawn. Did he know about Lorna? His face suggested he had the troubles of the world on his shoulders and he did not look well.

'Jack, about Lorna ...'

'Yes, old chap, I know.'

Frank felt relieved and decided to wait until later to say more about what had happened in Sedan.

'How on earth did you know I was landing here? It all must be so chaotic.' he asked Ingleby.

'Ah... well, old chap, Horton was suspicious of you possibly being a German spy, so he radioed ahead. Eventually, I got back to him, described you and he confirmed it was you, so I drove here. All these men are being sent all over the country just to give in their name before they are given leave. I'll take you straight home – my car is out the back here.'

'Just a moment, there are a couple of men I need to have a word with. Have you a pencil and a piece of paper?'

'No, sorry, old chap, but that private over there probably has.'

With a sheet of paper and a pencil, Frank returned to Pettit and Tom. They were waiting for their turn to see the doctor. He shook each man's hand in turn.

"I've just been told you're both off to Southampton, that's a bloody shame. Still, it won't be too long before you're home. Luckily, I'm being allowed to head straight to Chelmsford, so will be able to tell your families of your safe return before you can. So, if you give me their names and addresses, I'll drop into to see Mrs Pettit on my way and send a note to your folks, Tom.'

'That's very kind of you,' said Pettit. 'Give the old girl a kiss from me, won't you?' They all laughed.

'We've been through so much in not very many days, Frank,' said Tom, 'with more excitement than most people have in a lifetime. Hardly believable, is it?'

'Too true' exclaimed Frank, 'and, perversely, although it's been exciting and something like an adventure you might read in a comic or see on a film, the deaths are real – Captain Dawson, those on the road, my colleague and thousands more. We'll never forget this or each other and now I have your addresses, I'll write to you. We can't tell what will happen to us, but it's certain we'll see more action. Let's just hope we can also come through that.'

'Come on, you two,' shouted the sergeant.

Frank held out his arms and Pettit and Tom did the same. They briefly hugged each other and slapped each other's backs.

Frank re-joined Ingleby and they headed along the quay towards the car.

'Sorry, Jack, just one more thing to do.'

He searched for the woman in the red cardigan. She was near the harbour office but appeared distressed and was being comforted by another. Frank almost apologetically approached her.

'Mrs Stevenson?' he asked, politely. She broke away.

'Have you news of my son?' Her voice trembled in expectation.

'I do but I'm afraid Johnny isn't with us.' Mrs Stevenson recoiled into the arms of the woman with her.

'We had to leave him behind,' said Frank, holding out his hand as if to comfort her. 'He was bravely helping the soldiers he'd saved onto the steamer when he was swept away from us towards the shore. I am sorry.'

Mrs Stevenson staggered towards the quayside wall and sat down. Sobbing she reached into her handbag for a handkerchief and covered her face.

'It may not be as bad as it seems,' continued Frank. 'One of us saw his head above the waves and it was moving. He was drifting close to the beach and appeared to be floating on something, maybe a lifebelt. There's an excellent chance he could reach the safety of the beach.'

Mrs Stevenson gathered herself a little, taking the handkerchief away and squeezing it into her hand.

'Your son's a hero,' Frank continued. 'He's saved the lives of countless men rowing into shore time after time to get us away. It's a tragedy we had to leave him, but he's a strong lad. He'll get to the beach.'

'And then what, Major, were our men still on the beach?'

Frank hesitated.

'Well... no... I'm afraid we were the last ones to leave that particular area. It is most likely the Germans arrived soon after we left. They'll take care of him, I'm sure. After all, he's a non-combatant and nothing but a lad.'

'Will he be a prisoner or do you think they'll send him back?'

'No one can tell what they'll do. They should return him or at least give us word. Please be positive about it. Your lad seems a strong-minded young man. If he's reached the beach, he'll be fine and I'm sure he'll be home before you know it. He'll be decorated for what he did; make no mistake.'

She smiled thinly, nodded and wiped her eyes. Frank held her hand.

'Be brave about it and give your details to the army officer over there, so, if we hear anything more, we can contact you.' Frank returned to Ingleby, leaving Mrs Stevenson and her friend with the captain.

'That will be repeated all round the country,' said Ingleby, when Frank joined him in the car.

'Where to, sir?' asked the driver.

'Chelmsford, please. Major Shipley will direct you more precisely when we are near.' He turned to Frank. 'There'll be thousands of worried families. It will take months for us to find out what's happened to the men left out there, with many dead, of course, which will only make matters worse.'

'I'm writing to the family of one of the men who came out with me, but the other lives in Chelmsford. If you don't mind, Jack, I'll just pop round to see his wife, before you drop me home.'

'Of course, old boy. Now, I have been given scant details of what happened to Lorna, tell me more.'

'Firstly, Jack, she let slip about you and her. I am so sorry, you must be devastated.'

Ingleby looked down at his feet and sniffed.

'Yes, it has been difficult. Did she suffer? I heard it was a shot as you both tried to escape.'

'She was just unlucky; she tripped and fell. I looked back and saw her. She was killed instantly.' Frank decided to leave out much of the detail, but on the journey to Chelmsford he told the story of the lead up to their imprisonment and the escape. Ingleby said nothing throughout and when Frank had finished, the rest of the journey took place in silence.

***

Mrs Pettit looked out of her sitting room window when the car drew up. She turned and hugged her daughter when she saw a man in uniform open the rear door. They stood staring out as Frank came up the garden path. They moved to the hall and Mrs Pettit sank to her knees.

Frank knocked on the front door. He could hear a woman wailing from inside the house. He pushed open the letterbox.

'Mrs Pettit? He's alive; he's fine, I've recently left him.'

As the door opened, Frank could see Mrs Pettit on the floor. Her daughter knelt down beside her,

'Come on, Mum, up you come. It must be good news.'

Frank helped Mrs Pettit to her feet.

'We arrived in Shoeburyness this morning. We were one of the last ones to leave France. He's off to Southampton, but should be home in a couple of days.'

'Is he injured or anything?' asked the daughter, as she helped her mother onto the bottom step of the stairs.

'A slight wound to his shoulder, but he'll be fine. I promised him I'd let you know, as I'm on my way home to Roxwell. You've heard the news, of course? Some have not been so lucky.'

Mrs Pettit stood up, smiling through tears. She hugged Frank,

'Thank you so much for taking this trouble to come here and you say you were one of the last?'

'We certainly were and very lucky. We nearly didn't make it. We were under constant attack, but a little steamer and a brave young man reached us.' Mrs Pettit hugged him again and kissed him on the neck.

'Well, Mrs Pettit, I must leave you in peace and return to my own family. The very best of luck for the future.'

"Thank you. Thank you from the bottom of our hearts,' said Pettit's daughter, as she walked with Frank to the front gate. Neighbours appeared, concerned at first but relieved when Mrs Pettit called over that her husband was safe. They all waved as the car drove off. Frank sank into the back seat,

'Phew! That was much easier than with that poor woman at Shoeburyness. I wouldn't want to do that too often.'

Ingleby said nothing, but just patted Frank on his knee.

As they neared Frank's home, they passed The Hare and Hounds.

'I can't wait for a pint in there tonight,' said Frank, 'and to be with the family, meeting up with my friends from the village.'

'You deserve it, Frank, and you'll probably be the first home from France so you'll be the centre of attraction.

Frank reached into his pocket, pulled out the piece of paper on which he had written Tom's address and passed it to Ingleby.

'Could you do me a favour, Jack, and make sure this lad's family also receive the news that he's safe? He is more seriously injured. He'll be fine, but he might not be sent home quite so quickly.'

'No problem, old chap. Now I want you to take five days off then come and see me in London, say Wednesday morning next week.'

The driver pulled up outside Frank's house.

'Well done, Frank. Thanks for what you did out in France. We both feel sad about Lorna, but that Frenchman failed you both. A sorry business.' He held out his hand and Frank took it.

'Jack, when I next see you, make sure I tell you about that young lad whose mother I was talking to at Shoeburyness. He was called Stevenson and he saved my life and the lives of many more on that boat. He might be dead for all I know, but, either way, his efforts need recognition.'

'I'll attend to that as soon as I can, but it would help if you write out a report and I'll pass it on; you have my word."

As the car drove off, Frank walked round to the back door to surprise Joan, but it was locked.

'Well I'm buggered, what an anti-climax,' he muttered to himself.

He had no key for either the back or front doors. He looked through the kitchen window and saw evidence of Joan having been there earlier, with empty cups and saucers still on the table. The car was not in the driveway, but Frank knew George often made use of it.

He returned to the front garden and sat on the wall to wait. Soon, a bus came into view. The stop was about a hundred yards away. It dropped off one passenger. Frank stood up and waved at Joan. When she saw him, she dropped her shopping bag and ran towards him with her arms outstretched. He stood still with arms extended. She jumped into them and kissed him. He swung her round several times and, when he stopped, she kissed him again fully on the lips, as hard as she could.

Frank ran to pick up her bag and, arm in arm, they walked towards the house. Joan was skipping along; she looked up at Frank,

'You won't know this yet, but I had a telegram from Jack Ingleby to say you were at the French coast and I really hoped you'd be home, but it said on the wireless that thousands of men were either dead, captured or on the run in France. It also said that no more would be coming home because the Germans had reached the beaches.'

They stood by the front door and Joan felt for the key in her pocket. Frank held her in front of him,

'I was lucky. Ingleby picked me up when we landed at Shoeburyness and brought me here, but he didn't mention a telegram. Lorna was killed in Sedan, but I escaped. Thierry failed us, yet I don't know what happened to him.'

'I know about the girl. I had a curious letter from her father about what happened. It must have been awful. That poor girl. Anyway, Alvar Lidell said on the News that over a quarter of a million of our boys have been rescued. He said it was all due to the Navy backed up by an armada of small ships. That is a mighty effort. '

'That's right, love, we saw it all coming across the Channel. We were carried on a little steamer and pretty well the last to leave.'

Once inside, Frank collapsed into the armchair. Joan came and sat on his lap.

'It's so lovely to have you home,' she said as she cuddled in close to him. 'We've all been so worried. Everyone's saying this is a victory, and I suppose it partly is to bring that many home, but I think we all know worse is to follow.'

'True but we have hope now; it's a defeat but we're not defeated, if you think about it. We're here and they're over there; it will take a mammoth effort for them to reach us. At least we have a chance, especially with so many men still available to fight.'

George and Lizzie arrived home in the early evening. George had been studying in Chelmsford library, seeking out reference books, and had picked up Lizzie from work.

They were thrilled to see their father with plenty of hugs and tears. After dinner, they left for The Hare and Hounds.

The landlady provided free drinks all round to joyfully celebrate Frank's safe return. One after another the villagers came up to greet him. The family soon sought out the tranquillity of the snug where they sat on their own. Frank was beginning to feel the exhaustion of not having slept properly for more nights than he could keep count of. They were on the point of leaving when the door opened and Jack Ingleby came in, smiling.

'I expected you to be here, old chap,' he said loudly. 'I went to the house but not finding you in, remembered you said you would be coming down here. I had to call into your old house in Epping earlier and decided to return here.'

'Thanks, Jack, what would you like to drink?' asked Frank, moving to the bar.

'That can wait, Frank. I've been a bit devious, old chap, and detoured into Chelmsford.' He turned and opened the door and in walked Josie and Norman Walmsley followed by Harry and Phyllis Parmenter.

'I managed to squeeze them into the car after sending my driver to London on the train,' Ingleby continued. 'I had the Walmsley's address from when we moved your family there to escape from Hindley's men. They suggested we pick up Joan's mother and father and here we are.'

Frank was overcome.

'Jack, that's wonderful and so kind of you. Thank you so much.'

Josie hugged and kissed Frank.

'I'm glad those French lessons counted for something,' she said, smiling broadly.

'Saved my life, Josie. Saved my life.'

Harry, frail and using a stick, shook Frank's hand. Phyllis, looking sprightly in her best W.I. dress, gave Frank a kiss on the cheek.

'So glad to have you home, son,' she whispered, 'Joan has been so worried, but put on such a brave face when she heard the news from over there.'

Frank bought all the ladies a port and lemon and beer for the men. He wanted to propose a toast, but before he could do anything, Stan Hebden and one of Frank's former constables arrived, they had received a note left for them by Ingleby at the Police Station. The party was now in full swing and after several rounds of drinks, Frank had forgotten all about his toast.

Suddenly, Joan called for hush. She stood on a beer crate provided by the landlady.

'I would like to propose a toast,' she said, slightly slurring her words. 'You cannot begin to imagine what I feel like now Frank is back. I should smack Jack Ingleby's bottom for putting my husband in danger, but it's war and that's what these boys have to do. I would like you to raise your glasses to welcome Frank home. To Frank!' She toppled off the crate and was caught by Ingleby.

'To Frank!' everyone chorused, followed by, 'Speech! Speech!'

Frank cuddled Joan before climbing onto the crate.

'Thank you - thank you. It is so exciting to see you all and thanks very much, Jack, for taking all this trouble to bring those who mean so much to me here tonight to celebrate my survival, because that is what it is. The story of the last week or more would make a film so dramatic that many of you would say it was too far-fetched. What really happened to all of us over in France will become the stuff of legend – you mark my words. However, sadness is never far away to temper this happiness. Jack here has recently lost someone very dear to him. Jack, you have our deepest sympathies.'

The whole room echoed to, 'Hear, hear'.

'To continue being serious for a moment, I am enjoying being here with you fine folks because of two people. Jack, of course, has known me since I was a schoolboy in Somerset and brought you here tonight. Furthermore, I have met all of you, other than Jack, because of Marie. She was tragically taken from us, but her death meant I met Joan and Lizzie, who have given George and me so much love and helped us through such a difficult time. Of course, Harry and Phyllis, and Josie and Norman contributed in no small way. Tragically, Lorna, my companion in France, was killed during the German advance. I want you to be thoughtful for a few moments and think of two young, beautiful women who were taken from us in the prime of their lives.'

Everyone was holding back tears. Frank was momentarily overcome with emotion. He gathered himself and continued,

'I would like to say something else. I met Marie because of a man most of you know little about. My close friend, Eddie Wilson, went through a hell at Passchendaele that makes my little jaunt in France seem like a walk in the park. Also a young man, younger than my George, who may or may not be dead, is the reason I am standing here and his name is Johnny Stevenson. He's only sixteen. He bravely lifted scores of men, including me, off the beach at this place called Dunkirk. We owe him our lives. I just so hope he drifted ashore after being injured when falling overboard and will be picked up by the Germans. That is all I want to say, so let's all have another drink.'

Ingleby quickly took Frank's place on the crate.

'I would just like to add one little thing about this man here. Frank has worked for me for a number of years. Before this war started and since September last year, he has done many very brave things for this nation. I cannot tell you exactly what they are, but suffice to say they have been crucial to protect us all. He has faced death a few times before and has now experienced a difficult time in France. A long while ago he faced his own demons and came through that when many would have folded altogether. To you he is an ordinary fellow, but to my superiors and me he is a nugget – a golden nugget. Frank, old chap, we salute you and thanks.'

An enthusiastic singing of 'For he's a jolly good fellow' was followed by more drinks.

By midnight, Frank and Joan were in bed. For Frank it was the first decent bed he'd been in since he left the Fontaines' house in Sedan. For Joan it was just nice to have her husband home. She knew what he had gone through was probably quite unimaginable. She was longing to ask him all about it, but that would have to wait until the morning. Before that they had some catching up to do of another kind and she pulled Frank towards her and gave him a long and loving kiss.

***

Johnny came round trying hard to recall what had happened. His head throbbed and he was out of breath. He was inside a lifebelt, but how he came by it he was not sure. He was finding it difficult to keep awake. He was in shallower water now and the waves were less steep, but he was still some way out from the beach. He looked round and saw smoke rising from Arcadian in the distance. He remembered what had happened and shouted out towards her, but realised it was no use. He put his arms out resting them on the belt and lost consciousness again.

When he awoke he felt giddy and vomited some of the salt water he had swallowed. His head was sore from the blow.

He shivered; he was freezing cold from having been in the water for so long. He had taken time to drift in towards the beach due to the swell, but now the tide was beginning to turn and go out again. For a while he just bobbed around in circles and, when he looked towards the beach, saw he was the same distance away as he had been when he had first woken up. He made one more supreme effort, paddling furiously with his arms.

Almost an hour after he had fallen into the sea he could finally touch the sand with his feet and he stumbled forward. He was completely done in and felt faint again. He was shaking with the cold and his hands and arms were completely numb. He staggered into the shallows and ended up crawling on his knees. Once out of the water he collapsed with the relief and turned on his back gulping in the air, at the same time clasping his arms round his body trying to warm himself.

He still had the lifebelt round his waist, so he pushed it off with his hands and feet. He picked it up and kissed it saying, 'Thanks for saving my life' and threw it into the sea.

He sat up and in front of him was a pair of thick army trousers. He squinted as he looked up to see a rifle and the unmistakable uniform of German grey. A young face stared down at him and spoke in German. Johnny said nothing.

A second soldier joined them and the two Germans talked with occasional glances towards Johnny. They were arguing about him and pointing out to sea. Johnny assumed they were trying to decide whether he had come from one of the boats they had watched sail away earlier or was, perhaps, a local Frenchman.

'Englander?' one of them asked. Johnny stood up to his full height and pulled back his broad shoulders,

'I am,' he said, proudly. The soldiers held each arm and led him away towards the dunes.

To be continued ...